ALIGNMENT

To Jean,

Souvenirs de St Laurent,
Souvenirs de France.

Bonne lecture!

Best Wishes
TracyCxxx

ALIGNMENT

Tracy Chollet

First published in New Zealand 2017
Tracy Chollet
alignment.thenovel@xtra.co.nz
www.tracychollet.com

A catalogue record for this book is available from the National Library of New Zealand.

Alignment/Tracy Chollet -- 1st ed.
ISBN 978-0-473-38570-5 (paperback)
ISBN 978-0-473-38572-9 (Kindle)
ISBN 978-0-473-38571-2 (epub)

Book Layout © BookDesignTemplates.com 2016

Cover artwork and design © Gwenaëlle Chollet 2017

For my parents,
Fay and Jack Hammond

For my mother- and father-in-law,
Marie Louise and Marc Chollet

TURNER, George Selwyn – On April 7, 1986, at the Nurse Maude Memorial Hospital, dearly loved husband of the late Sarah, loved son-in-law of Iris, dearly loved father of Joseph and loved brother and brother-in-law of Ian and Jenny and loved uncle of Drew, Linda, Susan and Joanne, in his 60th year. Garden flowers only please, or donations to the Cancer Society would be appreciated and may be left at the service. The funeral service will be held in the Canterbury Crematorium Chapel, Linwood Avenue, tomorrow Friday at 2 p.m.

Christchurch
New Zealand

PART I

1

May 1986, Carnac

Isabeau was late. As she slowed her Renault 5 she noticed the man in a suit waiting at the end of the road. He was standing beside the gate of a small house, and he gestured for her to pull into the courtyard and park in front of the garage. He came over and opened the car door for her. She took a deep breath and got out of the car.

"Monsieur Tatibouet?"

"Oui," he nodded. "Mademoiselle Martin, I presume. It's a pleasure to meet you after our telephone conversations."

"Pleased to meet you too." Isabeau shook his manicured hand.

"You must be tired after your journey. I'll show you around and then leave you to settle in," he said.

"It's been a long week. I finished at the post office yesterday and I left Besançon at six this morning," said Isabeau, following him inside.

"As I explained on the phone, it's a small house. It should be suitable until you get yourself organized," he said, walking around the kitchen-living room area that took up most of the downstairs. He pulled open a curtain at one end that had been partitioned off to form an alcove bedroom. "You have two single beds here, or there's a loft bedroom with a double bed upstairs. If you need any other furniture, please let me know."

"It will be fine, thank you. The removal company's delivering my things on Monday afternoon."

"Here are the keys." Monsieur Tatibouet placed a set of keys on the bench beside the front door. He felt in his pocket and pulled out another key. "You may wish to inspect your mother's house before we meet on Monday," he said, holding out an old brass key. "I have an appointment available for you at ten o'clock."

Isabeau stared at the key. When she didn't take it, Monsieur Tatibouet placed it on the bench beside the others.

"I never met your mother. My predecessor, Monsieur Le Guen, had more to do with her. Her situation was ..." he hesitated, "unusual, but her estate is quite cut and dried. I look forward to seeing you Monday."

Monsieur Tatibouet left. Isabeau shut the gates and unloaded her suitcase and the boxes of bed linen and kitchen gear. She pulled out the sandwich left over from her afternoon tea stop and ate while she walked through the house and around the courtyard, trying to relax her shoulders.

It was getting cold. She finished her sandwich and came inside. She sat beside the bench on a stool she'd found in the garage, fiddling with the old brass key. The light dimmed. It was dark outside when she put the key back on the bench and went upstairs to make up the bed. Exhausted, she fell into it and pulled her familiar duvet around her. After twenty years she was back in Carnac.

She couldn't sleep.

May 1986, Christchurch

Joseph Turner placed the box on the wooden slab that ran along under the window and served as a workbench in the shed. It was faintly mottled maroon colour cardboard, roughly the shape of a shoe box but smaller. It opened with a flap at the end, on which there was a sticker with his father's name, the date of his death and a registration number. Inside, there was a thick brown paper bag that contained the ashes.

It was a blue-sky crisp morning. An early frost. He took his father's woollen Swanndri jacket off the hook on the door, pulled it on over his jersey and rubbed his hands as he walked around the woodworking machines and along the shadow board. Every tool was in its place. The tea-stained Best Dad mug was still on the shelf beside the window on the round rippled stain mark it had sat on for years. Beside it, the old hot water jug was plugged in. Joseph picked up the carpenter's pencil that was sitting on the workbench. He took a knife out of the drawer at the end of the bench and pared the wood back with a series of curls until the wide flat lead was apparent. He slipped the pencil behind his left ear.

"Had to die son, to get you off your guitar and back using my tools," he said, imitating his father's deep voice and chuckle.

The transistor radio sat on the window ledge. He turned it on. Station 3ZB. His father never changed it. He sat and listened to the eight o'clock news and the weather report.

There was plenty of wood neatly stacked on the shelves along the back wall. Joseph sorted through the pieces of pine, macrocarpa and rimu and put aside the nicest pieces of rimu, matching the grain as he measured them, trying to picture the finished box in his mind. He took his time to set the planer first. He rechecked the measurements. "Measure twice, cut once. You see, I haven't forgotten, Dad."

It felt strange to turn on the machine without his father there. He pushed the switch and stood back as the high-pitched noise filled the shed and drowned out the radio. He guided the first piece of wood along the planer table, turned the machine off and ran his hand along the smooth side of the wood. He smiled. It was a clean cut, and the wood had a nice sheen.

Joseph talked to his father while he continued preparing the wood, measuring and remeasuring, working slowly as he planed each piece. Outside, the sun moved around and thawed the lawn from silver to green. The shed warmed up, and he took off the Swanndri and put it back on the hook.

At the end of the day, Joseph opened the old beer fridge. The last three bottles of his father's home brew sat alone on the bottom shelf. He took one and drank the beer at the workbench while he inspected the even pieces of wood. When he'd finished, he slipped the bottle into the crate of empties in the corner.

In spite of her tiredness Isabeau walked at a steady pace along rue du Ménec. In the early morning light it seemed like a dream. She arrived at the northern edge of town, where the houses gave way to fields and trees and the road curved to the right, and came to the Ménec Alignments. She stopped. On the left of the road, the field of menhirs started, stretching southwest to northeast for more than a kilometre. The stones stood in eleven imperfect lines. They rose squarish, most of them tapering to the top, wearing time proudly in the simplicity of their shape, like sacred sentinels linking earth and sky. Lichen decorated them at random, but, for Isabeau, patience was etched into every pore of their rough surface. They were still waiting for her.

From time to time a car passed down the road, but it was early enough Saturday morning that there was no one else amongst the menhirs. As daylight bleached the sky she walked up amongst the rows of stones, weaving her way back and forth until she reached the central section, where the stones were smaller. In one of the middle rows, she crouched beside a menhir that had a more rounded shape. In the damp grass, she leaned into the cold granite and put her arms around the stone. It was still strangely comforting. "I have finally come back," she whispered to the stone.

When Isabeau reached the end of the alignments she took the path through the broom bushes, came out at allée des Alouettes and kept walking. It was a short distance to the old house. Pushing her hands into her jacket pockets, she fiddled with the brass key and her asthma inhaler. She stopped across the road from the house and studied it. The stone walls were in a sorry state, and on the roof some of the slate tiles were slipping. The paint on the wooden shutters and door was peeling. The grass was overgrown.

She still couldn't believe that the house belonged to her. The house where she'd spent the first nine years of her life. *With both my parents.* How those four words sounded strange to her now. In those days, Papa had worked in bars and on fishing boats. When he was home, there was cooking and cuddles, tickling and being tucked in. Mother was always there. She mainly stayed in her room; she mistrusted most people. It had taken Isabeau many years to understand it was mental illness: depression. And there was no one else. Papa had been a ward of the state. Mother was English, and at a young age she had lost both her parents in a plane crash. As far as Isabeau knew, she had no living relatives. She was without a family.

The house wasn't like the houses Isabeau looked at whenever she walked: homes where normal people lived out their lives, with family and friends, against clean painted surfaces, their belongings well-ordered around them. Like the Morels' house next door. The sight of their tidy house with its smooth walls and established garden filled her with the same childhood longing, even after twenty years. Their shutters were closed. Monsieur Tatibouet had mentioned they were away in America, visiting Chantal, their daughter. What would the Morels think when they knew she was back? What would she say when she saw them? She was no longer a child who could run to their house for a bandage when she scraped her knee, or for Madame Morel's freshly made butter biscuits on baking day.

Isabeau forced herself to cross the road and unlock the door of the old house. It was dark and cold inside. As soon as she stepped in the door she could smell it. The dirty scent, ever so faint, of Mother's Gauloises Blondes was still in the air. Her chest tightened. She walked around downstairs, opening the shutters and windows. The same wallpaper and paint. Nothing had changed. It was just dirtier, dustier, damper. In the bathroom, the ceiling was covered in a rash of disgusting mould, and the bath and basin were filthy with stains and webs of black cracks. The sink in the dingy kitchen was in a similar condition. According to Monsieur Tatibouet, the house had been rented out for several years, but when her mother died the tenancy had already ceased. The house was now empty, except for a square walnut table and two chairs now sitting like an old married couple who no longer needed to speak to each other.

What had happened to the old oak table she used to sit at with Papa in the evening? Isabeau tried to bring to mind his face and his thick black moustache that tickled her cheeks with extra kisses, to make up for the morning because he left early. When he wasn't on the fishing boats he would sometimes come home with green beans and cherry tomatoes from Antoine, his boss in the bar. The cherry tomatoes were like bright red marbles, with spider stalks. Papa would sprinkle fine Guérande salt on them, and they would sit at the table eating them as they topped and tailed the beans.

"Do you remember, Papa?" she said to the silence. "The beans had no strings and tasted of summer." Isabeau's hands instinctively repeated the action of snapping the end off a bean.

She took a deep breath and the stale air caught in her throat, making her cough. She spun around. She felt as if her mother was standing in the doorway, her face livid, staring at her like a black-eyed bird. Isabeau hurried out to the front step and took a puff of her inhaler. She wanted to close up the house and leave, but she couldn't help herself. When her breathing was more regular, she went back inside and slowly climbed the stairs. She tiptoed to her mother's bedroom and pushed the door open with her foot. The stained velvet curtains and 1960s flowery wallpaper were still there. The room smelled worse than the rest of the house. She quickly closed the door. Next was her own bedroom. Here, the brown wallpaper was gaping along the edges, and damp had eaten into the windowsill. Isabeau walked around and around the room. It seemed so small, and she felt suddenly very sad. She left the bedroom. There was only one more room: the spare bedroom where Papa used to sleep. She entered and stood there, her eyes closed, trying to imagine the old wooden bed with his clothes thrown over the end. She remembered searching through the pockets of his trousers, looking for spare coins when the kitchen jar was empty.

"Papa, where are you?" she sighed.

4

The chisel slipped. Joseph swore. He'd taken too much out. Again. He picked up the piece of wood and threw it. It hit the bottom of the shed door with a loud bang, making the glass in the pane at the top rattle. He pulled the pencil out from behind his ear and aimed it at the door too. Why didn't he just stick four pieces of wood together? Or buy a box, any box? Or use the cardboard one the ashes had come in? It would be lighter to travel with. At this rate he would have no choice. He kicked the leg of the workbench. "Bloody dovetail joints!"

Now he had used all the best pieces of rimu. "Yes, I know, Dad. If you'd been here you would have said 'put the nicest pieces aside for the moment, things don't always go to plan when you're out of practice'. I know. I know."

He turned the radio up. "Might as well have the best, Dad," he shouted above the music. "I'm butchering the best for you; hopefully I might make a bloody box in the process!"

He locked the shed, took the piece of wood inside to the fireplace and left the house, carrying his surfboard and wetsuit. He drove towards the coast to New Brighton and parked in the carpark on the north side of the pier. There was a good swell, and the waves rolled in high and regular. The usual cold easterly blew in off the Pacific Ocean, but there were several surfers already out on their boards. He recognized some of the winter regulars. He pulled out his harmonica from his pocket and sat in the car playing the notes of the new song that was forming in his head. It was like a stormy sea: angry waves crashing in, unstoppable. When he got into the water and paddled out on his board he was still humming. He couldn't get the tune out of his head.

For two hours it was good to be on his surfboard, watching the waves, waiting for the one with the right angle, trying to ride it, forgetting his father.

By evening, he was back in the shed.

Isabeau stepped back to take in the six and a half metres of stone, and started to sketch a rough form. A solitary stone amongst the trees, the Giant of Manio was the tallest menhir at Carnac. He was going to be her new embroidery project: blackwork in a shade of grey. There was a sadness about him. In his pitted surface she saw a large face, like a simplified Easter Island moai whose identity had been almost erased. An indentation on the left formed an eye socket, and another to the right was a nostril. Underneath, dark horizontal lines created a stern mouth.

It was secluded here, quiet. She could talk aloud to him, have whole conversations, in French or English. He was a good listener. While she sketched she talked about her new position at the post office and her courteous colleagues. She wasn't sure how to join their coffee break chats when they talked about their families and what they did at the weekend. It was no easier than it had been in Besançon. And then there was the question of what she was going to do with the Alouettes house. She wished making a new start was as simple as unpacking her belongings, but even that had lost its novelty; the unopened boxes were roughly stacked on the beds in the alcove in the little rental house.

Isabeau had come early, to have the Giant to herself. With the spring sun coming through the trees, she walked around the quadrilatère, the rectangular stone enclosure that stood near the Giant, and then returned along the forest path and out through the little carpark. She followed the road back along the pine trees and came to the Kermario Alignments. These stones were much bigger than those of the Ménec Alignments, and their size and shape accentuated the angles and hollows of the stone. As a child she had easily disappeared behind them, but she'd always been wary; they were gentle giants in sunlight, then dark stormy light would always transform them into ogres. In the corner stood a dolmen, massive slabs of rock sitting strongly, forming a house for the dead.

When she arrived at route du Pergatoire Isabeau found herself turning right towards allée des Alouettes. She went past the Morels' house, which was still closed up, and stopped in front of her own house. It was becoming a Sunday morning habit, almost a ritual. The days were lengthening, and when she unlocked the front door and opened the downstairs shutters and windows the house felt warmer.

In the living room she tried to imagine how it would look with fresh paint, new wallpaper and her embroidery chair beside the window. She'd had another appointment with Monsieur Tatibouet during the week. He knew nothing about what had happened to her father. He had raised his eyebrows when she'd said she wouldn't be selling the house yet. *Perhaps he thinks me mad, like Mother.* The thought started running through Isabeau's mind. She had found herself saying she wanted to completely renovate the house before she lived in it, and asking Monsieur Tatibouet if she could rent his son's house for longer. She walked through to the kitchen thumping her thigh. Why had she said that? "Stupid, stupid, stupid."

It was still early when Isabeau reached the town centre. She stopped in front of the bakery. Inside, two women were buying bread. There was something familiar about them. She studied them. Their faces were older now, and their hair was grey-streaked. She couldn't remember their names, but she recognized them. They were mothers of children who had been in her class. They would remember her too. Questions, that look. She'd had enough of it at the post office. She stood back from the window and turned away, pretending to look at a shopping list, until they had gone out of the bakery and headed towards Saint-Cornély's.

Isabeau entered the bakery. A young woman was tidying the counter. It was the first time that Isabeau had seen her there. She had black hair cut in a bob, and the fringe was pulled up at the front with a barrette. Isabeau ran her hand over her own thick brown hair, which was in a ponytail. She had tried on several occasions to style it at the front in the same way, but it never seemed to work. She could never get her hair to do what she wanted.

The woman was wearing a white blouse and black trousers, covered by a dark blue gingham apron pulled in at the waist, accentuating her figure. *She would look good in anything*, thought Isabeau, as she asked for a baguette. The woman put the bread on the counter, and Isabeau's eyes were drawn to the apron, to the decoration across the top of the pocket and along the hem. Cross-stitch. Isabeau smiled and shifted on her feet to get a better look at the pattern, wondering if the woman had made it herself. She thanked her and left. She wished she'd dared ask about the apron. She hoped the woman would be wearing it another day.

"So, you finally got it finished. Nice work. Your dad would be proud." Drew picked up the wooden box. "Didn't know you could do stuff like this." He studied the carved pattern on the lid.

"Neither did I," said Joseph. "It took me a while."

"You're really serious about this trip then?" Drew asked.

"You know I promised I'd take him."

"Puts a new meaning on the term 'guided travel'!" Drew joked. "I can understand why you don't want to take that thing." He pointed at the cardboard box on the other end of the workbench. "I've never seen anyone's ashes. I guess there's a first time for everything. Are you ready?"

"As ready as I'll ever be." Joseph opened the flap of the box, eased the bag of ashes out and carefully opened it. They both peered inside.

"Looks more like white river gravel," said Drew. "Sorry, Uncle George." He lightly touched the bag.

Joseph tipped it up and poured some of the ash into the box. He took his time, being careful not to spill any. "That's as full as I can get it," he said, closing the paper bag up again and sliding the lid onto the box. He took the second-to-last bottle of beer from the fridge and filled two glasses.

"Well, here's to your trip," said Drew, and raised his glass.

Isabeau drove towards the coast. From the centre of Carnac it was less than two kilometres, but Carnac Plage with its golden sand beaches seemed a world away from the alignments. She preferred the part of Carnac anchored in the earth: forests and menhirs, solid and trustworthy, rather than the ever-changing landscape of sand, sea and sky. The boulevard de la Plage was lined with cars, and the beachside apartments were filled with holidaymakers enjoying the balconies and the beach. Through the dunes and trees she caught glimpses of people paddling, swimming and lying on the fine golden sand. She followed the coast. It stretched and curled all the way around to the port on the river Crac'h at La Trinité-sur-Mer.

The café was still there, facing out towards where the trimarans were moored. There was an empty parking space nearby, but Isabeau turned left and parked further away. She sat in the car, spinning her inhaler around with her fingers, practising what she would say to the person behind the bar.

In the café, Isabeau ordered and stood at the counter to drink her coffee, sipping it as slowly as she could. By luck the owner had served her. She mentioned that her father had worked there. She tried to sound natural, as if she was saying it in passing. As if it wasn't important. The owner told her that he'd only bought the café two months earlier, and that before that it had changed hands several times. He had never heard of Paul Martin, so he asked a couple of regulars at the bar, but no one could help. Twenty years was a long time. Isabeau finished her coffee and left. Once she was back in the car, she started to cry.

She reached Carnac but kept driving. Circling the bay at Plouharnel, the road led straight to the Penthièvre isthmus that funnelled cars onto the Quiberon Peninsula. She'd always felt nervous driving across it. The peninsula was barely attached to the mainland. What if the sea breached the small strip of sand and land and it broke; the peninsula became an island, floated off? Papa would laugh. "Well, we could sail all the way to Belle-Ile-en-Mer then; we wouldn't need to take the ferry." It was his joke, but all his promises to take her on the ferry for a day out on Belle-Ile had never come to anything.

At the end of the peninsula, in the town of Quiberon, Isabeau walked around the streets, amongst the tourists, stopping to look in the windows of boutiques full of kites, beach gear and marinières, the long-sleeved striped t-shirts, as she headed in the general direction of Port Maria. She needed time to arrive in her mind as well as her feet.

She eventually found the port. There was a ferry loading for Belle-Ile; passengers were heading from the terminal up onto the ship and settling on the upper deck, while cars were being driven up the ramp into the hold. Isabeau stopped at the sea wall and stared at the ferry. She took a deep breath. The air was even fresher than at Carnac Plage or La Trinité: raw and salty, stripped of town and earth smells. The smell of her father when he'd just come back from sea. She wiped her eyes with the back of her hand. The ship left the port. Isabeau walked away. It would soon be the holidays, but she wouldn't come back to Quiberon.

Joseph drove and Drew was in the passenger seat. They headed west out of Christchurch, across the plains through Sheffield and Springfield and up into the mountains. Two cars followed. Drew's parents, Joseph's Aunt Jenny and Uncle Ian, were driving Joseph's maternal grandmother. Drew's sisters Linda, Susan and Joanne were in the other car.

Between the Torlesse and Craigieburn mountain ranges, they passed the limestone rock formations on the winter green slopes of Castle Hill. Joseph thought about the box with the rest of his father's ashes, sitting in the workshop. And Carnac on the other side of the world: the stones there that his father had often talked about, orderly, shaped and lined up by man thousands of years before.

They arrived late morning at Arthur's Pass and stopped at the bach his father had built from recycled timber. They lit the fire and sat around eating a lunch of garlic bread and the lamb casserole – George's favourite – that Aunt Jenny had made, recounting stories about George and talking about Joseph's impending trip.

"Do you think it's a good idea to go now?" asked Joseph's grandmother. "They're still talking about Chernobyl on the news every night."

"Don't worry, Nana, they're saying that it's okay to travel. It'll be fine. I promised Dad I'd go this year. I don't want to put it off."

"I can see your mind's set. At least you'll have warmer temperatures than this," she said, stretching her hands towards the fire.

"Uncle George sure had it worked out," said Drew.

"What do you mean?" asked Joseph.

"What with his jet-setting new lifestyle in two hemispheres, he'll have summer and spring all year round."

"Drew!" said Susan and Joanne at the same time, and everyone else half laughed, half groaned.

"Can't you take anything seriously?" said Linda.

"Well, by the time I get back, it will almost be summer," said Joseph.

"Take some time for yourself, Joseph. It's been a long hard year," said Aunt Jenny, giving Joseph a hug.

"Will do. I'm going to try and catch up with a guy I met in Perpignan at the music festival five years ago. He's in Nantes now; doesn't look too far from Carnac. I'd love to perform in France again, and even more so because Dad will sort of be there, at least a part of him."

"I always knew he'd make it there one day. I just didn't think it would be like this," said Uncle Ian, with a catch in his voice.

After lunch, they walked down to the old coach road, which wound through the bush above the main road. Joseph wore the Swanndri and carried George's old tramping pack with the cardboard box inside. He took his grandmother by the arm and walked at her pace. They stopped amongst the mountain beech in the same place where Joseph's mother's ashes had been scattered. He removed the urn from the backpack. Without saying a word, they formed a small circle.

Uncle Ian spoke first. "You loved this place, George: the bush and mountains. And Sarah did too. You spent many happy moments together here. Now you'll be together again, finally." He swallowed. "I miss you, big brother."

Everyone nodded silently. Then Uncle Ian took the box from Joseph, opened the paper bag and tipped some ash into the bush. The box was passed around the circle, and each person said a few words and repeated the gesture of scattering some ash into the bush. The box came back to Joseph. He stood for a long time in silence. His throat was tight. He couldn't speak. Tears ran down his cheeks.

"Goodbye, Dad."

He scattered the remaining ash over the moss-covered ground.

When Joseph arrived home later, the day had closed in on itself. He unlocked the shed. The air was as cold as the last bottle of beer in the fridge. He sat, numb, in the dark, drinking the beer. He sang one final song to his father.

It was almost closing time, but the newsagent's was still full of tourists looking at guides and maps and browsing books, in search of the perfect novel to read lying on the beach the next day. Isabeau had been on holiday for a week. She picked up the new *Broderie Aujourd'hui* magazine and flicked through the pages as she took it to the counter.

Hurrying around Saint-Cornély's Church, she resisted the urge to look at the magazine, and tucked it under her arm. She glanced across to the souvenir shop on the other side of the street and saw Corinne, who also worked at the post office, making her way past the stands of postcards. Isabeau stopped and changed direction, quickly heading back around the other side of the church. There wasn't a lot to say about her summer holidays. Staying home. Listening to music and the BBC. Discovering, to her surprise, that she was actually missing speaking English now that Mother was dead. Writing poetry. Walking. Today she'd been on her first day trip out with her bike. Going to the bakery was fast becoming the highlight of her day.

Isabeau had been going to the bakery in the morning and returning there in the late afternoon for a pâtisserie. That was the time Marianne was most likely to be there. Isabeau had heard Madame Dupont, the boulangère, call her by that name. Isabeau called her Marianne in the pretend conversations she had with her. In those conversations, she complimented Marianne on the cross-stitch aprons she often wore.

Isabeau ran the last strides to the bakery. The closed sign was on the door, and the other woman who worked there was removing the unsold pâtisseries from the display case. Damn. Until then, Isabeau had been happy with her day cycling around the quiet flat roads of the Brière Marshes, but now she wished she'd come home earlier. She was about to turn around when she saw Marianne coming through from the bakery into the shop area. When Marianne saw Isabeau she came and unbolted the front door. She was wearing a new apron, with a row of cross-stitch triskeles, the three-pronged spiral Celtic symbol so common in Brittany.

"You go, Julie," she said to the other woman as she let Isabeau in. "I'll finish up."

"I'm sorry to bother you," said Isabeau, a little out of breath.

"No problem. That's funny; I noticed there was only one piece of far breton left, and then you appeared. You've been buying a piece since you've been on holiday."

"Perfect, it's my favourite." Isabeau fiddled with the magazine. Marianne looked down.

"*Broderie Aujourd'hui*. That must be the new one? Great, I've been waiting for it to come out."

"I've just picked it up."

Marianne placed the far breton on a little piece of cardboard and wrapped it in paper. "Do you need bread as well? There's not much left, but I do have half a baguette."

"Thanks." Isabeau had plenty of bread, but she didn't say so.

Marianne twisted a square of paper over the end of the half baguette and sat it beside the pâtisserie parcel.

"I'd better let you get on with tidying up," Isabeau said, handing over her money. "You've got a new apron," she blurted out, and blushed. "It looks good, the triskele pattern. Nice idea."

"Thanks. I've just finished it. Since I've been here I haven't had much time for bigger projects." Marianne handed Isabeau her change. "So, you like embroidery too?"

"Yes. I'm doing some blackwork at the moment." Isabeau found herself saying it before she realized she had opened her mouth.

"I haven't tried blackwork. I'd love to see some. Well, anyway, I'm Marianne Fournier." She smiled at Isabeau and held out her hand.

"Pleased to meet you. I'm Isabeau Martin."

"You work at the post office, don't you?"

"Yes." Isabeau picked up her bread and pâtisserie.

"Well, enjoy the *Broderie Aujourd'hui*. I'm going to pick up a copy tomorrow."

"I will, and thanks for opening up for me."

"My pleasure. A demain."

"Yes, see you tomorrow."

10

Friday night in the Gladstone, wet jackets and scarves were draped over every chair. Cold rain stung the windows. The southerly blast had arrived in Christchurch, but everyone in the bar had forgotten the weather; they were turned towards the music. In three strides Joseph moved across the low stage and gripped the microphone. He held it towards the packed dance floor. "The mountains shake, the plain awakes, when we meet you pull the rug out from under my feet ..." When they had finished singing the chorus back to him, he took his harmonica from his pocket and cupped it to his lips. The dancers stopped, the room quietened and the harmonica notes rose above the wild song of the wind and rain. At the last note the crowd roared applause.

Joseph worked his way through his well-known songs. It was good to be back with the band: Mike on drums, Stevie on bass and Brendan on keyboards. And Drew was there, in the audience. Joseph didn't want to stop, and the band didn't need any encouragement to perform some extra numbers. He was almost breathless at the last song. He strummed his guitar while he addressed the crowd.

"I appreciate you coming out in this weather. To say thanks, here's one for the road: a sneak peek at a new song that'll be on my next album. See you in September, Christchurch!"

After the show, Joseph and the band joined Drew at the bar and they had a drink together. One by one, Mike, Stevie and Brendan said goodnight. Joseph took out his harmonica from his pocket and turned it over in his hands.

"I remember when your dad gave you that for your eighteenth birthday," said Drew. "I wanted a motorbike for mine, and here you were excited about a bloody harmonica. I'll never forget that."

"Have you still got the motorbike?"

Drew laughed. "Okay, point made! Anyway, it wouldn't be much good in this weather. Hope it's better on Monday for your flight."

"Should be. This is supposed to blow through. I'm counting on it to get the last jobs done around Dad's house this weekend."

"Don't you mean *your* house?"

"I haven't got my head around that yet."

"Well, we'd better get home then."

Drew went outside to bring his station wagon as close as possible to the entrance. As soon as they had loaded the gear and were both inside the car, the wind rose, shaking it. Drew turned the heater up. They drove along Durham Street, heading south towards the Port Hills. Christchurch was quiet. Drew slowed the car as they came to a red light at the intersection of St Asaph Street. The rain swept across the middle of the road at a forty-five-degree angle. He flicked the wipers on to fast.

"Hardly any cars around, and we still get the red light. I don't get it."

The light changed to green. Drew accelerated. At the same time, a car came straight through the red light on St Asaph Street. There was a screech of desperate braking. Joseph and Drew turned.

"Fuck!"

The car crashed into the passenger side and pushed Drew's car across the intersection.

One of the Morels' shutters was open. It was the first thing Isabeau noticed as she came through the bushes at the end of the alignments. The house had been closed up the Sunday before.

For twenty years she'd missed the Morels, and now they were there she was suddenly nervous. She wished their door would magically open, and they would step out and see her. She hurried over to her own house. In the living room she took out her inhaler and took a puff. When the tightness in her chest had eased, she opened her front door and peeked out. Maybe the Morels were still in America and someone had come to do something in the house. She walked around inside in the semi-darkness of closed shutters until she could stand it no longer. She went out to the front garden. All the shutters at the Morels' were open. She took a deep breath and walked over to their house.

"Isabeau!" Madame Morel exclaimed when she opened the front door.

"You remember me?"

"Of course. How could we forget you? And you haven't changed. Look, your long hair, just as beautiful as ever." Madame Morel opened her arms, embraced Isabeau and held her. She called over her shoulder, "René, come quick. There's someone here." She kept her arm around Isabeau and ushered her inside.

Docteur Morel came through from the kitchen.

"Isabeau! Mon Dieu!"

Isabeau was passed from Madame Morel to Docteur Morel, and he enveloped his arms around her.

"When did you arrive?" he asked.

"I've been here since May."

"We had no idea," said Madame Morel. "We've been in America. Chantal's married to a banker in New York. She needed complete bed rest for this third pregnancy. Little Matthew was born in August. But enough about us. I can't believe you're here. And ... you're here for good then?"

"I think so."

"Is it the first time you've come back?" asked Docteur Morel.

"Yes," said Isabeau, sighing. "It's been too long."

"And your mother?" Docteur Morel exchanged a glance with his wife. "How has she been? Is she well?"

"She passed away in January. An aneurysm. It was very sudden."

"I'm sorry to hear that, Isabeau," said Docteur Morel.

"So am I." Madame Morel squeezed Isabeau's hand, and they didn't speak for a minute.

Docteur Morel broke the silence. "What are you doing now you're all grown up?" he said, shaking his head. "You're so tall; I can't believe it. And we are older too: grey-haired grandparents."

"I'm Deputy Postmaster at the post office. I ... we – Mother and I – shifted around a lot, and then we were in Besançon for a long time. Things were a little better then. After she died, I applied for a promotion to come here, and much to my surprise I got it. And, I've inherited the house. It was a bit of a shock to say the least. I never even knew that it belonged to Mother in the first place, not to mention that she still had it."

"You're not living there, are you?" asked Docteur Morel. "It's in pretty bad shape."

"No. I'm renting Monsieur Tatibouet's son's house in town."

"What are you going to do with the house?"

"I'm not sure. I mean I ..."

"Oh, René, enough questions," Madame Morel interrupted. "Come through, come through, Isabeau. Here we are leaving you in the hall!" She put her arm around Isabeau's shoulders and led her through to the kitchen.

PART II

12

Behind the town hall, the cemetery, with its high stone walls, stretched down rue du Tumulus like a prison. On the southern corner of the wall a lone cross stood guard. Isabeau climbed the entrance steps beside the large wrought iron gates. She had started coming to the cemetery at lunchtime when it was quiet. There wasn't enough time to go up to the standing stones.

It was All Saints the next day, Saturday, and already pots of red, white and gold chrysanthemums, cyclamens and jars of colourful bouquets stood out against the grey gravestones and gravel paths. At the weekend, families would gather to honour and remember their loved ones. At this time, the cemetery almost became a place of life. Isabeau would stay away.

The gravel crunched under her feet on the short pathway to the west wall. Here, tiny graves were adorned with white-robed angels praying, pointing skywards and spreading their wings. Isabeau was drawn to a grave with a statue of a young girl sitting, with a bouquet of flowers in her lap, looking into the distance. *I think I know how you feel*, she wanted to say to the statue, but she heard footsteps on the gravel. Someone was coming. She carried on into the next row, amongst solid full-sized tombs, and stopped at a grave with no flowers. Bare. Just like Mother's grave in Besançon.

Isabeau headed back to work. Everyone at the post office was happy All Saints had fallen on a Saturday and they didn't have to work in the morning. She wasn't so sure. She had a lot to get through before closing time. Monsieur Poulain, the Postmaster, was ill, and she was in charge for the first time. "You deal with anything that comes up," he had sniffled into the phone. "I should be back on Monday."

Amongst the pile of correspondence to the post office itself that she had gone through in the morning, there was a parcel addressed to the Postmaster. Isabeau pulled it out again now, still unsure whether she should open it. There was something about it. The size of a fat book, it was very heavy. It had been sent airmail from New Zealand. Stamps featuring birds, fruit and minerals formed a perfect patchwork, and the carefully folded brown paper was taped and held tight with string that intersected over neat writing. The customs declaration was torn away, leaving only a corner of green paper.

The parcel gave slightly and revealed tissue paper underneath as Isabeau cut the string and ran the edge of the scissors along the tape. When she set the paper aside, it kept the form of the wooden box it had contained. The box was made of a reddish, unusual wood. It looked as if someone had spent a long time making it. The carved lid slotted snugly in to the box. She ran her fingers over the series of spirals around the edges. Strange. In the centre there was a row of rounded forms with flat bottoms that reminded her of menhirs. She turned the box over to inspect it, and the contents made a faint swish.

There was a letter under the box, and a photo: small and square with a white frame, a photo from the seventies. A man and a boy standing in front of snow-capped mountains and a bright blue sky. The man was tall and broad-shouldered and had thick brown hair. He had his arms wrapped around the young boy's shoulders. The boy had a big smile, and blond wisps of hair flicked out from under his woollen hat.

16 October 1986

Dear Sir or Madam,

I apologize for writing in English. My French is limited, and I trust you will be able to have this letter translated without too much difficulty.

I am writing to ask your help to fulfil the last wish of my father, George Turner, who wanted some of his ashes scattered at the standing stones of Carnac. He had planned to travel to Carnac in July, but at the beginning of the year he became unwell and was diagnosed with cancer. He still intended to travel, with my aid; however, his condition deteriorated rapidly and he died in April. I have spread some of his ashes at Arthur's Pass in the Southern Alps, and I promised him that I would scatter the rest at Carnac. My desire to put him to rest is overwhelming. However, due to unforeseen circumstances I am now unable to travel.

I would be deeply grateful if you could scatter these ashes at the standing stones. I know that this is a very strange request, but it reflects a heartfelt desire to carry out a promise that I made to my father. This will finally realize his lifelong dream of coming to Carnac, which began when, as a young boy, he saw pictures of standing stones in a book.

I am enclosing a favourite photo of my father and me taken many years ago. He was a strong man, who loved the outdoors, and he was also an avid reader. He had a great love of the Asterix books. When I was young, he would read these stories to me, laughing as he took on the role of his favourite character, Obelix, the menhir delivery man.

Thank you, in advance.

Yours faithfully,

Joseph Turner

Ashes. Isabeau couldn't control her hands; the letter was flapping like the wings of a bird. She squeezed the box and letter into a large envelope and pushed it into the back of her desk drawer, behind her bag. Her chest was suddenly very tight. She grabbed her inhaler and shook it, put it to her lips, pushed the end of the metal canister and breathed in.

"Isabeau, are you okay?" Corinne stopped in front of Isabeau's desk, her hands full of documents. Her eyes asked other questions while she waited for Isabeau to get her breath.

"It's just my asthma," Isabeau managed to say. "I'd better get all this tidied up before we close." She gestured to the papers on her desk.

All afternoon, Isabeau kept telling herself to place the parcel on Monsieur Poulain's desk and forget it, but she felt a compulsion to look at the photo again and reread the letter. At seven o'clock she put the envelope with the box of ashes and letter into her bag. She couldn't leave the dead man's ashes alone in the post office all weekend, especially at All Saints.

On the way home, Isabeau turned off the avenue and cut through to the bakery, hoping to see Marianne, even if it was only for a couple of minutes. The buzzer sounded as she entered, and Marianne looked up and smiled. While she was serving an elderly couple, Isabeau focused on the three embroideries above the shelves. Each depicted a different view of the Ménec Alignments, in blackwork. It was new for Isabeau to have her work on display. She was still amazed Marianne had persuaded her to let her put them up.

"Any plans for the weekend?" Marianne asked, when she was finished with the customers. "You'll be pleased to have your Saturday off."

"Probably stay home."

"Why don't you come for lunch on Sunday? I've been meaning to invite you for ages. It'll be busy here, but François' mother and Julie are going to take care of things." Marianne handed over Isabeau's usual baguette. "It would be an opportunity for you to meet François properly. He's got to help his father with maintenance on the oven in the afternoon, so we could do some embroidery together then."

"I don't want to be a nuisance. Weren't you going to the cemetery with François' family?"

"Change of plans. We're going tomorrow afternoon because the oven has to be done on Sunday." Marianne stopped. "Are you okay? You look pale. Madame Poulain came in earlier and mentioned her husband was off work. There's some virus going around."

"I'm fine. It's just my asthma."

"Make the most of the weekend to relax. Anyway, come on Sunday at one."

There was another late customer behind Isabeau, so she took her bread and called "merci" over her shoulder.

As soon as she arrived home, Isabeau changed into her flannelette pyjamas and a woollen jersey. She put on her favourite Jean-Jacques Goldman cassette and turned the gas radiator up. A chill still ran through her. She had some of the ashes of a dead man in her bag: a man she didn't even know. And it was the day before All Saints, which meant it was Halloween. Nobody really celebrated it in France, but Isabeau still knew it was when the spirits of the dead were supposed to come back to earth. She pulled out the photo and letter, then took the envelope with the box of ashes to the garage and left it on the shelf beside the door.

While a piece of leftover quiche heated, Isabeau cleared her poetry journal and pens from the kitchen table. She took out her atlas. Open, it covered half the kitchen table. Joseph Turner's letter sat beside it. New Zealand was alone in the atlas, the last map. It had been in the news a lot since the sinking of the *Rainbow Warrior* in Auckland the previous summer. Now she wished she'd paid more attention to what they'd said about the country itself: these long, skinny islands sitting in the ocean at the end of the world, like a forgotten appendix to the planet. So much water. She shuddered.

Isabeau reread the letter. *Unforeseen circumstances*? What could have happened to Joseph Turner that he was desperate enough to send some of his father's ashes to the post office in Carnac? Monsieur Poulain was a devout Catholic. What would he think about scattering the ashes?

She picked up the photo. Although Joseph Turner's father was dead,

Isabeau envied him. On the photo, he smiled from his happy childhood at her. All she had of Papa was the chipped bowl he'd always used for his breakfast coffee, and the rag doll, Cosette, he'd given her for her sixth birthday. She still kept Cosette hidden away in her bed. Now, her woollen hair was reduced to a few strands. She was worn out, like her memories of Papa.

Isabeau went to bed late. At three o'clock she woke and turned the bedside lamp on again. "A dead man's ashes are in the garage," she whispered to herself. She hugged the duvet tighter, and left the light on. She was supposed to be finding Papa, keeping the promise she'd made to herself again and again over the years; not becoming responsible for someone else's father, even if it was only ashes. But she couldn't stop thinking about George Turner. She could understand why he would be so drawn to the stones.

Her head was full of questions though. Why had the parcel turned up at All Saints and the day she was in charge for the very first time? As crazy as it seemed, did Joseph Turner somehow know how important the standing stones were to her? It was too much of a coincidence. Was it a sign that it was possible to find her own father?

13

The usual bowl of black coffee didn't make the slightest difference. Isabeau had hardly slept. Her shoulders and neck were tight, and she had a headache. She couldn't clear her head, couldn't shake the image of George Turner from her mind. He looked big and strong. He'd like the Giant. It was drizzling, but she had to get out. She needed to walk. She pulled tracksuit pants and a woollen roll-neck sweater on over her pyjamas. Nobody would know. She'd drive up to the house and walk from there. Isabeau twisted her hair up into a knot and tucked it into her beret. The key to the Alouettes house went into one coat pocket and her inhaler into the other. In the garage, the ashes were still on the shelf. "Good morning," she said softly to the envelope. She backed the car out and went to close the garage door. She returned to the shelf and stood, looking at the envelope. Finally, she picked it up and took it inside to the coat stand. "It's warmer in here. I'll be back later. I need to go to the stones."

As Isabeau followed the route des Alignements, deep inside herself she talked to the menhirs. She wanted to talk to George Turner too. She started speaking aloud – about what she was seeing, where she was going – and by the time she turned left into allée des Alouettes she wasn't sure if she was talking to herself or to George Turner. On the basis of the photo, he could be around Papa's age. What would George Turner think of the house? She still didn't know what she was going to do with it.

When she'd done her usual walk around inside the house and locked up again, the drizzle had stopped, but the air was still damp and cold. She walked quickly past the Morels' house, and was almost at the corner when she heard someone call. She turned. Docteur Morel was walking towards her.

"Lovely to see you, Isabeau," he greeted her. "We saw you pop in last weekend, but you were gone before we could catch you. How's your asthma?" He kissed her on both cheeks.

"Not too bad, thanks."

"I hope you've found a good doctor here."

"He's okay. But not as good as the old doctor I used to have."

Docteur Morel smiled. "Why don't you come in? This old doctor would love to catch up with you and hear about your plans for the house."

"I'm still sorting things out. Maybe I'll do some work on it first. I don't know ... I'm not sure if it's worth renovating."

"I think your father would want you to keep it." Docteur Morel followed Isabeau's gaze towards the house.

"Even though it belonged to Mother?"

"He often talked to me about how he liked it here. I got the impression it was the longest he'd ever been in one place." Docteur Morel stared at the house. "Anyway, the house is yours now." He looked as if he wanted to say something else, but before Isabeau could ask, the front door of their house opened and Madame Morel stepped out.

"Isabeau, wonderful to see you. Come in and have a hot drink," she offered.

"Thanks, but I'm going for a walk. I need some exercise and fresh air."

"Don't catch cold," Madame Morel scolded with a smile. "Come and see us when you've got time."

"I'll come and see you another day," Isabeau replied. "I'd better go before it starts raining again."

Isabeau crossed route du Purgatoire and took the right fork. She wished she'd accepted the invitation. She adjusted her scarf tighter against the cold air and concentrated on her walking, trying to relax her body, trying to take her mind off her breath. In Besançon the doctor was always telling her to keep warm, but she was just as likely to have an asthma attack if she stayed inside and became a prisoner of her own thoughts.

At the Kermario Alignments the wet standing stones formed dismal untidy lines against the grey sky. Each one seemed alone. Today she stopped at the dolmen in the corner near the road. Time had removed the mound of earth that had once covered the slabs of rock, leaving the grave bare. It was an empty tomb remembering a body. She stared at the simple burial chamber and thought about George and Joseph Turner.

The road led past the entrances to La Grande Métairie and Le Moulin de Kermaux camping grounds and the little windmill where tourists often climbed up to take photos. Here the stones ended and the pine trees kept Isabeau company until she arrived at the empty car park for the Giant of Manio. The path to the clearing was bumpy with tree roots, and the earthy smell of horse manure from the riding school bordering the woods hung in the air. When she arrived in the clearing her shoulders and neck felt better, but the weight on her chest was still there, and the ashes were still heavy in her thoughts.

"Bonjour, Monsieur le Géant," Isabeau said to the Giant, and she walked around the huge stone several times while she gathered her thoughts. "There was an unusual parcel at the post office yesterday. Some ashes of this man from New Zealand who wanted to come to Carnac. I think you would like George Turner."

Isabeau laid her hands on the Giant and felt the minute indentations and texture of his surface. It was like a mysterious Braille. She took a deep breath, closed her eyes and leaned back against the stone.

Docteur Morel came into her mind; the way he had looked when the conversation turned to her father, as if he knew more than he was saying. And then Isabeau remembered a particular autumn day long ago. Then, too, the air had been damp and cold.

She had been waiting for Papa in the stones, always waiting in the stones, as the day faded. He'd been coming home later and later, and he smelled different, like when he'd had a glass of wine. Her breath was making a whistling noise in her chest. She wished she'd taken the inhaler he'd picked up from the pharmacy for her. She headed back up the alignments and when she entered the house walked quietly to the sideboard. The inhaler wasn't in the drawer. She could hear her mother's footsteps on the stairs. Isabeau ran next door to the Morels'. There, Madame Morel knelt and put her arms around her. Finally Isabeau's words came out. "I can't find my inhaler. Papa's not home."

"René has one," Madame Morel replied, and sat Isabeau down. She went out of the room and came back with a new inhaler. She undid the packaging, clipped the canister in, shook it several times and helped Isabeau put it to her lips. "I'll leave it in the cupboard for you. If you ever need it, come and see me," she told Isabeau.

Isabeau's eyes opened suddenly as she remembered. Why did the Morels have another inhaler at the house? At the time it had seemed natural – he was a doctor – even though Papa had collected everything else from the pharmacy. The Morels must have organized the inhaler especially for her. It was a strange feeling to understand a minor detail from so long ago, something that had seemed insignificant. What else hadn't she seen that was obvious to the adults? Isabeau would have to ask the Morels about it.

Isabeau put down her embroidery basket and checked her pocket for her inhaler. She should have brought some flowers. She shouldn't have worn a skirt. It was too late; she'd already rung the doorbell.

"I'm so glad you've come, Isabeau. Come in," said Marianne, leading Isabeau through to the kitchen. She was wearing black trousers and a stretch top, and everything fitted in the right places. She wasn't afraid to show off her figure. Isabeau had never liked make-up, but she was intrigued by how Marianne did it: just enough in the right places. Marianne's cheeks were flushed, and she looked even happier and bubblier than usual.

"Can I help with anything?" asked Isabeau.

"You can give me a hand with setting the table," Marianne said. She took out a colourful tablecloth with a traditional pattern featuring Breton peasants: little men in breeches and women with aprons and lace headdresses. She handed Isabeau white plates, cutlery and crystal glasses for wine and water. "François's bringing dessert. And he's also bringing his friend Pierrot for lunch. He's a carpenter. He often helps out around the bakery."

Isabeau studied the knives and forks as she set them out – they had a slightly heart-shaped handle. Everything was beautiful in a simple way. Everything about Marianne's life was perfect. She made it look easy to be happy.

"I was going to wait till François got home, but I'm too excited. Look!" Marianne tilted her left hand towards Isabeau. The ruby and diamonds shone under the kitchen light, but not as brightly as Marianne's smile. "I always thought we'd get married, but I was so surprised when François gave me this yesterday."

"It's beautiful. Congratulations. Have you set a date for the wedding?"

"We're going to have an engagement party sometime in the new year, and we'll get married next summer, before François' parents retire and we take over the bakery completely." Marianne didn't stop smiling.

"It all sounds exciting."

"I'm glad you've come for lunch, Isabeau. Since I've been in Carnac

I haven't had time to do anything much except work," said Marianne. "Lots of people come into the bakery, but it's hard to really get to know people, to make friends."

Isabeau nodded. Marianne had no idea how true that was.

"Anyway, my mum's just rung. My family's thrilled. Mum and Dad love François, and they're good friends with his parents."

"Is that how you met?"

"My parents have a bakery near Angers, and François came to the bakery as an apprentice and boarded with us. His father thought he should get some experience elsewhere. But it wasn't until François came back to help out a couple of years ago that the romantic spark happened." Marianne made the gesture with her hands of fireworks going off.

"Love brought you to Carnac?"

Marianne nodded. "What about you? Was it love?" she asked cheekily.

"No. Well, maybe love for Carnac. I was born here, spent my childhood up beside the Ménec Alignments ... I have a house there."

"Lucky you. Why are you living in town then?"

"The house needs work."

Marianne's eyes lit up. "François' parents have bought a house for their retirement. When they retire we'll shift into the bakery, but I'd love to have my own place to do up, put my mark on. I love decorating."

"This needs lots of work. More than decorating. It's ..."

"You should talk to Pierrot. He does a lot of work on old houses. He may be able to help."

"I don't know if it's worth it."

"I'm sure he could help you with that. So, is your family around here then?" asked Marianne.

"When I was nine my mother and I went to live in Besançon." Isabeau wanted to say more, but the words were stuck.

"I have an aunt who lives there. She's been a French teacher at the Lycée Victor Hugo for years. It would be funny if she'd taught you. She's always joking about having illustrious neighbours because her apartment's in the town centre, around the corner from the house where Victor Hugo was born."

"I would've liked to study literature, writing. It didn't work out that way."

"Is your mother still in Besançon?"

'Yes ... she's buried there."

"I'm sorry," said Marianne. "And your father?"

"I don't know where he is. I haven't seen him for a long time." Isabeau's voice wavered. She pretended to study the figures on the tablecloth. She wasn't sure if she felt better having told Marianne or not.

Marianne was about to speak when the door opened and François entered, his arms full of bread. Just behind him was Pierrot. He looked about the same age as François. He was carrying a cake box and had a friendly smile.

"Hi ladies," François greeted them. "I hope we haven't kept you waiting too long. Pierrot's been giving us a hand. Today, the more the merrier." He laughed.

"Isabeau, you know François from the bakery – and this is Pierrot," said Marianne.

François and Pierrot tended their cheeks. Isabeau swallowed and stepped towards them. She turned to François first and then Pierrot. She felt even more self conscious with him. She hadn't been brought up being taught to greet relatives and strangers with a kiss, and everyone she knew, except the Morels, shook her hand. She was only just getting used to embracing Marianne.

As soon as they had finished, François grabbed Marianne around the waist.

"I couldn't wait. I told Isabeau," said Marianne, kissing him.

"I can see by your face," he replied. "And it won't take long for word to get around town this week, will it?" François winked at Isabeau. "Let's get started; I'm famished."

Marianne placed a plate with a block of foie gras in the middle of the table and added the toaster with an extension cord. "I'll toast the bread as we eat. It's better warm," she explained.

"Foie gras! You're spoiling us," Isabeau stammered.

"It's not every day we get engaged," said Marianne.

After the entrée, Marianne brought out a dish of flageolet beans and then the leg of lamb. She placed it in front of François to be carved. Printed on the side facing Isabeau was "Agneau de Nouvelle-Zélande." *New Zealand Lamb.* Isabeau stared at the words.

"Isabeau? You do like lamb, don't you?" asked François while he sliced the meat.

"Sorry?" Isabeau blinked.

"You do like lamb, don't you?" Marianne repeated.

"Lamb ... yes, lovely, thanks." Isabeau looked down at the slightly pink meat.

"Great. I hope you enjoy it."

"I sure will. I'm ravenous," said Pierrot. "I've been looking forward to this all morning. I haven't had much time to cook this week."

"Do you have lots of work on?" Marianne asked him.

"I'm finishing off a house in Sainte-Anne-d'Auray, when I'm not helping out around the bakery," Pierrot laughed.

"Isabeau was just telling me that she has a house up by the alignments, and it needs some work."

"Sounds interesting," said Pierrot.

"It's old, rundown," said Isabeau, shaking her head. "I'm not sure if it's worth doing anything with it. Perhaps I should just sell it."

"You'd be surprised what's possible. Some of the houses I've worked on have been in a terrible state."

"But this house is ... I ..."

"Would you like me to take a look at it, give you some advice?" offered Pierrot.

"Thanks, but I don't want to inconvenience you."

"No problem at all. I'd be happy to help."

"That's kind of you. I'll have a think about it." Isabeau took a mouthful of lamb and chewed it for a long time while the conversation changed topic. She didn't know what to think about letting Pierrot have a look at the house. And she felt his eyes on her from time to time. She tried to ignore it. If she thought about it, she felt the colour start to rise on her cheeks.

It was half past three when they finished lunch. François and Pierrot returned to the bakery, Pierrot promising to get in touch even when Isabeau said there was no urgency. Marianne and Isabeau did the dishes, then settled back at the table with their embroidery. Isabeau pulled out her embroidery of the Giant of Manio.

"That's going to be stunning with the grey you've chosen," said Marianne. I don't know how you do it, drafting your own patterns. A lot of people are noticing your embroideries in the bakery. I'm sure tourists would pay big money for them."

"I doubt anyone would want to buy them," Isabeau answered. "And I don't think I could part with them. Anyway, what are you working on? It looks like you've finished that little picture for François' niece?"

"I'm going to experiment with bookmarks – something to dress up the table at our engagement party. I'd like to sit one on each plate, with the name of the person and our initials on it. I can see it already," Marianne said, as she pulled out some strips of linen.

"If you need a hand ..." Isabeau made the offer before she'd even thought about it. She'd never worked on an embroidery project with anyone else.

"Are you sure?" asked Marianne.

"I'd love to help."

"I'd appreciate that. It gets hectic in the bakery before Christmas."

They talked while they worked, but Isabeau rarely looked up. Why had she mentioned the house? She should have kept it to herself. It felt like her own story didn't belong to her any more. She hoped nothing would come of Pierrot's offer.

When Isabeau arrived home in the early evening, she picked up the box from the coat stand. The parcel had been addressed to the Postmaster; it was Monsieur Poulain's responsibility to deal with the ashes. She should take them back to the post office in the morning and give them to him, she thought. She should.

Monsieur Poulain had rung to say he would be late. It would've been easier if he'd been there when Isabeau arrived, his usual early self, like in the scenario in her head. She opened the desk drawer and looked at her bag again.

"Monsieur Poulain," she whispered to herself, "this parcel arrived Friday. I took it home for safekeeping. I didn't want to leave it here over the weekend. It's somebody's ..."

"Good morning. Sorry I'm late." Monsieur Poulain came through the door, his woollen scarf tied several times around his neck and his brown checked cap pulled down over his ears. He stopped at Isabeau's desk, pulled off his gloves and stretched out his hand for the customary morning handshake.

Isabeau took a deep breath. "Monsieur, this ..."

"Mademoiselle Martin, good morning. Thanks for taking over on Friday. A little rest did me the world of good." Monsieur Poulain paused and surveyed the office. "Didn't want to take any more time off, though."

"Monsieur, good morning, I ... this ..."

"How are you? You look a little pale." Monsieur Poulain peered at Isabeau.

"It's just ... I ..."

Corinne came over. "Monsieur Poulain, good to see you back," she said. "How are you?" She glanced at Isabeau.

"Better, thank you, Corinne." He turned back to Isabeau. "Now, did everything go well on Friday? Did you want to say something?"

"Everything was fine, Monsieur."

16

Isabeau pulled out the writing pad she'd bought at the bookshop and put her name and home address at the top of the first sheet. If, by any chance, Joseph Turner replied and it was to the post office, Monsieur Poulain might find out about the parcel. She might get into trouble because she hadn't said anything about it. Monsieur Poulain called on her to deal with any correspondence that needed to be in English. If he'd opened the parcel he would have asked her to draft the letter. He wouldn't have even been able to read it without her translating. She tried to tell herself that she would be doing this anyway. She had been taking the box of ashes to work since Monday, in the wild hope there would be an opportunity to tell him about it. Three days had passed and she still hadn't said anything. She could hardly just bring it out now and say it had arrived on Friday. She twirled her pen. "Joseph Turner. Joseph Turner," she kept repeating. He didn't know her, yet it was as if he'd reached out directly to her from the other side of the world.

Dear Joseph was too informal, *Dear Sir* too formal. She crossed them both out and then underneath put *Dear Mr Turner*, and kept writing that down the page, like the lines of a repetitive poem. She took another piece of paper and doodled his name while she kept repeating it aloud, hoping that it would somehow conjure forth the right words for the letter.

I am writing in response to your recent letter concerning your father's ashes. The parcel has arrived safely in Carnac. As Deputy Postmaster, I have your father's ashes in my possession. I can imagine how disappointed you must be that you are unable to undertake this trip. I can assure you ...

On Saturday afternoon Isabeau still only had an unfinished copy. She scribbled phrases and then started again and again, and the balls of paper lay scattered on the floor, taunting her that she would never be able to finish the letter. It should have been a matter of a simple sentence or two, but she hadn't had a good night's sleep all week, and she wasn't sure what she could assure Joseph Turner. Now the box of ashes was sitting on the coat stand by the front door. She didn't know where else to put it. George Turner was in limbo.

In desperation, Isabeau took the box from the stand and carried it to the middle of the table. The photo stood up against it perfectly. She looked through the unpacked things in the alcove until she found a candle and an old candle holder. She arranged them on the table and lit the candle. The timid flame stretched upwards and danced gently from side to side, mesmerizing her with its irregular movement. It was a warm sight. The candle was good company, so was George Turner.

Isabeau started the letter again, forcing herself to write quickly without raising her pen. The words came more or less as they had in her rough copies. She didn't wait for them, or let any thought or doubt interrupt her, and forged on. Suddenly, she was finished.

Dear Mr Turner,

I am writing in response to your letter concerning your father's ashes. The parcel has arrived safely at the post office in Carnac. I read your letter with great interest, and I can imagine how disappointed you must be that you are unable to undertake this trip. As Deputy Postmaster, I have the ashes in my possession, and am waiting for a suitable occasion to scatter them around the standing stones according to your request. I understand why your father had this wish. The standing stones are a special place. I know them well, having grown up beside them.

Yours sincerely,

Isabeau Martin

If she didn't take it straight to the postbox she might change her mind. On her way, she went to the bakery. Julie was serving a customer. She didn't usually work Saturday afternoon. Only now, Isabeau remembered Marianne was going to Vannes with François' mother. She didn't go into the bakery, and as she headed past the church, she looked up at the statue of Saint Cornély sitting in the alcove on the west side. The legend was that when the Romans persecuted him and chased him, he turned them all to stone, thus creating the standing stones. She liked the story.

Isabeau went inside the church. She was drawn to the stand of burning candles, where the flames flickered like a silent choir. She placed five francs in the box, took one of the slender white candles, kissed it to a flame and placed it on a metal spike. For George. The letter was in her pocket. She sat and closed her eyes, trying to imagine herself casually walking up to the mail slot and slipping it in. Forty minutes later she was finally at the postbox. Her right hand clutched the letter and wouldn't move. She took a puff of her inhaler, then with her left hand pushed her right hand forward and separated the fingers. The letter dropped. As soon as it had left her hand she wanted to take it back.

17

Isabeau cleared the sideboard and placed George's box in the middle, adding the photo, letter and candle holder. All that was missing was flowers to complete the arrangement. "I've done it, George. I've sent the letter to your son." This was their secret. But the feeling of relief of having finally written the letter and sent it was short-lived. Should she have done it without saying anything to Monsieur Poulain? What if he somehow found out? Could she get in serious trouble at work: be demoted, or even worse sent to another post office? It had seemed too good to be true to get the position in Carnac in the first place.

And now she had to scatter the ashes. She tried to put the thoughts out of her mind. She needed to keep busy. She dropped her favourite Goldman cassette into the deck, pushed play and started picking up the balls of paper around the kitchen, moving to the music.

Banging. Isabeau wasn't sure for a moment if it was the beat of the music or someone knocking on the door. Nobody came to see her: only Marianne, who had called in once. Isabeau had been trying to get up enough courage to invite her for a meal – slip the invitation into the conversation as if it was the most natural thing in the world, like it would be for Marianne.

She tiptoed to the door and looked through the peephole. It was Pierrot, straightening his jacket with one hand. It looked like he was holding something behind his back with the other. He must have heard the music. She tried to breathe slowly. He knocked again, and Isabeau jumped. Her heart was pounding. "Just open the door, Isabeau," she told herself. She turned the lock, grabbed the handle and pulled. Pierrot stepped back.

"I wasn't expecting to see you ... this soon, for you to visit ... You must be busy," Isabeau blurted out. She held out her hand to greet Pierrot, then felt stupid. She should have tended her cheek. He stepped forward and kissed her on the cheeks anyway.

"I stopped in at the bakery and Marianne asked me to drop these off to you." Pierrot held out a small bunch of flowers. "She's just got back from Vannes, and bought a couple of bunches. She said you might like a few to brighten up your place."

"That's kind of Marianne, and you too, of course. Thank you."

"I was going to ring, then Marianne mentioned you lived this close," he said, shifting on his feet. "I hope you don't mind me turning up."

"Um, no."

"I've got a client who's just put his project on hold, so I thought I might be able to help you sort out what you want to do with your house," Pierrot said quickly.

"My house?"

"You seemed like you needed some help with this house of yours."

"Well, I ... do you want to come in?" Isabeau felt she had to ask.

"Thanks."

Too late, Isabeau realized the box of ashes on the sideboard. And her poetry journal and the rough copy of the letter on the table. She pulled off her cardigan and placed it over the box and other things on the sideboard.

"Sorry about the mess. I'm having a big clean-up; I've got a bit hot in the process." She gathered up the things from the table and put them in front of the box, hastily arranging her cardigan over it all. Her hands were shaking. "Please, have a seat."

"Nice sideboard," Pierrot said, watching Isabeau. "I love oak. I like to restore old furniture when I get the time."

After she had set the coffee maker going, the sound of water dripping through the filter and the coffee maker gurgling filled the silence. She remembered how he had been looking at her at lunch at Marianne and Francois' place. He was doing it again.

"I'm intrigued about this house of yours," he said.

"Well, as I said, I'm not sure if it's worth renovating or not. I might end up selling it."

"Renovating an old house can be daunting, but when you get a vision of what you want to achieve it becomes easier. What kind of work does the house need?" Pierrot fidgeted with his hands.

"I don't even know where to start." Isabeau stayed standing beside the bench.

"Have you had it long?"

"No. I only came back to Carnac six months ago: about the same time Marianne shifted here." Isabeau breathed deeply, and busied herself with pouring the coffee.

"Are you from around here then?"

"I grew up here. I spent a lot of time amongst the standing stones. Suppose it kept me occupied." Isabeau concentrated on keeping her voice even, natural.

"I used to roam around there as a kid with François during the holidays. Can't remember ever seeing you though."

"They cover a lot of ground," Isabeau said with a shrug.

"Around the alignments; that's a nice place to have a house."

"Yes."

They talked for a while about the alignments while they drank their coffee. When they'd finished, Pierrot got up and stopped beside the sideboard, studying it. "There's something about old furniture and old houses, like this sideboard, for example," he said. "They have their own character. You just have to know how to bring it out to its best advantage. I'm happy to help with your house and it's no bother at all. I love old houses. What say I have a look at yours with you? Perhaps that could help you sort out what you want to do? No obligation. I know it's a bit last-minute, but I'm free Tuesday. I don't have any plans for Armistice Day." He ran his hand along the front of the sideboard, inspecting the wood. His hand caught in her cardigan and it started to slip.

Isabeau's chest tightened. She stepped over and put out her hand to stop the cardigan from falling, draping it back over the box in the same movement. She said the first thing that came into her head. "Okay."

"Shall we say two o'clock?" Pierrot asked. "I'll bring some house magazines for you."

"Fine. Would you like more coffee?" Isabeau forced herself to ask the question.

"I'd better be going. I promised Marianne I'd put up some shelves for her."

Isabeau followed Pierrot to the door and gave him the address. He stopped at the coat stand.

"Nice stand. You've got good taste in furniture." He smiled at Isabeau.

"Thanks."

"Looks like you appreciate old things. I'm sure you can make your house special."

As soon as Pierrot had gone, Isabeau put the flowers beside the box and the photo, and cleared a space inside the sideboard. If there was a next time she would put everything away. She sat down at the kitchen table and leaned forward on her arms. "That was close, George."

Why did Pierrot seem so keen to help her with her house, Isabeau wondered. Was it more than just the house? She'd found herself agreeing before she'd realized. Why on earth had she agreed? He seemed nice, but she hardly knew him. She kept telling herself it was just a rundown house, like many he'd already worked on. She still had the uneasy feeling that she would be showing him her childhood.

She touched the box. Since she'd had the ashes, nothing was as usual. She had sent a letter to a stranger on the other side of the world, had a visitor and agreed to show the house to Pierrot. And she was talking more and more to a dead man's ashes.

18

Isabeau unlocked the front door of the Alouettes House, and in spite of the cold she opened the shutters and windows too. She wanted to go and ask the Morels about the inhaler, but first she had to get Pierrot's visit over with. One thing at a time. There was still three hours before he arrived. She was far too early, but she had found it impossible to settle to anything at home. She should have gone to the bakery and got his number from Marianne, said she wasn't well. She sat down on the doorstep and pulled her jacket around her. She was tired of the house being sad and forlorn. She was tired of being lonely.

"Well, George, what do you think?" Isabeau said to the box of ashes, wrapped in a scarf at the bottom of her bag. "I'll take you to the Giant later."

She had packed a thermos of coffee and a sandwich for lunch. To try and take her mind off Pierrot, she poured herself a cup, and sipped the hot liquid while she thought about Marianne's project. Marianne had given her a pattern, linen, thread and a list with six names. Isabeau took the list out of her bag. Tonton Aimé, a great-uncle; Christian and Sophie, her brother and his girlfriend; Pierrot, and two of Marianne's friends: Marie-Claire and Véronique. She knew the names off by heart now. She wanted to start with Tonton Aimé.

Tonton was a child's word for uncle. It was one of the names that had been thrown around by the children at school when they had talked of their families, often complaining of visits and gatherings, unaware of the good fortune they had. She peered over at the Morels' house. When she was a child she'd pretended they were her parents.

It was too cold to sit. Isabeau slipped the list back in her bag and left the front step to walk around the garden. Pieces of wood and paper were scattered on the ground, and withered convolvulus wound up the front fence. She gathered up the pieces of wood and carried them to the shed at the back of the house. She'd never really had a good look inside. Hoping to find an old bag for the rubbish, she pushed the door and it creaked open. The floor was covered with empty cardboard boxes, stained newspaper and a dirty blanket. In the corner, a pile of old mats hid a wooden box containing gardening tools. Amongst them Isabeau recognized a small fork and a spade. Her father's. She caressed the smooth wooden handles. They'd been there all this time and she'd never realized. She went back to the fence with them, pulled off the convolvulus and started digging.

Long bleached roots formed parallel networks in the earth. When Isabeau pulled hard on the white roots they snapped. She swore. She chose a fat one and loosened the earth around it, determined to ease it out without breaking it. She pulled gently, as though she was undoing embroidery stitches, sliding the thread right back to its beginning, and the root eventually slithered out completely. Victory. Each time she dug, more roots magically appeared, and her determination to remove them increased. It felt strange, but good, to have her hands in the earth and be clearing the small patch. It had never occurred to her before now that she could tidy the garden around the house; that this was her garden. This was her house. She didn't normally say that to herself.

The water wasn't turned on, so Isabeau brushed her clothes and rubbed her hands as best she could before installing herself again on the doorstep. The exercise had given her a good appetite and made the bread and cheese taste better than usual. Unused to the bending and crouching of gardening, her legs and back were sore, but it was a satisfying ache.

There wasn't enough time to go for a walk now. What if she left and wasn't there when Pierrot arrived? That might disappoint Marianne, and bring up more questions about the house.

Isabeau returned to the garden. She was still there when she saw a white van slow down on the road. Pierrot was at the wheel. She stayed crouched and continued digging. She wished she had her inhaler in the pocket of her jeans, and that they weren't all dirty now down the legs.

"Salut, Isabeau. I didn't expect to find you in the garden. Looks like you're raring to go with the house," he called. He was carrying a pad and pencil.

"No, not really … I thought I'd pull out a few weeds while I was waiting. I'll be finished soon. You go in and have a look." Isabeau gestured over her shoulder at the house.

She took her time finishing in the garden and putting the tools away, while Pierrot walked around the outside of the house and then inside. After his inspection, he met her in the living room, and showed her some notes and rough drawings.

"The house is pretty rundown, but it's got good bones," he told her. "The stone needs some attention. I know a stonemason who does a lot of this kind of work. I could also help you sort out a roofer. It wouldn't be a big job for them. Apart from that, it's amazing what some cleaning and new paint and wallpaper can do for an old house." He rubbed his hand over the wall.

"You make it sound easy. I can't really imagine what it could look like." Isabeau folded her arms across her chest.

"I restored a similar house in Pluneret, and you wouldn't believe the difference. They knocked out the kitchen wall and opened up the living area. You could do something like that here." Pierrot pointed towards the kitchen. "Take out this wall, and extend the kitchen and dining area right out. You'd be surprised how much the whole house would come alive from such a simple change, and how much bigger it would seem."

Isabeau walked over to the kitchen door and looked in.

"It all depends on what you need, though," continued Pierrot. "It's not about the house; it's about you. You should renovate it to match the way you live. Do you like to cook, to entertain?"

"Not really. I mean, I cook, but I don't often entertain." Isabeau tried not to think about how much she was stretching the truth.

"What kind of things do you like doing, then?" Pierrot asked.

"I like embroidery, and I read, and ... do a little bit of writing," she mumbled.

"Where do you do your embroidery? Sitting at the kitchen table, or in an armchair? Would an office or a corner for a desk be helpful?" Pierrot started sketching on his pad.

"Maybe." Isabeau followed his pencil strokes. "It's the light that matters for my embroidery. Sometimes I sit at the kitchen table, but mostly I prefer my armchair."

"It wouldn't take a lot to open up the kitchen and then in this living area create a corner for your desk with shelving for books and papers. You could put your armchair near the window," he suggested. "It's really the kitchen and bathroom that need the most work, but a lot of that is superficial." His enthusiastic voice filled the house.

While Pierrot took measurements, Isabeau tried to picture what he was explaining. He offered to draw up some plans, and she found herself agreeing. When he left, he handed her a pile of magazines, saying he could make it more economical for her by fitting it in quiet periods, around other work. It would take longer, but she didn't seem in a hurry.

Isabeau sat back down on the front step and sighed. Her head was full of Pierrot's ideas after all. She could almost imagine the changes he'd suggested. She hugged her bag on her knees, and talked softly. "George, you must have given lots of advice to Joseph when you were alive. What should I do with the house? Will it achieve anything?"

Silence answered her questions. She got up and walked to the Morels' house.

19

Before Madame Morel had even placed the white coffee cups on the table, Isabeau's question burst out.

"Madame Morel, I was thinking the other day about that time when I'd just got an inhaler and I couldn't find it."

Madame Morel paused, the sugar bowl in her hand. For a second, Isabeau wasn't sure whether she remembered.

"You were in quite a state." Madame Morel nodded, and looked Isabeau in the eyes.

"You had a brand new one, just like mine," Isabeau continued. "The other day it occurred to me that it was quite a coincidence that you had one here, all ready for me when I needed it." She concentrated on each word. It was important that she said this.

"René brought one home in case your mother misplaced your one and you were caught out, didn't you, René?" said Madame Morel, turning from Isabeau to her husband.

"Did you talk to my father about it?" Isabeau asked Docteur Morel.

"We didn't always have the opportunity to talk to him. I took it upon myself to get an extra one in case. You know, we used to worry about you," said Docteur Morel.

Isabeau took a big breath.

"Before my father disappeared, did he come and talk to either of you? Do you know why he disappeared? Where he went?"

Docteur Morel and his wife looked at each other.

"We used to see him from time to time. In the weeks before he disappeared, though, we hardly saw him," said Docteur Morel. "It came out of the blue for us too – that he left like that. Left you. So you haven't had any contact with him since then? Neither you nor your mother?"

"I didn't. And if Mother did, she never told me. You know what she was like. I really came to believe ..."

"What is it, ma petite?" asked Madame Morel, putting her arm around Isabeau's shoulders.

"... that he didn't care about me; that he didn't love me." The words tumbled out, taking Isabeau by surprise.

"I'm sure your father loved you very much," replied Docteur Morel.

"How can you be sure? He never wrote or tried to find me," Isabeau started to cry.

"How do you know that?" asked Docteur Morel, his voice kind and gentle.

"We were never listed in the phone book, but I'm sure that if he had tried, he could have found us."

"When you and your mother left, we had no idea where she was taking you." Docteur Morel cleared his throat. "The only thing she said to us was England. What if your father believed your mother had taken you back to England, and tried to find you there?"

"England? That's ridiculous! She always said that she hated England and that there was nothing left back there for her. Although I don't think there was much in France for her either."

"Have you ever tried to find your father?" asked Madame Morel.

"I wrote to him several times. I sent the letters here in case he returned. They came back. I figured he didn't want me any more, otherwise why would he have left me with Mother?" Isabeau took the tissue that Madame Morel offered and wiped her eyes, then blew her nose. "When I started at the post office, I searched for his name, but couldn't find anything. I kept putting off coming back here, and then Mother needed looking after."

"It was like a miracle when you turned up," said Docteur Morel.

"The real reason I came back is to find him. But I don't know where to start," Isabeau sniffed.

"Well, I saw your father in a bar in Pornic a few months after he left," said Docteur Morel.

"Pornic! That's not very far."

"It was along the waterfront," Docteur Morel explained. "It was called Le Bar des Pêcheurs or something like that. I was in a hurry to visit an elderly friend who was unwell, and I saw your father through the window. When I called in on the way back he was gone. I'm afraid I never saw him after that."

"Perhaps you could start looking there," suggested Madame Morel. "He may have worked there."

In a bar in Pornic. So close. It seemed like a cruel joke. Isabeau didn't know whether to laugh or cry. The pressure was building up between her eyes, like a third eye at the bridge of her nose. She needed to get away, to be alone. "Thank you, Madame Morel, Docteur Morel, for the coffee and the information." She stood up. "I must go. I still have some things to do in the house."

Upstairs in her old bedroom, Isabeau slumped down against the wall and pressed her hands over her eyes, but the pressure wouldn't go away. She felt small again, like when she used to crouch in the corner behind the wardrobe, wanting to make herself disappear. Her head filled with the past. She had come home from school and the front door had been open. She had gone to the bathroom. Something was strange, not right. Papa's toothbrush wasn't on the little shelf of the wooden cabinet. It wasn't inside either, and his old razor was also gone. The night before had been the first time Isabeau had seen him in a few days. She filled an old beer bottle with water, and took a piece of camembert and some baguette. She could hear Mother upstairs, moving towards the staircase. Isabeau ran out the door and crossed the road, and only slowed her pace when she'd gone through the bushes to the menhirs. She was still there when the sun had lost its heat and it felt like the time Papa usually came home. It was eight o'clock when she came through the front door: the big hand on the kitchen clock was right on the twelve.

Mother was sitting at the kitchen table, staring at a piece of paper in her hands. It looked like Papa's flat scrawl. She crumpled it, took a box of matches from her pocket and set the paper alight in the ashtray, then she lit a cigarette and went up the stairs. Isabeau poured the last trickle from the beer bottle on the flames, and wisps of smoke wafted upwards. All that was left was the bitter smell of burnt words.

2 0

As a teenager, Isabeau had waited for years with mad hope for a reply to the letters – all twenty-three of them – she had sent to Papa. Perhaps a reply would appear in the same random way that he had disappeared. But her letters came back to her. Return to Sender. It became a long one-way conversation with herself. Now, as she waited for an answer from Joseph Turner, she wondered if her expectation that Papa would reply had ever completely faded.

If Joseph Turner wrote back, it would be a sign that it was all right that she hadn't scattered George yet. Each day she lifted the lid on her letterbox and said the same thing to herself: "Don't be stupid. Are you expecting that he's going to write back?" But she wanted him to. And Christmas was approaching. The post office was getting busy, with more and more mail. If only one of all those letters could be from Joseph Turner.

The letter from Papa had never come, but a letter from Joseph Turner did – one Saturday, after a long morning at work. Isabeau had gone straight home. She would go to the bakery later, she decided. She walked past her letterbox at first, and then came back. Two envelopes: a bill and an airmail envelope with large neat handwriting. Chest tightening, her thoughts racing, she put the letter in her coat pocket and walked slowly to the bakery, trying to loosen her shoulders, her torso. She needed a little time to gather herself, and there was always something reassuring about seeing Marianne, chatting to her.

Marianne was behind the counter serving a customer. Isabeau wanted to tell her, to shout out to everyone that she'd received a letter, an important letter, even if she was too scared to open it.

Finally, Marianne finished with the customer. "Pierrot dropped in to see François last night," she said to Isabeau. "Sounds like he's got lots of ideas for your house, and he's almost finished some plans. He said that it would be an interesting project to work on. You must be excited!" She clapped her hands.

"There's nothing finalized yet. I'm still not sure what I want to do. I've done some more bookmarks for you, though."

"Why don't you bring them round Tuesday evening? François has a

Bakers' Guild meeting. It's much more fun to work together."

"Thanks, that would be nice."

Isabeau asked for a baguette, and while Marianne served her, she ran her fingers across the letter in her pocket, gently feeling the outline of the stamps and the corners of the envelope.

On the way back home, Isabeau's steps quickened. She burst in the door. "There's a letter from Joseph!"

She put George's ashes and the photo on the kitchen table and sat down. She held the letter for a long time, and then she sliced down the fold of the envelope with her sharpest knife. The single sheet of paper was decorated along the top with a series of quirky drawings, all named: a little kiwifruit and a kiwi bird, a rugby ball, a fern, a sheep and the islands of New Zealand.

Dear Ms Martin,

I couldn't believe it when your letter arrived. I can't express my thanks enough for scattering my father's ashes. I am relieved and happy to know that his dream has been fulfilled, especially by someone who appreciates the standing stones. I'm deeply grateful to you for helping me.

I try to imagine what it is like in Carnac amongst so many standing stones. I have never seen such a sight. I've been looking at my father's books about megaliths, and my cousin, Drew, also brought me some from the library. Perhaps I'm asking too much, but I would appreciate if you could send me some photos of the standing stones where you have scattered my father's ashes.

I was very surprised to get a letter with such good English. If I ever do come to Carnac one day, I would like to meet you and thank you personally.

Thank you again. This letter cannot express the gratitude I feel.

Yours sincerely,

Joseph Turner

Isabeau picked up the photo of Joseph and his father. Exactly how old was Joseph Turner? In his twenties or thirties? Isabeau wished he were twenty-nine, the same age as her.

He thought she'd scattered the ashes.

"Are you mad at me that I haven't scattered you, George?"

When the time is right.

Isabeau blinked at the photo. If was as if the voice had come from inside and outside of her at the same time. Was she going mad, like her mother? She relit the little candle. Words came into her mind. She quickly found some paper and started scribbling.

Dear Mr Turner,

Thank you for your letter. I often think of your father and the importance of my task – fulfilling his wish to come to Carnac. I hope he is happy. I thought the best place to scatter his ashes was at the Giant of Manio, a six-metre-tall megalith that stands alone in the forest. It is very close to the alignments, but it is a more private place.

It is cold in Carnac now as we approach Christmas. The standing stones, called menhirs here, are sometimes shrouded in mist, which gives them an even more mysterious appearance. I spent a large part of my childhood playing amongst them. Although I also lived for many years in the east of France, I can't imagine living anywhere but here.

I can speak English because my mother was English, and my father, although French, spoke English too. Funny as it may seem, I've never been to England. My mother is dead now, and I don't know either of my parents' families. My own father is gone too, so your request has particularly touched me.

I do not have any photos at the moment, but I will try and send you some very soon. I am curious about New Zealand. Your faraway country seems exotic. I know very little about it.

Yours sincerely,

Isabeau Martin

She dropped her pen and stared at the page. She rarely talked about her parents, and here she was telling a stranger on the other side of the world about them. Isabeau looked at George and Joseph with their simple smiles. It was as if they were saying *Just send the letter. Don't complicate this.* Before the reality of what she was doing caught up with her, Isabeau walked briskly to the post office. She stopped at the airmail slot, suspended all thought and dropped the letter in.

"I did it," Isabeau said to herself, and hurried home to tell George.

Now she had to scatter the ashes.

2 1

It was nine o'clock, but felt like midnight. Isabeau slowed down at the Kermario Alignments and pulled into the side of the road near the dolmen. There was no one: just the wind, the watching moon and the stones – silent and dark – standing like monsters, as if in a second they could come to life. It wouldn't take long to throw the ashes into the dolmen; if only she hadn't decided to scatter George at the Giant. In the forest, it was more private, almost a sanctuary, but the very idea of that was turning against her in the dark of moving shadows and a fleeting moon.

That morning she'd waited at the Giant. With George in her bag she'd sat in the clearing, thinking about him and her part in his life, or more particularly his death. Silently, she had talked to him. It couldn't be rushed. She was about to slide the lid when a group of tourists arrived. They stayed for half an hour. She waited. More tourists, and each time they left more came, in ones and twos. All morning she grew colder, until finally she was alone with George. Isabeau breathed in, readying herself. She could do it. She just had to wait a few seconds longer. Then she heard more voices from the path. It was too late. She went home. Guilt had her in its jaw all afternoon; as if she were a bone, and it wouldn't let go of her. It was her own fault that she had to come back in the night.

The car park leading to the Giant was deserted. The trees guarded the night, their branches moving in the wind. They were animated in a way that Isabeau had never noticed during the day, when they were part of the restful summer green or winter bare landscape. They were black and alive now, their shadows forming anguished shapes across the sky as if they were warning her of some hidden danger, carried on the wind so she couldn't comprehend what or where it was. The only thing she knew was that the fear was in her.

Isabeau ran down the path. She pulled out her inhaler from her pocket and desperately sucked in as she stumbled forward. A dog barked in the distance. A gust of wind whipped the trees and filled the night with an evil swish. Something cracked on the path behind her. She looked over her shoulder and ran faster. Her foot caught in a tree root and she fell forward, clutching the box to her chest. Her head hit the dirt, while her right shoulder took the full force of the impact. The box, sandwiched between her and the ground, completely knocked the breath out of Isabeau, and shook her soul. There was something terribly wrong with her presence here in the dark night; she felt like she was committing a crime. She hurt all over, but she picked herself up, trembling, and ran back to the car still holding the box.

"**A**ny plans for Christmas and New Year, Isabeau?" asked Marianne.

"Not sure," said Isabeau, thinking of her meagre plans, such as they were.

"Our engagement celebration's at midday on Sunday the fourth at Saint-Laurent-de-la-Plaine. I hope you can make it," Marianne beamed. "You could come for the weekend."

"Are you sure?"

"I'd love you to be there and to meet my family. Pierrot's coming – he could bring you."

"I'd love to come, but I think I'll come on my own. I might stop off in Pornic on the way. I'm not sure yet."

"If you want to come Saturday and stay the night, I can organize something at the lodge where François' sisters and Pierrot are staying or perhaps you could stay with us," Marianne offered.

"Thanks. I'll let you know."

Marianne's onion soup was warm and comforting, her company also. Isabeau thought of George at home, and Joseph in New Zealand. Was he alone right now? Or eating with a friend? Or a girlfriend, or even a wife?

Isabeau was happy to let Marianne talk. She was full of excitement about her engagement: the party, the menu, what she'd wear and who would be there. Every time she mentioned François, her eyes lit up, and she twirled the ring on her finger. Then she began to talk about her family and their bakery.

"My brothers and I always had to help out. We got up to a lot of mischief. Once when it was the plum tart season, in August, we put all the plum stalks into the tart for our old teacher. There was all hell to pay when Papa found out. He laughs about it now, but he didn't at the time. Neither did we when we had to clean the bakery from top to bottom!"

"What do your brothers do?" Isabeau asked. There was only one, Christian, on the bookmark list.

"My eldest brother, Christian, is an engineer, and he works in Angers," Marianne said, pausing, her brow furrowed in a way Isabeau wasn't used to seeing. "My other brother, Thierry – he was just a year older than me – was in a horrible car accident." Her voice wavered.

"I'm sorry."

"It's a while ago now," Marianne said. "It's hard though, especially when it's Christmas or a celebration like the engagement party and he's not there. Times like that will always be a mixture of happy and sad."

"You must miss him." Isabeau didn't know what else to say.

"Yes. Anyway," Marianne's voice brightened, "at the party you'll be able to meet my parents and Christian, everybody from the bookmarks."

"I've finished the latest batch."

"Did you bring them with you?"

"No, I'd like to surprise you. You can give me the last ones," Isabeau offered.

"Really?"

"Yes. I'm enjoying doing them. Would you mind if I added a couple of extra touches?"

"Not at all. That sounds great. I don't know what I'd do without you! The bakery at Saint-Laurent gets busy, but nothing like here."

After dinner, they cleared the table and Marianne took her embroidery basket and a fat *La Redoute* catalogue, and they sat back down at the table. She opened the catalogue in front of Isabeau at a page featuring a model in a fitting black dress and short bolero jacket. "This is the outfit I was telling you about for the engagement party," she said.

"It's perfect for you."

"What are you going to wear?" Marianne asked.

"Probably trousers and a blouse." Isabeau flicked through the pages of the catalogue.

"Let's have a look," said Marianne. "I saw a dress that would suit your green-brown eyes. They're so unusual; I can never quite make out what colour they are. Here it is – this would look gorgeous on you! You could have your hair down and some nice earrings."

She held the crinkled page up in front of Isabeau. A deep lilac jersey dress hugged the model's curves. The neckline was draped, and sequins adorned the shoulders. The soft material was gathered around the waist, and hung flatteringly to mid-calf.

"I don't look anything like that model, and I don't really wear dresses."

"Isabeau, you're beautiful. It would look great. You're helping me with the bookmarks; I'd love to help you sort out your outfit for the party."

The order only took five days. Marianne told Isabeau that the parcel had arrived when she called in at the bakery, and insisted that Isabeau pop around after dinner for a try-on. François was working late, making Christmas chocolates.

When Isabeau arrived, the dress was ready on a hanger.

"It's an amazing dress, but I don't think it'll look good on me," Isabeau said. The neck was very low, and the style well fitting around the waist.

"You'll look gorgeous in it. You have a nice figure, Isabeau, hidden under your loose pullovers and cardigans. You should show it off more!"

Marianne made the exaggerated pose of a fashion model, and Isabeau couldn't help but laugh.

"It's just not my style. I prefer clothes that are comfortable and practical – jeans and trousers – and I don't have much opportunity to dress up."

"Comfortable and practical is okay for when you're biking, walking or renovating your house, but sometimes it's nice to dress up in something really feminine. Look, try it on, that's the best way to see." Marianne put the dress in Isabeau's hands and directed her towards the bedroom.

In front of the mirror there, Isabeau held the dress up, then she took off her roll-neck jumper and jeans, and carefully eased it down over her body. The material was soft. She stared at herself in the mirror. Was it really her?

"You should dress like this more often," said Marianne as Isabeau walked back into the kitchen. "How can I put this?" She adjusted the neckline and straightened out the waist. "I think you need a new bra. We can have another look in the catalogue." She smiled.

Isabeau blushed.

"Try this on over the dress," Marianne said, handing Isabeau a cropped jacket.

Thirty minutes later, Marianne had her black outfit on and Isabeau was standing beside her in the dress, wearing a pair of high heels, one of Marianne's necklaces, matching earrings and make-up that Marianne had applied in amazing deft strokes. It was like playing dress-ups.

23

Isabeau walked home. It had been a long day at work helping Monsieur Poulain with all the extra work that Christmas entailed. She hadn't even been home for lunch. The post office was full to the seams with mail-bags overflowing as if it were Santa's workshop, and she wondered if it was possible that somewhere inside one of them there was a letter for her. Everyone else was talking about the strikes and demonstrations that were starting to take over France: students in high schools and universities mobilizing against the proposed educational reforms. And now the railways were on strike. She only hoped that didn't affect the mail getting through. She'd arranged Joseph's letters around the box of ashes on the sideboard, and George continued to keep her company. Her Christmas wish was simple. She would content herself with another letter from Joseph. Looking in her letterbox had become a daily ritual of anticipation and disappointment.

Along the avenue, the light seeping through the cracks in the closed shutters shone warmly in the winter evening. Decorations sparkled out into the dark from the houses with open shutters, and occasionally Isabeau caught a glimpse of a Christmas tree, in pride of place, waiting in its fleeting splendour. In spite of the cold she slowed her step. She was a moth at the window of Christmas.

Through the windows of the crêperies and restaurants, the diners looked happier than they did during the year. Revelling in end-of-year dinners, they laughed longer and louder as they celebrated together. It was easier to be unhappy when it was an ordinary day. It was easier to pretend.

Even if they were shorter, Isabeau satisfied herself with her daily chats at the bakery with Marianne. She waited behind customers ordering Christmas bûches and extra bread, or buying boxes of chocolates made by François and his father. Marianne was now doing all the packaging of the chocolates, as François' mother was having trouble with her arthritic hands. Isabeau had taken over the bookmarks. It was taking her mind off Pornic and Papa, and the project was a change from her blackwork embroidery.

When Isabeau reached the bakery, Marianne wasn't there. Julie was tidying up. Isabeau bought the last baguette and looked at the brightly coloured shelves draped with garlands, where gold and red boxes of chocolates were the best decorations.

On the rest of the way home, she thought about buying the Morels some chocolates for Christmas. Arriving at her gate, she glanced at her letterbox. A little corner of red envelope was poking out. She grabbed it. Christmas trees and decorations, surrounded by birds and ferns, decorated the edges of the envelope. Isabeau recognized the tidy printed handwriting.

The envelope was square and heavy. It held a letter and a card that featured a beach and a tree with bright red flowers. According to the explanation on the back, it was a pohutukawa, New Zealand's native Christmas tree.

"Look, George! A Christmas card and letter from Joseph." On the photo, he smiled back at Isabeau. Tonight he looked like he knew.

Dear Ms Martin,

Thank you for your letter. I was very happy to receive it. I have a lot of time on my hands, and wanted to reply. It makes me feel connected to my father writing to you. This is my first Christmas without him. You wrote of the cold misty days in Carnac. Here, we're enjoying a good summer and the days are long and hot. Great weather to go to the beach. Today the temperature is 28 degrees.

I have put little drawings on my letter again. They represent some New Zealand things, such as the kiwi, a nocturnal flightless bird that is a symbol of our country. I have only seen one, and it was in captivity! Did you know that New Zealanders are also called Kiwis?

I like to draw, but it's just a hobby. I'm a musician and composer. I play the guitar, harmonica and keyboards, and I love to sing. I write most of my own material. I've made a few albums, and I came to France five years ago to sing at a festival in the South. I've always wanted to come back to perform. I love your country. If I had come to Carnac, I would have made the most of it and renewed the music contacts I had over there.

Do you like music? And if so, what kind? I could send you a cassette of one of my albums if you're interested. I love French music: in particular, classic singers like Edith Piaf, Brel and Charles Aznavour. I have always wanted to understand the lyrics, so I learned some French at high school, and did a couple of courses at university. My aim was to be able to sing in French. I'm not very good, though! I would love to learn more about modern

French music and artists, and I would appreciate it if you had any suggestions.

I've had a lot of time to listen to music because I was in a car accident with my cousin. I still need to rest, but I'm finally starting to feel better. Before my accident, I used to do a lot of biking and surfing.

I hope this letter finds you well and enjoying the festive season with your friends and family, and that you're not suffering too much from the cold. I also want to take this opportunity to wish you a Merry Christmas and Happy New Year.

Yours sincerely,

Joseph Turner

An accident. Isabeau had imagined all sorts of strange scenarios that could be unforeseen circumstances, but none of them had involved a simple accident. It must have been serious if he wasn't able to travel. She felt a sense of relief for Joseph Turner that he was getting better.

And Aznavour! Joseph Turner liked Aznavour. Isabeau put on one of her Aznavour cassettes, arranged George in the middle of the kitchen table and danced, holding the card close to her, thinking of Joseph Turner on the other side of the world.

24

In the days that followed, Isabeau's colleagues bought presents, and ordered oysters, foie gras and smoked salmon for their Christmas feasts. At work she listened to their plans for family get-togethers on Christmas Eve and Christmas Day. She bought extra treats from the bakery, inventing excuses to call in twice a day. Marianne gave her instructions to get to Saint-Laurent-de-la-Plaine, thirty kilometres south of Angers, and the location of the bakery and the lodge where she'd booked Isabeau a studio for the night. She repeated her invitation for Isabeau to stay at the bakery, but Isabeau preferred to be on her own. She offered to bring the bookmarks with her to Saint-Laurent. She didn't want to back out.

Marianne had given Isabeau carte blanche with the bookmarks, and Isabeau worked on them every evening, adding more details and a border down the sides. As she embroidered, she listened to Aznavour and spoke to George and Joseph, and little by little her voice found the right words for a letter in reply to Joseph. She should write back before Christmas if she wanted to wish him Merry Christmas, she knew, but as the days passed and the pile of finished bookmarks grew, Isabeau realized that the best present to herself would be to write the letter on Christmas Day, even if it meant that her wishes arrived late.

At the bookshop, she bought a Christmas card and postcards of the menhirs for Joseph, and presents to herself – new writing paper and a Waterman pen – and sat them beside George on the sideboard. On Christmas Eve, much to Isabeau's surprise, Marianne gave her a small parcel, telling her to open it on Christmas Day. She was touched and eager to return the gesture. She just had time to find an embroidery book with cross-stitch designs at the bookshop and drop it in to Marianne.

Late on Christmas morning, Isabeau put on an Aznavour cassette and prepared the table: George in the middle with the photo and Joseph's letters, surrounded by little candles. Lastly, she added her own present to herself and the gift from Marianne.

Isabeau took out her father's breakfast bowl and ran her fingers over the discoloured hand-painted china. She held it to her cheek. If she hadn't hidden it from Mother, she wouldn't still have it. It was an old

Henriot bowl from Quimper with a blue and yellow pattern and the traditional Breton peasant woman.

Isabeau sipped her coffee from the bowl and ate two pains au chocolat before she slowly opened the presents: first, the correspondence set and pen. She was pleased that she'd said yes when the shop assistant had asked if she wanted them gift-wrapped. The cream writing paper and envelopes were thick and water-marked; she didn't care if they were heavy to send to New Zealand. The pen, sitting in a box with white satin lining, was ink-blue tortoiseshell with gold trim, and pleasantly heavy and smooth in her hand. It seemed almost too luxurious. "For once, George, I have indulged myself," she said to his photo.

Isabeau examined the writing material again, then placed it all carefully on the table beside George. Next, she picked up Marianne's gift. It fitted snugly in the palm of her hand in its pink shiny paper. Isabeau held it for a long time before she opened it.

It was a velvet jewellery box. Inside the box sat a pair of gold and purple earrings, a perfect match for the dress. Isabeau felt as if they had some magic power, because as soon as she put them on she wanted to brush her hair and wear her party dress. She gave in to the urge and went to change. She walked around the kitchen in her new dress and Marianne's shoes, swinging her hair from side to side. Unaccustomed to high heels, she changed her gait several times, until she was walking more naturally. It was good practice for the engagement party, she thought. She sat down and moved her body and head, adopting different positions as if she was taking part in a conversation. She said aloud the names of the others who would be at the party, and pretended she was listening to Pierrot talk about the plans for her house: plans that he was going to bring with him.

It was a party with herself. The little objects on the table – letters, paper, pen, a photo – and George were good company. She was ready to write.

Dear Joseph Turner,

Thank you for your letter and Christmas wishes. It was a lovely surprise, and I enjoyed the drawings. It's a real pleasure to receive your letter. New Zealand must be an interesting country. Having Christmas in summer seems very strange. I can't imagine going to the beach. It's cold and dark here in Carnac. The houses and streets are decorated and lit up.

I'm pleased to hear you're feeling better after your accident, and I hope you can get back to biking as soon as possible. I like biking too, and when the weather permits I bike around Carnac. In summer, I went for some day trips around Brittany with my bike on the rack on the back of my car. I like to stop and bike around when I find a quiet spot.

I don't do any drawing as such, but I do a little sketching for my blackwork embroidery. Embroidery is my passion. I've done many embroideries of the menhirs. At the moment I'm busy preparing bookmarks for a friend's engagement party at New Year in Anjou.

I listen to a lot of music, and I'm also a big fan of Charles Aznavour. In terms of more modern artists, my favourite is Jean-Jacques Goldman. Like you, he writes his own songs. You may also be interested in Michel Sardou, Daniel Balavoine, François Feldman, Michel Berger or Catherine Lara and France Gall. Other classic artists are Jean Ferrat and Brassens. I would very much like to hear some of your music.

In your first letter, you talked about your father reading Astérix to you. Do you still read comic books? Do you have a favourite? I read them too, but I also like to read novels.

You asked me for some photos. I hope postcards are all right. I am enclosing a postcard of the Giant of Manio, and also some of the Ménec and Kermario Alignments that are very close to the Giant.

Merry Christmas and all the best for the New Year.

Sincerely,

Isabeau

Isabeau looked at her sewing basket. She wrote her wishes on the card she'd bought, and before she could ask herself a hundred questions about whether it was a good idea, she was stitching a menhir on a strip of linen.

"I've done it, George. I've written back to Joseph."

Well done. Isabeau heard the words in her head. Was it George? But it sounded like Docteur Morel and Papa too. She should scatter George. But since he'd arrived things had changed for the better, as if he was helping her: with the house, finding Papa, everything. *When the time is right.* She thought back to those words. She felt as if she had to find Papa first. For that she had to go to Pornic. Today, however, Isabeau didn't want to think about that.

Isabeau had left early on an impulse. Everyone was preparing to celebrate New Year's Eve. But suddenly, all she could see was another year gone, still waiting, and she didn't want to wait until the engagement party to go to Pornic. At work, she could tell they thought it was strange when she'd asked to leave early. But Monsieur Poulain had said yes. All through December she'd been working extra hours; it was easier when you didn't have to prepare Christmas for family.

On the passenger seat was her small overnight bag and her handbag, containing Joseph's letters and the photo. She might stay the night in Saint-Brevin-les-Pins, she thought. She almost wished she'd brought George with her, instead of putting him away in the sideboard.

She passed the sign for Guérande and turned off, heading towards the medieval town. It sat solidly behind its walls and moat, surrounded by the ring road, which was almost empty. From the small car park beside the main gate she entered the town beneath the towers. Rare shoppers were on last-minute errands for New Year's Eve. It was a stark contrast to the summer high-season hustle and bustle Isabeau remembered. Then, the sunny streets inside the walled city had been packed with holidaymakers. It was a bone-chilling two degrees today. She forced herself to keep moving, and headed down the main street to the square. The crêperie where Papa used to take her and the shop full of postcards, which she'd loved as a child, were still there. She went in and spent a long time looking at the postcards, before buying one of the salt marshes.

In the crêperie, the waitress installed Isabeau in the back room beside the crackling fire, and came back five minutes later with her hot chocolate and lemon crêpe. Isabeau pulled out Joseph's Christmas card and read it again. She found herself wondering what it would be like sitting there with him, sharing this special place. Would he think it strange if she sent him a postcard? She was full of the hot sweet drink and crêpe. The flames of the fire reminded her of her candle, and her new pen was sitting in her bag.

Dear Joseph,

Hello from Guérande. I'm stopping off here for New Year. It's very cold, and the town is quiet. Guérande's famous for its salt marshes, and the walled city, which was built long ago to protect this precious mineral, still stands today. My father used to bring me here during the holidays, and always used this salt in his cooking. This weekend I'm going to my friend's engagement party in a little village near Angers. I hope you're well. Happy New Year.

Sincerely,

Isabeau

Should she send it? Her postcard made it sound like she was on a proper holiday, with plans. It sounded like she was doing something other people did – people who had more than one friend – rather than making this cold lonely pilgrimage to Guérande and Pornic.

Back down the main street, Isabeau stopped at the boutiques filled with traditional hand-painted Breton pottery, china decorated with colourful swirls and patterns in a similar style to that of Papa's bowl. In the shop that sold salt boxes, she was drawn to one with a picture of the two-tower main entrance of Guérande, with the name of the town written underneath. She could imagine it in one of the kitchens in the magazines Pierrot had lent her. Perhaps it could even go in the kitchen of the Alouettes house. Isabeau bought it, along with a large bag of gros sel and a smaller one of fleur de sel, the finest salt crystals, which form on the surface of the ponds.

It was only a short drive from Guérande to the industrial city of Saint-Nazaire. Isabeau followed the motorway past mundane apartment blocks as it wound around in a gracious curve to the long, high bridge across the Loire. It was framed by the port installations and dockyards, where a massive cruise ship was being built. Isabeau tried to keep her eyes on the road. The bridge was beautiful, but the size of it scared her. Someone had told her that it was built high enough across the Loire to let the luxury liner *France* pass under, should it return to the port where it had been built. She didn't know if it was true, but she liked the story. The *France* was now called the *Norway* and sailed in the Caribbean. "Things can change," Isabeau shouted, as her car hurtled down the other side of the bridge.

On the South Loire bank, the houses had orange tiles and ochre plaster. Brittany, with its granite and slate, suddenly seemed far away. Saint-Brevin-les-Pins was the town on the other side of the bridge. She would return there later and look for somewhere to stay the night. First, she needed to go to Pornic. It took another twenty minutes until she turned off to Pornic and was heading for the port, where fishing boats were snoozing in the late-afternoon low tide. It wasn't hard to find the café along the waterfront. It was almost empty. The only customers were a couple of men leaning against the bar, gesturing and pointing out to sea. The barman, who looked to be in his early twenties, was listening. He would be too young to have known Papa.

Isabeau pretended to study the menu on the window, and then she walked away along the port. At the end of the main street, she continued on the walkway. She came to a gap in the rocks where the wooden causeway was suspended above the water and the waves surged. She forced herself to keep walking, to not look down. It was like when Papa had taken her to the tidal dam over the Rance River, and they had stopped on the bridge. Looking down, Isabeau had been frightened that the little whirlpools would suck her in, but she couldn't stop gazing at them.

The short walkway ended at a playground and car park, both deserted. Isabeau took the road back to the port. She could get in her car and leave. Partir, partir, leave, like Papa. The words drummed in her head. Surely he couldn't have been this close to Carnac and not come back? If she didn't go back to the café, where could she go from here? She thought of George and pictured the photo of him. *Just go and ask.* The words came into her head.

Isabeau shivered and rubbed her hands. She walked briskly to the café, entered, ordered a coffee and forced herself to drink it slowly. Instead of leaving the money on the table, she went up to the counter to pay. The barman counted the change onto the bar and wished her a good day.

"Merci." She picked up the change. "I'm looking for a man called Paul Martin. He may have been a customer here or perhaps worked here in the sixties. I know it's a long time ago now."

"Sorry mademoiselle, I've only been here for a few months," he replied, barely looking at Isabeau as he dried a glass.

She wanted to slap him.

"It's extremely important." Her voice came out louder than she expected.

The barman looked up.

"Madame Laval's owned the bar for years. If he worked here, she'd know."

"Please," Isabeau said, "I need to speak to her."

"She doesn't live far from here." He nodded to the right. "Go along the port, cut through rue du Môle and then take the steps up l'escalier Galipaud. At the top, in the square, opposite the Tabac Presse, is rue Tartifume. She lives there, in the house with the new blue-painted shutters. All been done up at the end of summer. You can't miss it."

Isabeau thanked him and left.

In rue Tartifume there were several houses with blue shutters. One of them stood out, though, with its bright new paint. Isabeau studied the door, her hands firmly in her coat pockets, her left hand fiddling with her inhaler. She was going to run out of breath. She was about to turn around when the door opened. "Merde!" she gasped, and stepped back. The elderly woman opening the door also raised her hand to her heart.

"I'm so, so sorry. I didn't mean to give you a fright," Isabeau stammered.

"I was just going to the baker's." The woman left her hand on her chest.

"I'm sorry," Isabeau said again. "Madame Laval?"

"Yes?"

"The barman told me to come here."

"Is there a problem at the café?" the woman asked, frowning.

"No. I ... I'm looking for a man who may have been a customer, or possibly worked in your café in the sixties. Paul Martin."

"That's going back a while now. Let's see. Yes, he worked in the bar for a couple of years. It was when my husband had his hernia operation; he was unwell for several months." Madame Laval looked closer at Isabeau.

"Do you have any idea where he went, or where he might be now, by any chance?"

"When he left the café, he worked on a fishing boat for a while. Used to come into the bar, and lived above the poissonnerie in a studio with his wife, Ghislaine. I heard they went to Nantes."

Isabeau felt her face fall.

"Are you all right, dear?" asked Madame Laval. "Would you like to come in?"

"You said he had a *wife*?"

"Ghislaine was a lovely girl – worked at the poissonnerie and helped clean the café when we got busy. They kept pretty much to themselves, though." Madame Laval looked confused. "I'm sorry, there's not much else I can tell you. Are you sure you wouldn't like to come in?"

"Thank you. I must be going. Goodbye."

Isabeau ran back down the street, across the square and down the steps towards the port. She reached the bottom and collapsed, breathless. Bent over, between sobs, she sucked on her inhaler, but even that couldn't bring back the breath she needed.

Isabeau threw her bag on the bed in the cabin and turned the electric heater on high. The pizza she'd bought was sitting on the table next to a bottle of cider and a crème caramel dessert. Corinne and the others from work back in Carnac would have Champagne chilling in the fridge while they finished preparing platters of seafood. Their friends would soon be ringing the doorbell, offering flowers or wine, all of them dressed up, the full works, ready for an evening of fun and laughter.

Why hadn't she stayed in Carnac? Isabeau felt numb. Ghislaine? Had Papa been with her all those times he hadn't come home? She paced up and down in the small kitchen of the cabin. She couldn't stay in one place. She put her coat and beret back on.

In July, Saint-Brevin-Les-Pins had been a refuge; it had been pleasantly cool cycling around in the shade of the large pines. Isabeau had stopped then beside the holiday village and watched the children jumping in the pool while their parents sunned themselves on the chaises longues. Today, the pool was covered over, and only three other cars were parked around the holiday village.

She headed straight down the road to the beach. The sand was smooth, hard and easy to walk on, but the wind stung her swollen eyes and cut to the bone as if it wanted to punish her. She was back at square one, or even worse. Just more questions. Why? Why? Why? The word accompanied every step. The scream escaped.

"Why did you leave? I loved you. *I hate you.*"

At last, she had said it.

The bakery was a few houses to the left of the church square. Down the alley at the back Isabeau found the garage door with the pink ribbon Marianne had tied to the handle. The garage gave access to a courtyard where large yellow bread containers were stacked in a corner and clean white aprons and tea towels filled the washing lines. Isabeau walked slowly around the washing to the kitchen door. She tapped on the glass pane and stood rubbing her forehead. Her neck was tight, and a headache was lurking behind her eyes. After Pornic and Saint-Brévin it had been hard enough returning to work for a day. She still didn't know how she'd managed to get through it and then drive to Saint-Laurent-de-la-Plaine.

Marianne came through the door at the back of the kitchen.

"It's good to see you," she said, opening the door and embracing Isabeau. "Bonne année. Come and sit down. You look tired. What did you get up to on New Year's Eve?"

"Nothing much. I ended up going to Pornic earlier than I planned, and then stayed the night in Saint-Brevin. Bonne année, Marianne. I wish you and François an amazing year and especially a magnificent wedding."

"Thanks, Isabeau. I wish you everything you want for this New Year. I don't know what that is," Marianne laughed, "but I hope you get it. It's going to be a great year. Look how it's starting off, with you in Saint-Laurent. I'm so happy you could come."

"I can't believe I'm here," Isabeau sighed.

"My parents are napping," said Marianne. "This is the busiest time of the year for them. Maman should be up soon, but Papa will sleep longer. He probably won't be up before I take you to the lodge. Christian and Sophie are around, though." She turned as a tall young man with hair the same dark colour as her own and a shorter blond young woman came through the door that led out of the kitchen. "Here they are." She said to them: "Christian, Sophie, come and meet Isabeau."

"Great to meet you," Christian said to Isabeau. "Marianne's been talking about your embroidery. Sounds like she's finally met her match. Used to drive us mad – she's had a needle in her hand since she was born, this girl. She likes to make her point!" Christian ruffled his sister's hair. "I'm sure she lets everyone know what a pest I am."

Christian was much taller than Marianne, but he had the same round face, and Isabeau could also see how alike they were on the family photos that covered the kitchen wall. Several showed Marianne flanked by two boys. Isabeau recognized Christian. The other one, with finer features, had to be Thierry.

Marianne talked, barely pausing, as she got out coffee cups and cleared piles of flattened cake boxes from the kitchen table so that they could all sit down around it.

"François' parents are driving over tomorrow with his grandparents, but his two sisters, with their husbands and children, are arriving this afternoon. They're also staying at the lodge. Isabelle and Jean-Paul are coming from Brest. They've got a little boy, Cédric. And Charlotte and Sébastien have two children, Elodie and Nicolas. Sébastien's a teacher, and they've recently shifted to Normandy."

"Has Pierrot arrived?" Isabeau asked. She hoped he'd had a change of plans and wouldn't be arriving until the next day. She needed to gather herself before she saw him and before he started talking about the house.

"Not yet. I don't think he'll be too late, though. We'll bring some pizzas and quiches over tonight and have a meal together in the dining room. I've also invited Tonton Aimé. Then, tomorrow, you'll get to meet my grandparents and my friends Marie-Claire and Véronique."

Isabeau tried to match the people with the names on the bookmarks. If only meeting them was as simple as embroidering their names quietly at home. The name *Ghislaine* started to throb behind her eyes. Her headache was getting worse.

"I'll get some of Papa's chocolates," said Marianne, heading through the door to what looked like the dining room. She came back, followed by François, sat a soup tureen in the middle of the table, and lifted the lid with a flourish. Inside there was a jumble of knobbly rochers, pralinés, caramels and large round chocolates that Isabeau had never seen before. "They're seconds, but just as good. Try one of these." She pointed to one of the round chocolates. "Papa created them: layers of nougatine and praliné."

Isabeau took one of the chocolates and ate it slowly. When she had almost finished, a tall brunette woman came through the door. She was elegant and attractive, like Marianne, but older.

"Maman," said Marianne, "Isabeau's arrived. Isabeau, this is my mum."

"Welcome to Saint-Laurent," said Madame Fournier. "Marianne's been telling us how helpful you've been, although she's keeping the project under wraps." She opened her arms to Isabeau and embraced her. "I'm glad you're trying some of Eugène's chocolates. Please help yourself," she said, motioning to the soup tureen.

Isabeau sat back down and took another one. She sucked the smooth delicate chocolate until there were only miniscule nuggets of crunchy nougatine left. Exquisite. And Madame Fournier's welcome made the chocolate taste even better, more special. If only her headache would stop. If only she hadn't gone to Pornic.

It was only a short drive from the village to the lodge, a renovated water mill in the valley of the Jeu River, but Isabeau was relieved when Marianne offered to show her the way. As soon as they were in the studio unit, Isabeau opened out the parcel of bookmarks on the small table. Gold thread stood out on the dark blue linen, and contrasted with the borders and the small red heart under Marianne and François' initials. Isabeau had also added the date.

"You haven't seen them for a while, but you did say I had free rein," she said.

"They're gorgeous," said Marianne. "Perfect. I love following patterns, but you're so good at improvising. They're going to look amazing with the gold napkins."

"You're lucky you can decorate the restaurant as you like," Isabeau said, trying to concentrate on the conversation. Her head was pounding. She sat down on the bed.

"Papa supplies all the bread and many of the pâtisseries for the restaurant," explained Marianne. She looked up. "Are you okay, Isabeau?"

"I've got a terrible headache. I haven't been sleeping well lately."

"I hope you haven't been up all hours of the night to finish these." Marianne gestured towards the bookmarks on the table.

"It's nothing to do with the embroidery. I had some unexpected news." A weight was pressing on Isabeau's chest. "The reason I went to Pornic was because I was looking for my father. Our old neighbour,

Docteur Morel, told me that he'd seen my father in a bar in Pornic after he disappeared. I went to the bar, and it turned out that he worked there years ago. The old lady who owns it had no idea where he went after that, but she told me that Papa was married to a woman called Ghislaine. I don't understand." As soon as Isabeau said the name Ghislaine, the sob rose in her throat, and she couldn't stop it from coming out. "I'm sorry, I didn't mean to ..."

Marianne sat down on the bed beside Isabeau and put her arm around her.

"It's okay," said Marianne. "It's better you're having a good cry now rather than holding it in and being miserable during the celebration tomorrow. When my brother Thierry died, I cried so much that I thought there couldn't be any tears left. I wondered if the grief could kill me." She offered Isabeau a tissue. "Your parents were divorced then?"

"No, as it turns out they weren't even married, but I didn't know that until I inherited the house. My mother was unwell; she never talked about my father."

They heard cars pulling into the car park.

"That must be one of François' sisters, or Pierrot," said Marianne. Why don't you lie down for a while, and I'll see if I can get you something for your headache. We won't be eating till eight. If you're not up to joining us, I'll bring you some dinner."

Isabeau lay down and pulled the duvet up around her chin. She closed her eyes and tried to think only of Marianne's family and their welcome. Precious pleasant thoughts. Marianne came back with two tablets and a glass of water, and then slipped out again, promising to check on her before dinner. The paracetamol slowly took effect.

It was seven o'clock when Isabeau woke up, for a few seconds confused about where she was. She was still tired, but the tension had eased. After a shower, she curled up on the bed and waited for Marianne. If she didn't have dinner with the others, her headache would take over again, she knew, and it would be too hard to turn up at the lunch the next day. When Marianne returned, Isabeau let Marianne lead her along to the dining room. Isabeau concentrated on the names and visualized the bookmarks as Marianne introduced her to her father and François' sisters, their husbands and children. Pierrot was also there. At least he was a familiar face, but Isabeau was still relieved that she found herself at the other end of the room while he was engaged in a conversation with François.

They were about to sit down at the table when the door opened and a slim elderly man, wearing an immaculate suit, a bow tie and a black felt hat, entered.

"Tonton Aimé!" exclaimed Marianne.

Tonton Aimé greeted everyone around the room, and when he came to Isabeau he squeezed her hand between both of his as he spoke. "I hear you've come from Carnac, the land of menhirs and dolmens. I've always been fascinated by that place. There's something magical about it."

"Yes, Monsieur, very magical," replied Isabeau.

"Oh, please don't *Monsieur* me," he told her. "Just call me Tonton: everyone else does." He took a seat beside her.

Marianne and Madame Fournier brought trays of pizza and quiches to the table, and everyone started eating while they continued to chat. Isabeau observed and listened. The conversation came around to the New Year, and there was laughter as tales were told of past resolutions.

"Alors, ma petite Isabeau de Carnac, have you made any resolutions?" asked Tonton Aimé, turning his chair towards her. "I've smoked for fifty years. I thought I couldn't change my habits after so long, but then last week while I was visiting an old friend whose wife has just died, I ran out of cigarettes. He wanted to talk, and all I could think about was that I needed to buy another packet. I haven't had a cigarette since. It's funny – it doesn't seem that hard any more. Perhaps the time was right. I'm sorry if I'm boring you."

"Not at all." Isabeau really meant it.

"And do you smoke?" he asked.

"I have asthma. I've never been tempted to try."

"What's going to be your resolution – or resolutions – then?"

"I have no idea."

"There must be something, even some little change you want to make in your life. You know, sometimes the smallest things have the biggest effect."

Isabeau looked hard at Tonton Aimé. It was exactly like Marianne and the embroidery magazine, and the parcel.

"Well," she pondered. "I'll try to answer all my correspondence promptly."

"I might write to you and see," Tonton Aimé chuckled. "I'll check up at the wedding."

"I don't know if I'll be invited."

"Of course you will be, my dear," he said.

The dress was lying on the bed. Isabeau had put on the earrings that Marianne had given her, but she was still in her new underwear and tights. A car stopped outside. She grabbed the dress and pulled it over her head.

There was a knock at the door.

"Coming." Isabeau adjusted the dress as she went to the door.

"Gorgeous!" Marianne beamed. "All ready for your make-up and hair. How are you feeling?"

"Better, thanks. I didn't wake up until ten o'clock."

Isabeau had slept surprisingly well, and she was managing to keep the headache at bay. Thoughts of Ghislaine were still intruding, but now she had other things to think about: the way everyone had made her feel welcome the day before, as if it was the most natural thing that she was part of the gathering, and Tonton Aimé's talk of resolutions, and the bookmarks that she would soon see on the table.

Marianne sat Isabeau in front of the wall mirror and started brushing her hair. "What do you prefer, something sophisticated or something sexy?"

"I don't know if I'm capable of either of those kind of styles."

"Your hair is gorgeous," Marianne replied. "Mine's so straight. I wish it was wavy like yours." She swept Isabeau's hair up and around, holding it in different styles before she finally suggested leaving it untied. "I've hardly seen you with your hair out," she said. "You've always got it in a ponytail. What about a change? The make-up will help. Less is best."

Marianne applied foundation, blusher, eyeliner, mascara and lipstick to Isabeau's face. When she'd finished, Isabeau didn't recognize herself.

"A toast to Marianne and François." Monsieur Fournier raised a small wine glass towards the couple. "Health and happiness to Marianne and François," rang out around the table. The straw-coloured wine, syrupy sweet, slid down Isabeau's throat.

"Don't be tricked by this little sweetie," Tonton Aimé told Isabeau, smiling. "Quarts-de-Chaume seems innocent enough, but it's a traitor. Visitors to our region often get caught out." He tended his glass towards

Isabeau.

"It's very good." She clinked her glass against his.

"And while we're making toasts," said Marianne as she stood up. "To Isabeau, my friend from Carnac, who's an expert embroiderer, a true artist and a good friend, because she made the beautiful bookmarks that you have in front of you." Marianne raised her glass. "And when you're at home reading, I'm sure you'll appreciate Isabeau's handwork and think of this occasion today."

Isabeau's cheeks grew warmer, and she didn't know whether it was from the wine or the attention. "To Isabeau." Everyone raised their glass, and Marianne came over and embraced her. When Marianne was back at her seat, she took out her camera and aimed it at Isabeau. Pierrot, sitting across from Isabeau, was also staring at her. Isabeau gave a quick smile, then picked up the menu sitting under the bookmark and pretended she was studying it.

The conversation buzzed around Isabeau, and the platters of oysters, prawns and crabs emptied. She quietly watched Marie-Claire and Véronique, who were talking. They looked relaxed and at ease. Isabeau straightened her shoulders and leaned slightly forward, the way she'd held herself when she was practising in her outfit at Christmas. Her thoughts were interrupted by Pierrot, who was offering her a pair of pliers to break the crab legs. He held them out across the table.

"Did you have a good time in Pornic?" he asked. "Must have done you the world of good. You look great."

"Thanks." Isabeau felt herself blush again.

"Have you seen anything you like in those magazines?"

"There are so many beautiful houses in them." Isabeau hesitated. "It's hard to say, although there's an article about kitchen renovations in a house similar to mine, where they opened up the kitchen and living space like you suggested. It looks great, very homely."

"I've done some rough plans and prices," said Pierrot, "I'll give them to you later. And I was talking to a joiner friend in Vannes. He's been working on some kitchen cupboards, and the order's been cancelled. He's willing to give them to me for a good price. They're light oak and could be adapted to your kitchen. I think you'd like them."

"Are you renovating a house, Isabeau?" asked Tonton Aimé, overhearing their conversation.

"Yes," she said. "But it's in a terrible state."

"It won't be for long if I get my hands on it," laughed Pierrot.

"Sounds like you have more on your plate than correspondence then – plenty of resolutions hidden away," remarked Tonton Aimé.

"I don't know if it's worth doing anything with the house though," Isabeau said, and took a sip of wine.

"Houses are like people: when you give them love, they shine," said Tonton Aimé.

After the meal, Marianne insisted that Isabeau join her family back at the bakery.

They sat around the large table in the dining room. Monsieur Fournier put a match to the paper and wood that had been prepared in the stone fireplace and brought out packs of tarot cards. It didn't take long for two groups to form, cards to be dealt and two games to get under way, one at each end of the table.

"I don't know how to play either," Madame Fournier reassured Isabeau as they settled in armchairs by the fire. "Tonton Aimé's always offering to teach me, but I've never liked card games."

"He's very nice," said Isabeau.

"He's a lovely man. He married very young, and sadly his wife and daughter both died in childbirth. When Eugène and I got married he was living here in the bakery. After we had children he shifted out, but he's always been close."

"He never remarried?"

"No, he's been a widower for a long time."

Like the kitchen, the walls of the dining room were covered with family photos: Marianne and her brothers playing in the snow, in their communion robes and in family portraits with their parents and grandparents. Tonton Aimé featured in several. Isabeau studied the largest picture. Marianne's parents were on a bench, and behind them, Marianne was between Christian and Thierry. They were all smiling. The perfect happy family. Marianne must have been about eighteen, and Thierry not much older. Isabeau wanted to tell Madame Fournier that she was sorry about Thierry. It was so simple but seemed very hard to say.

While the cards were being put away, Isabeau helped Madame Fournier bring through a large pot of pistou soup and charcuterie, including home-made pork and prune pâté, cheese and bread. They all squeezed around the table, and the simple dinner tasted as good as the luxurious festive fare they had eaten at lunch.

In spite of the late hour, when Isabeau got home she sat up in bed and took out her journal and new pen. The drive home had given her time to think, and for once she was happily tired. It was the kind of tiredness that came from staying late at a long gathering just to be with people, the tiredness Corinne and her other colleagues complained off when they had had a busy weekend. Madame Fournier had invited her to return. And Isabeau wanted to see Tonton Aimé again. She hoped she would be invited to the wedding. In big letters across a double page of her journal, she wrote *RESOLUTIONS*, and started a list.

> *Answer correspondence promptly*
> *Study Pierrot's plans and estimates*
> *Visit the Morels more often*
> *Invite Marianne soon*
> *Wear skirts and dresses*
> *Try different hairstyles*
> *Buy some plants for the garden at the house*
> *FIND PAPA*
> *SCATTER GEORGE*
> *CHANGE CHANGE CHANGE*

She took a piece of paper and continued writing in list form *I must scatter George, I will scatter George.*

28

Madame Morel sat a dish of mushroom vol-au-vents in the middle of the table.

"I saw that carpenter friend of yours at the house again. When is he starting?" she asked Isabeau.

"I'm not sure. He was having another look at the kitchen," Isabeau explained. "There's still nothing finalized, but I'm considering leaving him to it. He's got lots of ideas. He's suggested ripping out the wall between the kitchen and living room to really open up the living area."

"That would make a huge difference to the house," said Docteur Morel. "It sounds like a great idea."

Madame Morel served the vol-au-vents and passed a dish of mixed vegetables to Isabeau.

She pondered Docteur Morel's words while she savoured a mouthful of crisp pastry and creamy mushroom sauce. She'd come to the stones and the house from the other side, via rue du Tumulus, and stopped at the massive Saint-Michel tumulus. She'd even walked up and around the little chapel on the top, a place she seldom visited. Then she'd come straight to see the Morels. She hadn't been next door to her house, hadn't done her usual tour. She'd been forcing herself to do things differently since the engagement party, sometimes buying a loaf instead of a baguette.

The weekend before, when she'd briefly seen the Morels, instead of hesitating or refusing politely, Isabeau had accepted their invitation to come to lunch today, to share a galette des rois, the traditional cake eaten for Three Kings' Day on the sixth of January. She'd added this to another list she'd started: the list of changes she'd successfully made. While they ate, Isabeau told them about Marianne and François' engagement party. She thought, however, of only one thing. Ghislaine. Did the Morels know her, by any chance? At the end of the meal, Madame Morel served the coffee and opened the box of chocolates Isabeau had brought them from Saint-Laurent. They all sat back a little in their chairs. Time was running out.

"I went to Pornic at New Year," Isabeau finally said.

"Did you find out anything about your father?" ventured Docteur

Morel.

"I saw the elderly owner of the café you told me about. She said Papa worked there for a couple of years. She wasn't sure where he went after that – perhaps to Nantes." Isabeau paused. "Do either of you know a woman called Ghislaine, by any chance?"

"What's her surname?" asked Docteur Morel.

"I don't know. The lady said she was Papa's wife. I don't understand." Isabeau put her head in her hands. Tears came, and her shoulders started to shake. Docteur Morel handed her a clean handkerchief from his pocket.

It felt like she'd come back to cry twenty years too late.

"I can't think of anyone by that name," said Docteur Morel. "To be honest, I wondered if your father was seeing someone – if that explained why he left. It might be this woman you're talking about. Nantes would be a good place to start looking then. Perhaps your father's still there?"

"I doubt it. Since I've been working at the post office I've searched for his name many times."

"I have a cousin in Nantes who's been doing a bit of work as a private investigator since he retired from the police force," said Docteur Morel. He's used to tracing people, and he often talks about all the contacts he has. I'll ask him if he can look into it."

"Do you think it would be possible?"

"I'm sure he won't mind. You'll have to be patient though. Sometimes these things take time," said Docteur Morel with conviction.

29

The post office was still overflowing with mail. In January – the month for sending best wishes for the New Year to friends and family – the cards kept coming, day after day. Isabeau had sent the only card she had to write, to Joseph. Now she waited. He had to reply. She'd said she wanted a copy of his album. But as the days went by, Isabeau felt as if her hope was reduced to grains of sand slipping through the hourglass of patience. More and more it seemed it would be a bad omen if she didn't receive a reply before the end of the month.

Isabeau wandered up and down the Ménec Alignments, and felt that they were waiting too. And at the cemetery, the little angels were a sadder shade of grey in the winter light.

Snow arrived. The temperature dropped to minus nine, and much lower elsewhere in France. The country was paralysed by the cold, and then more strikes. At the post office, those two subjects were all they talked about. The cold weighed heavy and sharp on everything, and it took all Isabeau's energy, and the radiator working overtime on high, to stay warm. Black ice made it difficult to go out. She stayed home and concentrated on her embroidery. Listened to the BBC and talked to George. Waited for the letter.

Apart from work, going to the bakery was the only time she left the house. Marianne was searching magazines and books for ideas to decorate the little linen bags she'd bought for the dragées, the sugar-covered almonds traditionally distributed to wedding guests. The wedding had been set for July in Saint-Laurent-de-la-Plaine. Isabeau had offered to help. She wanted to be useful.

The cold and snow continued. Each time Isabeau looked at George, the word *patience* came to mind. *Be patient, Isabeau.* She repeated it aloud several times a day. By the 29th, there still wasn't any letter, and her resolutions were starting to seem worthless. Her impatience rubbed off onto the house project. She wanted something to happen. Something to change. She contacted Pierrot, gave him the key to the Alouettes house and told him to go ahead with the kitchen, and to organize a stonemason and someone to repair the slate tiles, but everything was blocked by the cold.

31 January. Miraculously, the letter arrived just in time. It was waiting in her letterbox when she arrived home from work Saturday lunchtime. In fact, it was not a letter but a small parcel. Inside the parcel were a gift-wrapped smaller parcel, containing a cassette of Joseph's music, and a letter decorated with drawings. Across the top, instruments were lined up, and notes spilled down the sides and formed a musical score at the bottom with *A Song for the New Year* written across it.

Isabeau counted to ten, made herself a large cup of coffee, took out three chocolates from the box Madame Fournier had given her and opened the parcel. She held the cassette up in both hands. Joseph smiled at her from the photo on the jacket. He still had blond hair, and his nose, large and straight, dominated his long face. He was handsome in an unusual way. He could be around her age.

"Windblown". A lump formed in Isabeau's throat when she read the name of the album. She remembered the wind at the beach at Saint-Brevin-Les-Pins on New Year's Eve. She opened the cassette case and slid the cassette and jacket out. The songs were all written by Joseph. She moved her player to the table and put the cassette into the left deck. There were piano notes and the haunting melody of a harmonica, then Joseph's voice.

"Breathe deep and easy all across the land

Let the sun set and lie tired on the warm sand

In something this good, this beautiful

God must have had a hand ..."

Dear Isabeau,

Many thanks for your Christmas wishes and the postcards. They give me a better idea of the standing stones. Thanks also for the beautiful bookmark. I will treasure it. When your postcard from Guérande turned up shortly afterwards it was an added surprise. It looks a fascinating place. I would love to visit the region one day and discover it all for myself.

As promised, I'm sending you some of my music. It's my third album, and the one I'm happiest with because I wrote all the material. I recorded it last year before my accident. I hope you enjoy it. Since I've been writing to you I've been listening to a lot more French music, in particular Charles Aznavour, trying to understand the words. It's difficult!

I hope you've had an enjoyable Christmas and break. We've had great weather. It was 25 degrees on Christmas Day. We had a big family barbecue at my aunt and uncle's house near the beach. It was good to go out there for the day and spend time with them. We talked a lot about my father, and remembered the great times we had with him as a family.

I've also been reading a lot lately (the bookmark is very useful): especially mystery novels and some books on France. I enjoyed the time I spent in Perpignan when I performed at the music festival there. I hope you enjoy the cassette. On the cover, you get to see me! It would be nice to be able to put a face to you, especially as I am enjoying our correspondence. It's doing me good to have something else to think about.

The low temperatures in France have been in the news here. I hope you're managing to stay warm.

Sincerely,

Joseph

All afternoon and evening Isabeau listened to Joseph's music. By midnight she had lost count of how many times she'd turned the cassette or reread Joseph's letter. It was doing him good to have something else to think about. "He's not the only one, George," she said. She looked at the photo Marianne had taken of her at the engagement party, happy that she'd asked Marianne for a couple of prints of it. "He'll never know I don't usually look like that." She took her cassette player up to bed and lay in the dark listening to the songs, falling in love with the music.

30

"No reply – No reply – No – re – ply – no – re – ply." With each syllable, Isabeau pushed a pedal, her voice growing in intensity and her legs working hard. After the winter break from biking, it felt good to be back on her bike. This was the longest gap there had been in Joseph's correspondence. It had been several weeks. Had she really sent that last letter, and dared to include the photo? She'd kept the rough copy of it, and when she reread it, she cringed. There was so much about herself and the Alouettes house and her plan to renovate it, and how the menhirs were important to her. Maybe this was where it ended. After all, Joseph had trusted her, and she was misleading him. She didn't deserve more.

Finally, Pierrot was starting on the kitchen, and he was going to contact the stonemason. Isabeau had thought she'd stay away. It would be too hard: the house, and also Pierrot. She was never quite sure how to act around him. Now she found herself biking up to the house to do some more gardening. She'd borrowed decorating books and gardening magazines from the library, trying to think of the house as a piece of linen and imagine what colours and stitches she could add to it. She'd also taken to looking at gardens around town, and was going to ask Madame Morel for some advice. She would pop in and see the Morels now, she thought. Maybe Docteur Morel had heard back from his cousin. Each time she had seen them it had been the same. "Nothing yet. It may take time, but don't give up."

She followed the worn path beside the Ménec Alignments. The stones were quiet, waking to the morning light, the space still their own before the visitors arrived. "Wish me luck," she called to them.

Pierrot was at the house, getting his toolbox out of his van. Before greeting him, Isabeau stopped at the gate and studied the house. He hadn't even started, and it already looked different, better. It took her a minute to realize that the slate tiles on the roof now formed a regular even pattern. The slipped tiles had been repaired.

"The roofer's been?" she asked Pierrot.

"Yes, during the week."

"I can't believe what a difference that already makes."

"I told you it wasn't that bad. Wait till the stone's been tidied up; that'll make a huge difference. It may take a while for the guy I know to come and do it, but he'll make a good job, and it won't cost a fortune."

Isabeau parked her bike against the fence.

When Pierrot kissed her on each cheek, he pressed for the slightest time longer than usual. Maybe it was that they were getting to know each other better. But then again, maybe she was imagining it. Leaving him to his preparations, she took out the gardening tools. She needed to keep busy, very busy. She didn't want to back out of the house project now. Her legs were sore from biking, but she pushed Papa's spade hard into the earth. She had no power over whether Joseph replied, but she wasn't going to let this damn convolvulus get the better of her.

When Pierrot called from the front door, Isabeau glanced at her watch. She'd been outside almost two hours.

"I'm stopping for a break. Coffee and croissants on me," he said.

Isabeau sat on the front step and Pierrot astride an upturned wooden box on the grass. He talked about his other projects. Isabeau listened. He was so sure about his work and the house. That was what she needed.

Once they had finished, Pierrot headed straight back to dismantling the cupboards in the kitchen. Isabeau also had a mission. She went next door.

Madame Morel answered the door.

"Come through. René's doing his crossword puzzles – or perhaps he's snoozing already," she laughed.

"The carpenter's started this morning, and I'm working in the garden," said Isabeau, following her into the kitchen.

"I saw the van there and thought it looked like something was happening," said Docteur Morel, getting up from the kitchen table. "That's great news."

"If you want help with the garden, I can give you some cuttings and plants," offered Madame Morel.

"I'd appreciate that," Isabeau said. She turned to Docteur Morel. "I'm sorry to bother you again about this, but I was wondering if there's been any news from your cousin in Nantes?"

"I'm afraid not. I thought I might've heard back from him by now, though. I'll give him a ring."

He went to the phone, picked up the battered address book beside it, flicked through to the letter B, and dialed. "Salut Lili. Comment ça va?

Oh, you were, were you? Well, this couldn't be better timing then, could it?" Docteur Morel listened intently, nodding and saying "oui" several times, then asking "whereabouts in Nantes is that?" He wrote down an address, then soon after said goodbye and hung up. There was a slight smile on his lips.

"We're waiting with bated breath, René," said Madame Morel.

"Lili was busy on a couple of important cases and then came down with the flu," Docteur Morel told them, "but all good things come to he, or she, who waits. Unfortunately he can't find any trace of your father at present. However – and I don't know how – he did find a record of him at this address." He handed Isabeau the piece of paper. "You now have a lead."

"**P**ierrot called in to see François," Marianne said to Isabeau. "You must be pleased he's started on the house?" Together, they walked down the alley to chemin er Goh Fetan.

"I think so. At least something's finally happening," Isabeau replied.

"And I'm pleased you've started on the sachets," said Marianne, following Isabeau through the gate.

Isabeau lifted the flap of her letterbox. There was a long airmail envelope there, with a row of suns and sailing boats across the bottom. She slipped the letter under her arm and concentrated on stopping her hands shaking while she opened the door.

"Here, let me help you," offered Marianne, taking the baguette and the letter from under Isabeau's arm and sitting them on the table when they got inside. Marianne glanced at the letter as Isabeau took it as casually as she could.

"That looks interesting. And nice stamps. New Zealand! That's a long way. Do you have friends there?"

"Not really. It's just someone I've got to know recently."

"Have you ever been there?" Marianne asked.

"I've never been out of France."

"Would you like to travel?"

"For so long I only thought about coming back to Carnac, so I've never really thought about going anywhere else," Isabeau said as she tucked the letter away in the drawer of the sideboard. She picked up her embroidery basket, pulled out three linen sachets from it and placed them on the table.

"I love the different colours. They look amazing," said Marianne. She picked up a sachet with "M & F" embroidered in lavender, the wedding date in ink blue and a heart in raspberry pink. The next sachet was orange, yellow and blue, and the last one was different shades of green.

"I thought it would be fun to have them all different colours rather than the same," said Isabeau. "That way you can have something simple like this that will still stand out."

"That's a great idea. It's going to be a big job, though."

"I'm happy to help, and I'm pleased to have a different kind of project to do."

"Really?"

"Yes."

"Are you sure?"

"Let that be my wedding present to you and François. You have enough to do."

"That would be the best present, thanks. As hard as I try, I don't have a lot of free time, especially with François' mother being unwell now," replied Marianne.

Isabeau had already prepared lasagne for dinner the evening before. While she took it out of the fridge, Marianne picked up one of the decorating magazines sitting on the bookcase and flicked through it. "Lots of ideas in these that you could use in your house," she said. "I'd love to see it."

"Maybe when it's looking better."

"Mind if I have a look through your music?" Marianne picked up Joseph's cassette from the top of the pile. "This looks different. Can I put it on?"

Isabeau almost dropped the dish of lasagne as she was putting it in the oven; it slipped out of her hands onto the rack.

"Who's the singer?"

"He's a New Zealand singer-songwriter." Her secret was starting to reveal itself. *Breathe slowly*, she told herself. Joseph's voice came on, and in spite of the distance it was as if he was there with her, telling her she could tell Marianne about him.

"He's not bad looking, to say the least," Marianne smiled. "Did your New Zealand friend send it to you?"

"Actually it's him, the singer. He sent it to me ... Joseph."

"He sounds as good as he looks. I can't understand what he's saying, but the music's beautiful."

"I got it at the end of January, and I've been listening to it a lot. All the songs are as good as this one."

"How do you know him?"

"It's a long story," Isabeau said. "He sent an enquiry to the post office, and it all happened from there." She hoped Marianne wouldn't take this question any further. *Please*. Although she hadn't lied. Just summarized.

"Makes your work sound interesting," Marianne said. "You never talk about it." Isabeau could hear the questioning tone in her voice.

"It's just a job, not like the bakery for you. You look like you're in your element. I don't like to think about work when I'm not there."

"Anyway, he has very kind eyes," Marianne continued. "He's good-looking, don't you think?"

"He must have a girlfriend, and be chased by women fans," Isabeau said, to her own surprise.

"Have you asked him if he's got someone?"

"No! We don't talk – I mean, write – about those kind of things."

"Well, maybe you should," teased Marianne.

After the meal, Marianne put Joseph's cassette on again, and his music accompanied them as they pulled their needles back and forth and snipped and counted. There was always one more stitch. It was eleven o'clock when Marianne left. Isabeau took the letter and cassette player upstairs and snuggled under her duvet. She'd told Marianne about Joseph. It was like embroidery thread, she thought. Once the cotton came loose from the paper that secured the hank, it could unravel. Since George's arrival things had been like that.

There was a house theme across the top of this letter, and, along the bottom, a beach scene with the sun shining and sailing boats.

Dear Isabeau,

I'm sorry it's taken me a long time to reply. I've been shifting the last of my things back home and having some renovations done to Dad's house – which is mine now – not to mention starting to sort through all of his stuff. After I got out of hospital, I went to my aunt and uncle's for a while, and then my cousin Drew came to stay with me to help me get a few things done. We used to flat together and have always been close, but it feels good to be on my own again and writing songs. When I'm writing music, I forget everything else: all my worries and cares. Do you have an activity like that? I'm glad you're enjoying my album. Music is a universal language!

You mention that you have a house and that it's near the standing stones. It's funny how you grew up there, as if you were meant to receive my father's ashes. And you are going to be renovating too. I hope it goes smoothly for you.

Thank you for the photo. It's nice to be able to put a face to you. You're not like I expected. I guess I imagined some stuffy postmistress the first time you wrote back, but you don't look at all like that! We must be about the same age. I'd love to meet you one day.

It's been a hard year for me, losing my father and having my accident. Some of it is only just sinking in, especially as I'm on my own for the first time in a while. Your letters have connected me to my father, and I really need that. My mother died when I was very young, and my father brought me up alone.

When I sent the ashes, it was out of desperation. The promise I had made to my father weighed heavily upon me. Several years ago, I read an article in the local newspaper about an American family who sent some of their mother's ashes to the Chief Postmaster in each world capital. She had prepared to go on a world tour several times in her life, but each time had to cancel the trip because of ill health. The family were happy because they received many replies detailing what had been done with the ashes. Once I'd sent off Dad's ashes, I worried that I'd done a foolish thing, but it has turned out to be good.

It's still summer here. Drew spends a lot of time sailing, and I've been out to watch. My Uncle Ian has a boat-building business, and Drew works for him. Growing up, I spent a lot of time with them around boats. Christchurch has a big port and two main beaches: Sumner and New Brighton, very different from each other. It's a very spread-out city, and where I live in the south of the city the Port Hills dominate the scenery and you can't actually see the coast.

I look at the European temperatures in the newspaper each day and try to imagine what it's like over there. You're going towards spring, and here autumn is approaching.

Next time I'll send you one of my other albums, when I'm more organized.

Sincerely,

Joseph

32

Isabeau straightened her cotton jacket and looked at her watch. She rang the doorbell and waited. The house was quiet. She rechecked the number on the piece of paper Docteur Morel had given her and took another look at the map of Nantes. It was Saturday afternoon Easter weekend. After work, she'd driven straight to the house in rue Henri Cochard. She'd been studying the map of Nantes all week. All that effort just to ring a doorbell. Should she leave a note or try the neighbours? What would George say? *Put a note in the letterbox. It's that simple.* It was that voice again: old and calm like Docteur Morel, yet it wasn't exactly his voice either. She rubbed her eyes. Was she imagining it? She took out her notebook and ripped off a page.

It wasn't far to the centre of Nantes. Leaving her car where it was, Isabeau headed down rue Pitre Chevalier towards the Erdre River where it met the cours des 50-Otages. This big city was a different world to Carnac, yet Nantes was also full of stone. Elegant buildings in tuffeau lined the wide avenue of the cours des 50-Otages. Isabeau took off her jacket as she walked. The sun was shining. Spring had arrived – daffodils and high temperatures – and daylight saving was starting the next day. After the bitter winter, she almost felt like she was on holiday. She followed the cours des 50-Otages until she reached the tram line, and stopped to watch the Saturday bustle of people carrying bags of shopping and getting on and off the tram. What would Marianne or the Morels do if they were here? Marianne would definitely go shopping. Isabeau slid the photo from the engagement party out from between Joseph's letters in her bag. She headed towards Place Royale, which led up to rue Crébillon and the fashion boutiques.

At the fountain in Place Royale the water glistened in the sun. Isabeau sat down on the edge and trailed her hand in the water. Papa would like this fountain. Could he somehow still be in the city? Could she pass him in the street? Would she even recognize him?

She wandered up rue Crébillon and half way up saw the Passage Pommeraye. Curious, she entered and explored the boutiques, marvelling at the architecture and many statues decorating the three-level covered passage way. Then, on rue Crébillon, Isabeau admired the beautiful clothes in the boutique windows. Etam was full of casual summer clothes that were not expensive. A white t-shirt caught her eye and drew her into the shop. A young blond woman was searching through the rack of t-shirts. Isabeau imitated her movements. The woman picked out three t-shirts and went towards the changing cubicles. Isabeau took a striped grey one and entered the adjoining cubicle. When she tried it on, she slid her hair out of its ponytail.

She carried on to Place Graslin, dominated by the theatre with its columns. On the opposite side of the square, she looked in the window of La Cigale, an art deco brasserie that she'd seen in magazines. It was too classy for her on her own. Instead, she cut through to rue du Calvaire, and went into Monoprix, where she bought a bottle of water and a sandwich in the supermarket section. She then wandered around the store's clothes and accessories section, and decided to buy a dark grey headband.

"I have things to show Marianne," Isabeau hummed to herself as she descended rue du Calvaire, wearing the striped t-shirt and the headband. The two purchases were her Easter treat to herself.

Now, what would the Morels do? Isabeau could imagine them strolling along, Madame Morel's arm through her husband's. They were everything her parents weren't. She studied the map of Nantes. They would go to the Botanic Gardens, she thought. Isabeau followed the tram line east, stopping at the castle before she reached the Gardens, opposite the station.

Here, families with young children were enjoying the fine weather. New parents pushed prams, and toddlers eager to explore pulled at their parents' hands. She took her time around the circular paths and ponds, walking slower than her usual pace, then found a bench in the sun and sat. She pulled out Joseph's last letter and reread it several times.

It was the longest and most detailed letter he'd sent. She had replied almost straightaway, writing a longer letter too. She pondered why it was becoming easier to write about herself to a person she had never met on the other side of the world.

When Isabeau had finished, she followed a family to the Jules Verne monument on the eastern side of the gardens. She studied the monument while around her a steady stream of people stopped to look at it. It was comprised of a bust of the writer and, around the base, two children reading Verne's *Extraordinary Voyages.*

Isabeau looked down. On the gravel beside the monument was a bird, quivering, dying. Nobody was taking any notice of it. She felt sick. She wanted to look away, but she couldn't. Suddenly it seemed like a bad idea to come to Nantes. A bad idea to have left the note.

33

The days were lengthening. Isabeau spent May Day pottering in the garden at her house. The beds at the front of the house were starting to look like a real garden now that they contained some hydrangeas and other plants from Madame Morel. Isabeau kept stopping to look up at the slate roof, admiring the flat uniform tiles. Pierrot had gone away for the long weekend so she had the house to herself. It seemed crazy, but she kept thinking about turning it into a bed and breakfast. She needed a distraction. There was no news from Nantes, no reply to the note. But she was beginning to worry more that there was no reply from Joseph.

"Why doesn't he write?" Isabeau asked George. "Did I get too personal? He probably thought it was pathetic, me telling him about my embroidery and writing poetry." Or, worse still, she thought, he could have somehow read between the lines and guessed she hadn't scattered the ashes. *Sometimes these things take time.* The voice was there again, old and wise, like Docteur Morel talking about his cousin from Nantes getting back to him. At the same time it was as if it was George talking to her. And the voice was right. At the end of the week, the letter was there, like a magical surprise sitting in her letter box.

"George, it's here!" This time, the envelope was decorated with tiny planes that swirled and dived around birds and clouds. Isabeau wished the birds didn't remind her of the dead bird in Nantes.

Dear Isabeau,

Once again, I have to apologize for taking so long to reply. It's a long story, so perhaps I should start at the end with the most amazing part – I'm coming to France in July! Can you believe it? I'm not sure I can myself. I would have written sooner, but I wanted to wait until I was 100 percent sure if I was coming or not.

My cousin Drew does a lot of sailing, and he's coming to compete in a part of the Tour de France boat race around the Atlantic coast and the Mediterranean. One of Drew's sailor friends has just been appointed partner in a law firm and is reluctant to take time off now, and Drew's talked me into buying the spare ticket. He came up with the idea that we could come to Carnac first, before his sailing begins. I don't think it's convenient for him, but he's insisting.

We plan on coming to Carnac 2–7 July, and I wondered whether, if you're not going to be away on holiday, we could meet. Do you know of any good hotels or bed and breakfasts that have rooms on the ground floor, or don't have too many stairs? Since my accident, I haven't been too good on my legs. I would be grateful if you could send me the details, and I could take care of the bookings from here.

I read with interest about your embroidery. I'd never thought of it as being such a creative activity. What you said reminded me of a cross-stitch picture my mother made before I was born, which Dad kept on the wall. It's a scene of a house with a tree on each side and birds. Growing up it didn't mean much to me, because it had always been there, and when Dad died I put it in a box and almost threw it out. After reading your letter, I got it out and looked at it in a completely different light. I can't remember anything about my mother, because she died when I was two. All I know about her is from what Dad and other family members have told me over the years. I've hung the picture up again.

As for poetry: I can relate to that. Writing song lyrics is similar to writing poetry. Most of my songs are based on my personal experiences. I've been struggling a bit to settle back into my old habits of composing, and I'm hoping the trip to France will give me a fresh perspective and kick-start things.

I would love to meet you, not only because of Dad but also because I'm really enjoying corresponding with you. It would be good to meet and carry on the conversation in person! Perhaps it would be easier to organize something by phone? If you send me your number I could call you. I was going to send you another of my cassettes, but perhaps instead I could bring it with me when I come to France and give it to you in person.

I look forward to hearing from you.

Yours sincerely,

Joseph

"George, Joseph's coming to France. He's coming to Carnac," Isabeau whispered, her voice getting louder. "I'll have to scatter you now."

34

It was warm on the front step. Isabeau stared at the hydrangeas along the fence.

She still hadn't written back to Joseph. He was needing to organize accommodation. Waiting for a reply. What did he mean by *not too good on his legs*? Because of the accident, did he have trouble bending one knee, or both of them? Was he on crutches?

Repeating the resolution that she had mentioned to Tonton Aimé about trying to answer her correspondence promptly didn't make any difference. Every time she took out her writing pad, she only managed to write more sheets of resolutions about the ashes. *I will scatter George. I must scatter George.* What would Joseph think if he knew? She couldn't wait any longer, even if it felt like George wasn't ready yet. How could she ever explain that to Joseph?

Isabeau closed her eyes. George was in her bag. Perhaps she should walk to the menhirs and scatter him now. Anywhere. Did it really matter if it wasn't the Giant? She pulled her bag towards her and hugged it hard.

"George, what should I do?"

"Isabeau."

"Docteur Morel!"

"I'm sorry. I didn't mean to give you a fright. You look preoccupied," he said gently, and stepped back.

"I was just thinking. Everything seems so complicated." Isabeau pushed her bag under her legs.

"I wish I could give you some answers to all the questions about your father," Docteur Morel said. "Nothing would please me more."

"When I think things are better, something unexpected comes up and I'm back to square one."

"So, no luck with that address in Nantes? Nobody's made contact with you?"

"Nothing. I doubt I'll hear anything now. It was kind of you to help, but there doesn't seem much point pursuing it."

"Well, as I said, sometimes these things take time. Something may still turn up."

Isabeau wished she could believe Docteur Morel's confident voice.

"I feel like time's running out. Docteur Morel, have you ever wanted something and perhaps been able to have it, but at the same time you've been too scared to do anything?" Isabeau paused. "I'm sorry I'm not being very clear."

"I understand. Yes," he chuckled, "when I first met Marie-Luce. I couldn't take my eyes off her, but I was too scared to talk to her."

"What happened?"

"A friend of mine sent her a note pretending to be me, inviting her to go to a dance," said Docteur Morel. "He thought it was a great joke. At the time, I hated him for it, but she accepted, and I had no choice but to go through with it."

Isabeau couldn't help but smile.

"I'll leave you to have a think then. It's a nice day for it." He gestured towards the sun and started to walk away. After a couple of steps, he half turned back. "Don't ask yourself too many questions though, Isabeau. If you're always asking questions, there's no space for the answers to come." He turned back around, waving as he walked away.

Riding back into town, Isabeau continued to think about what Docteur Morel had said. For the next hour she would not ask herself a question, she declared to herself. She would only make affirmations. She pushed harder on the pedals. A faster rhythm always helped to clear her head. One, two, three, four: something familiar and simple. Un, deux, trois, quatre, Jo – seph, one, two, three, four, Jo – seph. I – want – to – see – him. She was picking up speed down rue du Ménec. I – will – write – back. I – will – meet – Joseph. Suddenly, Isabeau felt as if she could take off.

"Looking for accommodation?" Marianne glanced at the leaflets in Isabeau's hand.

"Sort of. My New Zealand friend, Joseph ... the singer. He's coming with his cousin to Carnac for a few days in early July. He's asked me to find them somewhere to stay." Isabeau put the leaflets she'd picked up earlier from the Tourist Information Office on the counter.

"We've got a spare room, you know," Marianne told her. "And we won't be around much. We'll be busy getting things ready in Saint-Laurent for the wedding. They're welcome to use our place. We're happy to accommodate anyone who sings that well and is a friend of yours!"

"Thanks. I'll keep it in mind. I've also got a room – well, you know, the alcove downstairs – but I think they want to be independent. At the moment I'm looking into all the options." For the first time, Isabeau was wishing the little house had two proper bedrooms.

The main brochure had an extensive list, categorized by facilities and prices. Isabeau ate her sandwich while she walked around the streets looking at the hotels and the bed and breakfasts. They were all two or three storeys high, and it was hard to tell if any of them had rooms on the ground floor. Maybe one flight of stairs would be okay.

Would she see much of Joseph, apart from a quick meeting? She could invite him and Drew for a meal.

Down chemin du Douet, Isabeau stopped in front of a small hotel, Le Ratelier, with an inviting courtyard, vine-covered stone walls and blue and pink hydrangeas lining the entrance. It was pretty, and wasn't far from where she was living. She should go in and ask if they had ground floor rooms. She carried on.

At home, Isabeau went straight to the alcove and paced up and down, trying to imagine it without the unpacked boxes stacked on the beds. She knew a little about Joseph, but nothing about his cousin, except that he sailed. What would they do for five days?

She needed to talk to George.

"What should I do?" Isabeau held the box of ashes and rubbed her finger back and forth across the row of menhirs on the top. The voice came again, familiar and elusive, from inside her and outside at the same time. It always went away just as she felt she was about to have a sense of where it came from and whose voice it was. Now *it* was asking questions. *What do you want?* "I want to invite Joseph to stay with me," Isabeau declared.

She sat at the table, listening to Joseph's music while she looked at the photo of him as a boy with George. She tried to imagine Joseph and Drew at the table, laughing and talking. With her. It suddenly seemed as if everything was reduced to a single question. What if? Isabeau grabbed her new writing paper and pen. She wanted to chase the questions, send them packing, to leave space for the answers, like Docteur Morel had said. She wrote quickly.

Dear Joseph,

What a surprise! I can't believe either that you will be coming to France. In July, I'll be on holiday, and I don't have any plans. It would be great to meet you. I'm enclosing the accommodation guide for Carnac. I've highlighted those hotels close to the centre or the standing stones. However, most of them have stairs. All the contact details are in the booklet, but if you need any other help at all please let me know.

Otherwise, I have a spare room, and you're both welcome to stay with me. It's not spacious – more of an alcove really – but it would be big enough for two, and it's on the ground floor. The little house I'm renting (while my own house is being renovated) is right in the centre of Carnac, and not far from the alignments. It would be handy for you and Drew to get around. I will, of course, understand if you prefer to stay in a hotel, and we could still meet.

I would love to see your mother's embroidery. It must be a very special memory of her. I've been thinking a lot about your father, and I'm curious to find out more about him. There are many questions I want to ask you. It will be easier to ask you in person, rather than by letter!

I've been doing more embroidery for my friend Marianne, who got engaged at New Year. I'm helping decorate the little sachets for the sugar-covered almonds, called dragées, that are traditionally given out at weddings, christenings and communions. I like to listen to your music when I'm doing my embroidery. The days are getting longer, and I've also been working in the garden up at my house near the alignments. The renovations have started.

I look forward to hearing more of your plans. If I can help in any way,

please don't hesitate to ask. I would be very happy to have you both to stay.
    Sincerely,
    Isabeau

Isabeau added a P.S. and put her phone number, and at the top of the letter started drawing a chain of triskeles. She continued until she had decorated all the borders of the page. She pushed the letter and brochures into a large envelope and placed it under George. "Make sure I send it, please," she told him.

At first it had been easy. Isabeau had tackled a couple of boxes of embroidery magazines and old books. She had managed to sort through them after work during the course of the week. But now the kitchen floor and table were covered with opened boxes, china and crumpled newspaper. Instead of decreasing, the mess was spreading, and taking over the house as if it had a mind of its own. She wondered how everything had ever fitted into the boxes to start with. And how she was going to get through it all. As well as her own things, there were still boxes of Mother's belongings to be dealt with.

Isabeau picked up one of them. Pieces of an English blue and white tea set nestled in discoloured newspaper. She unwrapped the cups. Maybe this had belonged to her grandparents. She thought of Joseph and his mother's cross-stitch. She emptied out the whole box onto the sideboard, pushing George and the letters to the side to make enough space.

The doorbell rang. Isabeau put George and the letters away, pulled on a pair of tracksuit pants over her pyjamas and arranged her hair behind her ears. As soon as she opened the door, Marianne stepped forward.

"Special delivery," she said, holding out an envelope. "I thought I'd see you this week, but I've somehow missed you every day. I wanted to give you the wedding invitation. And I thought that you might need more thread for the sachets." Marianne pulled out several hanks of thread from her bag and handed them to Isabeau.

"Thanks, good timing. I'm starting to run out," Isabeau said, and put the thread on the coat stand.

"Can I come in?" asked Marianne. "I've also got something for afternoon tea." She patted her bag. "Thought you might need some energy what with all the work you're doing on the sachets."

"Of course. I – the house – we're a bit of a mess though."

"No, you look great. I like it when you have your hair loose, a little wild." Marianne followed Isabeau inside and surveyed the half-emptied boxes and the contents scattered around the kitchen. "You weren't exaggerating about the house. Where did all this come from?"

"I've never got around to unpacking completely." Isabeau pointed towards the alcove.

"Any more news from your New Zealand friend?" Marianne asked, poking her head around the alcove curtain.

"Not yet. He and his cousin can stay here if they want, but they'll probably prefer a hotel or bed and breakfast. Anyway, this unpacking really needed to be done." Isabeau tried to sound convincing. Scenarios kept flashing in her head. Joseph phoned to tell her that it was all a joke, or that there had been another change of plans – as sudden as the decision to come in the first place – and he wasn't coming after all. It was too good to be true. She was afraid of him coming, and afraid of him not coming.

"This looks like a pretty good establishment to me – it'll be much better for them than staying in a hotel."

"Do you think so?"

"Don't look so serious," smiled Marianne. "I'm sure your friend would rather stay with you than in a hotel. Would you like some help to get things sorted?"

"That would be great, thanks."

"I love doing this kind of thing and decorating. It's fun. And you've got some nice old character furniture. This looks good." Marianne picked up one of the cups off the sideboard and examined it.

"At the moment it's not much fun. I'm creating more chaos than order," Isabeau sighed.

"One thing at a time." Marianne moved her hands as if she was a conductor. "Open box, sort entire contents, fold box and put out."

"If only it were that simple!"

"It is. May I?"

"Please, be my guest," replied Isabeau.

"Well, to start with, we need a rubbish box," Marianne said, tipping out a few magazines from an almost empty box, "and to repack some of the stuff to get it under control, and then we can go from there." She gathered up some pieces of crumpled newspaper. "And some music will help get us in the mood. What do you think?" she asked, picking up Joseph's cassette.

"Perfect," said Isabeau.

"When I shifted to Carnac, I had a big clean-out of most of my things.

It felt really good. I've just got to finish sorting through my clothes. I'm not quite dressing the same now I'm working in the bakery."

"I was going to sort through everything when I left Besançon, but there wasn't time. It was all a bit too much. I still haven't finished sorting through all my mother's things."

"The first thing is to decide what you are going to keep, because the less stuff the easier it will be to get organized and decide where to put it all."

"You make it sound so easy."

"It is, but you have to be in the right frame of mind. Why don't I hold things up, and you tell me if you want to keep them. We could start with something easy like the books and magazines in these boxes, and then we could tidy your bookshelf."

"Okay."

"First, though, can I use your bathroom?"

"Sure."

As soon as Marianne was out of sight, Isabeau grabbed the box of ashes and Joseph's letters as quietly as she could and ran upstairs to hide them in her wardrobe, right at the back.

A couple of hours later the living room and alcove were looking more ordered. Isabeau couldn't believe how much they had emptied and sorted; they had flattened the empty boxes and put them outside beside the rubbish bin.

"That's better," said Marianne, undoing the little parcel she had deposited on the bench earlier and setting out two chocolate religieuses on the table. "I think we deserve our afternoon tea now."

"I don't know how you keep your figure working with all that temptation. Must have been great growing up in a bakery," Isabeau said.

"The secret's not to start. When I first helped make chocolates, Papa said I could eat as many as I wanted," Marianne laughed. "The first day I did, but I didn't eat any after that for a while!"

"Your parents are amazing."

"Yes, I'm very lucky. What about your family – do you have any grandparents or other family?" asked Marianne.

"I used to wonder, but my mother was an only child, like me. Her parents were killed in a plane crash when she was young, so she was brought up by her grandparents. I never knew them, and I don't think I have any other relatives on her side. She was English, but she never went back to England. I've never even been there. My father lived in foster homes. I have no idea about his family. Perhaps my parents were attracted to each other because both of them had nobody else."

"Where did they meet each other?"

"In France, I think. But it didn't last. And then my father left." Isabeau pulled the top off the religieuse and bit into it.

"You might have some family in England, you never know."

"I doubt it."

"It's a shame you didn't get anywhere with finding your father when you went to Pornic," said Marianne, licking chocolate custard off her fingers. "It's nice the Morels have been helping you. Have you had any news from that address in Nantes that you told me about?"

"No, still nothing."

"Perhaps something will come up. I hope so," said Marianne. "I think you need something more pleasant to think about – like something nice to wear to the wedding." She pulled the *La Redoute* catalogue from her bag.

"How much stuff have you got in that bag?" Isabeau teased her.

"I thought you might like some help with your outfit." Marianne sat the catalogue on the table. "You've ended up doing the sachets single-handedly. I'm feeling a bit guilty about that, and I enjoyed helping you put together your outfit for the engagement party. I used to work in a clothes shop, and I miss it."

"I can't wait to see your dress."

"It's all sorted," Marianne said, as she started looking through the catalogue. She had turned down the corner of several pages. "Now, what about what you're going to wear?"

"I could wear the jersey dress again."

"You need something more summery. I could help you have a look through your wardrobe?"

"It's not really worth it. I don't have a lot of clothes."

"I might have some clothes that would suit you, give your wardrobe a bit of a boost. We're about the same size."

"Thanks. Can I borrow the catalogue? I can have a look later when I've got some time."

"Sure. Make the most of it. You never know when you might have the opportunity to dress up a bit."

"**H**ello. No, you're not disturbing me. I was expecting your call."
Isabeau snipped the thread on the finished sachet and put her
scissors down. Joseph's voice was singing to her.

"It's nice to hear your voice – you talking. I already know what you
sound like singing. Actually I was just listening to your cassette."

As much as she tried to tell herself that a conversation was only one
word after another, like stitches, Isabeau still had no idea what she
would really say if Joseph phoned. When she embroidered, she
controlled the needle, the colour, the size and order of the stitches. She
wasn't always in control in the same way when she was talking to other
people.

Marianne had been back twice to help her continue with the
unpacking process. Papa's bowl was now in pride of place on the
sideboard, alongside pieces of the tea set, on a cloth Isabeau had stitched
when she was a teenager. Some framed embroideries were grouped on
the wall. In the alcove, the remaining boxes were stacked in the corner.
The little house was more pleasant, more ordered. Isabeau felt more in
control, but not when she thought about Joseph.

The music finished, and Isabeau sat in silence. She rubbed her hand
along George's box. The phone rang and she jumped.

"Allô, Isabeau."

"Pierrot?" She hoped she hadn't sounded too disappointed.

"I haven't seen you for a while."

"I've been busy here; I haven't been up to the house much." It was a
half-truth. She'd been going up there late for walks and peeking at the
kitchen.

"I wondered if you'd seen the progress." He paused. "The kitchen's
finally taking shape. I need to know if you want to add a shelf beside the
bench. Could we meet at the house Saturday afternoon around four?"

"Sure."

Isabeau said goodbye to Pierrot and hung up the phone. "Do you
really think he'll call, George?" she said, with a long sigh.

The kitchen and living room were now one open space. The light reached everywhere, and the freshly plastered walls and oak cupboards made it entirely different from the dark and poky kitchen of Isabeau's childhood. It looked brand new and homely.

"It's a different house – completely new," Isabeau stammered. She almost wanted to cry, in a happy way. Things were happening that she couldn't have even imagined a year earlier.

"I thought you'd be pleased," Pierrot said.

"I don't know what to say. Thank you." Isabeau walked around, taking in the new space. "You haven't given me the bill yet for the final payment. We'd better settle this before you start on the bathroom."

"Don't worry, I'll get on to it. We should celebrate. We could have a crêpe at the blue crêperie near where you're renting in town? On me. I'll be rich once you've paid me." He laughed. "What about next Saturday?"

"I'm not sure, um, I ..."

"It would be a great opportunity to talk in detail about the bathroom."

"Okay ... thanks."

"Great, I'll pick you up at seven."

When Isabeau got home she curled up in her armchair and pulled out some embroidery threads. Red, the colour of passion. Yellow, for friendship. She thought of Pierrot standing in the kitchen. She still wasn't sure she should have said yes. What would Joseph be doing Saturday evening? Why did she think about him so much? Even if he came to France, he would go away again. Pierrot would too, when he'd finished the house. He worked all over Brittany.

The phone rang. Pierrot must have forgotten something.

"Allô, Pierrot." There was silence at the other end.

"Hello, Isabeau? I'd like to speak to Isabeau Martin. Je voudrais parler à Isabeau Martin."

It was the voice from the cassette. Isabeau bit her lip.

"Hello. Allô." The voice was louder. "Isabeau?"

"Yes. Joseph? Sorry, I was expecting a call from someone else and I was ..."

"I hope I've pronounced your name right."

"That's right, Iz – a – bo," Isabeau enunciated slowly.

"I got your letter, thanks. It's hard to imagine that you're in Carnac and we're finally talking ... Isabeau?"

"Sorry."

"I hope I haven't rung at a bad time. It's a bit hard with the time difference; it's very early morning here."

"No, not at all. I was just doing some embroidery."

"Your written English is excellent, but it's still a surprise to hear you speak. Thanks for the information about accommodation in Carnac, and for your offer to have us to stay."

"That's fine, really."

"Are you sure it wouldn't be too much inconvenience having both me and Drew for that long?"

Isabeau looked at George on the table. *Go on, say something,* she heard.

"Not at all. I'd be pleased to have you both, and there wouldn't be any problems with stairs at my place." There was a short silence. She didn't like to mention Joseph's crutches until he said something about them. "You're most welcome to stay with me, but please feel free to stay somewhere else if you want; whatever suits you."

"Thank you, you're very kind." He sighed faintly. "I'm sure your place will be perfect. The travel agent's finalizing the train from Paris at the moment. He said that the closest would be to Auray, and he's booking a train that arrives early afternoon: 1.15 p.m."

"It's only twenty kilometres away. I can pick you up," Isabeau offered.

"Thanks. I'm looking forward to meeting you." Joseph's voice wavered slightly. "I really appreciate how much you've done for me and my dad."

"You're more than welcome. It will be nice to meet you too," Isabeau said, concentrating on keeping her voice steady. "And we'll be able to have a good look around the alignments."

"That'll be great, especially having a few days to take it all in. How long are your holidays?"

"I have all of July."

"So you'll have plenty of time for other plans then, as well."

"Yes, plenty."

"Well, the train booking will be sorted out this week. If there are any changes, I'll be in touch. Otherwise I'll see you on the second, at a quarter past one at Auray."

"I look forward to it."

"Thanks, Isabeau. I'll see you soon."

"Goodbye, Joseph," Isabeau said softly. She wasn't sure if he heard it before the phone clicked. The line droned.

Everything was accelerating, flowing more freely. Isabeau wasn't sure what she was moving towards, but she felt herself carried along. She started to spring-clean, forcing herself to complete one task after another. She was surprised at what she'd been able to achieve since Marianne had given her a hand with the unpacking. The garden up at the Alouettes house was taking shape, and she'd even bought some pots of geraniums for the courtyard at the little house in town, and planted some herbs in the strip of earth along the wall. Pierrot had to postpone their meal at the crêperie because of some out-of-town work he had on. It was a relief.

There was still no reply from Nantes. It didn't matter during the day, but at night questions about her father and finding him played themselves out in Isabeau's head. When she couldn't sleep, she talked to George. "I must scatter you. Joseph will be here soon," she repeated with conviction, but every tomorrow there were things to do: finishing the last sachets and trying to work out a menu for Joseph and Drew's stay, as well as a programme to fill in their five days. Stuffed tomatoes or bolognaise? Quiche or pasta? Visit the standing stones the day they arrived, or wait until the next day? As soon as Isabeau had decided something, she changed her mind. How could anything be right if she was deceiving Joseph? What would she say?

Another letter from Joseph arrived. Isabeau's stomach sank. He must be writing to tell her about a change to his plans – she would be left to spend July in a tidy house and pretty garden, alone.

But he was still coming. It looked like he'd made the card himself, and there was more decoration than writing: menhirs, fireworks and bottles fizzing, as if it was a party invitation to his arrival. Only three weeks away.

Dear Isabeau,

It will be great to escape winter for a short time. We often have cold crisp clear days in Christchurch, but lately it's been grey and foggy, sad weather. I long for some sun, and soon I'll be in Carnac! I can't wait. I'm really looking forward to it. I hope Drew and I won't be too much trouble. The train tickets are booked. See you at Auray, 2 July at 1.15 p.m. Again, thank you.

Sincerely,
Joseph

Isabeau turned the card over in her hands while she walked to the bakery. Joseph hoped they wouldn't be too much trouble! She'd spent weeks spring-cleaning the house, her life. For once – like other people – she actually had an inconvenience to concern herself with.

As she arrived at the bakery, she still had the card in her hand.

"More news from New Zealand?" asked Marianne.

"A card from Joseph." Isabeau slipped it into her jeans pocket.

"When did you say he was arriving?"

"July second. They go to Brest on the seventh for the boat race," Isabeau explained.

"Just before the wedding; that works out well," Marianne said, pointing to the baguettes then the boules as she spoke.

Isabeau nodded for a boule.

"Yes, and on that subject I've finished the sachets, if you want to come and see them."

"I'll be down in about half an hour. Julie should be okay on her own."

"Close your eyes and give me your hand." Isabeau led Marianne from the front door to the kitchen table. "You can open them now." The sachets formed a spiral of colour on the table.

"You must've spent hours working on these!" Marianne picked up different sachets and examined them, then came back around the table and embraced Isabeau. "They're beautiful. It's the best wedding present you could ever give us. Thank you."

"It didn't take as long as I thought, and I've really enjoyed doing them. If you give me the dragées I'll fill them and tie them up with ribbon."

"Talking of finished things, now that your kitchen's completed, I'd love to see your house."

"It looks good, completely different," Isabeau told her. "I'll show you some time." She sat down beside Marianne. "And Pierrot and I are going out to the crêperie to celebrate."

Marianne raised her eyebrows.

"It's not really a date. He's nice, but we're more sort of like friends."

"I think he'd like to take you to the wedding. He's mentioned it to

François."

"Has he?" Isabeau picked up a sachet and pretended to study it.

They packed the sachets back into Isabeau's basket, and Marianne took the *La Redoute* catalogue from the shelf. "There's a special twenty-five percent reduction offer on at the moment. Sounds like it might be a good opportunity for you to get something to wear for going out. What do you think?"

"I've had a look at it, but I don't really know where to start."

"No problem."

Thirty minutes later, Marianne had helped Isabeau choose a skirt, shorts, singlets, a dress – short and well-fitting – for the wedding and even some new underwear. She started to pack up, but Isabeau couldn't leave the catalogue alone now. She looked longingly at the nightwear section. What would she wear when Joseph was staying?

"I think I need something new to sleep in," Isabeau said. "I haven't got anything to wear when I have house guests."

"You sleep in the nude?" Marianne said with a big smile.

"No, I mean I haven't got anything like that." Isabeau ran her hand over the pages where the models wore cool cotton pyjamas that showed a lot of their tanned skin. She wanted Marianne to tell her they would be perfect.

"Well, I think that's exactly what you need for house guests!" Marianne pointed to a model wearing a cotton dressing gown casually open over pyjamas with a low-cut t-shirt top.

After Marianne had left, Isabeau brought George downstairs and put Joseph's music on. Then she searched through her basket to find sachets with green, blue and brown colours, similar to the colours of the clothes she'd ordered, and laid them around George in a circle. "Only twenty-one days to scatter you, George." It seemed a shame to scatter the ashes so close to Joseph's arrival. Perhaps she should tell Joseph and let him do it. Just the thought of it gave her a sinking feeling of panic deep in her stomach.

Isabeau took out the pages of writing paper she had tucked into her journal. Now there were six of them, all covered with the same phrases written out in a jumble of small and large writing: *I must scatter George, I will scatter George.* On one of the pages, where there was a little space, she added *I must tell Joseph, I must tell Joseph.* Folding the pages, she slipped them back into her journal.

Isabeau was trying to feel in control as she laid out her new clothes on the bed. She'd even bought new sandals, with a heel for a change. And Marianne had given her a skirt and top. A denim mini skirt. A halter-neck top. Isabeau had never worn anything like it in her life, but Marianne had said she thought Isabeau would look great in them and she could try them on and see. What kind of outfit would be best for the crêperie? Isabeau's stomach was unsettled and her chest tight. What if Pierrot asked her to go to the wedding with him? She glanced from the mirror to George on her bedside cabinet.

"Look at me, like a teenager on a first date. You're not allowed to laugh, George!"

Have fun, Isabeau. Enjoy yourself; you deserve some fun. It sounded like the kind of thing Marianne or Docteur Morel would say.

The dark green singlet had fine straps and hugged her body. With the mini skirt from Marianne it was too tight, too exposing. Instead, Isabeau chose the long gathered skirt she'd bought. Over the top of the singlet she put on a green shirt, leaving it open. She was doing up her sandals when the doorbell rang. Pierrot was punctual.

He'd had a haircut, and he was wearing jeans and a white shirt that looked new. He tended freshly shaved cheeks to greet Isabeau, and put his hand on her shoulder when he embraced her. Walking up through the alley and along the street to the crêperie in the still, warm evening, Isabeau was surprised how good it felt to be out after the activity of the preceding weeks. Her hair spilled forward. To resist her habit of pushing it back behind her ears, she held the strap of her small shoulder bag with one hand and slid the other into the skirt pocket. She wasn't walking as she normally did. Maybe it was the new sandals.

The crêperie was in rue Colary. Isabeau went past it every day and often looked in, but she'd never entered, never passed through the small courtyard or sat beneath the vines. Tonight, she was in the restaurant. They were soon seated at a corner table with menus, looking down the selection of fillings: from basic butter or cheese to more sophisticated combinations. She decided on a spinach and goat cheese galette, while Pierrot ordered a classic cheese, ham, mushroom and tomato galette and a jug of cider for them both. Isabeau watched the other patrons carefully. At the next table, a couple of older American tourists were trying to ask the waiter the difference between galettes and crêpes. Isabeau wanted to lean over and explain.

Pierrot coughed softly. "You look very serious, Isabeau."

"Sorry, I can't help but overhear the conversation at the next table." She lowered her voice. "Those tourists are having trouble understanding the menu. They've never eaten crêpes before."

"Your English is good."

"My mother was English."

"Perhaps you could help them," he said, gesturing to the couple.

The waiter's voice rose as he explained in basic English and pointed to the different sections of the menu. "Galettes are savoury crêpes: ham, cheese, you know. Crêpes are sweet, for example chocolate and sugar." Isabeau turned back to Pierrot.

"So now I know you speak English," he said. "I didn't know you were half English. Tell me something else about yourself." He settled back in his chair and studied Isabeau.

"Well, there's not much to say. I don't really feel English at all. I can speak English but I'm more French," she said, pushing her hair back behind her ears. "I work at the post office. I love to embroider – I think you know that. I listen to music, bike and walk, and sometimes I write poetry." Isabeau had surprised herself. She resisted the urge to open her bag and fiddle with her inhaler under the table. "Your turn."

"Let's see. I love my job, and I love to make things with my hands. It's not just about buildings. I like transforming a person's life by changing their house and their environment. I like music too. I've never tried to embroider, but I once wrote a poem at primary school about a turtle."

He smiled at Isabeau, and it was hard not to smile back.

"And you live near Auray, don't you?"

"Yes, I've got a house; I'm doing it up too. I could show it to you sometime."

"You're pretty busy – just when you've got time." Isabeau wanted to change the subject. "And you spend a lot of time in Carnac."

"I grew up here, and my parents are here. I've got three brothers, but they're scattered around Brittany. I see quite a lot of them, depending where I'm working."

"You move around a lot."

"Jobs come up in different places. I don't like sticking to the same place. And what about your family? You said you inherited the house."

Isabeau hesitated. "It was my mother's house. And I haven't seen my father for a long time."

"Do you have any brothers or sisters?" he asked.

"No."

"Cousins, aunts, uncles, grandparents?"

"No."

"You must have some family."

"No, I don't think so."

"It must be strange having no family at all," pondered Pierrot. "Have you ever had any pets?"

"I used to have a cat, Caillou, but he disappeared."

Isabeau was saved from any further questions by the waiter, who placed their galettes in front of them.

"This looks good," Isabeau said. "I didn't realize how hungry I am. I went for a ride up to the house this afternoon to water the garden."

"I can see the house is starting to win you over," Pierrot remarked. "You spend a lot of time there and at the menhirs."

"Lately I've been thinking about whether it would be possible to turn the house into a bed and breakfast."

It had just come out. Isabeau hadn't planned on announcing that to anyone – especially not to Pierrot. She was getting a bit carried away. She thought of the first time she'd mentioned renovating the house, and how those words had since become reality.

"You seem pretty hungry yourself," Isabeau added. He had a large piece of galette poised on his fork.

"I helped François around the bakery this morning, and then this afternoon, as a matter of fact, I got myself organized to start on the bathroom at your house." Pierrot looked pleased with himself.

"I didn't expect that so soon. I haven't even paid you yet for all the work you've done. I hope you'll give me the bill before too long."

"I'll have it ready next week for you." Pierrot looked right at Isabeau. "I can see this house is pretty important to you."

"Yes." Isabeau looked at her plate. Her cheeks were hot.

"Well, it's all going to look brand new," he continued.

"That's what I want. Something fresh." Isabeau struggled to keep her tone light.

"It's funny, because since I've known you, you've changed, like the house. You're looking different." Pierrot shifted in his seat and fiddled with his cutlery.

"I don't know if that's a compliment or not." Isabeau wanted to get out her inhaler. She was short of breath. She put her hand to her face, pretended she was scratching her mouth and took a deep breath as quietly and naturally as possible.

"It certainly is," he said.

A compliment. Isabeau thought of Marianne and tried to keep her breathing steady. She sat back in her chair and looked around, as if she came to the crêperie often, as if she got compliments regularly. They both finished their galettes. Asking the waitress for the menu and deciding on what kind of crêpe they would have for dessert brought a welcome change to the conversation.

They were eating their dessert when Pierrot brought up the subject of the holidays.

"What are your plans?" he asked. "Hard to believe that the holidays are almost here."

"I've got a friend from New Zealand and his cousin coming for a few days at the beginning of July, and I'm going to show them around," Isabeau told him. She was pleased to have some plans of her own to share. "Then I'm going to do some day trips and go biking. What about you?"

"I'm going hiking in the Cévennes with my brother and some of his friends, and then we're heading to Corsica."

"That sounds fun."

"I love hiking, and it'll be great to catch up with my brother. I'm also looking forward to the wedding and being François' witness. Actually, I was wondering if you'd like to go with me."

Isabeau pictured the invitation, at home on the sideboard, where the photo of George and Joseph had sat. They both came to mind, and Joseph's face lingered. She'd never met him, but she couldn't stop thinking about him.

"That's nice of you to ask me ... do you mind if I get back to you on that?"

"Not at all," said Pierrot.

Isabeau could see he looked a little surprised.

They lingered over coffee, and it was eleven o'clock by the time Pierrot walked Isabeau back down the alley. He broke the silence.

"This is a bit of a cut-throat alley."

"I'm not usually out at this time," Isabeau said.

Tonight, the alley really did feel a little dangerous, but it wasn't because of the darkness. When they arrived at Isabeau's door, Pierrot turned towards her. Did he expect her to invite him in?

"Thanks. I had a good time," Isabeau said. It was true.

"Me too. I'd like to do it again." Pierrot stepped towards her.

She didn't move. "Thanks again for all you've done on the house."

"It's not finished yet. I'll be there off and on till the end of July." Pierrot's eyes were sparkling.

Isabeau tended her cheek, and his cheek came towards her lips, but then he turned his head slightly and his lips met hers and pressed lightly. She pulled back just before he did.

"I'll be in touch," he said.

Isabeau stood on the spot. She couldn't move. She'd forgotten to breathe.

"Goodnight, Isabeau," he called, and climbed into his van.

Her hands were shaking, and it seemed to take her forever to open the door. Her heart was pounding. She was breathless. Her first kiss.

Isabeau sat on the doorstep in the sun with George beside her. She brushed her hair with long slow strokes. She was finally on holiday. The house was in order. The sachets were finished. She tried to breathe slowly, gently taking in the warmth of the calm evening and Joseph's music in the background, but she still couldn't stop her troubled mixed-up thoughts. What did the kiss mean? How should she act the next time she saw Pierrot? And Joseph and Drew were arriving the next day. Tomorrow. The days of lost opportunities were gone. The road to hell was paved with good intentions. To scatter George on the eve of Joseph's arrival would be an insult to him. "What am I going to do with you? Where will I put you?" Isabeau asked George.

It was only five days, and they would be gone. But that wasn't a reassuring thought. They would go away again and it would all be over, gone – like Papa. And she had to tell Joseph she hadn't yet scattered his father's ashes.

PART III

41

1.14 p.m. In one minute the train would arrive. Isabeau still wasn't sure how she would greet Joseph and Drew, and whether she was dressed suitably – in the same clothes she'd worn to the crêperie. She'd been waiting twenty-five minutes and been to the toilet three times. Behind her, a billboard advertised the local thalassothérapie; it showed a close-up of a beautiful woman relaxing "le bonheur les yeux fermés". Happiness with your eyes closed. Isabeau closed her eyes and repeated the slogan, but it did nothing to help the pressure in her chest and the panic in her stomach. Nothing was right any more. The good feeling Joseph's letters had given her over the preceding months was evaporating under the midday sun. George was hidden in her bedroom. It was too late now. She didn't even have time to return to the toilet.

Two young women waiting on the platform chatted and laughed. They looked carefree and impatient for the train to arrive. Isabeau felt envious. There were also travellers waiting to board the train to travel further down the line, to Quimper. Everyone was going about their business. No one paid Isabeau any attention. It seemed incredible to her that no one noticed how nervous she was. She felt in her bag for her inhaler and couldn't stop herself from taking a puff.

The orange and silver Corail train appeared down the track and slid along the platform, filling the station from one end to the other. There was no turning back now, no running away.

The doors opened and travellers descended from each carriage, some heaving large suitcases for the holidays, others with tote bags slung over their shoulders. The train would only stay in the station a couple of minutes, but everyone was orderly, waiting their turn. Isabeau's eyes flicked up and down the platform. There was no one remotely resembling Joseph. The ticket inspector, who was standing beside the first-class carriage at the head of the train, reached up and lifted something down, then opened it out. It was a wheelchair. Then he reached up again, and took some bags and backpacks. Two men, both tall and blond, were in the doorway of the carriage. The shorter of the two had his arm around the other man's shoulders, and leaned heavily on him while he descended the step, hopped onto the platform and reached the wheelchair. The other man put the bags on a trolley. Isabeau was mesmerized by the movement, and she couldn't take her eyes off the man in the wheelchair: his shorts, his legs – leg. His right leg. A shiny scar ran down from the knee, the skin puckering on each side like a giant zip. The left leg of his shorts hung mostly empty. Empty. Part of him was missing.

Her eyes returned to his face. Joseph. Not good on his legs. Leg. Why had he used the plural? Isabeau winced. Everything she'd prepared to say to greet them – every single syllable – was gone. She saw the wheelchair and Joseph's face in a freeze frame. As her eyes refocused, she saw that he was staring at her and slowly advancing, beside the other man, who was pushing the trolley.

"Isabeau?"

"Joseph?"

"Enchanté. I'm pleased to meet you after all this time. This is my cousin Drew, well, Andrew, but everyone just calls him Drew."

Isabeau shook hands with Joseph. The skin on his hand was slightly rough.

"Joseph's explained to me a hundred times how to pronounce your name, but I'll probably still get it wrong," Drew laughed. "Is – o – bee … No, hold on. Is – a – bo." Drew grabbed Isabeau's hand with both his large hands. He had a mischievous grin.

"Don't take any notice of Drew," said Joseph, looking from his cousin to Isabeau. "He has everyone on. Anyway, it's very kind of you to have us both to stay."

"It's no trouble really … I've been looking forward to it," Isabeau stammered. It was hard not to stare at his stump. Joseph was in a wheelchair. He only had one complete leg. And George didn't know.

"I'm very pleased to meet you – the person behind the letters I took to the post office!" exclaimed Drew. "And you have a lovely name and accent."

"Thank you. My English is a bit rusty though. It'll be good for me to have the opportunity to speak more."

Joseph had lost weight since the photo on his cassette, and his hair was shorter and more tousled, his features drawn. He looked tired. Drew was big – he must have been almost two metres tall – and muscled, and his thick curly hair made him seem even more of a giant. They were both wearing Bermuda shorts, white t-shirts and similar pendants strung on leather cords, which looked like they were made of bone. Drew's was a fish-hook shape and Joseph's more of a spiral. Isabeau had never seen anything like them.

She led the way back down the platform, through the station building and out into the car park. Only one leg. Only one leg. She'd presumed he was on crutches. How stupid could she be? But why hadn't he said?

"My car's over there. It's small. Do you think it's all going to fit in?" Isabeau asked, as she pointed to her car.

"Don't worry about a thing," said Drew. "I'll take care of it all and get everything in the car. The bike rack will be perfect for the chair."

"I'm sorry," said Joseph. "I've been having problems with my artificial leg and got an infection. My arm's not strong enough to use crutches all the time. So, here we are. Me and my chair." Joseph tapped the side of the wheelchair.

Isabeau opened the car, and Drew put their bags in, while Joseph wheeled up beside the passenger seat and hoisted himself up – standing for a second – and into the car. He had a small pillow with him, and he positioned it under his stump. Drew took the chair, folded it up and pulled out a strap from a pocket on the side of his bag to tie it to the bike rack, with the ease of someone who'd done it many times before. Then he somehow squeezed himself into the back with their backpacks. How strange it was to have two men organizing themselves and their belongings into her car. It had never been this full. Isabeau breathed slowly, down into her stomach, but her left hand was playing around with her inhaler in her bag.

They headed down the route Nationale towards Carnac, and Isabeau tried to concentrate on the road. She could see Joseph out of the corner of her eye. She should say something, she realized.

"Did you have a good trip?"

"It was long," Joseph said, "but we stopped for a couple of nights in Singapore and had a night in Paris. Everyone's been really helpful. Drew has a contact at the New Zealand Embassy. He met us at the airport and helped with transport and getting around. It made a big difference."

After the turn-off, they headed down route du Purgatoire towards Carnac.

"Funny to see ferns along the side of the road. So far away, and something so familiar," Drew said, scanning the roadside.

In the rear-view mirror, Drew filled up the back seat. She remembered the ferns Joseph had drawn on his letter and how he'd said they were a symbol worn by sportspeople. Drew looked fit and athletic; she could imagine him in such clothing. "You have lots of them in New Zealand?" she asked.

"Yes, little ones like these but also large native ones," Drew said with enthusiasm. "You should see them down the West Coast. They're amazing."

"We'll soon see some of the menhirs," Isabeau told them. "The road's going to take us down along the Ménec Alignments: the biggest and my favourites." They came past allée des Alouettes, and Isabeau slowed down. "There are well over a thousand stones just here, and about three thousand standing stones in total around Carnac. We'll come back to visit them, but would you like to stop now?"

"Shit, so many of them. Oops, sorry," Drew said.

Joseph was silent. He stared out the window. Isabeau could see there were tears in his eyes.

"It's probably better to rest up and come back tomorrow, eh, Jos?" said Drew, patting Joseph's shoulder.

Joseph nodded.

A few minutes later they pulled into Isabeau's courtyard, and Drew and Joseph were again organizing themselves while Isabeau watched. Drew took the wheelchair off the rack, unfolded it and placed it beside Joseph's seat, then dealt with the bags. Isabeau showed Drew through to the alcove. It was on the ground floor, but what about the doorstep? And would there be enough space for Joseph to manoeuvre around the bed or into the bathroom? But Drew didn't seem fazed. He simply pushed the beds together to make more space, and Joseph had no problem rolling up the step. Isabeau could see he was used to his chair. He went into the alcove, and she could hear him and Drew deciding on where they would put their bags.

When they sounded like they were done, she showed them the bathroom.

"It's quite small, I'm afraid."

"Don't worry," said Joseph. "I can leave the chair outside and hop a few steps, with Drew's help. I really only need a stool or chair in there to help with showering."

Drew helped Joseph into the bathroom, and Isabeau went to make coffee. She needed to do something. Drew joined her at the kitchen bench.

"Joseph's tired," he said quietly. "The trip's taken it out of him, but he'll be right after some sleep."

"It's a long way to come."

"Sure is. Thanks for what you've done for him. Your letters have helped over these past few months."

"I thought Joseph must be on crutches," Isabeau admitted.

"He didn't tell you?"

"No. Well, sort of. He talked about an accident, but only said he wasn't good on his legs. He didn't mention that he'd lost part of one."

"I thought you looked surprised at the station." Drew shook his head. "By now he should've been walking with his artificial leg, at least most of the time. But he's had some problems with it. It takes a while to sort out the size and fit. Joseph's had to learn some patience." Drew raised his eyebrows in a comical way, but Isabeau could see that behind the humour he was serious. "For the trip, it was better to stick to his chair. He can't push it himself for long distances, because his arm was also hurt in the accident – fortunately it was his left arm – and the strength's only just starting to come back."

"Will he be okay?" Isabeau asked.

"I know that he will. I'm not sure that he believes that himself yet, though. He almost pulled out of this trip at the last minute, but he's had enough time on his own. He needs to get back in the world, and to be here. Coming to Carnac is really important for him. He was close to his dad."

"I know."

"It's really kind of you to have us," Drew concluded. "Thanks."

Isabeau pulled out a quatre-quarts she'd bought from the bakery, and they sat around the table. Joseph and Drew had had a sandwich on the train, they told her, but Drew didn't refuse when Isabeau also offered baguette, butter, ham, cheese and pâté. He made himself little slab sandwiches, and encouraged Joseph to eat more.

"I hope the coffee's not too strong?" Isabeau asked.

"Perfect." Drew took a large sip and stretched back in his chair, watching Joseph from the corner of his eye.

"If you want to have a sleep this afternoon," Isabeau told them both, "please feel free to ..." Her voice faltered. "... make yourself at home."

"Thanks, but maybe we could go for a walk and get some fresh air instead, then we can unpack and get to bed early," said Drew.

"We could go for a walk around town," Isabeau suggested.

"That would be great. We've been cooped up in planes and trains for the past few days," said Drew.

They went up the alley single file, Isabeau leading and Drew pushing Joseph, and came out to the street.

"Not much space for pedestrians around here; just as well there are no cars coming," said Drew, and quickly pushed Joseph up the middle of the street. They headed around Saint-Cornély's, the main square and the Tourist Information Office, and stopped on the northern end in front of the Museum of Prehistory.

There was a wheelchair access sign. Joseph looked at it. "Might come back for a visit," he said.

"It's well worth it," said Isabeau. "It will help you to understand the standing stones better, and the whole progression from men being nomads thousands of years ago to settling in one place and farming the land."

"That's an impressive way of putting down roots!" laughed Drew. "And here I thought Obelix had something to do with it?"

"Didn't you drop out of history at school?" Joseph rubbed his hand across his forehead and sighed in mock despair.

Isabeau laughed. She felt relieved to see Joseph finally smile.

"And there aren't just the standing stones in Carnac. There are also dolmens, and a tumulus not far from here." She pointed north-east.

"A tumulus? What's that?" asked Drew.

"It's a grave mound," explained Isabeau. "Basically a massive mound of earth and stone. This one's got a little chapel on the top."

"I'd love to see that. Is it far?"

"Maybe about a kilometre."

"What do you say, Jos?"

"Sounds good to me, but it's up to you. You're the one pushing."

"Let's go. I've got a bit of history to catch up on. And this is much more interesting – with our local guide here, thanks Isabeau – than stodgy old sixth-form history with Mr Patterson!" Drew turned Joseph's wheelchair around.

They set off past the town hall and the cemetery, and continued until they came to the turn-off for the track to the tumulus. This was a different pace for Isabeau. She almost felt like a tourist. She glanced at Joseph. He'd been very quiet since they'd arrived. It had been easier to talk to him in her letters. Drew was doing most of the talking. He chatted continually, expressing his curiosity about everything around him. As they approached the tumulus he whistled.

"You weren't joking when you said it was massive."

The track up to the chapel was bumpy and stony, but Drew insisted on pushing Joseph up to the top, saying that he needed to stay in shape for the sailing.

At the top, they walked around the chapel, admiring the view of Carnac and the surrounding countryside.

On their way back they looked at the shops and went past the bakery. Isabeau saw Marianne there, cutting a large far breton into pieces. She left Drew and Joseph to look at the window display, and slipped inside. Before she knew it, they'd followed her in and were looking at the pâtisseries in the display case.

At the counter, out of their hearing, she greeted Marianne. "Well?" Marianne asked.

Isabeau motioned over her shoulder. "Joseph's the one in the wheelchair."

Marianne's eyes widened, and for a second she seemed flustered.

"Are you okay?" Isabeau asked.

"Sure. He reminds me of someone, that's all."

Marianne didn't have time to say any more before Joseph and Drew came up beside Isabeau. Marianne held out her hand to Joseph and spoke slowly in English. "Pleased to meet you."

"Enchanté." Joseph took her hand.

"Joseph, Drew, this is my friend Marianne," said Isabeau.

Marianne shook hands with Drew, and looked set to ask a question when she was interrupted by Julie calling her from the back of the shop about an order she was filling. Marianne turned to Isabeau and reverted back to French.

"I'm sorry, but I have to tend to this. Drop in tomorrow and say hello." Marianne said "goodbye" to Joseph and Drew and went out the back of the shop.

Julie came to the counter. She passed over two baguettes, and Joseph insisted on holding them on his knee. Before they left, he pointed at the embroideries on the wall. "Did Marianne make them?" he asked Isabeau.

"No, I did. Marianne asked me if she could display them. She thought tourists would like them. She loves embroidery too; that's how we became friends."

"They're beautiful."

"Thank you."

"I can't wait to see the real thing up close." His eyes took Isabeau in. "I can't quite believe I'm here."

"I know. It doesn't seem real to me either."

42

Isabeau put the dish of melon slices in the middle of the table and sat down. She'd kept it simple: rock melon for entrée, ham and potato salad for the main, a selection of cheeses, and strawberries for dessert. She might more or less throw the same thing together, on a tray, for herself on a summer's evening. Tonight, presentation and order were important. She tried to enjoy the juicy melon and relax her shoulders, but tension was creeping up her neck, and a headache was forming.

Joseph took one piece of melon and refused a second helping. Drew made up for it by eating three pieces, and devoured chunks of baguette with the ham and salad. "This bread's amazing," he said. "I didn't think I was hungry, but this is so good." He prodded Joseph. "Come on. We've got to get some meat back on your bones!"

Drew was still doing all the talking. Isabeau was beginning to wonder if Joseph was in fact happy to have come to her place. Perhaps she wasn't doing things as she should. She offered the bowl of salad to him again.

"It's very good, thanks, but I'm afraid my appetite isn't over the jet lag," he replied.

It was only half past seven when they finished. Joseph pushed his chair back and yawned. Drew excused himself from the table and returned with two plastic shopping bags. Smiling, he handed one to Joseph and out of the other one pulled a flat parcel wrapped in gift paper. "For you," he said, handing Isabeau the parcel with a flourish.

"Me?"

"For having us. You didn't have to. We appreciate your hospitality, and if you ever come to New Zealand you'll be most welcome. Won't she, Jos?" Drew said as he sat back down.

Isabeau's mouth dropped. She didn't deserve this. She couldn't help but think of George, still upstairs.

"Go on, you can open it now," said Drew, nodding towards her.

She carefully lifted the tape and opened the gift wrap to discover a box containing two wooden spirals fitted together to form a large oval. The wood had a reddish tinge, just like George's box. She placed the spirals on the table.

"They're to sit hot dishes on, and you can arrange them in different ways. It's rimu, a New Zealand native wood," explained Drew, fitting them into a pattern to show her.

"It's beautiful. I've never seen anything like it ..." Isabeau ran her hands over the pieces. "Thank you."

Before she could say anything else, Joseph handed her another parcel. It was wrapped in paper almost the same colour as the dress she'd worn to the engagement party. Inside, nestled in tissue paper, was a dark lilac sweater.

"I hope it's all right. I thought you must like that colour, but I wasn't sure about the style, and I guessed the size," said Joseph, briefly raising his eyes to meet Isabeau's gaze.

"It couldn't be more perfect." Isabeau stroked the sweater. It was lambswool, baby soft, and she couldn't resist rubbing it against her cheek. Sitting on the wrapping paper, there was something else. It must have been tucked in the sweater. "This too?"

"It's nothing really, after all you've done for me, and for having us," said Joseph.

It was a small delicate box. The lid was decorated with a shiny spiral inlay: a bright mixture of blue and green with a hint of pink. It was paua shell, Joseph explained. She opened the box by swinging its lid to the side.

"It's like a little treasure box," said Isabeau. She could picture the earrings from Marianne nestled in it.

"You look like a kid at Christmas," said Drew.

Joseph and Drew were both watching her. Her mouth was dry. She should thank them properly, but she was nervous. She wasn't used to this.

"It wasn't necessary, but thank you." Isabeau forced herself to stand up and turn towards Drew. It was easier to start with him. "In France, when you receive a present, you say thank you by kissing the person on the cheeks, like when you greet someone."

"That's a nice custom," said Drew. "Sorry we haven't shaved!" He entered into the spirit of it, placing his hands on Isabeau's shoulders and turning his cheek.

Drew had a way of making her feel at ease, like Marianne. Isabeau liked him. She kissed him quickly. Next was Joseph. Now, her movements were no longer happening of their own accord. It was taking all her concentration to appear natural, and she wasn't sure she was succeeding. She didn't want Joseph to see how uneasy she felt. Another secret. How many could you hide before they burst out?

"The sweater will be very useful, and it's beautiful. Thank you," Isabeau said to Joseph. She took a couple of steps towards him, and he swivelled his chair around to face her. "Thank you for the box, too."

She bent down and kissed his cheeks as lightly as she could. She felt him respond with his lips on her own cheeks at the same time, as if he knew how to do things in France. On his cheeks, underlaying the day's sweat, there was the faintest smell of aftershave, something fresh and inviting that she recognised. But before she could discern what it was, she was straightening up, and it was all finished.

Drew stood up, as if on cue.

"You must be tired," Isabeau said to both of them. "Please feel free to go to bed if you want, or have a shower."

"Thanks," said Drew. "It's been a big day. I think I'll turn in now, and have a shower in the morning." He headed towards the alcove. "Goodnight."

"Me too," said Joseph. "I'm ready for bed."

"Do you have everything you need?" asked Isabeau.

"If you have any more pillows, by any chance, that would be great."

"I've got another couple spare upstairs. I'll just get them."

Joseph was waiting when Isabeau came back downstairs with the pillows under her arm.

"Here," she said, giving them to him. "I hope you sleep well."

"Thanks. I'm a little jaded. I hope I'll be better company tomorrow, after I've had some sleep." He pressed the pillows on his knee. "Goodnight, Isabeau."

"It's okay. It's good that you're here. Goodnight." She smiled at him, and, inside, she smiled to herself. She'd finally said something right.

She still hadn't said the most important thing, though. She would have to tell him in the morning. Before the charade escalated. She hadn't lied outright in her letters – only by omission – but if she didn't tell him now it would be worse. She'd missed her chance with Monsieur Poulain, and there had been no turning back.

Isabeau lay in bed, studying the treasure box and stroking the sweater. She tried to remember the scent of Joseph's aftershave. She wanted to know what it was. She imagined capturing the smell somehow and keeping it in the box, like a genie in a bottle. She closed her eyes. Her headache was worse. She hadn't travelled thousands of kilometres like Joseph and Drew, but she was exhausted. She wished she had the fatigue of a long journey to pound her into peaceful sleep.

"George, Joseph's arrived," she said quietly. "He's here. His leg is horribly scarred, and the other one is half missing. His arm is also hurt. It must've been a terrible accident." She lowered her voice even further. "How do I do tell him I haven't scattered you?"

There was no answer, only the sound of snoring from the alcove below.

43

A bed creaked in the alcove. Isabeau could hear Drew and Joseph stretching and yawning, all the sounds of waking up.

Drew appeared first, with a wide grin on his face. "Good morning. Bonjour! I need to practise my French before I get to the race, get into the swing of things."

"Bonjour, Drew," Isabeau replied, and smiled back at him.

"You've been up to the bakery," he said, surprised, as his eyes took in the croissants and fresh baguette in the middle of the table. "I didn't hear a thing."

"I crept around to prepare breakfast. The coffee's ready, and there's butter and jam for the baguette."

"I've only been in France a couple of days and I'm already beginning to understand what they say about French food." Drew rubbed his hands together.

Joseph soon appeared too, and wheeled into the space at the table where Isabeau had removed the chair. His hair was standing up. He looked better than he had the day before, but still tired. Isabeau was staring, she realized. He pushed his hands through his hair and patted it down. "Bonjour. Sorry, I must look a sight. And we've slept so late," he said.

"It doesn't matter. We're in no hurry," Isabeau replied.

"Sounds perfect. I'm sure Dad would be pleased we've made it here, even if I'm not the one to have scattered his ashes. I'm really looking forward to seeing the standing stones up close and exactly where Dad is," said Joseph.

Isabeau took a deep breath. This was it. "Well, I took him to the alignments several times, and to the Giant of Manio, the tallest menhir in Carnac, which sits alone in the forest, but I have to say that I found it difficult to –"

"I'm sorry," he interrupted her. "I know it was a big ask to put on your shoulders."

"No, it's not that, it's ..."

Joseph tilted his head to one side. This was her chance.

"It was ..."

The phone rang. Isabeau went to answer it. The person calling introduced himself as Olivier Boulanger and asked to speak to Joseph.

"It's for you, Joseph. Someone called Olivier Boulanger."

"Thanks," he said, wheeling over to her. "I hope you don't mind that I gave your number to Olivier. I wasn't sure that he'd call."

Joseph took the phone, and Isabeau sat back down at the table next to Drew.

"I could get a call too," he told her. "From a sailing friend. I gave him your number, just in case."

"That's fine."

"Anyway, tell me about these standing stones. Uncle George used to show me pictures, but still I never imagined there were so many of them. Guess I've always been more interested in the sea."

"Carnac's special," she said. It's the biggest megalithic site in Europe. They still don't know exactly why men aligned all these stones in the ground." She wished she could hear what Joseph was saying. It was obvious that he was pleased to talk to this Olivier Boulanger, who must speak fluent English, given the way Joseph was talking and laughing.

"It's incredible," said Drew.

Isabeau continued explaining about the different alignments: Le Ménec, Kermario, Kerlescan and the smallest, Le Petit-Ménec. After a few minutes, Joseph hung up.

"Is that the music guy you were telling me about?" Drew asked as Joseph came back to the table.

"Yeah, the one I got to know in Perpignan. He's been listening to the cassettes I sent and thinks I could be good for the summer festival in Nantes. He was wondering if it would be possible to meet up there. Anyway, sorry, Isabeau," Joseph turned towards her, "to interrupt our conversation. You were saying?"

"That's okay. That's great news for you. I'm not surprised he likes your music."

"Thanks." Joseph looked at Isabeau.

"So, the menhirs. It's ... the Giant of Manio, the tallest menhir in the forest ... we have to go there."

"I can't wait," he said. "Once we've had a shower we'll be ready to go."

They finished their breakfast, and Joseph and Drew went to have a shower and get ready. Isabeau bit her lip. Why didn't she say it? Say it. Say it. Say. It. She clenched her fists and quietly stamped her feet on the floor. Maybe she could say it when they went to the stones.

"Your father's here." Isabeau swept her arm around the clearing, taking in the Giant and the quadrilatère. "There's a little bit of him here. He's here now, everywhere: a part of all this. I thought about scattering him at the Ménec or Kermario Alignments, but it seemed more appropriate here. More private. I thought he'd like the Giant. Your father looks tall in the photo you sent ... like the Giant."

Isabeau concentrated on the exact meaning of the words. It wasn't a lie. One word more here or there and it wouldn't be true. She'd brought George here so many times that it was almost as if he'd become part of this place, she tried to convince herself as she spoke. It was true, but just not in the way Joseph thought.

"You couldn't have made a better choice, Isabeau." Joseph spoke softly as he touched the Giant. They had been to the Ménec and Kermario Alignments on the way, and walked around the menhirs. Joseph had been pensive. He'd stopped often and touched the stones. Even Drew wasn't talkative. How could she break their sacred silence with her confession?

Joseph and Drew moved in closer to the Giant, and instinctively Isabeau did the same, until they were standing around the stone, in almost a triskele, thought Isabeau. Joseph bowed his head and closed his eyes, and his lips moved like he was saying a prayer. Isabeau silently repeated her mantra: George was here, everywhere, now he was part of this place. It was like he had somehow come home. That was what she wanted Joseph to see in her eyes.

From the kitchen window, Isabeau watched Joseph and Drew at the table in the courtyard outside, as they wrote postcards and chatted. Joseph had his back to her. She just had to be careful that Drew didn't catch her watching out of the corner of his eye.

They had spent the morning at the Museum of Prehistory and bought the postcards on the way back. She had refused their offers of help to prepare lunch, so they had settled outside to write while she worked in the kitchen.

Isabeau ripped basil leaves and scattered the shreds over the tomato slices. Maybe she would have the opportunity to say it. Maybe somehow it would happen. If not, she only had to hold out for three more days, then she could scatter George at the Giant, and it would almost be as if she'd already done it. Three more days. Why didn't she feel more relieved?

Joseph pushed the postcards across the table. He took out a notebook and seemed to scribble in it, then he pulled a harmonica from his pocket and put it to his mouth. He repeated a few notes, each time with a different rhythm, and Drew picked up the tune, humming with exaggeration. When Joseph launched into a song, it set Drew singing with gusto. What he lacked in musical ability he made up for with enthusiasm. He was so carefree. And he was on holiday with Joseph. She envied Drew. She sighed and turned back to the bench, then jumped as the phone started ringing. Hopefully it wouldn't be Pierrot.

The voice that answered her greeting was similar to Joseph and Drew's. The man introduced himself as Simon, and asked for Drew.

"He's my sailing friend," Drew told Isabeau as he came to the phone. "Must be some last-minute details."

As she listened to his side of the conversation, Isabeau heard Drew's frequent "ahas" and "yeahs" suddenly stop, and his tone became serious. "Oh no," he said. He started asking questions about someone called Jeremy, and then about who would be there and for how long, and where they were staying. "I'll get back to you as soon as I can," he said, and hung up.

Isabeau followed Drew back out to the courtyard and started setting the table.

"What's up with Simon?" asked Joseph.

"It's not Simon; it's Jeremy," said Drew. "His sister's in hospital. She was having some routine surgery, and there were complications. They've put her in an induced coma, and they're not sure if she's going to make it. Jeremy's flying home tomorrow. Simon's coming to sail as planned." Drew scratched his forehead. "Bugger, I know he was really looking forward to hanging out with you."

Joseph didn't say a word.

During lunch, it was Drew's turn to be quiet. For the first time Isabeau found herself leading the conversation. When they were finished, Drew stacked the dirty dishes on the tray while Isabeau made coffee. She was going to come back outside to wipe the table down, but just inside the kitchen door she stopped. Joseph and Drew had returned to the theme of their previous conversation.

"It doesn't matter about Jeremy," said Drew. "You know there'll be a big crowd, and there should be plenty of people around to give you a hand ... if you need it."

"I don't want to count on strangers, and worrying about me is only going to distract you. I know how important this race is to you. I should never have come. It was a crazy plan, now that I think about it." Joseph sounded angry.

"Aren't you forgetting that this trip isn't only about the sailing?" asked Drew. "It was about coming to Carnac for your dad. Isn't that worth it – to see the standing stones and pay homage to him? It blows me away, to think he's here. And Isabeau's amazing too. I'm sure there'll be a solution."

Joseph stared straight ahead. Drew waited for him to speak.

"I don't need to follow the race. I could just stay in one place and then meet you again in Paris for the flight. I'll be out of your way," said Joseph, seeming calmer. "It would give me some time to write some music. Being here's giving me inspiration. And you need to be able to concentrate on your sailing. I could go to Nantes; I'm sure Olivier could help. It'd be a great opportunity to catch up with him."

"Look, I'll try some of the others and then we can take it from there," said Drew.

His voice dropped, and Isabeau strained to hear the rest of their discussion as the coffee maker gurgled. She stepped out into the courtyard.

"Another great meal, thanks, Isabeau," said Drew. "Do people always eat this much? At home we often just grab a sandwich for lunch."

"This is nothing, really. The midday meal's important in France." Isabeau smiled. She often had a sandwich for lunch too, but she wasn't going to admit that.

"I need a walk," said Drew. "I think I'll pass on coffee and head off for a bit of an explore on my own, if you two don't mind." He stretched and yawned.

"Go ahead. Make the most of it," said Joseph.

Drew followed Isabeau into the kitchen and asked where he could find a payphone. He wouldn't accept her offer of her own phone, so she gave him directions to the post office, and he headed out. She left the dishes and went outside to join Joseph, who was writing in his notebook again. This could be the chance she was waiting for. Her first time alone with him. She might not have long. She stared at the notebook. On the open page, she saw words set out like little poems and musical notes and scribbles.

"I've listened a lot to the album you sent me," she said. "I really like it."

"Speaking of which, I promised you another one. I'll just get it." He went inside and when he returned handed her a cassette.

"Merci beaucoup." She turned it over in her hands. "'South' – interesting title. I can't wait to hear it."

"It's a bit about New Zealand, about my experiences," said Joseph. "It all gets mixed up in the songs. Not sure how the next album will turn out; my life's changed so much." He looked down.

"From your letters, I thought you were on crutches," Isabeau blurted out. The wrong words were coming out of her mouth. And she hadn't kissed Joseph on the cheek when she had thanked him for the cassette.

"I'm sorry. I guess I was a bit vague about it. At first it was too hard to say, and then time went by. I think I was trying to avoid admitting it to myself, as if I would wake up one day and it would all have been a bad dream, like wishing when you're a child." Joseph squeezed the wheels of his chair. "And I should have walked off the train with my artificial limb, my prosthesis, closer to normal. I almost pulled out at the last minute. Almost."

"It's true what you say," Isabeau replied, "sometimes it's too hard to say things. I wanted to ... I mean, as a child I had a lot of secrets. I used to share them with the menhirs."

Joseph looked up at Isabeau. She breathed in and was about to tell him about the ashes, but in the split second that followed he spoke again.

"I didn't want to make things difficult. I had this overwhelming feeling that if I told you, it would all become too complicated; it would change something, maybe everything. You would write back and politely say that there was nothing available on the ground floor, and little by little the dream would come undone. And that would be the end of that."

"I know what you mean."

"And I wanted to meet you. It's not just that I'm grateful to you for scattering Dad's ashes. I was still in the hospital when your first letter arrived, and Drew brought it in to me. It was good to write to you – to someone who didn't know about the accident, someone outside of that. I felt like I connected with you."

Isabeau couldn't stop looking at Joseph. His eyes were stone grey.

"When I had my accident I was working on a new album, and thinking about going on tour again when I got back from France. Performing again is going to be a big step for me – literally. I need to try and find a fresh perspective. Drew badgered me until I agreed to come on this trip. He seems to think I had to come here in order to move forward. Maybe I do."

She should say it.

"Sorry, I'm rambling on like this."

Now.

But he was speaking again.

"Anyway," he said, and seemed to be trying to sound brighter, "here I am, and it's great to see Carnac and the menhirs. It's inspiring. And now that I've had a couple of nights' sleep, it feels good to be here." He raised his hands in a gesture sweeping around the courtyard.

Isabeau stared at his hands.

"And I can't believe Olivier rang. I'm not sure if I'm ready now, but I'd love to perform at another festival here. The one in Perpignan was a great experience, and from what Olivier says Nantes sounds amazing. He's going to contact me again before I leave. How far is Nantes from here?"

"Just under a couple of hours by car. It's a beautiful city." As Isabeau spoke, she squeezed her hands under the table. The conversation was moving away from her opportunity; it was slipping through her fingers. She looked at the notebook again. It had a cherry blossom-patterned cover that looked Japanese. "That's a beautiful notebook," she said.

"Picked it up in Tokyo," Joseph said. "I carry one most places I go. I'm always filling them up with bits and pieces." He glanced at Isabeau as he flicked through pages with doodles of musical notes and phrases. In parts, where there was more writing, it looked like one of her journals. "You said something in one of your letters about writing poetry," he continued.

"I write a little," Isabeau admitted.

"Songs and poetry – there's not really a lot of difference." Joseph pulled his harmonica out of his pocket and started to play a tune. Isabeau recognized it from the album he'd sent. She wanted to go and get her journal and note down the short poem that was writing itself in her head.

Secrets
Secrets are shy.
They seep down
through the cracks of silence
and disappear.
You can't coax them out
of your conscience
just like that.

Instead, she pushed her chair back and closed her eyes, as if she was enjoying the music in the afternoon sun. She'd missed her chance. If she opened her eyes Joseph would see they were wet.

Isabeau lay in bed waiting for noise downstairs. After breakfast they were going back to the alignments, and she was going to show them her house. Only two more days and life would be back to normal. She would be alone again. It seemed as if Joseph and Drew had only just arrived, and now it was past the halfway point: their stay was coming to an end. She wondered what Joseph was going to do while Drew was sailing. If he stayed on longer there would be more time to tell him about the ashes.

Drew received another call during breakfast. It was Simon again. Then Isabeau washed the dishes while Drew helped Joseph into the bathroom. Drew came straight back and picked up the tea towel.

"Sorry I'm preoccupied with these phone calls. I'm trying to sort something out for Joseph. It's not that he needs help all the time – he's pretty independent now – but I'd prefer that he has someone around who can help if need be. I don't want him to overdo it." He kept his voice low.

"Please don't worry," Isabeau replied. "You obviously care about him a great deal."

"We've always been more like brothers than cousins."

"He's lucky to have you and your family."

"He spent a lot of time at our place when we were growing up, and we've always been close. And when he got hurt, I was the one driving. A drunk driver ploughed into us, crushed everything on the passenger side ... including Joseph. I only had a few cuts and bruises. It's hard to understand how one person can come out of an accident so damaged and the other walk away virtually unscathed." Drew grabbed a bowl and dried furiously.

Isabeau stared at the plate in the soapy water and washed it again.

"Jos is talking about staying on his own somewhere, or going home. I'd just prefer him to have someone with him if he needs it, if you know what I mean," said Drew.

"You said there would be plenty of people at the race?"

"There could be, but until we get there, to be honest, I'm not sure. And Joseph doesn't want to be reliant on strangers." Drew's voice had gradually returned to normal.

Isabeau put the bowls away in the sideboard. She passed her hand along the top, where George's shrine had been. George's face came into her mind, and there was that voice again. *Offer, Isabeau. It's not complicated.*

"There's no need to apologize. I understand," said Isabeau. "If Joseph doesn't want to ... He could stay on here in Carnac, while you go to your race. Perhaps he would appreciate a longer time with his father – I mean, to have longer around the standing stones."

She couldn't get enough air into her lungs. "I'm sorry: my asthma," she said. "My inhaler." She pointed upwards and then hurried up the stairs.

Once her breathing was under control, she lay on her bed for a short while. She took George from her bedside cabinet and opened the scarf that he was wrapped in. "I've offered, but I don't know if I can go through with this," she whispered.

When she came back downstairs, Drew was waiting in the kitchen and sat her down at the table.

"Are you okay? I wasn't intending for you to offer. That's not why I was telling you all this. I didn't plan on talking about it. I'm just feeling bad that we've been a little preoccupied since yesterday, and not very good company. And until that call Joseph was starting to look more relaxed."

She nodded, feeling unable to speak.

"Please don't worry. Something will come up. I'm still waiting for a couple of people to call me this evening," said Drew.

Pierrot's van was parked in front of the house. Isabeau slowed her car. Her hands were tight on the steering wheel. It was too late to turn around and make up an excuse. She parked, and as they were crossing the grass, Pierrot came out the front door.

"I wasn't expecting to see you here," said Isabeau.

"A pleasant surprise! I wasn't expecting to see you either," Pierrot said, and kissed Isabeau on each cheek. "I've got a couple of quiet days, so I'm making the most of it. I thought I'd work on the bathroom ceiling."

He stepped closer to Isabeau, and she felt herself blushing. Joseph and Drew were watching.

"These are my friends from New Zealand, Joseph and Drew," she said to Pierrot. "I'm just going to show them around the house. I hope you don't mind if we look around while you're working."

"No problem, I'll just carry on.

Pierrot shook hands with Joseph and Drew and then excused himself and went to his van. He came back with two pieces of wood and placed them against the steps to make a ramp. Joseph gave the thumbs-up sign, and Drew said "thanks, mate".

Pierrot went back inside and started measuring wood in the corner of the living room, where he had all his tools and materials, but Isabeau could sense him watching them while she showed Joseph and Drew the newly opened-up kitchen and living room.

"So this is where you grew up, Isabeau?" asked Joseph.

"Yes, until I was nine." There was so much more she wanted to tell him.

"And how long will it take to finish the house? When do you think you'll move in?"

"Depends on lots of things. I'm in no hurry. I might turn it into a bed and breakfast," she told them.

Isabeau wanted to kick herself as soon as she'd said it.

"And what's upstairs?" asked Joseph. "The bedrooms?"

"Yes. There's not really anything to see up there."

After they had had a quick look around the rest of the house, Isabeau suggested a walk to the Kermario Alignments.

"We'll leave you to it," she said to Pierrot.

"Should make some progress on the bathroom before my holidays. I'll be heading away a week after the wedding," he told her. "July's going to go quickly. It's not long until the wedding. Have you –"

"It's probably easier if I meet you there. I'm not sure what I'm going to do for the rest of the holidays. I may not even be around Carnac by then." She tried to ignore how far she was stretching the truth. It was true that she had no idea what she was going to do after Joseph and Drew left, though.

"Okay then. I'll look forward to seeing you there. From what François has said, it sounds like it's going to be quite a wedding."

"Knowing Marianne, I think you're right."

*

They left the house, crossed route du Purgatoire and turned into route du Kerlescan, where it was quieter. Drew pushed Joseph along the wide band on the side of the road. When they reached the alignments, Drew went over to the menhirs. Joseph and Isabeau stayed beside the dolmen.

"It must've been amazing growing up so near to all this history – almost part of it," said Joseph. "I didn't imagine people living so close to them."

"They were such a part of my life, I never really thought about it. I don't know what it's like for other people in Carnac, but I couldn't imagine life without them."

Joseph nodded in agreement.

"They're silent, only stone, but they ... You can ... sorry, I sound silly." Isabeau was trying to say so many things, and the most important thing wouldn't come out.

"Not at all. It is a special place. I haven't even been here long and I can feel that. Now I understand why Dad was so fascinated by Carnac. I really feel connected to him here."

"Your father must be ... would've been sad to know that you've had an accident."

"I think he would be pleased to know that I've finally made it here, even if the circumstances are nothing like what he would have imagined. Anyway, I'm sure he would be pleased that I know you." When he turned towards Isabeau and she met his eyes, he didn't look away.

Isabeau pushed her hands into the pockets of her jeans. "It's a shame that you can't stay longer," she said. "I don't think you can get tired of the menhirs. It's like they have so many secrets. I'm sure there are other ones that you have to discover. I feel like I have other things to tell you – to ask you. I have so many questions about your father. And now the days have gone by and you're almost going."

"Yes, it is going by quickly."

Isabeau turned towards the stones. They were big and strong, like George. *Give me strength*, she thought.

"What are you going to do while Drew's racing?"

"Well, I'm thinking about maybe staying in one place, making the most of it to write some music."

"You could stay on in Carnac for a while if you want," she said. "I haven't got anything planned for the rest of the holidays." Isabeau bit the inside of her lip and stared at the menhirs. She'd forgotten her inhaler. She mustn't think about it.

"That's kind of you, but Drew will be racing for two weeks, and I don't want to impose on you for that long."

Impose on her. Merde. She had finally got up the courage to offer, and he didn't want to impose on her. She wanted to cry.

Drew came striding back before she could say anything.

"Hey, you two look like you're at a funeral," he said. "Come on, it's going to work out one way or another."

"I was just telling Joseph that he was welcome to stay longer," Isabeau said.

"Sounds like a great offer to me, Jos. Why don't you stay on here, and if anything comes up we could organize some kind of transport."

"I could drive you," Isabeau added. So little thought, so much spontaneity this week. It was new and liberating and very frightening. Then she thought of George, and it was as if he was there with her. She needed more time. Suddenly she was saying the words that were in her heart. "If you want to stay on here, even for the two weeks, you are more than welcome. I would really like you to."

"Maybe it would be the best option after all," said Drew.

"Are you sure, Isabeau?" Joseph asked.

"Yes."

"It would be a good opportunity for me to write some songs, here at Carnac, beside the menhirs and near Dad. I've been wanting to do something new since the accident. And maybe I'd have the chance to meet up with Olivier."

"We could do some sightseeing, and you'd still have plenty of time to write. We could go to Nantes for the day if you want," Isabeau offered.

"You're very kind, Isabeau. But I still need to be pushed sometimes, and also a bit of a hand – well more like a shoulder really – to get in and out of tight places, like the bathroom."

"Sure, no problem. I can do that."

Words burst forth. Isabeau didn't know where to start; there was so much to write in her journal. She wrote about a day spent sightseeing, about Joseph and Drew and Isabeau: the Isabeau who had nice clothes, who had flowing hair and who held herself like she had done at the engagement party. She drove Joseph and Drew along the Grande Plage, wandered with them along the jetty at La Trinité-sur-Mer, admiring the trimarans, offered to push Joseph so that Drew could make the most of the boats, anchored herself to the chair and concentrated on pushing Joseph. She only glanced for the briefest of seconds at the café where Papa used to work. She wasn't going to let looking at a café spoil this day.

Driving Joseph and Drew around the Gulf of Morbihan, she started to understand how you could admire the scenery of land and sea, shining under the summer sun. She listened to Drew's sailing stories. She suggested lunch in Vannes, and they agreed. Outside on the terrace of a little restaurant beside the old port, she mopped up the sauce from her moules frites; the mussels had never tasted this good.

In the evening, she graciously accepted Drew and Joseph's offer to treat her to dinner at the crêperie at the bottom of rue Colary. Tonight, she didn't seek refuge in the kitchen. She didn't hide. She wasn't watching. She was part of something. She savoured the tiredness that comes from a good day. As they ate, she looked at Joseph front on. She smiled at him, and laughed at Drew's jokes. And Joseph laughed too. And that was the best part of the day. In bed, she snuggled into her pillow and whispered "Joseph, Joseph." His name was soft. She tried to remember what his cheek was like. She kissed her pillow goodnight.

"Easy does it, Isabeau."

Drew was carrying most of the weight of the bed as they manoeuvred it on its side through the kitchen door. They were taking it to the garage in order to make more room in the alcove. The sun was already beating down, and it was the hottest it had been since Joseph and Drew had arrived. Isabeau's hands were clammy. The bed started to slip. "Ouch." It had scraped her leg. She sat down to take a rest on one of the outside chairs.

"Are you okay?" asked Joseph. He moved towards her and placed his hand on her shoulder. She could feel the warmth of it through her t-shirt. She forgot about her leg.

"It's okay, thanks. Nothing serious."

"I think I can handle it from here," said Drew, lifting the bed towards the garage. He came back with a little smile on his lips. "Now you'll be able to prepare breakfast for Isabeau, Jos: just get up and whizz around," he joked. "I think you must have had other plans when you invited Joseph to stay, eh Isabeau?"

Isabeau's cheeks were hot. She went to the kitchen to catch her breath and finish preparing the meal that would be their last together as the three of them. She didn't want to think about Drew leaving. And then she was feeling nervous about his friends, who were coming to pick him up early afternoon, in time for dessert and coffee. She was just starting to get used to Joseph and Drew, but she didn't know these people at all. Was she underdressed or overdressed in the skirt and shirt she'd chosen? The carefree outing of the day before already seemed long ago. She forced herself to concentrate on the entrée. "Just wash the lettuce, Isabeau. Cut slices of baguette, spread goat cheese over them and put them under the grill." She repeated the instructions under her breath as she went through the tasks. The stuffed tomatoes were already cooking in the oven, and she'd put the rice on.

"That smells good," said Drew, entering the kitchen. "You're spoiling us. I really came along for Joseph and Uncle George, but I've had an amazing time too. I just want to say thanks for everything."

"I haven't really done anything."

"Probably more than you realize. Ever since we've arrived, I can feel a slight change in Jos: a shift. He's talking about writing new songs. That's always a good sign."

"Music seems to be a big part of his life."

"It's always been like that."

"I'd better take these out," Isabeau said, and pulled the tray out of the oven.

"You're a great cook, Isabeau. I'm sure Joseph will be in capable hands," Drew said. He winked at her with a cheeky look.

She didn't meet his eye, but began to arrange the food on the plates.

"What are you two up to?" asked Joseph at the kitchen door.

"I'm watching how to assemble this," replied Drew. "It looks better than cheese on toast. And I've been telling Isabeau to make sure you prepare her breakfast every morning and to keep you on your toes – sorry, on your guard!"

While they ate, Isabeau wanted to tell Drew how it had been for her to have him there. How she liked him and the way he joked. How, apart from Marianne, he was the first person she'd been around who could put her at ease like that. How he and Joseph were the first people she'd ever had to stay, and she didn't want him to leave. Instead, she asked questions about sailing and the race. Otherwise, she might start crying.

She was putting the strawberry tart from the bakery on the platter when she heard loud voices outside: English. Suddenly, the voices were in the courtyard. Isabeau watched from the kitchen window. A young man with dark skin and a red-haired woman were greeting Drew and Joseph, and there were yells of "good to see you". The redhead was slim and attractive. And she hugged Joseph. Isabeau tried to breathe slowly and relax her shoulders, to tell herself that she was in her own house, but that didn't make her feel any more at ease. She busied herself with getting extra cups, dessert plates and spoons, then went to the sideboard and got her inhaler too, in case. She heard steps coming towards the door. She slipped her inhaler into her pocket.

It was Drew.

"Lucy and Matt have arrived. Come and I'll introduce you," he said. "Let me take that." He picked up the tray and motioned for Isabeau to go ahead. In the courtyard, he placed the tray on the table and held up the platter with the tart. "Look at this. Isabeau's been spoiling us."

"Not really," Isabeau shrugged.

Drew put his arm around her shoulders and took a couple of steps towards the newcomers. It was as if he had sensed what she needed him to do.

"Isabeau, this is Lucy and Matt, who've come to whisk me away. Matt and I will be sailing together, and Lucy's a freelance journalist. She's going to cover the race."

"We've heard about you," said Lucy. "What an amazing story. It's nice to meet you." She smiled and took Isabeau's hand warmly.

"It's nice to meet you too," Isabeau replied, making an effort to sound as if she meant it.

They made room around the table. Why did Lucy sit beside Joseph, and lean in to talk to him? Drew had said that she was just a friend, but was there more? Isabeau sat back and watched everyone as they talked, trying to look as if she was enjoying dessert, and nodding and smiling as soon as anyone looked at her. When everyone had had a second cup of coffee, Drew set about getting his bags. Suddenly everything was being squashed into the rental van, and Matt was looking at the map and asking directions to get onto the road to Brest. He and Lucy said goodbye to Isabeau and Joseph, and got in the van. Drew stepped closer to Isabeau.

"It's been memorable for me," he said. "I'll see you again in a fortnight when I come back for Joseph. Have fun! Thank you, Isabeau." He took her firmly by both shoulders. "I think I'm getting used to these French habits," he said as he kissed her on the cheeks.

Everybody laughed, and Isabeau let herself be caught up in the humour. She had to. It wasn't the time, wasn't the place – it never was – to burst out crying.

"Make the most of it," said Drew, hugging Joseph. "Look after yourself, mate, and take care of Isabeau."

"Don't worry about me, I'll be fine," said Joseph.

"I know. You're going to have a great time," said Drew, patting him on the back.

Joseph and Isabeau waved as the van headed down the street and turned into avenue du Roer. Once it had disappeared, he offered to help tidy up the kitchen. Isabeau washed and Joseph dried. Side by side, they chatted about Drew and his sailing.

"I'm putting these away as best I can," said Joseph. "If you can't find something you'll know it was me." With the tea towel over his shoulder he placed the last of the plates on the pile in the cupboard.

"Thanks. Do you feel like getting out for a wander around town?" asked Isabeau.

"Sure. It's too nice to stay inside. If you can give me a push to get up to the square, I should be okay after that. My arm's getting stronger."

Isabeau pushed Joseph slowly up the alley and then up rue de Ker Anna. They moved around the main square, manoeuvring through the crowds on the narrow footpaths. They were in no hurry as they looked in the windows of the art boutiques and souvenirs shops full of regional specialities.

Outside a shop, Joseph stopped at a stand of embossed leather bracelets decorated with common French names set against silver dolphins jumping in the waves. He turned the stand around, reading out some of the names.

"Pity they don't have Isabeau."

"It's not common. It's very odd – I mean, old."

"I think it's very poetic. Why did your parents call you Isabeau then?" asked Joseph.

"My father really liked the name." Isabeau scanned the names on the bracelets. "What about your name? Here it is. There's only one left," she said, pointing to the Joseph bracelet.

Joseph stretched up and took the bracelet to examine it. "I was named after a good friend of Dad's. They used to go hunting in their youth. Dad got attacked by a wild boar once, and Joseph saved him. Then my name sort of got transformed to Jos: I hated being called Joe." He held up the bracelet to the light. The dolphins shone in the afternoon sun. "I'll take it," he said.

"Something to remember Carnac," she said, trying to keep her voice cheerful as she stared at the empty hook on the stand where the bracelet had been hanging.

After Joseph had bought the bracelet, they ended up in front of the brasserie. Its courtyard was full of holidaymakers relaxing under sun umbrellas.

"My shout," said Joseph. "I feel like a cold beer."

Once they were settled at a table, Isabeau sat back and watched the tourists passing by. Carnac looked different.

"What would you be doing for your holidays if we hadn't turned up?"

asked Joseph.

"Maybe I would have gone to Guérande, Saint-Brevin or around there. It's not far. I like to go biking when I can." Isabeau took a sip of her lemonade.

"Sorry, it's not much of an option for me at the moment."

"This is fine. It's nice to stay around here."

"Yes, this is the life. It's great to escape winter." Joseph sighed and closed his eyes. He held his head skyward as if he wanted to soak in the sun, to warm something cold inside. Isabeau watched him and tried to take a photo in her mind.

On the way home they stopped at the bakery.

"Bonjour, hello, hello. How are you today?" Marianne greeted Joseph with a big smile.

Joseph responded in French and then left Isabeau to talk to Marianne while he had a look around the bakery.

Marianne turned to Isabeau. "I'm glad you've called in. I've got the dragées ready. It's about time I gave them to you. I'm going to Saint-Laurent in a couple of days."

The dragées! How could she have forgotten about the wedding when she'd offered for Joseph to stay on? Suddenly Isabeau felt a little short of breath.

"They're out the back. Come with me." Marianne gestured over her shoulder to Joseph to wait. "Excuse, one moment." She grabbed Isabeau by the hand and pulled her through the opening out to the corridor.

"What time is he leaving then? It is today, isn't it?" Marianne lowered her voice as she spoke.

"It's a long story," Isabeau said quietly. "It's worked out that he's going to stay for another two weeks, while Drew's racing."

"Two weeks! He'll still be here when we get married then," Marianne said. "That's great news."

"Yes, aah ... the wedding. Well, I'm sure he won't mind staying on his own while I come to the wedding." Isabeau felt a sinking feeling deep in her stomach. She'd have to see if Joseph minded. Until then, she'd been quietly excited about the wedding. Now, she wasn't so sure. Why did things always have to be complicated?

"Why don't you bring him with you?"

"To the wedding?"

"It would be great," said Marianne. "He could get to experience a

French wedding. And remember, you know there are a couple of spare sachets!"

"Are you sure?"

"Yes. I'd love him to come, and I'm sure my family would be pleased too."

"Your family – really?"

"Yes." Marianne picked up the boxes of dragées and handed them to Isabeau. "I'm inviting him. And I'll sort out the lodge. I'd love Joseph to come. Wouldn't you?"

Isabeau could see that Marianne wasn't just being polite.

"What about Pierrot? I didn't say I'd go with him; I just said I'd see him there. But still."

"Mmm, that's a bit tricky. What say I talk to François? I think Pierrot will understand. It's not every day you have a friend from so far away staying, and Pierrot will have other opportunities. Maybe you could go out for another meal soon with him?"

"Thanks. I'd appreciate if you could speak to François. There's just one thing though: promise me you won't talk to Joseph about his father – he might get upset. He died recently, and Joseph was very close to him. He came to Carnac as a sort of homage to him, because his father had always wanted to come here."

"Don't worry, I won't mention a thing."

Joseph was studying the pâtisseries when they came back into the shop. Marianne put two round cakes in a box and handed them over the counter to him.

"For you and Isabeau," she said. "Traditional Breton cake, kouign-amann, much much butter." She wouldn't take any money for them. "Have fun, and don't forget to bring the dragées!" she added to Isabeau. "I'll see you in Saint-Laurent, if I don't see you tomorrow."

4 8

After dinner, it was still warm and sunny in the courtyard. Joseph played his harmonica, stopping regularly to scribble in his notebook. He'd been talkative during dinner, reminiscing about his father, but now it was as if he was in his own little world. Isabeau closed her eyes and listened. She was pleased to sit without talking. She was going over and over in her mind what had happened when they had come back from their walk.

Joseph had said "Can you lend me your shoulder?" as if it was the most natural thing in the world for Isabeau to walk up beside the chair and let him put his arm around her shoulders and lean his weight on her as he hopped into the bathroom.

Joseph asked again now. "Isabeau, do you mind lending me your shoulder, please?" Maybe he said that at home to others, but Isabeau couldn't remember him using the expression with Drew. *Can you lend me your shoulder?* If Isabeau concentrated on those words, it was easy to forget the reality of it all: the effort to appear natural, as if she wasn't affected by being so close to him. And it was a pleasant thought that perhaps she was the only one he said that to. That they had their own language, something that belonged just to them.

Isabeau wanted to fetch her journal and write about Drew leaving and what was happening with Joseph, but she took an embroidery magazine and pretended to look at the pictures while she listened to the soulful notes of the harmonica. She glanced up at her bedroom window. George must be happy that Joseph was down in the courtyard with a concentrated look on his face, and that his lips almost curled into a smile from time to time. Isabeau had two weeks to find the right time, the right way to tell Joseph about his father. But first, she had to bring up the subject of the wedding, to see if he would like to go with her. It was almost as if she was asking him out – but she wasn't, of course. Tomorrow she would mention it casually when they bought bread, as if it wasn't that important.

49

When Isabeau awoke it was as if Joseph's music was still within her, and she hummed to herself. Below, in the kitchen, there were other noises: the sound of a cupboard opening, followed by the soft chink of china, water running and a kitchen chair scraping on the tiles. She pulled on her new gown, grateful to Marianne for insisting that she bought a cotton dressing gown as well as pyjamas. She crept halfway down the stairs, and the smell of coffee was like a cue to descend into the kitchen. The day before, when Drew had left, she had just carried on, but this morning it was as if a new act in the play was beginning, and this was the moment when she had to step onto the stage.

"Bonjour Isabeau, ça va?" Joseph said.

"Bonjour Joseph, ça va merci. Et toi?" Isabeau laughed because it was the easiest thing to do, and she didn't know what else to say. It was as simple as that, for once.

"Breakfast, le petit déjeuner, will be served in five minutes," he announced.

"You went up to the bakery?"

"It was slow going at first, but some old guy came along and took pity on me, gave me a hand. I have to say, the locals are very friendly. Coming back was easier. And I believe these are your favourites." He pointed to some pains au chocolat on the table, beside a baguette viennoise.

"How did you know?"

"Between Marianne's schoolgirl English and my French we managed to have a little conversation. Once we got the bread and pastries sorted, I think she told me she was leaving very soon. I'm not sure for where. She kept talking about a wedding – her wedding, maybe. And, it's strange, but I think she invited me. I must have got that wrong."

"No, it is her wedding. Not this weekend but next. Marianne said yesterday that you're welcome to come with me. I was going to talk to you about it."

Joseph was looking at Isabeau's dressing gown. She pulled it around herself a little more tightly.

"Well, breakfast looks good," she said.

"I've put you on the other side of the table so I can get around," he explained.

"You don't have to do all this."

"I want to."

"Thank you. It's just I'm not used to having someone prepare breakfast for me."

"Well, make the most of it while I'm here!" Joseph said, as he filled Isabeau's bowl with coffee. "There has to be an advantage to having me around. I'm sorry about this wedding. If I'd known you had it lined up I would have made other arrangements. I don't want to spoil your plans. I could stay here for a day or two while you go."

"You're not spoiling my plans. I don't really have any."

"You're not going with anyone in particular then?" Joseph spoke slowly, and Isabeau thought there was a little emphasis on *anyone*. Or was she imagining it?

"Pierrot – you know, the builder who's working on my house – he's a good friend of François and Marianne, and he asked me to go with him, but I –"

"Sorry, of course. I understand." Joseph looked uncomfortable.

"There's nothing definite. We're just friends."

It was important that Joseph knew this. Isabeau remembered when Marianne had talked about bringing Joseph to the wedding; Isabeau had seen that the offer had come from her heart.

"Truly Joseph, I'd love you to come to the wedding." She dipped the pain au chocolat in her coffee and bit into the half-soaked buttery pastry while she steadied herself. She thought of George. Did Joseph somehow feel his presence too? Is that why he had wanted to stay?

"Thank you. I hope I won't be a nuisance." He busied himself with refilling his bowl with coffee.

"Any plans for today?" he asked. "I'm not meaning that we have to have any, of course."

"What would you like to do?"

"That beach at Carnac that we drove along with Drew looked great. I'd love to spend a day there, but it doesn't have to be today. If there are other things you'd like to do I'm happy to tag along."

"Sure, why not? I'm not a great swimmer, though." Isabeau didn't want to admit that she never went swimming.

"I was thinking of more walking and taking in the sea air. We could find a café and have lunch."

Joseph insisted on doing the dishes while Isabeau had a shower. It was another hot day. Back upstairs, when she looked in her wardrobe, the green halter top that Marianne had given her caught her eye. She slipped it on with her new short denim skirt. She felt half naked, but also a little bit what it must be like to be Marianne. She studied herself in the mirror. Was that all she was doing with Joseph: playing a part? Or was this really her too?

She'd left her hairbrush in the bathroom. She sneaked down the stairs and listened. Joseph was in the alcove. She tiptoed across the kitchen. The alcove curtain suddenly opened, and he appeared.

"Looks like you're ready for the beach," he said, and smiled.

"I need my brush," Isabeau mumbled. She grabbed it and headed quickly back up the stairs, her heart thumping. She couldn't take the outfit off now. "George, George, help!" she muttered. She picked up her inhaler, took a puff and tried to breathe slowly. *Calm down. Calm down, Isabeau.* Was that her or George talking?

"Ready when you are," called Joseph.

"I'll be down in a minute."

She was shaking slightly as she put her sunglasses and the notebook and pen from her bedside cabinet in her bag. She had to focus on something. This wasn't the time to have an asthma attack. She was supposed to be looking after Joseph. When she came downstairs, he was already waiting by the car, his backpack on his lap.

"Are you going to be okay with attaching my chair?" he asked.

"I think so. I've watched Drew doing it."

"I'll put your bag in the car." His hand brushed Isabeau's as he took it.

Suddenly Isabeau wanted him to touch her again. She wanted to touch him. And then the moment was gone, and Joseph was getting in the car. In a few days he would leave too. Her eyes watered. Isabeau pulled the strap tightly around the chair and fastened it as slowly as she could, to give her eyes time to dry.

They went past the old salt ponds towards the coast, and were early enough to find a parking space at the start of the boulevard de la Plage, which ran the length of the Grande Plage. Isabeau concentrated on untying the chair, wheeling it around and placing it next to the car for

Joseph to get into.

It was their first outing together. It was the first time she'd worn a halter top. Maybe the passers-by weren't looking at Joseph, but at her in the halter top. She wished she'd at least put a shirt on over it.

Across the road, there was an opening in the dune that separated the beach from the esplanade. The fine sand formed soft furrows. They stopped beside a cabin with chairs and bicycles for hire, and Isabeau pulled Joseph's chair backwards until they reached the firmer sand.

"Would you like me to keep pushing?" she asked. "You've already had plenty of exercise today, getting up the road to the bakery."

"No, I'll take over from here," said Joseph. "I may be a bit slow, though. I'll let you know when I get tired. Thanks."

Advancing at a snail's pace was perfect. One little step at a time. Isabeau couldn't do this in a hurry.

The beach was quiet. A few people were lying in the sun, while parents and young children played in the water. Cheerful yellow and white striped tents were lined up in a row, waiting to be rented. The morning had a lightness that would dissipate in the intensity of the afternoon heat, when the beach would fill with bronzed bodies. The sand darkened towards the sea, where a fine line of foam separated land and water. From there the sea stretched away, still, little sailing boats forming a series of white triangles on its calm surface.

Isabeau and Joseph made their way towards the water. Isabeau's shoulders were pleasantly warm under the sun, and suddenly the halter top didn't feel out of place. She stopped, took off her sandals and threw them in her bag. She studied the small shells on the sand and bent down to gather some, like she used to do with Papa when he brought her to the beach.

"Perfect," Joseph called out.

Isabeau looked up. He was holding his camera and had already taken the photo.

"Another one," he said, and pointed the camera at her again. "Smile!"

"I'm not at all photogenic."

"Looked good to me."

Isabeau tried to give her best smile, and when Joseph had taken another photo she bent down again and picked up another shell.

"A souvenir for you," she said, handing it to him.

"Thanks. I love the sea," he told her. "I can't keep away from it at home – used to be in the water all the time. I could sit here all day."

They moved back from the water, and Isabeau sat down beside Joseph. He put on a cap, pulled out a bottle of cream from his bag and rubbed some on his arms and around the back of his neck. He held out the bottle to her. "Would you like some cream? I don't want your shoulders to burn. They don't look like they've had much sun yet."

"This is the first time I've worn this top ... this summer." She squeezed some cream into her hands and rubbed it on her arms.

"Here, I'll help you with your back," Joseph offered.

Isabeau stared at the sea and tried to calm the excitement rising inside her like a wave forming as it moved towards the beach. She held her hair around to the front while Joseph's hand traced down the middle of her back and then massaged the cream out across her shoulders. She closed her eyes.

"That looks like it's all covered," he said. "Sorry, it's a bit sticky for your hair." He shifted forward in his chair and gently placed a loose strand of hair over her shoulder. "Your hair is beautiful."

"Thanks for the cream," she said, pretending to scan the sea, the horizon.

"You're welcome," Joseph said, and put the bottle away.

Joseph started humming and took his notebook out of his bag. Isabeau pulled her journal out too.

"You brought your notebook. Great," he said.

"This one's plain compared to yours. No Tokyo chic, just French stationery style."

"It's not what's on the cover, it's what you put inside that counts."

Isabeau turned to the side, pulled her knees up as far as she could and tilted her journal back. She started to write. She wanted to capture the moment. She wanted time to slow, to almost stop. She wanted to keep sitting quietly with Joseph, listening to the song he was humming, being with Joseph. With Joseph.

When he closed his notebook, it was almost lunchtime, and all she'd written were more poems about lost opportunities.

"Funny how I feel closer to Dad in Carnac than I did when I was at home," he said. "Maybe it's because I'm not so focused on my own problems here. Or maybe it's because this place was so important to him and part of him is here – I don't know. I can see new possibilities. It's like a whole album is forming in my head, dedicated not only to Dad, but also to Carnac. Sorry, once I get started I lose track of time. You must be hungry. Shall we go get some lunch?" He gestured in the direction of the restaurants and cafés behind the beach.

They went back down the beach and came out on the boulevard. On the other side of the road, the restaurant on the corner had an outdoor terrace level with the pavement. As Isabeau and Joseph crossed the road, the waiter caught Isabeau's eye, smiled, and started to remove chairs. Joseph gave him a wave and called "merci".

They ordered a seafood platter. Isabeau was surprised how hungry the sea air had made her. She licked her fingers, which tasted of the oysters, prawns and shrimps. The conversation was also a feast. She devoured Joseph's stories about outings to the beach with his father, and later as a teenager with Drew and their friends: swimming and surfing, and spending Christmas around a barbeque under the summer sun.

Instead of having dessert, they headed off into the small streets behind the beach in search of an ice cream. Isabeau knew the perfect place. They wandered past boutiques full of sandals, spades and inflatable toys. She sensed that navigating through the thick holiday crowd was making Joseph tired, and took the handles of his chair and started to push. He didn't say anything, and they merged with the flow of the pedestrians. They made their way around to avenue des Druides and stopped at the corner in front of an ice cream parlour where there was a line of holidaymakers along the counter. The smell of freshly made waffle cones was in the air.

"Here," she said, "L'Igloo. Their ice cream is amazing, and there's plenty of choice. I loved coming here when I was a child."

"Looks good. Smells good." Joseph manoeuvred closer to the counter and watched as the man working on the waffle irons filled them with batter and then removed the hot waffles, quickly rolling them into the shape of a cone. "And more than 170 flavours! Is that possible?" Joseph scanned the long board listing the available flavours. "What's your favourite?"

"If you can guess, it's on me."

"Let me see." Joseph advanced and read through some of the flavours. "I bet you're partial to something fresh, like strawberry or passionfruit. Or maybe you're more of a chocolate girl – or something crazy, like ... curry? Curry ice cream. I can't believe it!"

"You only have one guess," Isabeau teased.

"Okay ... strawberry."

"Wrong," she said. "Classic dark chocolate. What do you like?"

"Aha – now *you'll* have to guess!" Joseph laughed.

"Maybe it's a bit obvious, but I'll say kiwifruit."

"I do like fruit ice cream," he admitted. "But today I'll go for praliné. It's not a flavour we have at home. If I lived around here I think I'd be down here every day trying something different."

Isabeau sat on one of the ice cream-shaped seats with Joseph beside her, and they watched the passers-by. A young girl with dark curly hair, in a pink and white spotted sundress, stood out in the crowd. Between her mother and father, she held their hands as they stopped to buy an ice cream. Isabeau studied her. At that age, Papa had brought her here.

She wanted to share something about her father with Joseph, to tell him about their outings to the beach and other good things, like cooking with him. But she also wanted to tell him about how he left. Her chest tightened. Joseph's voice was there beside her. "Sorry?" She'd lost track of what he was saying.

"I wonder how Drew's getting on," he repeated. He was studying her as he spoke.

"Sorry, I was thinking about my father ... Yes, I hope everything's going well for Drew. I can imagine him on the trimarans we saw at La Trinité-sur-Mer."

"Did you use to come here with your father?" Joseph took off his sunglasses. He looked at her in a way that made her want to answer.

"Sometimes," she said. "It was a real treat. He also used to take me to La Trinité-sur-Mer. He was a barman in one of the bars along the waterfront, and he also worked on fishing boats."

"You wrote that he was gone. When did he die?"

"He didn't. He went – left – when I was nine. He disappeared one day, and I never saw him again." Isabeau stared at her ice cream and took another lick. She didn't want her chest to tighten any further.

"What was he like?"

"I'm not sure any more; it's been so long. He was a good cook. I liked being in the kitchen with him, helping prepare meals. But he wasn't like your father. He wasn't often at home. And my parents didn't get on. I don't know where he is now, or if he's even alive. I don't really know anything at all."

"Maybe one day he'll come back."

"I've always hoped, but it hasn't happened."

"You must miss him. My dad's only been gone a year, and it seems like forever."

"I know."

"What about your family? In one of your letters you said that your mother was English. And do you have any brothers or sisters?"

"Yes, she was." Isabeau stared at the ground. "And no, I don't have any brothers or sisters."

"Sorry, I didn't mean to pry. Maybe I shouldn't have asked."

"Yes, you should have."

"I'm glad I did, then."

He didn't need to say any more than that.

50

Joseph's clothes were casual but good quality, the black cotton underwear incredibly soft. There were a lot of socks. The ones for his stump were all white: some thick, some thin.

There was a noise in the courtyard. Isabeau quickly pushed everything into the top of the machine before Joseph appeared in the doorway.

"Thanks again for offering to do my washing," he said. "I'll have some clean clothes for Nantes tomorrow."

"You must be looking forward to meeting Olivier."

"It's motivating me to work on my music. In fact, there's something I'd like to play for you." He held out his harmonica. "It's dedicated to my father."

"I just need to pop upstairs – won't be long."

From her bedroom window, Isabeau peeked at Joseph downstairs, playing his harmonica in the courtyard. She took George and held him while she listened to the music. She should carry him downstairs, put him on the table and tell Joseph.

"Are you coming?" he called. "I've got a surprise for you. Isabeau?"

His voice was full of trust. She tried to steady herself and breathe slowly.

"Sorry, I didn't mean to hurry you, especially when we're having a lazy day," he said, as Isabeau stepped out the kitchen door.

"I was just looking for something," she said. For some courage to tell the truth, she thought. She hated herself. For once, something special was happening to her. Someone special. It was all her fault if she couldn't enjoy it.

Isabeau sat back in her chair and concentrated on the music. She recognised the little tunes Joseph had been humming for a few days, connected with highs and lows as if they were meant to be together from the very start. The melody was the stones at sunset, the train retreating, Papa walking out the door, an empty shelf in the bathroom, the haunting sadness of farewell, but Joseph had made it beautiful. Tears started to form in her eyes. She wanted to go to the bathroom and cry, but the music compelled her to stay. Joseph followed the rough score he had recorded in his notebook and after the last note rubbed his sleeve across his eyes before he looked at Isabeau.

"I'm thinking of calling it 'Farewell'," he said.

"It's beautiful." She was afraid to say more. The pressure behind her eyes was building.

"I haven't finished. I have another one. It's for you."

The tune was light and happy, like the wind skipping over the waves at the beach, but there was also a hint of something sadder. Isabeau wanted to understand what the music was saying, but the notes slipped through her, making her giddy. She felt as if she was stumbling through her emotions, falling, falling into something unknown. If the music weren't so beautiful she would have been afraid of it. When the song was finished, she saw that Joseph was staring at her.

"Excuse me, I need my inhaler," Isabeau said, breathless. She ran into the kitchen, shaking and wheezing, and rummaged through the drawers of the sideboard. Of course she'd left it beside her bed. She raced upstairs, taking the steps two at a time, stumbling.

"Isabeau, are you okay?" Joseph called. He was at the bottom of the stairs. She heard him swear softly at himself.

Gradually her breathing eased. "It's just asthma," she answered, as loudly as she could. She put her face in her hands.

She wanted to disappear into the oblivion that had been life before George arrived, but at the same time she wanted to go downstairs and listen to the music. She wanted to put her head on Joseph's shoulder and cry and cry and cry, and let out everything that had been building up tight and strong inside her.

"I'll make some coffee and take it outside. There's no hurry, just whenever you're up to it," he called.

She couldn't move. Joseph must think she was mad. Perhaps she was. After all, she talked to the ashes of a dead man; a dead man's ashes were in her bedside cabinet. Joseph's father. And yet she couldn't tell Joseph about them.

He started singing in the courtyard below. "Hold back the sea, the tide's going to invade my heart, love awash in me ..." The song was on the cassette he'd just given her. The lyrics took Isabeau's thoughts in another direction. Who had he written that for? Everything was in the music today. Suddenly he stopped and launched into a different tune. Twinkle Twinkle Little Star. She started to hum, got up and moved over to the window. She could see Joseph picking little daisies from a plant that grew beside the garage and arranging them in a cup. She had to go back downstairs.

"George, give me strength."

Isabeau crept down the stairs to the bathroom and splashed water on her face before she went outside. Joseph advanced towards her and pulled her chair out for her.

"I noticed you had an inhaler, and Drew said your asthma was troubling you the other day. One of the guys in my band has asthma. I've seen it come on in him pretty quick too. I'm sorry if the music upset you."

"I started getting asthma as a child," she said, "and it's never really gone away. Your music's beautiful, moving. It reminded me of Papa, and made me think of your father too. It does sound like a farewell." She felt as if she was going to burst into tears, but held it in. Her eyes moistened. There was a band of tension behind her eyes in a part of her face and head that she didn't normally feel, and it hurt. She stood up and couldn't move, couldn't speak. Joseph pushed his hands on his seat and raised himself up, tall.

Isabeau hadn't seen him standing upright this still before. Like he had two whole legs. He leaned on the table and hopped forward, holding out a handkerchief from his pocket. She stepped forward to take it, and her foot tripped on the table leg. She came crashing into Joseph and knocked him backwards, to the ground, ending up almost on top of him.

"Are you all right? I'm sorry, so sorry. So sorry. So sorry." She started to pull away.

"I'll be fine," he said, catching his breath. "I'm getting used to falling since I lost my leg. I'm more worried about you."

She was shaking. Joseph put his arms around her. She let herself relax against him. She didn't want him to look into her eyes. Inside, she was still falling. Falling into love.

51

"Where's La Cigale?" Joseph followed Isabeau's finger on the map.

"Not far: straight up the street. You can't miss it, on the left in Place Graslin. It's a landmark restaurant in Nantes," she explained. "Will you be okay to get up there?"

"I've got plenty of time. Shall we meet back here at half past twelve and have lunch together? Whatever the outcome of this meeting, I feel like celebrating."

"Yes, let's do that. Good luck. I hope it goes well."

Joseph headed up rue Crébillon. He had purpose, thought Isabeau. It was there every time he talked about his music, and today it was in his arms, as he slowly but surely pushed the wheels of his chair and advanced up the street. Isabeau could see that he was stronger than he had been when he first arrived. She wanted to follow him. At the same time, it was a relief to be on her own, to be out of the house and have a change of focus. She kept thinking about when she had fallen on him and about being in his arms, wishing they had kissed. She didn't know how to act, so she was trying to pretend it hadn't happened.

Joseph had taken it all in his stride. If he had been hurt, he certainly hadn't let on. He'd insisted on making lunch, and sent her off to have a nap in the afternoon, joking that he had to make sure his chauffeur was in shape for the trip to Nantes. Isabeau had lain in bed and listened to him singing softly while he did the lunch dishes. It could have been the sweetest lullaby. But things were unravelling. She didn't know how much longer she could hold herself together. She'd managed for the few days with Drew and the day at the beach, but her usual self was starting to show now. And no one, not even Joseph, could love her. And she hadn't scattered George, and she had lied. Everything was defined by that. And now, there was more to hide. The feelings she had for him. Her eyes could give it away. Could she hide that till he was gone? Gone. In the end it wasn't going to make any difference, because he would leave.

She watched Joseph disappear. What was she going to do for the rest of the morning? She walked up to the Etam boutique, browsed around the shop, tried on a short skirt and bought it, hoping she'd dare wear it while Joseph was still staying with her. That only took twenty minutes. She wandered around the Passage Pommeraye, window shopping, but she couldn't stop thinking about rue Henri Cochard. She couldn't come to Nantes and not go there. It was like an itch that had to be scratched. George would want her to go. Maybe even Joseph would, if she could bring herself to talk to him about it.

Isabeau kept walking, concentrating on her body, breathing into her stomach to relax herself and drive the idea of purpose down into her feet, into each step. Once she'd listened to a BBC radio programme about mind over matter. It made her uneasy. It was too close to home. Today she wanted matter over mind. Her walk started to feed a sense of determination inside her.

When she arrived at the house, the shutters were open. Isabeau rang the doorbell, and heard footsteps coming down the hall. A man wearing old jeans and a shirt splattered with paint opened the door. "Bonjour," he said matter-of-factly.

Isabeau forced herself to speak. "I'm sorry to bother you. I left a note here at Easter, and I haven't had an answer. I thought I would try again."

"A note?" he said, waiting for Isabeau to go on.

"I'm looking for someone called Paul Martin. Apparently he lived here years ago. I wondered if you may've known him or have any information about where he is now." Isabeau slid her hand into her bag and felt for her inhaler, held it in her hand.

"Friends were staying here at Easter for a month. They kept the mail for me, but I don't know what happened to your note. That name does ring a bell though." The man rubbed his stubbled chin. "This house belonged to my grandmother. She's in a rest home now. I used to come here for the holidays. There's a separate flat on the third floor." He pointed upstairs. "Perhaps this man was one of the tenants. What did he do?"

"He worked in a bar in Pornic, and he was a fisherman. He might have been with a woman called Ghislaine," Isabeau explained.

"You're right. There was a couple from Brittany. The guy used to tell me stories about the fishing boats and being away at sea."

"How long did they stay, can you remember?" Isabeau could hear the eagerness rising in her voice.

"Not sure. Maybe a couple of years. I think they were here two summers. I was at school at the time."

"Do you know where he went after that? Where he could be?"

"I'm afraid not. My grandmother might know something. I could ask her," he offered, and asked for Isabeau's phone number and address.

Isabeau scribbled down her details and thanked him. She walked back slowly towards the centre of town. Each step was a syllable, and she alternated the phrases in French and English. Je – l'ai – fait. I – did – it. By the time she reached Place Royale, Joseph was waiting.

"Isabeau, good news!" he greeted her. "Olivier wants to put me on the programme for next summer. Can you believe it? He's listened to the albums I sent, and is keen. Now I'd really love to take you to lunch. That Cigale place where I met Olivier was something. I've never seen a place decorated like that. With his help, I booked us a table." Joseph was tilting his head slightly to the side, and his eyes were taking in her face.

"Congratulations," she said. "That's amazing. You must be thrilled. I don't know if I'm dressed up enough for a place like that though."

"The place is pretty fancy, but the dress seemed quite casual to me. You look fine."

This time, Joseph took Isabeau up on her offer to push his chair. At La Cigale, two waiters with black bow ties and waistcoats, and long white aprons over their trousers, held open the swing doors, and she followed Joseph through to a table beside the window. She stared at the walls, which were covered in ornate woodwork, mirrors and tiles in the art nouveau style. The cicada symbol was everywhere.

"Olivier was great," Joseph said. "I haven't seen him for years, and we still connected. I can't believe he wants me to perform. When I was at the festival in the South it was a low-key affair, and it happened more by chance. Nobody knew me then: certainly not in France, and not in New Zealand much either. I used to dream about this kind of thing, that one day I would come back and perform in Paris or a big city. And now it's going to happen, and it's come almost out of nowhere. A few months ago I didn't even think I'd be coming to France, and here I am."

"Sounds like the Nantes festival is quite big. I think your music could be very popular in France. People listen to a lot of music in English, you know."

"Olivier was particularly interested when I said I was writing songs dedicated to my father and based on my experience at Carnac – this personal link between Brittany and a country so far away."

"Did you tell him about the ashes?" Isabeau felt her chest tighten.

"Well, I told him Dad had always wanted to come to Carnac and that I'd come to honour him. At the moment, I'm not sure I want to share the story of the ashes with everyone, so I left it at that. I also said that I wrote to Carnac for some information and the letter fell into your hands, and that's how I came to know you."

"I understand. I would want to keep it private too, and it's probably better not to say too much. It could shock some people. Most people in France are buried. Cremation isn't common – let alone scattering ashes. It's not something that's done in the Catholic Church." Isabeau felt hot, even in the cool of the restaurant. She took a few sips of water and picked up her menu.

"I did wonder how people would react to that," said Joseph. "Anyway, it's nice to be able to share this good news, to celebrate with you," he concluded in a quiet voice. "Shall we have a look at the menu? The dishes that are going past look good."

He ordered chicken with mashed potatoes "made the way Grandma used to", and Isabeau decided on salmon. While they waited for their food, they sipped pineapple juice and studied the restaurant.

"Olivier said it's classified as a historic monument," Joseph commented. "It's almost an art nouveau work of art in itself."

"It's like being in another world." Isabeau looked around. "I've always wanted to come here."

The restaurant and outside terrace were full, and the other diners were all engrossed in their conversations. Most of them looked like they were on holiday too, enjoying the summery weather. Waiters and waitresses moved back and forth from the terrace to the bar. Isabeau was grateful for the surroundings. She was scared to look at Joseph too much, afraid her eyes would give her away.

The waiter brought them their meals, and Joseph raised his glass of pineapple juice.

"Here's to Nantes and next summer. I'll send you tickets," he said. "Maybe we'll eat here again." It almost sounded like a question.

He pressed his glass softly against hers. Isabeau's throat and chest were tight. She couldn't imagine what things would be like a year from then. Joseph was going to leave. He wouldn't send tickets. She hadn't scattered George.

"You've got that faraway look that you get sometimes," said Joseph.

"I've always been a bit of a ... daydreamer. I was thinking about what an incredible place this is. If it wasn't for you I wouldn't have come here."

Isabeau felt the need to get her inhaler out and have it in her hands. If she could do that and Joseph wasn't looking at her, maybe she could tell him. He was waiting for her to say something.

"My salmon's delicious," she said. "What about your chicken?"

"Definitely as good as my grandmother would have made – maybe better. And she was a good cook! She used to make roast chicken, crispy potatoes and corn fritters. Always had an apron on, and her house smelled of baking. She lived near my school, so I'd go there after school until Dad got home, and when he had to work late."

"Sounds like she looked after you well."

"She did, and she still does."

"And what did your father do?"

"He worked on the railways."

"In the photo, he looks really strong."

"Yes, he was. He was very active and did a lot of tramping too. He was always taking me into the mountains. That's where my mother ... was killed. In a climbing accident."

"I'm sorry. I wondered how she died."

"Thanks, I can see you mean it. And you? What about your grandparents?"

"Oh, I don't – didn't – have any grandmothers, grandparents. My mother lost her parents in a plane crash, and she was brought up by her grandparents, but I never knew them, and my father was a ward of the state. My parents were both sort of like orphans, in a way, so there was just them. No one else. My dad had to work late a lot too, and he was often working on fishing boats. I played around the menhirs."

"That must have been hard on you and your mother."

"Yes. She struggled with that and lots of things. She was ... sick."

"I'm sorry. What kind of illness did she have? I hope you don't mind me asking." Joseph looked at Isabeau, directly in the eyes.

They both stopped eating. She didn't want him to think she was like her mother, but she needed to say it.

"She suffered from depression, and she would get paranoid about a lot of things. She shut herself away and didn't go out much. Her French was pretty limited, so it never improved."

"I'm really sorry," said Joseph. "And that's why you spent so much time amongst the standing stones?"

"Yes."

"Now I understand why you know the alignments so well."

Isabeau cut a piece of salmon and concentrated on eating. If she kept looking at Joseph she didn't know what she might say. And it wouldn't be right, there in La Cigale, with all those people, on a beautiful summer day, when Joseph had just received such good news. Saying anything about the ashes would have the same effect. It would spoil everything. The band of tension behind her eyes might take over again. Something might start that she couldn't stop.

Joseph took a mouthful of food too and when he had finished spoke again. "This mashed potato is the smoothest I've ever tasted. I definitely have to have a dessert today. Everything the waiter's taking past looks good. What about you?" His voice had taken on a softer tone, like the day before when they'd fallen – a tone that pulled Isabeau back, pulled her towards him. He smiled at her.

"Me too."

"I saw there was crème brulée on the menu, I can't resist that. Or then again there's tarte au citron." He sighed. "There were some in your friend Marianne's bakery. It's not long till her wedding now."

"Only a few days. I still have to put the dragées in the little sachets I embroidered."

"I'm happy to give you a hand." He stretched back in his chair. "I don't know what Drew's up to, but I hope he's having half as good a time as me."

Isabeau sat on the doorstep brushing her hair. Joseph was still asleep. They hadn't intended to stay late in Nantes, but had visited the castle after lunch, and then wandered around the cobbled alleys, full of little restaurants and boutiques, in the Quartier Bouffay. Isabeau had found it easier than sitting opposite Joseph at La Cigale; to be at his side, walking slowly beside the chair and pushing it from time to time, sharing his amazement at the old buildings around them. He sometimes ran his hands over the stones, and said "Christchurch's not even 150 years old. It's hard to imagine that people have walked in these streets and touched these stones for centuries."

They were still there in the evening and were tempted by a busy crêperie, La Crêperie Jaune. They sat at an outside table and watched the cook, an older woman, through the counter window of the kitchen.

"She's just like my Great-Aunt Gertrude with that shift dress and pinny," laughed Joseph, as the woman threw handfuls of cheese, ham, mushroom and tomato onto their galettes. They ate them with sweet cider, and Isabeau giggled as Joseph told her stories about his great-aunt.

He talked a lot about family: a family like the Morels' and Marianne's. Isabeau listened as if she knew about such things. It was ten o'clock when they sat back in their chairs, fully stuffed with chocolate almond crêpes that had been served with vanilla ice cream.

In the car on the way home, Isabeau put a Goldman cassette on, and they sang along to the choruses, Joseph trying to learn the words. After the last song, he started to talk again.

"I feel as if I've been going on about me and my music all day. I hope you're not sick of it. Tell me all about you."

The house was all Isabeau had to talk about. But then, somehow, she was talking about her parents. In the dark of the night, she wanted to confide in Joseph, to let the things deep inside her out, like the air that whistles through the valve on a pressure cooker. It made her breathless, yet she didn't think of her inhaler for once. Driving in the dark, in her small car, it felt like they were in their own little universe. The night surrounded them, sucked out some of her story, swallowed up the pain. Papa. Mother. The menhirs. Beside her, Joseph listened. She didn't want the drive or the day to end.

Now, this morning, Isabeau worried about what she'd told Joseph, that she'd said too much. But she still hadn't told him about his father's ashes. Her past had hijacked the silence, the opportunity. She was her own worst enemy. And she had a new past constructing itself: a past that had nothing to do with her parents. The day in Nantes was part of it. Joseph was all of it. If only it wasn't founded on deception. It would all disappear. Like Papa. She pressed the brush harder against her scalp and down through her hair. Only ten more days. Then Joseph would leave. She had to tell him before he did.

"I can't believe I've slept this late," he said, rolling up behind her. "I'll get straight into preparing breakfast. I'm all fired up to get back to my songs after seeing Olivier, especially while I'm here in Carnac, in this atmosphere ... and with you."

When they finished breakfast, they installed themselves at the table outside, Joseph with his harmonica and notebook and Isabeau with her journal.

Joseph cleared his throat. "I'd love to see some of your poetry. I presume it's in French? Do you write in English at all?"

"Most of it's in French. There's only the odd poem in English. But it's not very interesting. It wouldn't be of any interest to you – or to anybody else. It's too personal." Isabeau shut her journal.

"Perhaps that's why I'd like to see it," he said, raising his eyebrows. "And I'm always on the lookout for poetic material to use as lyrics."

"It isn't any good. And it isn't for anyone but me."

"I get that. It took me a while to be confident about singing my own songs to other people. How long have you been writing poetry?" He glanced at her journal.

"Since I was a teenager. What about you – how long have you been writing music?" Isabeau asked in turn.

"Pretty much the same. I started when I was at high school," Joseph reflected, "although I'd been learning the guitar and piano for years. Dad used to talk about how my mum loved to sing and how her voice filled the house. Music made me feel somehow closer to her. Tell you what, I'll show you a new song, if you show me something you've written. Is that a fair deal?"

"Fair?" Isabeau put her journal on her knee. "You're a professional.

You're writing it to share with others from the start. My writing isn't in a state to be shown to anyone. It's very messy!"

"Messy – I like that," he said. "Probably describes most of what's in my notebooks. I noticed that you've got quite a few journals in your bookcase. You must have a lot of poetry if you've been writing since you were a teenager."

"It's just for me," Isabeau said slowly.

"You might be surprised how, when you share something, it can take on new meaning, and if it resonates with others, it can be really positive." Joseph flicked through his Tokyo journal, stopped at a page and opened it out. "Here, O most privileged one," he said with an exaggerated flourish. "You've already had the world première of a couple of pieces of music; you can also be the first to have a look at this. It's not finished, but the essence of what I want to say is there. For the moment, the others are top secret." He adopted a tone of mock seriousness. "I'll show them to you one day."

Isabeau couldn't help but smile.

"No pressure." Joseph raised his hands. "If you don't want to show me, you don't have to. I'm happy to share this with you anyway." He pushed the journal towards Isabeau and insisted with his eyes that she pick it up. There were lots of cross-outs, and doodles like the drawings that had decorated his letters.

She took in the words he had written:

Sing to me, cry to me
over the big blue sea.
Send a bird with a bare branch of pain
I will paint the leaves on with love and care
and send it back again and again.

"It's beautiful," she said. "Like the songs on the albums you've given me. You're very lucky to be able to give others so much pleasure with your music." She tried to stop thinking about the words he'd written, she might start crying again, and the need to fetch her inhaler would take over.

"I'm sure your poetry's beautiful too. Don't underestimate yourself. Have a think about it."

Isabeau lay in bed. The house was quiet. She couldn't sleep. She sneaked downstairs, looked through her journals and took four of them back to bed. The little poems she'd written at the beach were scribbles, worthless. She wished she had happy poems to choose from. She could write something about the time she was having with Joseph, but then she couldn't show that to him either. With everything she'd confided to him, he might guess that too much depended on him now. She pulled George out.

"Please, George, help me. Joseph showed me some of his writing. It was beautiful, as if he knew exactly how I feel. Maybe if I could show him something, then I could tell him about you."

At half past one Isabeau was still searching for a poem. She kept leafing through the journals. In desperation, she grabbed one with a dark blue cover again and opened it towards the middle, like splitting a deck of cards. There were two long poems on the pages; each featured a lot of cross-outs. Her eyes were drawn to a short poem, in English, written diagonally across the bottom corner of the right-hand page. Far too personal. Isabeau shut the journal, put it back on her bedside cabinet and turned out the light. She lay in the dark and tried to sleep. Tried to forget the little poem. But it wouldn't leave her alone. She turned the light on again and looked for it.

Soliloquy
This dog solitude
needs walking
every day.
She wants to be fed.
The bitch
gnaws the bone,
sharpens her canines.
I am the leash.
I am the bone.

Isabeau copied the poem in the best writing she could muster at two in the morning. It looked sad sitting in the middle of the page, so she added a row of menhirs. She went back downstairs as quietly as a mouse and crept over to the curtain. She opened it just a crack and peeked through. Joseph was snoring. He was lying on his back, with Drew's pillows placed around him, as if he was sleeping in the clouds. His face was relaxed and his lips moved slightly as he exhaled. She tiptoed closer to the bed. She wanted to touch him, to move the pillows and take their place, then put her head on his shoulder and lean in against him, like when she'd fallen on him and felt the full length of his body.

He stirred. Isabeau froze and then stepped backwards out of the alcove. She sat the poem on the kitchen table at his place, and stood there for several minutes. Then she picked up the sheet of paper again. Upstairs, she hid it in her bedside cabinet with George.

Isabeau didn't like to say no. She would have preferred to go elsewhere. Anywhere but Quiberon. But Joseph had been studying the map while she'd slept late, and he was intrigued by the peninsula. She hadn't shown him any poems, and she hadn't told him about his father. She didn't know how to say no to this.

When she came downstairs, dressed for the day, he'd even prepared a picnic as well as the usual breakfast. Because they'd developed a loose rhythm of quiet days at home interspersed with outings, it must have seemed the most natural thing for him to buy extra bread when he went for his morning bakery visit, and then to make sandwiches ready for a day out. She sipped her coffee slowly.

"Sorry I've slept so late," she yawned. She felt as if she hadn't slept at all.

"Doesn't matter," he replied. "I was the one who had the sleep-in yesterday. We've got all day. I hope you don't mind going to the coast again?"

"In your letters you wrote a lot about going to the beach. I guess you're used to it, coming from a country of islands," said Isabeau.

"Yes, the sea's everywhere." Joseph made a sweeping gesture with his hands. "Like Carnac, Christchurch is on the coast, and near a peninsula too. The scenery on Banks Peninsula is amazing. And there's even a village there, Akaroa, that was colonized by a boat of French settlers. If they'd arrived earlier and negotiated a treaty with the Māori chiefs, who knows – maybe I'd be French!" he joked.

"It sounds exotic, nothing like Quiberon."

Isabeau found herself wondering what it would be like to go elsewhere, even to the other side of the world. Maybe she could do this. Everything was easier with Joseph. There was something almost precarious about being with him, but she also felt safe. Upstairs, she held George for a few moments before they packed the car. "Promise me this will be okay today, George, please." But there was no answer. She put the box back in her bedside cabinet and returned downstairs.

They drove straight to the town of Quiberon to look around before they explored the beaches and coast. They parked the car and headed into the main street. Outside a shop packed with t-shirts and other holiday clothing, Joseph stopped at a rack of marinières.

"I've always wanted one of these," he said, looking through the long-sleeved striped tops. "I think I'll go for a red one. All I'll need now is a beret and a baguette," he laughed. "Drew won't recognize me when he gets back."

He went into the shop to try it on. There was only just enough space for his chair inside the door, and he took off his sweatshirt and pulled the marinière on over his t-shirt. It was too big. The shop assistant handed Isabeau a smaller size for him. She pretended to look at a rack of t-shirts, and out of the corner of her eye she watched Joseph as he tried the smaller size. When he raised his arms, his t-shirt lifted, and the pale skin on his chest and stomach contrasted with the light golden tan on his arms. He bought the marinière and kept it on.

Through the shop window, they could see that the clouds were advancing and hiding the sun. Outside, the temperature was cooler. They went back to the car to get their jackets, and Isabeau slipped her inhaler into her pocket. The wind was coming off the sea now, and in the port the waves crashed along the sea wall. They stopped and looked across the port. A ferry, coming in from Belle-Ile, docked behind the terminal.

"Shame the sun's gone," said Joseph, pulling his jacket around him. "Where did that ferry come from?"

"Belle-Ile, over there. Belle-Ile-en-Mer, if you want the full name." Isabeau pointed out to sea. "There's a regular ferry service. Belle-Ile is one of the bigger islands off the coast."

"What's it like?"

"I don't really know. My father always promised to take me there on the ferry."

"And you never went? You've never been since?"

"No."

"I'm sorry," he said. "I'd like to take you, but I guess it wouldn't be the same. And I'm not sure today would be a good day to go, the way the wind's risen."

"Thanks for the thought anyway." Isabeau tried to force a positive note into her voice. She took a puff on her inhaler.

"Is your asthma playing up?"

She nodded.

"Let's go and find a warmer spot for our picnic," he suggested.

They drove back down the peninsula to one of the beaches on the eastern, more sheltered, side and parked facing the sea. Joseph pulled a thermal top from his bag.

"Here, put this on under your jacket," he told her. "I always carry one of these. At home, you can never trust the weather. It can change dramatically at the drop of a hat, worse than this. I don't want you to have another asthma attack." He pushed the top into Isabeau's hands. She took her jacket off, and he held it from behind while she slipped the thermal top on over her t-shirt.

They settled beside the car for their picnic, but the promise of a warm summer day had disappeared.

"The other day you said your father was a fisherman, as well as working in bars." Joseph said.

"Yes."

"I guess it's hard not to think about him here." Joseph pointed to the sea. "As soon as I see the mountains I can't help but think about my dad – and my mum."

Isabeau swallowed.

"Have you ever tried to find him?"

"That's really why I came back to Carnac. There was the house too, of course. But I'm not having much luck with finding him. All I've found out is that there was another woman. Ghislaine." Isabeau felt raw from the sea air and the words that had escaped, fading into the cold wind.

"Well, I hope you find him."

Joseph put his arm around Isabeau's shoulders. She could tell him about George now. She'd said so much already. What difference would it make if she admitted that she had the ashes at home?

"You see, I ..." Isabeau started to wheeze.

"You need your inhaler."

"I ..."

"Your inhaler, Isabeau."

She pulled it out of her pocket and sat dumbly. Her hand wouldn't move. Joseph took it from her, shook it and gently put it against her lips. She breathed in. It was as if everything she'd wanted to say was being pushed back into her. She was numb with cold.

"We need to get you home and warm you up. It's moments like this

I wish I could ... I have an automatic car at home now; it's easier." Joseph directed Isabeau towards the car and poured her a cup of coffee from the flask.

She sat in the car, cupping the mug in her hands, and slowly sipped. Before she knew it, he was standing behind the car, holding himself up and putting his chair on the bike rack, then he hopped around and slipped into the passenger seat. He was panting.

"You managed to put your chair on the back," was all she could say.

"Yes. My arm and hand are getting stronger. My securing technique isn't up to Drew's, but it should hold till we get home. Don't go too fast!"

Joseph wrapped the picnic rug around Isabeau, turned up the car heater and waited while she finished her coffee.

When they arrived home, Isabeau curled up in her armchair with the rug. Joseph took out his harmonica and played softly. Each note said "close your eyes". She turned on her side and brought her legs up, snuggling into the chair. She could no longer hold up the weight of her own body, her head, her eyelids.

She awoke with a start, feeling as if she had been falling. Joseph was at the stove. He turned around.

"Perfect timing," he said. "Dinner's almost ready. It's simple, but I thought it would be good to eat early." He lifted the lid on the pot.

"Have you made soup?"

"It's pretty basic. I've just used what I could find in the cupboard: a can of chopped tomatoes with some garlic and onion and the leftover basil," he explained.

"Smells really good. And whatever's in the oven does too."

"I threw all the bits and pieces in the fridge on the baguette and put it under the grill. It's easy to make something tasty when you've got French cheese."

"You're a good cook."

"I had plenty of practice," Joseph said with a shrug. "Dad did his best, but he wasn't very good in the kitchen. I spent a lot of time at Drew's place, and my Aunt Jenny taught me how to cook."

Later, in bed, the sound of the sea rocked in Isabeau's head. She held the piece of paper with the poem and couldn't stop reading it. Taking her Christmas pen, she added "Dear Joseph" above the poem, and below the menhirs she wrote "Thank you" and signed her name. She tiptoed downstairs and placed it on the table.

Joseph was setting the table for breakfast. Over his jeans, he was wearing the marinière. He had rolled up the sleeves, and had a red cotton scarf around his neck. As usual, the bone spiral was around his neck, and today the leather bracelet stood out on his wrist. Fresh croissants and a baguette filled the middle of the table, beside a little jug holding flowers from the courtyard. The poem was gone.

Halfway down the stairs Isabeau was a statue, watching through the banisters. He took one of the flowers and put it on her serviette, surveyed the table and then headed through into the alcove. Before she had time to go back up the stairs, he returned with a pad and pen. He drew notes across the top of the paper and wrote a few words, ripped off the page and sat it upright in front of her bowl. She strained to read what he'd written, but before she could make out any of the words, he screwed up the sheet of paper and started on another one. This time he stopped and put the pen to his chin. Isabeau held her breath. Suddenly she couldn't repress a cough. She rushed down the stairs. "Good morning. Need to get to the bathroom," she spluttered.

When she came back out, there was no piece of paper near her bowl. "Your marinière looks good," she said, glancing at Joseph's notepad and pen on his knee. The top page was blank.

"I didn't know how long you were going to sleep." Joseph looked at the notepad too. "I was going to note down some ideas for songs. Did you sleep well?"

"Not bad, thanks."

"I won't suggest any seaside picnics today."

"Anyway, I have to get the dragées ready. I'd sort of forgotten about them, and now the wedding's on Saturday."

"I'm more than happy to help."

"That would be great, thanks."

"In fact, it's my turn to say thanks. I had a little surprise this morning, very unexpected. Can I keep the poem?" asked Joseph. "It's powerful."

"If you want to." Isabeau felt her face redden. "Breakfast looks good again. You're spoiling me."

"About this wedding, I was wondering what I should wear. At home, it's mostly suits and ties for weddings. I haven't got any clothes like that with me."

"I'm not sure. I don't think you need a suit though." Isabeau wished she'd asked Marianne.

"I've got a good pair of trousers and a white shirt," Joseph said.

"That should be okay."

After breakfast, Joseph did the dishes, while Isabeau laid out the sachets, ribbons and boxes of dragées. As soon as he'd finished washing up, he moved in closer and surveyed the sachets.

"May I?" he asked, picking one up and examining it. "They're amazing, all these different colours. What's this tradition about?"

"I'm not exactly sure why brides and bridegrooms give sugar-coated almonds to their guests. I think they're a symbol of everlasting love and fertility, or something like that." Isabeau blushed. She turned away from him a little as she shifted the ribbon and sachets around, rearranging them. "They're also given out at christenings and first communions."

"How many sachets have you made?"

"One hundred and twenty-five."

Joseph whistled. "It's going to be a big wedding."

"I think there'll be 123 guests. You'll be number 124, unless Marianne's invited other latecomers. She likes to plan everything, and she asked me if I minded doing a couple extra, just in case."

"Well, I'm happy to be a 'just in case'!" laughed Joseph. "I never imagined going to a French wedding. How do we fill them?"

Isabeau picked up a pink and green sachet and a few dragées, and cut off some dark green ribbon. "About this many almonds: a mixture of pink and white ones. Slip them in, choose a ribbon colour and tie it up with a nice bow. I've cut off a piece of ribbon as a guide. This length is good." She handed Joseph a piece of blue ribbon. "Your turn."

Joseph took the guide piece and picked up a yellow and red sachet. He hesitated before the collection of different coloured ribbons.

"Maybe I should just put the almonds in the bags and you do the ribbons."

"Whatever colour you choose will be fine."

"Are you sure?"

"Yes."

"Isabeau, it's nice of you to take me to the wedding," he said. "I hope it truly hasn't mucked up your plans." He picked up the orange ribbon reel. "And that you weren't really supposed to go with someone else, or maybe you have a boyfriend who's not around – who's on holiday or something like that." He unrolled the ribbon, taking time to measure the length.

"No, no, I don't have a boyfriend ... at the moment."

She picked up another sachet, counted the dragées into it and glanced at Joseph. She remembered how Lucy the redhead had hugged him.

"And what about you? Do you have a girlfriend, at the moment?"

"No, I don't have anyone, either. I was in a relationship for a long time, but it had just ended before the accident. Now it seems like a whole new ball game." Joseph was studying the sachet in his hands.

"From what you've told me, I don't think your mother would've minded if your father had lost a leg, or been in a wheelchair," Isabeau said. "There are so many more important things." She was surprised at how sure her voice was.

"Thank you," Joseph said, and looked at her with his soft grey eyes. "Well, we'd better get back to these, otherwise we'll never have them ready." He smiled, and held up a dragée as if he was going to eat it. "What do they taste like?"

"You'll have to wait until the wedding to sample them."

He put the almond closer to his mouth, laughing.

"I'll tell Marianne if you eat any!" Isabeau was laughing too.

Joseph slid the dragée into the bag, tied it and quickly reached for another sachet. "I'm getting into the swing of this. Shall we have a competition?"

For half an hour they worked without talking much. When Isabeau slipped the dragées into the last sachet, Joseph counted up his pile and shouted "Sixty-four! I've won. What's my prize?"

Isabeau wanted to tickle him.

"You can try *one* dragée!"

Putting their bags in the car felt like setting off on a journey, an adventure. It was different to the outings they had undertaken. They had spent the day before at home, relaxing and writing, and getting their bags ready. They had made a quick trip to the stones, then spent the evening sitting in the courtyard till late. The time had gone, slowly and quickly and surely. After the weekend of the wedding there would only be three days left, Isabeau realized. She would have to tell him then. That was all there would be left to do. Perhaps he would hate her.

She had to block out thoughts of the ashes. The wedding was enough to deal with. It was getting easier to be with Joseph on their own, but there would be a lot of people at the wedding, including Pierrot. And what if someone asked why Joseph had come to Carnac, and he ended up explaining the full story?

Joseph thought the reason they were going to go to Saint-Laurent-de-la-Plaine via Guérande was sightseeing – visiting the town from where she'd sent him the postcard – but it was more than that. Isabeau wanted to share with him the special place she used to go with Papa. The good times.

It was market day in Guérande, and the town centre around the church was full of stalls laden with cakes, cheeses, and fruit and vegetables in ripe summer colours. Joseph took his time to study the range of goods, and they bought two baguettes, cheese, peaches and fat cherries for a picnic lunch. They ambled down the main street amongst the holidaymakers, looking in the shop windows. Joseph went into one of the shops and bought a salt pot and a small bag of fleur de sel.

"Looks like the salt you use at home," he said. "It's a good souvenir to take home: a little bit of Brittany and this day spent here with you." He tucked the parcel carefully in his pack.

They drove to Batz-sur-Mer, then took the narrow built-up roads through the salt marshes. In the basins, where the seawater had evaporated, low dividing walls created a series of rectangles, each with a pile of salt on the side.

"They're all at different stages," Isabeau explained. "As the wind and sun evaporate the water, the salt is gradually raked up into piles. It's a natural product, not refined at all. The salt you bought, fleur de sel, is the top part and the finest."

"I've never seen anything like it," said Joseph and reached for his camera.

Further along, a harvester was working in one of the ponds. Standing on the low dividing wall, he used a long-handled wooden rake with easy regular movements. Isabeau stopped the car, and they wound down the windows. Joseph took several photos.

"Must be this sea air: suddenly I'm starving," he said. He broke a couple of pieces off one of the baguettes and offered one to Isabeau.

The fresh bread was like cake, the cheese creamy and soft, and the peaches and cherries the perfect juicy dessert. They licked their sticky fingers and laughed about their red-stained mouths while they watched the harvester continue his work.

After the detour through the salt marshes, they headed towards Nantes and crossed the Loire to take the southern route. They stopped often for Joseph to take photos, and it was half past four when they arrived in the church square at Saint-Laurent-de-la-Plaine.

Around the back of the bakery, the garage door was open, and they could hear talk and laughter coming from the courtyard. Entering it, they saw that it was full of plastic outdoor tables that had been pushed together. Isabeau didn't know most of the people seated around them. At least Pierrot wasn't there, she noticed. She gave a small sigh of relief. Marianne and François were between two couples who looked about the age of Marianne's parents. Marianne looked around and saw Isabeau. She came straight over, followed by François and Christian. Before Isabeau could start introducing Joseph, Marianne embraced her and then also kissed Joseph on the cheeks.

"It's great to see you both. Joseph, this is my François, and my brother Christian," she said slowly, and then repeated the names.

"Welcome, Joseph. It's really great you could come," said Christian, in perfect English, with a friendly smile.

Marianne ushered them towards the table and introduced them around to good friends of her parents and two cousins, Valérie and Hervé, with their partners, and also to François' parents, who Isabeau knew from the engagement party. Marianne's parents joined them. Madame Fournier opened her arms to Isabeau.

"It's good to see you again, Isabeau. We're glad that you've brought your friend, Joseph," she said. Then she shook Joseph's hand, and pushed the chairs and sun umbrella out so that Joseph could fit more comfortably.

There was something about Marianne's parents' manner towards Joseph that reminded Isabeau of Marianne's reaction when she had first seen him. Before Isabeau had time to wonder about it, the two of them sat down beside Joseph, and Isabeau was amazed to learn that they spoke some English. Madame Fournier explained to Joseph that her best friend at high school had married an Englishman, and that she and Monsieur Fournier had regularly visited the couple in England. "It's a shame they weren't able to come to the wedding," she said. Madame Fournier was curious about New Zealand, and questioned Joseph in a mixture of French and English. His answers in French were short and simple, and he made mistakes, but everyone listened patiently and helped him with words and expressions. Isabeau was happy to sit and listen. She squeezed her wrist under the table, hoping no one asked why Joseph had come to France and how he knew her.

There was the sound of someone coming in through the garage, and everyone looked around at the same time.

"Bonjour chers amis," called out Tonton Aimé. "Always have to come in through the back way! What kind of a place is this?" he joked as he joined them.

Everyone laughed, and he made his way around the table, soon arriving at Isabeau.

"How wonderful to see you again," he said. "I've been looking forward to hearing about your resolutions." He looked at Joseph.

"This is my friend, Joseph, from New Zealand," Isabeau said.

"Enchanté, Joseph," said Tonton Aimé, half bowing as he extended his hand.

He took a chair standing against the bakery wall and pulled it up to the table close to them, but as he was about to sit down Marianne's father pulled him aside to talk, so that he ended up seated at the other end of the table. Isabeau hoped she had the opportunity at the wedding to talk to him.

At seven o'clock, Marianne and her mother set out tuna tarts and a selection of salads on the kitchen table, and everyone helped themselves, buffet style, before tucking into cheese and Monsieur

Fournier's strawberry tarts. When they had finished, Isabeau unloaded the boxes of sachets from her car, and then Marianne suggested that she take everyone who was staying at the lodge to their accommodation.

At the lodge, Marianne went into the office and came back with a young woman, Sandrine, who handed out keys and directed everyone to units. Joseph and Isabeau waited.

"Now, you two," said Sandrine, leading them to the unit at the end. "You're in this studio: one storey, with a sofa bed. Everything's on the ground floor, as instructed. It will be a squeeze, but there should be enough room."

Marianne and Isabeau looked at each other.

"There must be some mistake," said Marianne. "When I phoned, Monique said it was possible to have a *two*-bed unit with *one* bed on the ground floor."

"I think a double bed on the ground floor was marked on the booking sheet," said Sandrine, with a puzzled frown on her face. "We do have a folding bed, but there's not enough room to bring it in here." She glanced at Joseph's chair.

"I'm pretty sure I said two beds." Marianne sighed. "Is there a spare bed in one of the other units?"

"No, they're all full."

Joseph looked back and forwards between Sandrine and Marianne, trying to follow the rapid French.

Isabeau turned to him. "There's a slight problem with the accommodation. We were supposed to have a two-bed unit, but we've been assigned a studio unit with a double bed."

"I'm sorry to be all this trouble," said Joseph. "I don't mind if there's no other option here – it's only for two nights – but I don't want to put you on the spot. I'm happy to stay in a hotel close by, if that's not too much fuss to organize."

"No, please don't worry. It's not necessary. It's fine, really."

"I'm sorry about this," Marianne said to Isabeau. "I thought it was all sorted."

"It's only a couple of nights." Isabeau wanted to emphasize the words without appearing to.

Joseph joined in with his limited French: "ce n'est pas grave."

"Are you sure?" asked Marianne.

"Yes," Isabeau and Joseph answered at the same time.

"Okay, well, if you both don't mind. I hope you sleep well." Marianne smiled at Isabeau. She squeezed her tight as she kissed her goodnight and whispered "Thanks again for the dragées. Good luck."

The sofa bed dominated the space, leaving only enough room for the television and a coffee table. The bed head served as the bench and concealed the small kitchen area, with its table for two. The bathroom was off to the side.

"Well, it's cosy," Isabeau said.

"I think it would be better if I folded up my chair and left it beside the door," said Joseph. "I may need to borrow your shoulder."

"Sure."

"But on the plus side, the kitchen area's so small that I'll be able to lean on the bench or table to get around. About the bed –"

"It's okay, really," she said. "I don't mind sharing. It's more that I'm worried about you. I might be a nuisance for your space and comfort. I know you need lots of pillows." Isabeau blushed, remembering when she'd peeked in on Joseph asleep at home. "I don't want you to be uncomfortable."

"I'll be fine," he assured her. "Anyway, on that subject, I think I should get to bed. I want to make the most of tomorrow. I used to be able to stay up till dawn, but since the accident I need my beauty sleep. Ladies first for the bathroom," he offered.

Isabeau took her toilet bag, pyjamas and dressing gown into the bathroom. She wanted to stay under the shower for a long time, but Joseph was waiting. The double bed was waiting. She'd never slept in the same bed as anyone before.

"I'll take the wall side, if you don't mind," said Joseph, who was sitting on the bed when she came out.

"Not at all. And you can have these." She passed him the spare pillows.

"Thanks." Joseph stared at the pillows. "I need one under my leg, and I normally pack them around me. I know it's a bit strange."

"It's not strange." Isabeau thought of Cosette, hidden in her bed at home.

"I have this pillow ... habit," Joseph told her. "It's got worse since I've been in hospital. Between that and my snoring, I don't know if I'll be a good bedmate." He laughed.

Isabeau couldn't help but laugh with him.

"If I can borrow your shoulder, I'll have a quick wash and then we can get to sleep," he said, more matter-of-factly.

Isabeau helped Joseph to the bathroom and then eased in between the sheets. Her heart was racing. She closed her eyes and pictured him sleeping as she tried to calm her thoughts, her breathing, her body. When he called from the bathroom that he was finished she almost jumped. He was wearing pyjama shorts and a fresh white t-shirt, and his hair was slightly wet. When he put his arm around her shoulders, he smelled of aniseed and toothpaste.

"It's been a long day," he said. "Tomorrow will be my first French wedding." He breathed out slowly.

"Mine, too. It's the first wedding I've ever been to."

"Really? Well, I'm glad I'm sharing it with you."

"Me too."

With each step from the bathroom to the bed, their bodies moved closer together. Isabeau could feel his warm skin through his t-shirt. They stopped at the bed, and he turned and leaned towards her, leaving his arm around her shoulders. She couldn't take her eyes off his face. He would leave soon. She still hadn't told him. She pulled back.

"Well, we'd better get some sleep," she said, pretending to yawn.

Joseph sat on the bed and manoeuvred himself over to settle into position, slightly on his side, facing towards Isabeau. His left arm lay over the spare pillow, almost as if he was hugging it. She switched off the light, slipped under the sheet and turned away from him into her pillow. Damn. Another missed opportunity to tell him the truth. She wiped her eyes with the back of her hand and sniffed as quietly as she could.

"Here," Joseph said softly, as he reached up to a box of tissues on the top of the bedhead. He pulled one out and handed it to Isabeau.

"Thanks."

He passed her another tissue. His hand met hers, and didn't let go.

Joseph was on his back, breathing heavily, the pillow locked in his arms. Isabeau turned and watched him for a few minutes. He started to stir, stretched and opened his eyes.

"Bonjour," said Isabeau.

"Bonjour. Have you slept well?" Joseph pushed the pillow against the wall and put his hands behind his head.

"Yes, thanks. And you, and your pillows?" This morning Isabeau felt shy, but also a little cheeky. She'd slept surprisingly well.

"Not bad, thanks. But this pillow here," Joseph punched the pillow, laughing, "I think he snored quite a lot. You'll have to give him a whack if he does that again."

"I'll do that." Isabeau smiled.

"Back to the serious formalities: what time does this wedding start, again? Did Marianne's mother say half past ten? That's early."

"Yes, for the civil ceremony at the town hall, then there's the church service, followed by a reception – the vin d'honneur – for everyone at the ceremony, and then there's the wedding breakfast, which leads through to the evening and dancing. I don't know if all French weddings are like that, but Marianne said that in her family they have what they call an all-day wedding."

Joseph whistled. "It's certainly worth the trip then. And Marianne's family are so friendly. I can't believe how welcome they made me feel, as if I'd been invited from the start."

"Yes, I know what you mean."

"I'd better get up and see about my breakfast duties. I'll need your shoulder, but I'll do the rest."

"Marianne said they would deliver something for breakfast to the door."

When they opened the front door, cool air entered. Light rain was falling. There was a bag of croissants tucked beside the door.

"Luckily they covered them," said Joseph. "Shame it's raining. But I think breakfast will be perfect."

The small town hall was two hundred metres from the bakery, opposite the cemetery. The rain had stopped by the time they arrived.

Amongst the group of people waiting, Isabeau spotted Marie-Claire, who she remembered from the engagement party. When Marie-Claire saw her, she waved at Isabeau and Joseph to come over. Isabeau felt a little tight in the chest and tight in her dress. She pulled the back down and smoothed the sides as they crossed the road. She wanted to look in the mirror again to check her make-up. It had looked easy when Marianne had shown her, but today she felt as if she hadn't got it quite right.

"Isabeau, your dress is fine," Joseph whispered beside her. "You look great."

"I –"

"Beautiful."

Isabeau slowed her steps and squeezed her clutch bag. Earlier in the morning, when she'd come out of the bathroom, Joseph had wolf whistled, saying "I hope I scrub up as well as you." His eyes had moved over her body in a way that made her feel slightly uncomfortable and happy at the same time. When he was ready, in his white shirt and dark trousers, the left leg neatly folded underneath, she was almost too scared to look at him.

"Good to see you, Isabeau," said Marie-Claire, and then she introduced them to her boyfriend, Benjamin. Isabeau felt good to have someone to introduce in return. It was good to have Joseph by her side.

"Véronique is helping Marianne," said Marie-Claire. "It was getting a bit crowded, so we decided to come around here. They shouldn't be much longer. Hey, here they come now."

Marianne and François appeared around the corner of the cemetery, followed by their parents and family members. Pierrot was walking beside Véronique, Marianne's witness. Everyone clapped and whistled as the group approached. Marianne and François were smiling. They were a handsome couple, and today happiness made them even more beautiful. Marianne's dress was perfect: a princess dress in pearl white. The fitting bodice formed the slightest of v shapes, and was capped with a bow on each shoulder. Under the full skirt, Isabeau could just make out satin slippers, like ballet shoes. Marianne had let her hair grow, and it was drawn in at the nape of her neck with some small white roses that set off her dark glossy hair and matched the bouquet of roses she was carrying. François was clipped and shaved, smart in a black suit and a crisp white shirt, which formed a canvas for his silk tie. His buttonhole had a white rose like the ones in Marianne's bouquet.

They waved and headed to the side entrance of the town hall, to climb the stairs to the room where they would be married.

Isabeau glanced at Joseph.

"I'll be fine. It's a glorious day." He gestured to the sky. "No, seriously. I don't mind waiting here. The rain looks like it's going to hold off. You go."

"We men will get acquainted," said Tonton Aimé, walking up beside Joseph and extending his hand. "And I have an umbrella, if need be." He twirled the black umbrella he was carrying. "It's not a very big room up there, and the stairs don't agree with my knees. I'll leave the space for the young ones. Anyway, I'll have a seat right up the front in church." He turned to Isabeau. "Yesterday I wanted to have a chat with your friend," he told her. "I understand now about the correspondence, but you didn't tell me that your resolutions dealt with such faraway places and other languages, which you can obviously speak very well."

"We'd better be quick," said Marie-Claire. She pulled Isabeau's hand, and Benjamin followed them. "Let's go."

"Don't worry, Isabeau," Tonton Aimé assured her, as he stood by Joseph and watched them go. "I learned English at school, sixty years ago!"

"What was that like?" Joseph asked, as soon as Isabeau came back out of the town hall, and they joined in the procession making the short walk to the church.

"Really nice. The deputy mayor, who married them, is some relation of Marianne's father, so she talked about them in a really personal way."

"We don't do this town hall thing in New Zealand. Most people get married in church."

"Who does the civil part then?"

"The priest or minister marries you both legally and religiously. It's all done at once. You can go to the registry office to get married if you don't want to get married in a church."

"That sounds less complicated." Isabeau found her steps matching the speed of Joseph's chair. "What did you and Tonton Aimé talk about?"

"I think he wanted to know why I came to France."

"And what did you say?"

"I explained about Drew's race and that my dad had always wanted to come to Carnac."

"Your father?" Isabeau wanted to pull at her dress again. She put her hands behind her back.

"Relax, Isabeau. I remembered what you said and didn't tell him about the ashes. I said we were sort of penfriends."

"Penfriends?"

"Yes, penfriends." Joseph laughed. "He knew the words 'pen' and 'friend' and kept nodding, but I'm not sure how much he understood."

They stopped at the square in front of the church. There was a big crowd, and people were starting to enter. Madame Fournier came over.

"There's a ramp," she said, leading Isabeau and Joseph along the church to a side door at the front. She accompanied them into the church and seated them at the end of the second row.

"We don't want to impose," Isabeau said.

"It's a huge pleasure for us to have you and Joseph at the front with us," said Madame Fournier. She laid her hand on Joseph's shoulder. "Excuse me, it's time to fetch my parents." She walked back down the aisle and returned with her parents and Tonton Aimé. She settled them beside Isabeau and Joseph, then slipped into the front row with Christian and Sophie.

The church filled quickly. The wedding march started, and the talking hushed. Marianne walked in on the arm of her father, followed by François with his mother. When they stopped at the front of the church, they turned to welcome everyone.

Joseph was concentrating on what Marianne and François were saying. Isabeau glanced down at his hand on his knee beside her. She wanted to touch his hand and to look at him the way Marianne looked at François.

The priest gave his welcome and talked about the sacredness of the wedding vows, then the service continued with prayers and communion, interspersed with readings from the Bible and songs. Marianne and François repeated their vows and signed the church register. An hour later, they led the way out of the church, looking more relaxed. They talked and joked with the crowd, and encouraged people to follow the photographer's instructions and come forward for different family group photos on the steps of the church. Isabeau had never imagined there was so much involved in a wedding – and it was only midday.

"Come on everyone: all our friends now," called Marianne.

Marie-Claire, Benjamin and other friends moved forward. Pierrot and Véronique went together.

"Isabeau, Joseph, you too," Marianne said, motioning them over. They went to the edge of the steps, at the other end of the group to where Pierrot was standing. The photographer directed the group to move towards Joseph and Isabeau and to bunch up. Standing behind Joseph, Isabeau smiled, took a deep breath and placed her hands on his shoulders. She pressed a little more. Joseph bent his right arm and laid his fingers on her hand. She didn't dare move.

Everyone headed off on foot again, in a good-natured procession, to the village sports hall, where a room had been set up for the vin d'honneur. Long tables with white tablecloths were covered with glasses of wine and fruit juice, and the outside doors were open. There was a big crowd. Many people from the village, who had been at the church service, were also invited to share in the celebratory drink. Isabeau scanned the room for Pierrot. He and Véronique had stayed together since they'd been at the town hall; now they were talking to a group of people that looked like some of François' cousins and friends. They were near one of the drinks tables. She caught his eye.

"You stay here," she said to Joseph, "I'll go and get our drinks. What would you like?"

"Wine, thanks. Looks like it might be a good one."

Isabeau made her way through the crowd to the drinks table near where Pierrot was standing.

He turned towards her. "So, here we are," he said.

"I haven't had the opportunity to say hello to you."

"No." Pierrot glanced at Joseph.

"I didn't expect Joseph to still be here." She gave an audible sigh. "There was a change of plans – things out of his control – and he ended up staying while his cousin went off to sail. Marianne insisted I bring him to the wedding."

"I heard. She told me all about it. It looks like he's a good friend. A really good friend."

Isabeau nodded. She didn't know what to say.

"Well, enjoy the wedding," he said, with a half-smile, but his eyes weren't smiling.

"Thanks, you too. I'd better get our drinks." Isabeau picked up two glasses of wine and took her time to make her way back through the crowded room to Joseph. She felt as if she could feel Pierrot's eyes on her. She tried to breathe slowly.

While they sipped their wine, a queue formed in front of Marianne and François: guests lining up to congratulate them, with much kissing and handshaking. Isabeau led Joseph over to join the line. When it was their turn, Marianne bent down to Joseph and said, "I'm really happy that you're here with us, Joseph. You remind me of my brother."

Isabeau and Joseph moved on and took their drinks outside.

"Did Marianne say 'frère' – something about a brother – to me?" Joseph asked Isabeau as soon as they had found a spot on the grass.

"She said you reminded her of her brother."

"I don't think I look anything at all like Christian," said Joseph, a little surprised.

"No, you don't. She must mean her other brother, who was in a car accident. He's dead."

At the restaurant François' cousins welcomed Isabeau and Joseph and led them to their seats at the end of the bridal table, beside Marie-Claire and Benjamin, and Valérie and Hervé and their partners. Down the other end were Christian and Sophie, and the table filled with other cousins and friends. Pierrot and Véronique were seated on each side of the bridal couple's chairs. Turned towards each other, they were deep in conversation. Isabeau breathed a sigh of relief, and then she smiled. A sachet of dragées sat on each plate, creating a colourful display against the white plates and linen.

"They look amazing," said Joseph, following her gaze.

"Thank you. Merci beaucoup."

He picked up the sachet from his plate. "You must be very happy to see your work like this."

"Yes." *Happy.* She really did feel happy.

"I'm really proud of you."

Isabeau smiled at Joseph.

"And I've only known you nine months."

"Nine months? Is it that long?"

"Yes, but it feels like much longer."

The other tables were perpendicular to the bridal table. At the middle one, François and Marianne's parents were seated with the grandparents and other aunts and uncles. Tonton Aimé gave Isabeau a wave. François and Marianne entered, greeted by applause and whistling. Soon after, waitresses served the entrée of melon with Parma ham, and everyone settled down to eat. The large room was filled with chatter. When the course was finished and the plates were being cleared away, a group of Marianne's aunts and uncles, each with a piece of paper in their hand, got up from their seats and went to the end of the restaurant, where a microphone had been set up. They stood in a semicircle around the oldest aunt, who spoke.

"We've watched François and Marianne's romance grow," she said, "and I've written a special song in their honour."

"What's happening?" Joseph asked, struggling to follow the French.

"I'm not sure," answered Isabeau. "She says she has a special song for the newly-weds."

The tune was familiar to Isabeau, although she couldn't think of the name of the song. Joseph nodded in a way that showed he knew it too. There were many laughs as the aunts and uncles sang through their comic rendition of François and Marianne's courtship. At the chorus, they encouraged everyone to join in, singing "François aime Marianne, Marianne aime François." Joseph was carried along too and sang enthusiastically. Everyone at their end of the table gave him the thumbs-up as the song finished, to clapping and feet stamping. Marianne's father raised his glass and sang a toast to the aunt. The family joined in, and suddenly many of the men were hurrying over to the aunt and forming a line to embrace her, one by one. Joseph turned to Isabeau.

"What's that all about?"

"I have no idea. I've never seen anything like this." Isabeau felt like a foreigner, like Joseph. Marie-Claire and Benjamin looked similarly surprised.

"The Fournier weddings are always like this," Valérie explained to them. She spoke slowly so that Joseph could follow what she was saying. "If it's a woman who's performed, then all the men have to go and kiss her. If it's a man, then all the women go. The last person to kiss the person who's performed has to sing something themselves. That's why there's a rush. It's a bit of a joke, but you two had better go," she said, turning to Joseph and Benjamin.

Marie-Claire gave Benjamin a nudge.

François and Christian came past and gestured to Joseph, waiting for him to wheel out from the table, and they all headed off with Benjamin and Hervé to join the queue. There was some good-humoured jostling as Tonton Aimé and another older man, who Valérie explained was Tonton Albert, let the younger men go in front of them.

When they came back, the waitresses were serving the main course. Everyone settled down to enjoy the brochet au beurre blanc. Hervé spoke across the table to Joseph.

"Hey Joseph, sounds like you can sing," he said. "I don't think it would be a problem if you were last in line. You should go after me next time."

"Sing?" repeated Joseph with a bewildered look on his face.

Hervé slowly repeated what he'd said.

"My job – singing is my job," Joseph said, in simple French, and he mimed holding a microphone and singing.

"You'll have to sing something," replied Marie-Claire, pointing towards the set up microphone.

"Peut-être, perhaps," replied Joseph, which was met with loud laughing and whistling from their end of the table.

Tonton Albert stood up and moved slowly over to the microphone. He was almost as round as he was high, and his braces were thin stripes over his beach-ball body. He introduced himself and then began to recount the first time he'd met François at the bakery, when François had dropped the tray of fruit tartlets he had been carrying. Tonton Albert shook with laughter as he spoke and wove so many details into the story that it was impossible to know what was true and what he'd made up. Everybody was laughing so hard they were crying.

When he had finished, an aunt raised her glass to sing a toast. Next minute it started again: the scraping of chairs. This time, women were heading towards Tonton Albert. "There's no way I'm singing," said Marie-Claire, pushing her chair back. She grabbed Isabeau's hand and they rushed to join the queue in front of Tonton Albert, who wiped the sweat off his bright red cheeks between kisses.

Next, François' niece and nephew, Elodie and Nicolas, took the stage. Charlotte, their mother, pulled out a little table from the side and stood them on it, and they sang a song they'd learned at school. Then Christian took the microphone. Playing the flute, he was joined by François' cousin, Xavier, on the violin, and they performed three short pieces of Mozart. As soon as they were finished, two aunts helped an elderly great-aunt to the microphone. They stood by her side while she dedicated a song to Marianne and François, singing softly in perfect tune. The room was hushed as she sang, and the waitresses waited at the side to clear away the dishes. After the last frail note, everyone erupted into applause.

Once again, Marianne's father sang a toast, and this time an orderly line of men formed in front of the great-aunt to gently kiss her. Hervé stood up and motioned to Joseph. "Come on, we'd better get in before we're last – or perhaps you want to sing?"

"Would you like to sing?" Isabeau asked him.

"Peut-être," he said with a shrug and headed off with Hervé.

Isabeau watched them join the end of the line and saw Joseph let Hervé go in front of him. The cheese platters arrived, and the waiters refilled the bread baskets with pieces of baguette and slices of round country loaves, and brought new bottles of red wine. Hervé and Joseph returned to the table, laughing.

"Good wine, good wine," said Hervé with his broken English, pointing to one of the bottles of wine. "Good for singing!"

After dessert, everyone relaxed as they waited for coffee.

"Well, I guess it's now or never," said Joseph.

"You're really going to sing?"

"Peut-être." Joseph winked at Isabeau and left the table.

Isabeau's eyes followed him around the restaurant. She felt nervous for him. He stopped at the microphone. Christian went over to him, and they had a short conversation, then Christian helped Joseph to lower the microphone. Hervé called out "Allez Joseph!" and started clapping. Joseph pulled out his harmonica from his pocket.

"C'est pour Marianne et François," he said.

He raised the harmonica to his lips and started to play. "L'Hymne à l'amour". Everyone began to clap, and as they stopped Joseph's voice picked up from the harmonica, singing with almost perfect pronunciation and diction. Xavier joined Joseph, playing the melody with his violin. Joseph's eyes met Isabeau's, and she couldn't look away. The song ended, and Xavier turned and applauded Joseph. Everyone went wild, clapping and stamping their feet, chanting "une autre, une autre". Xavier and Joseph talked briefly, while the applause stopped in one last ripple. Isabeau tried to calm herself.

This time the violin and harmonica started together, tentatively at first, until they were in unison with each note of "Ne me quitte pas". Then Joseph started singing again. There was a hush of surprise and then audible whispers around the room.

When they finished, Xavier embraced Joseph amidst the clapping and wolf whistles, and Marianne and François came over to thank them both. As Monsieur Fournier started the toast, women grouped around Joseph. Marie-Claire stood up, and Isabeau followed her. Everyone around her was patting her arm and complimenting her on "son copain", her boyfriend. Marianne hugged her. "That was incredible, Isabeau." Isabeau's throat was tight, and the tightness was descending towards her chest. She didn't know if it hurt or she was happy. Her hands were sweaty, and suddenly she couldn't move her feet. Marie-Claire nudged her forward, saying "Let Isabeau through. Did you see how he sang for her?"

"It was for Marianne and François," said Isabeau.

"Sure, but he only had eyes for you!"

Isabeau was suddenly at the front of the line. She brushed Joseph's cheeks with a quick kiss.

"Hey, that's no way to kiss your boyfriend. C'mon – a real kiss," said someone behind her, pushing her back towards Joseph.

"Allez!" called the group of women around Isabeau, laughing and joking.

Joseph was smiling, looking right at Isabeau, as if there was no one else in the room. Isabeau bent down again and kissed him on the lips. She felt his lips press back. She didn't move. When she pulled away and stood up, her cheeks were burning.

She was too hot. She needed to go outside, get some fresh air. But Marie-Claire had taken her arm and was walking back to the table with her. Xavier accompanied Joseph back to their table too, and Isabeau was grateful that he stayed to chat with him. They talked in a mixture of English and French, while her racing heart slowed. She could feel

Pierrot looking at her. She avoided his gaze, pretending to follow Joseph and Xavier's conversation. After ten minutes, Xavier patted Joseph on the shoulder and stepped over to talk to François.

"You brought your harmonica to the wedding?" said Isabeau.

"Yeah, I like to have it in my pocket."

"That was beautiful – the song," Isabeau stammered. "I didn't mean to ... everyone was egging me on."

"It's okay." Joseph turned more towards her. His face was flushed, and he was smiling. "It was –"

Before Joseph could finish, Tonton Aimé had come over and was squeezing his hand and embracing him, repeating "magnifique, merci". He looked at Isabeau.

"What a talented penfriend you have."

"Oui."

The children had tied balloons to Joseph's chair. Elodie was on his knee, laughing as Joseph circled back and forward to the music, while Nicolas and Cédric ran around them, squealing with delight. Joseph was laughing too.

Isabeau watched the children. She envied them. Another four days and Joseph would be leaving. She felt an ache in her chest. She thought about the ashes. She kicked the leg of the table under the cloth and picked up Joseph's glass of wine. He'd hardly drunk any of it. She sipped the contents. At the end of the song the children ran off to their parents. Joseph rolled over towards Isabeau. His smile was still dancing.

"Helping me finish my glass. Thanks."

"Sorry, I'm a little thirsty and it's muggy." Isabeau fanned her face with her other hand.

"I haven't had this much fun for a long time," he said. "But you look pensive all of a sudden."

"Do I?"

"A little sad," he added. "I think you need to dance."

"I was thinking about how quickly the holidays are going."

"The wedding's not over yet. The night is young, as they say. You haven't even danced. You can't come to a wedding and not dance. Come on." Joseph held out his hand.

"Thanks, but I'm not really good at dancing."

Joseph looked down at his chair.

"It's not the chair. I've never really danced much."

"You love music. Please, I'd really like to dance with you."

Marianne came over.

"Hey Isabeau, I haven't seen you on the dance floor yet. Come on."

"I'm not a good dancer."

"No excuses," she laughed, and she whispered in Isabeau's ear. "Go on, take your chance."

The word *chance* rang in Isabeau's ears. *Chance, chance ... change*. She held out her hand and, before she could withdraw it, Joseph's warm fingers tightened over hers.

"I used to love to dance," he said, "but this is the first time since I've been in my chair. I think that makes us even."

The tempo of the music increased, and everyone started to move. Marianne grabbed Isabeau's other hand and followed François to the centre of the dance floor. Marie-Claire and Benjamin joined them, arms and bodies moving to the beat, and then Pierrot and Véronique advanced to the circle they'd formed. Joseph was beside Isabeau. She closed her eyes and concentrated on the rhythm.

The song finished and the lights dimmed. The band played softly. "Time for something romantic for the newly-weds," the vocalist announced. François took Marianne in his arms. They were barely moving, their eyes closed and their arms wrapped around each other. Soon the floor was full of slow-moving couples, glued together by love and the mellow music of "Laisse-moi t'aimer".

Joseph put his hands around Isabeau's waist and coaxed her closer, onto his knee. Through the fine material of the dress it was as if his hands were on her bare skin. Marianne turned her head, opened her eyes and winked at Isabeau. *Chance, change, chance, change.* They were hidden in the middle of the dance floor, and she could feel Joseph's breath on her cheek. He shifted, and her head nestled on his shoulder. The skin on his neck was warm and smelled of the wide open beach and the shells they'd gathered, the sun and a hint of sweet Anjou wine. He put his arm around her waist and with his other hand gently moved the chair back and forth, turning slightly. She closed her eyes and let herself relax. When the final refrain died away she realized that he was taking them outside; they were descending a ramp. The air was fresh and the music distant as the band started into a faster song. She could hear Joseph's heartbeat. She opened her eyes. They were on the terrace.

"I almost fell asleep." She moved to stand up.

"Stay close," said Joseph, putting both arms around her waist.

"I don't know about this." Isabeau couldn't look away from his eyes.

"In bed last night I couldn't stop thinking about kissing you," he continued. "But part of you keeps your distance. Sometimes, it's easy to read you, but then it's as if a curtain comes down and you're far away, somewhere I can't get access to. And I don't think it's because I'm in a wheelchair. You look sad again. What is it?"

"Nothing ... you're leaving Wednesday. You're going. There's so much left to say."

"Don't say any more."

He kissed her.

Isabeau relaxed and lost herself in the kiss, soft and slow. She didn't hold back. No pretence: just her as she was and the present moment. Nothing else.

She pulled away, breathless. He would know that she hadn't been honest all that time. Even worse, he would know that she loved him.

There were footsteps, voices.

"Oh, didn't know you were here," said Marianne, grinning.

"We wanted some fresh air," added François.

Isabeau stood up quickly.

"Il fait chaud," Joseph said, pointing inside.

"Yes, it is hot. It's nice out here, but I guess we'd better not neglect our guests," called Marianne over her shoulder, as she took François' hand and they returned inside.

"We'd better get back. I'm sorry, I don't know about this," Isabeau stammered.

"Isabeau, we've only just got here," said Joseph, taking her hands and not letting go.

"Here, on the terrace?"

"No, this kiss."

"Yes, but you're going."

"You make it sound like the end – when we're only beginning. I'll be back for the festival next summer. We can keep writing. I'll phone." Joseph touched her cheek.

"A lot can happen in a year, and it's not certain you will come back for the festival. Perhaps it won't eventuate."

"Isabeau, I don't need the festival to come back. I would come back to see you," Joseph said, standing up.

"You may have intentions, but people leave and don't always come back. And there are so many things unfinished: things to be said, things between us."

"What do you mean between us? There's nothing. Don't create a barrier."

"I'm not creating anything. It's already there."

"It's okay, Isabeau, calm down. Come here," he said, taking her hand. "You're right. There are things I want to tell you, to share with you, that I haven't dared say."

Things *Joseph* hadn't dared say. Everything was so wrong. Isabeau pulled away and ran. She found herself in the car park. She opened the door of her car and collapsed on the steering wheel. She couldn't stop the sob that rose up.

She didn't know how long she'd been there when Marianne tapped on the window and opened the car door.

"What happened? I think Joseph's worried about you."

"I'm sorry." Isabeau started to cry again. "Your engagement weekend and now this."

"It doesn't matter. Is it because we interrupted?" asked Marianne. "You looked so happy together."

"It's nothing to do with that."

"What is it, then?"

"He leaves on Wednesday. He's going."

"Yes, but by the way he looks at you, I'm sure he'll be back," said Marianne in her calm voice. "All the more reason to make the most of him while he's here. Come on," she said, not giving Isabeau the opportunity to answer. She put her arm around Isabeau's shoulders and eased her out of the car, walking her slowly back across the car park.

Isabeau's eyes were sore, bloodshot, no doubt. How could she face Joseph? What had he and Marianne been saying? She didn't have time to think about it. Joseph was coming towards her, and he joined her and Marianne as they walked back. Marianne kept her arm firmly around Isabeau's shoulders.

They stopped at the doorway, and before any of them could speak, Tonton Aimé appeared and grabbed Isabeau's hands. He led her towards the dance floor. The music was loud and the disco lights were flashing. "My turn for a dance," he shouted in Isabeau's ear. "I've given up waiting for a waltz; it's going to have to be one of these modern numbers. Since I've stopped smoking I feel like a spring chicken."

Isabeau was suddenly surrounded by bouncing bodies. Tonton Aimé was shaking and waving his arms as if he was scaring birds off a cherry tree. Isabeau started to giggle. She couldn't stop, and she started imitating Tonton Aimé's movements. She wanted the beat of the music to take over. Joseph, Marianne and François gathered around them; now they were all laughing and dancing like Tonton Aimé. When the music stopped, she was breathless, empty, exhausted.

"Maybe one dance is enough," said Tonton Aimé, offering his arm to

Isabeau and leading her back to their table.

Joseph and Marianne followed. Tonton Aimé pulled up a chair and sat himself down between Isabeau and Joseph. "Tell me, young man, how come you've come all this way to sing to Isabeau?" He pretended to sing.

Isabeau held her breath waiting for Joseph's answer.

"You sing for Isabeau, for her," Tonton Aimé repeated, pointing to Isabeau.

"It's a long story. And I've come a long, long way, but it's worth it," said Joseph.

Isabeau translated, and Tonton Aimé smiled.

Isabeau could hear her heartbeat loud in her body. The spare pillow was still between them, but Joseph was close in the bed.

"I haven't had a night this late for a long time. What a day," he said softly.

"I'm sorry," Isabeau whispered.

"What?"

"I spoiled the evening."

"Don't be sorry. I had the most amazing time today. Merci."

Isabeau pushed down into her pillow and tried to make herself small, like she had done when she was a child and wanted to disappear – except this time she wasn't scared about something bad. Joseph reached across and touched her arm. Silently, her hand took his. She couldn't help herself; she turned towards him. He pushed aside the pillow between them, brought her hand to his cheek and held it there. Then he removed his hand from hers and placed it on Isabeau's face. Her fingers stroked a feather caress on the stubble on his cheek, and his hand repeated the movement on her face.

"Do you want to play the mirror game?" he asked.

"The mirror game?"

"My hand will follow your hand. Only go where yours goes."

Isabeau gave the slightest nod. Her hand skimmed Joseph's lips and he kissed her fingers, as his hand copied hers. She traced along his shoulder, down his arm, hand and fingers and back up. Joseph took the same path. Their hands moved slowly in rhythm, a silent journey over each other's bodies, never leaving the skin, as if they were attached. Each of Isabeau's movements was hesitant, but she didn't stop. She didn't want to break the spell or the touch of his hand on her body. She didn't look away from his eyes, and for the first time she saw the colour blue in them, dissolved in the grey.

Isabeau caressed below Joseph's throat, staying high on his chest. She wanted his hand to go lower, gently, to feel what it was like, but she didn't dare. She placed her hand above his heart and felt the warmth of his hand in exactly the same place. Then she followed down Joseph's side and leg as far as his knee. He wasn't wearing a sock. She stopped.

He swallowed. She wanted her hand to say what was so hard to put into words. How she loved that part of him as much – maybe more – and she knew what it was like to be broken, at least on the inside. It was as if Joseph was somehow also touching that part of her, drawing it to the surface, taming her while his eyes told her not to be afraid.

Isabeau's hand felt safe resting on Joseph's hip, under the material of his t-shirt on the solid bone. His hand, nestled on her hip in the curve of her waist, awakened a craving, a curiosity in her. Joseph tilted his head to one side, waiting. Her hand traced a curve from his hip across his stomach and back. She felt the hair beneath the soft cotton of his shorts. His breath caught and his eyes flickered, and suddenly she was aware of her own breathing. It had been slow and calm, until then. What would it be like to slip her hand under the elastic band of his shorts, or slide it up the inside of his thigh?

She traced up his torso and burrowed into his armpit. Joseph squirmed. He was more ticklish than she had expected. Soon, they were giggling, thrashing around using both their hands, their bodies moving closer together. Then it happened. Joseph's hand brushed her breast and they were half laughing, kissing, pressing against each other, their bodies touching in all the places Isabeau's hand had been too shy to go.

60

From twelve o'clock cars arrived at the lodge, and Marianne and François' close friends and family gathered in the dining room and covered courtyard, around the trestle tables that had been set up with the barbecues. The meadow was too wet for the planned picnic, and it looked like there would be more showers during the day. But nobody cared about the rain. Isabeau helped Marianne and Marie-Claire carry containers of potato salad and taboulé, and bread and cheese from the bakery van. Christian lit the barbecues, and Monsieur Fournier opened bottles of wine for the apéritif.

They had only spent a day with these people, and some of them Isabeau hadn't even really spoken to, but they all called her and Joseph by their first names, the way you greet an old friend. They mimicked Joseph singing, and clapped and patted him on the back, and complimented Isabeau on the sachets. Tonton Aimé called Joseph "penfriend". So much had changed in the space of a day and a night.

Isabeau and Joseph sat outside in the courtyard, where there was more room around the table. Joseph took her hand and held it on his knee. She tried to talk and smile, as if nothing had happened in the past twenty-four hours. As if Joseph wasn't the first to take her hand and hold it on his knee in front of so many people. As if the axis on which her world turned hadn't shifted. All the time she couldn't stop thinking about the night before: about Joseph's hand elsewhere on her body, kissing, feeling his body – all of it – against hers. And how she'd fallen asleep with her head on his shoulder. And then there had been more kissing in the morning when they'd woken up. Everything was getting out of control. She didn't know how to stop what was happening between her and Joseph, and she wasn't sure any more that she wanted to. What would happen in the evening when they got home?

They took their time over lunch. Monsieur Fournier and Christian cooked the meat, and plates of merguez and steaks were passed around. Marianne went from group to group, talking to everyone. Isabeau watched out of the corner of her eye as she sat down beside Véronique and Pierrot. The two of them had spent most of the evening dancing together. Isabeau crossed her fingers and made a silent wish that they were getting on well and that Pierrot really liked Véronique.

At five o'clock everyone pitched in to clean up. All too soon it was time to drive back to Carnac.

"Come again to see us. We'd really like that," Marianne's mother said to Joseph. They knew of his hopes to come back for the festival. They all wished him bon voyage, and Marianne promised to ring Isabeau as soon as she returned to Carnac, at the beginning of September, after their long honeymoon.

Isabeau and Joseph were both tired after the drive home. They lingered after dinner at the kitchen table, talking about the wedding while darkness slowly descended outside. Isabeau's eyelids were heavy, but she didn't want to move. If they just stayed a little longer, she might be able to talk about the ashes, she thought. If only she could just curl up in bed, lying against Joseph, and let the words tell themselves, in a way that didn't shatter the magic of the weekend.

"You look as if you've had it," said Joseph. "I need to get to bed too. Thanks again for the great weekend. I had an amazing time." He came around the table to her. "Goodnight."

Before Isabeau could say anything, he took her face in his hands and leaned in towards her. His lips were warm and tasted faintly of the barbecue lunch and wine. Then his hands were in her hair, and she opened her mouth fully and she was kissing him back and putting her hands around his neck. When they finally paused and pulled slightly apart, their foreheads still touching, she could feel his breath on her cheeks.

"I guess it's back to our own quarters tonight," Joseph whispered.

"I guess it is," Isabeau said, ignoring the questioning tone in his voice. She forced herself to stand up. "Thank you, for an unforgettable weekend. Goodnight."

Isabeau felt an inevitability as she and Joseph went about their routine; each gesture and word was now one of a limited number, and had added meaning because of it. Only two more days. The sense of waiting was heightened by the fact that they were expecting a phone call from Drew. The following day would be busy with his return and with preparing for their departure.

Joseph told Isabeau that he wanted to spend some time alone at the stones, to say goodbye to his father. They decided to head off after an early lunch – Joseph to the stones and Isabeau to her house.

An idea was growing in her, taking strength from her conscience. She would take George with her, so that he could be close when Joseph said goodbye to him. She had to do something. And maybe, just maybe, an opportunity would somehow present itself, and she would find the courage to tell him. It was crazy, desperate, but she didn't know what else to do.

Drew phoned at lunchtime. Lucy and Matt were dropping him back in the morning, he said, on their way to Normandy to catch the ferry to England. Isabeau offered to have them all for lunch, in spite of Drew's protests that it would be too much trouble. As soon as she got off the phone she wished she hadn't offered.

Isabeau wrapped George in a scarf and packed him in the bottom of her bag with a journal and pen, then added an extra jumper on top. Joseph was already waiting for her beside the car. He asked her to drop him off in the car park at the Giant of Manio.

She drove as slowly as she could, but still it only took a few minutes to drive there. Joseph told her he would make his own way back.

"Will you be okay? I don't mind waiting for you," Isabeau offered.

"Thanks, I should be fine. I'm so much stronger now, and it's important I do this on my own. I'll meet you back at your house. I hope that won't be too long for you, though."

Isabeau sat in the car and watched him roll away. Cars were pulling in and out of the car park. Joseph would have plenty of company at the Giant.

Isabeau reversed. There was a loud toot, and she braked. She'd only just missed the car. Her heart was beating fast and tight in her chest. She had to get out of there.

At her house, she walked around inside, running her hands over the smooth new plaster until her heart stopped thumping. It looked so different now. New house. New Isabeau. She needed to be the new Isabeau today. In the living area, Pierrot had stacked some pieces of wood for later use, and his ladder sat in the corner beside two boxes of rubbish. Everything was neat and tidy. She tried to take in the sense of order, let it make her feel more in control over her sense of panic. She went and sat on the front step, pulled out the box from the bottom of her bag and covered it with the jumper on her knees.

"Joseph's at the stones, George, saying goodbye to you," she told him. "He's not far. He's here with you. Drew comes back tomorrow, and then they take the early train to Paris the next day. I have to do something today or tomorrow." She sat silently for a few moments, staring at the little box in the scarf. "Well, say something, won't you?" Silence. She carefully rearranged the scarf until she could see a little of the wood.

There was still no answer. No words in her head.

She leaned back against the door frame, drew her knees up and hugged the box. She was tired of complications and tired of not being able to do this. She closed her eyes.

When she woke, it took her a few seconds to realize where she was. Her neck was sore. How long had she been asleep? Then she saw Joseph coming along the road.

It could almost have been a dream. A bad dream. He waved and called her name. Why was he already back? What time was it? Merde! Shit! Isabeau gave a quick wave and headed inside. Then she realized that her bag was on the front step. She dropped her jumper and stuffed George under some rags in one of Pierrot's boxes in the corner.

"Isabeau, are you okay?" called Joseph.

"Yes, yes," Isabeau stammered, returning to the doorstep.

"Are you sure?"

"I fell asleep and then I woke up feeling as if I was going to have an asthma attack. I thought I'd left my inhaler on the table here, but it must be at home."

Isabeau put her head in her hands. She couldn't look at Joseph. Now she really might have an asthma attack. He laid his hands on her shoulders.

"You'll be okay. Sometimes we can't control our own bodies. Hey, I know that feeling." Joseph gently massaged her shoulders and started to recount his afternoon, as if he was telling a story to calm a child.

"I had the most amazing time: incredibly peaceful and exhilarating at the same time. At the Giant, I finally said goodbye to Dad. Coming back I felt strength in my arms, like I used to have, and the road didn't seem long. All the time I was talking to Dad in my head. I told him about you and the wedding. I felt that I was at peace with him, and with myself. And then all I could think about was seeing you."

George was in the corner, sitting in a box of rubbish. Isabeau had to say something now. Instead, Joseph spoke again.

"There's someone coming through your gate," he said. "Looks like the neighbours."

"What?"

Docteur and Madame Morel greeted them both with a big smile.

"Bonjour, Isabeau," said Docteur Morel. "We thought we'd come over to say hello. We haven't been around much this month; we've been up to Rennes a few times. You have company, I see." He turned towards Joseph as he spoke, and Madame Morel followed his gaze.

"This is Joseph." Isabeau cleared her throat. "From New Zealand. Joseph – Docteur and Madame Morel, my neighbours."

"Very pleased to meet you, Joseph from New Zealand," said Docteur Morel, taking Joseph's hands in a double-handed grip.

"Why don't you two come over for coffee?" asked Madame Morel when she shook Joseph's hand. "It would be good to speak some English. Haven't had a decent conversation with anyone since we came back from America. You'll have to excuse us if we're a little out of practice."

"That would be nice, thanks." Joseph nodded and smiled at the Morels.

"I haven't quite finished in the house," said Isabeau.

"Why don't you come back later," Madame Morel said. "I have some fresh brioche from the bakery, perfect with a coffee. And that reminds me. Your friend Marianne from the bakery – how did the wedding go? It must have been this weekend."

"It was beautiful," said Isabeau.

"An amazing experience," added Joseph. "I've never been to anything like it."

"Well, come and you can tell us all about it over coffee," Docteur Morel gestured for Joseph to go before him.

In the Morels' house, they settled around the kitchen table. When they had finished talking about the wedding, the Morels were curious about Joseph and what he'd been doing since he'd been in France.

"I'm pleased to hear that you've been making the most of the holidays and your friend's stay to get out and about, Isabeau. That's great," said Madame Morel, studying Joseph.

Isabeau nodded but was silent. She was thinking about what she would do when they left the Morels' and how she would get Joseph in the car first and then retrieve the ashes.

"You must have known Isabeau for a long time," said Joseph to the Morels.

"Yes," said Madame Morel, "and we are very pleased she's come back to Carnac. What about you, young man? How did you get to know Isabeau? Isabeau, you've kept your friend here a big secret."

Isabeau blushed. Joseph shot a glance at her and shrugged his shoulders.

"It's a long story, but basically I got to know Isabeau through her work. I sent a query to the post office and she answered it. The rest is history, as they say, and here I am. But I'm leaving Wednesday. My time's up already." He glanced at Isabeau again.

"We've seen television documentaries on your country," said Docteur Morel. "It looks very beautiful. It must be very different to Carnac."

"There isn't the history like here," Joseph said. "Especially a place like Carnac. My father was fascinated by this place – its history – and always hoped to visit it. I guess that's what brought me here."

Isabeau felt suddenly faint. She didn't know if it was because she feared Joseph might talk about the ashes or because they were in the rubbish next door.

"Isabeau, are you okay?" asked Docteur Morel.

"We had a big weekend at Marianne's wedding," Joseph said.

"I think it's all catching up with me," Isabeau said. She felt lightheaded and a little nauseous. The feeling passed, and then her chest started to tighten and her breath came out in a wheeze. She tried to take a deeper breath and her chest tightened further, and she felt the feeling of panic rise in her. "My inhaler's at home," was all she could say.

"I think we'd better get you home," said Joseph.

"I'm not sure that Isabeau should be driving," Docteur Morel said to Joseph.

"I'm afraid I can't." Joseph looked down at his own legs.

Isabeau sat staring ahead, concentrating on her breathing, trying to stay calm.

"Why don't I drive you both home in Isabeau's car?" Docteur Morel offered. "I can wait and see that she's okay and then walk back."

"Are you sure?" asked Joseph.

"I think it's probably the easiest solution."

"It's not too far?"

"I sometimes walk into town, but I've been a bit lazy lately. The exercise will do me the world of good. Anyway, I think we'd better get going."

Isabeau heard the conversation around her. She couldn't think. She couldn't move. She wanted her inhaler. How had she left it at home? She just nodded when Docteur Morel said they'd take her home. Before she knew it, they were leading her out to the car, and Joseph was attaching his chair and getting in.

At home, her inhaler was sitting on the sideboard. She dropped her bag there and it slumped without the weight and bulk of the box. She had let Joseph down. Now, she'd also let George down.

Docteur Morel helped her use her inhaler and kept her calm, waited until her breathing had eased. When he finally left, Joseph thanked him profusely and suggested Isabeau go upstairs and have a lie down.

"I'll see what I can rustle up for dinner," he said. "I'll call you when it's ready. I think you need an early night before everyone disembarks tomorrow, and Wednesday's going to be an early start."

Isabeau eased into her bed. Her breathing was better, but inside she felt sick.

There were only a few hours until Drew, Matt and Lucy arrived. Isabeau needed an excuse to go out. She thought about it during breakfast. If she was quick, she could drive up to the house and get George. She suggested to Joseph that a couscous would be a good idea for lunch. It would be easy; she could buy a prepared one. She just needed to pop to the supermarket. Joseph agreed that it sounded like Drew's kind of food. But he insisted on coming with her to do the shopping. In less than an hour they were back from the supermarket, and Isabeau couldn't think of another excuse to go out. Joseph was staying close. She tried to tell herself that it was as if George was at the menhirs, almost like she'd scattered him there, but in her house, still in his box. It didn't work. He was in the rubbish. How could she tell Joseph now?

"What do you want me to do with these?" Joseph held up a bowl of tomatoes.

"Just slice them and scatter some basil over them."

"You French certainly know how to turn something simple into good food."

Joseph was wearing the marinière over his shorts again.

He'd been there almost three weeks, Isabeau suddenly realized, and she didn't have any photos of him.

"Penny for your thoughts, Isabeau," Joseph said.

"I was just thinking, I really should buy a camera. I don't even have a photo of you from the holidays."

"Don't worry, I'll send you some." Joseph made the gesture of taking a photo, then grabbed her hand and pulled her towards his chair. He kissed her. "There's something I want to ask you. Why don't you come out to see me at Christmas? I know it sounds crazy, but I can't stop thinking about showing you around where I live, all the places I love. The house has plenty of room; you'd have your own bedroom. I'll sort out the ticket. It would be my present, in gratitude for all you've done."

"I haven't thought about Christmas yet," she said. "I don't know if I'd have enough leave, or if I could take time off then. It's not an easy time at work, and we're expected to take most of our holidays in July or

August."

There was a toot outside. Isabeau almost jumped. The van pulled in, and Drew appeared at the kitchen door. He hugged Joseph. Matt and Lucy followed, both as newly tanned as Drew, laughing and talking all at the same time. Isabeau watched Joseph and Lucy while she busied herself with preparing the table and apéritif. Then the three newcomers settled around the table, and Isabeau slipped into the seat she'd kept beside Joseph.

"How have things been here?" asked Drew. "Looks like you've had a great time too. You're both looking good."

"Where do I start?" answered Joseph. "I've – I mean, *we've* – done so many things." He turned towards Isabeau. "We've looked around the standing stones many times, of course, been to the beach, to Quiberon and to Nantes, where I met up with Olivier, who organizes the Summer Festival there. And last, but not least, we went to a wedding last weekend."

"You've packed a lot in," Drew said. "Even a wedding! You're starting to make me wish I'd stayed here."

"And to top it all off, Olivier's really interested in my music and wants me to perform next summer at the festival."

"That's great news," said Drew. "Good on you. Who knows where that might lead?"

Lucy and Matt also congratulated Joseph.

"Thanks. It's been an amazing two weeks. We've had a great time." Joseph put his arm around Isabeau's shoulders.

Drew, Matt and Lucy all looked at Isabeau and Joseph.

"Tell us about the race. It sounds like it was great," Isabeau said. She wanted them to stop staring.

Drew launched into a description of the race, the different stages and the conditions at sea. Matt and Lucy joined in, and the three of them were soon reminiscing amongst themselves. Joseph whispered in Isabeau's ear, "Please say you'll come for Christmas." Isabeau didn't reply.

Talk of the race continued during lunch, but as soon as they had finished eating, Matt and Lucy had to leave. They had to get to Normandy for the ferry crossing to England. Isabeau had mixed feelings about seeing them go. Saying goodbye to them brought Joseph and Drew's departure the next day one step closer.

She left Drew and Joseph to catch up while she finished tidying the kitchen. She had to keep busy. She helped Drew bring the other bed back in, and then he and Joseph began to organize their bags. She should have told them she had something to do, she thought. But now it would seem strange if out of the blue she said that she had to go out.

She would pick up George on the way back from the station after dropping them off tomorrow, she decided.

After dinner, Drew insisted on doing the dishes on his own. From the courtyard outside, they could hear him singing away while he washed.

"What do you think about coming to New Zealand at Christmas?" Joseph asked her again.

"Your offer's very kind," she said. "But there's the problem of holidays. I couldn't have long. And I don't think I could have you pay for my ticket." She stumbled through her words. It wasn't what she'd wanted to say, but it was too late.

"It would be a present for me if you'd come."

"I have to –"

Drew appeared from the kitchen.

"Dishes are finished," he said. "I think I'll turn in now. It's going to be a long day tomorrow, with an early start. Goodnight, Isabeau. Don't forget to set your alarm for five." He headed back inside.

"I know it's not easy at that time of the year in your job," said Joseph.

"I'll have to think about it." It was too late to say anything else.

"Sleep on it," he said. "We'd better turn in too."

He kissed Isabeau slowly, as if he also wanted time to stop.

The alarm clock rang. Isabeau had lain awake most of the night, worrying about George, dreading the departure, the regrets eating away at her sleep. She forced herself to get up and get dressed.

Joseph and Drew were moving around downstairs. Suddenly, she heard Joseph's voice rise in a strange intonation.

She came down the stairs. Drew was putting their bags beside the door.

"Bonjour," he said, in the most serious tone Isabeau had ever heard him use. "Joseph needs to talk to you, but we haven't got much time. We can't afford to miss the train."

Joseph's face was tense. "I'm sorry to bother you with this, Isabeau, but where did you say you scattered my father's ashes?"

She felt herself go pale.

"At the Giant. I told you all about it the first day we went there. Why are you asking me this now?"

"You did tell me, but it all seems a bit vague now. And I haven't liked to ask, but you never said what you did with the box."

"Well, I –"

"These papers fell out of one of your journals," he said. "I wasn't meaning to pry or read anything; I was just slipping in a little note for you." He held up the sheets containing her scribbled lists of intentions to scatter George.

She put her hand out to steady herself against the table.

"Have you really done it?"

"What do you mean?"

"Have you really scattered my father's ashes? Yes or no?"

Isabeau bowed her head.

"Have you?"

"No."

"Why didn't you do it? Why didn't you tell me? Where are my father's ashes, then?" Joseph's voice rose with each question.

"I didn't mean to. I mean, I meant to; I honestly did. I went to scatter the ashes and then I couldn't. I meant to go back and do it, so many times, but I couldn't bring myself to. I tried to tell you, several times. I tried, even last night, but it was too late."

"I know it was an unusual request, but you never said it was a problem! You didn't do it." There was anger and disappointment in Joseph's every word. "And then you pretended that you had!"

"I couldn't bring myself to ..." she forced herself to breathe, to speak. "At first it freaked me out to have the ashes in the house, then something happened. It was as if your father wanted to be here with me. I think he talked to me. I kept hearing him. It was as if he wasn't ready to be scattered. I know it sounds crazy. It was as if he was helping me find my father, and –"

"This isn't about your father!" Joseph banged his chair. "It's about mine."

"Look, I'm sure this can be worked out," said Drew. "We don't have much time. We can't miss the train. Or maybe we should change our booking?" He looked from Joseph to Isabeau.

Joseph ignored Drew. "Where are my father's ashes, then?" he asked again.

"They were here before," she said. "But I took them up to my house on Monday, so that they would be with you at the menhirs, even if you didn't know it: so that your father could be with you in some way. Then you surprised me. The ashes are still up there."

Joseph just stared at her for a second.

"What was I thinking when I sent my father's ashes?" he shouted. "I should never have trusted this – trusted you, a *stranger* on the other side of the world. I should have waited and done it myself. I was too impatient with this bloody accident."

"Look, I know there's not much time, but maybe it's not too late." Drew's brow creased into a frown. "It's 5.20, and our things are ready. It takes about twenty minutes to get to the station at Auray, doesn't it, Isabeau?"

"Yes," Isabeau answered automatically.

"We could get Dad on the way to the station, scatter him before we leave. We have to get him. Or maybe I should just take him home again!" Joseph glared at Isabeau. He gulped down the rest of his bowl of coffee and pushed away his half-eaten piece of baguette. He headed off to the alcove, his face set and jaw clenched.

"You should eat something," said Drew, pulling out a seat for Isabeau, "while we put our things in the car.

She wasn't hungry, but she let Drew sit her down. Tears welled in her eyes.

"This is all going to be okay when Joseph calms down," Drew tried to reassure her. "And if the worst comes to the worst, we could try to postpone our flights for a day or two. You could help us sort that out, and the train tickets."

"Of course," said Isabeau.

Her hands were shaking, but she drove. She didn't know how she was managing to even breathe. Joseph and Drew kept looking at their watches. They stopped at the house, and Isabeau got out like a robot. She put the key in the door and entered. She saw the empty space. She blinked. The kitchen had been cleared out.

She blinked again, hoping that when she opened her eyes the kitchen would be as she'd left it the other day, with Pierrot's gear in the corner. But when she did so, the ladder, the pieces of wood and the boxes of rubbish were still gone. She wasn't imagining it. Everything was gone. The floor was bare.

She walked around the room. She rushed upstairs, hoping that Pierrot's gear was somehow up there, but the bedrooms were empty too. Outside in the shed there was nothing of his. She rushed inside again, in the mad hope that she had somehow missed them – the boxes would somehow be somewhere in the house.

"What is it?" asked Drew, coming through the door.

"It's gone. The box where I put George's ashes. Pierrot must have come early, yesterday, to take his stuff away. I don't understand. He said he was going to continue working on the house until the end of the month."

"Breathe slowly," said Drew. "Where exactly did you put the ashes?"

"In a box of ... rubbish in the corner, when Joseph surprised me the other day. There was also a ladder and some pieces of wood. He must have come and taken it all away." She wrung her hands. "What's Joseph going to say?"

"I'll deal with him," said Drew. "I'll be back in a minute."

Isabeau closed her eyes. Joseph and Drew's voices swept over her in waves.

" ... delay our departure for a day or two ... Isabeau's in a state about this. Can't you see how she is?"

"I trusted her ... the sooner we get out of here ..." Joseph started to swear.

She wanted to cover her ears and block out everything. She couldn't open her eyes. She couldn't get enough air into her lungs.

She realized Drew was shaking her gently by the shoulders.

"Isabeau, have you got your inhaler?"

She motioned to the car. Drew came back with her bag. She put her inhaler to her lips and sucked in everything: air, hurt, tears, Joseph's stormy eyes looking at her, his voice raised in anger. Drew waited until her breathing quietened.

"We'd better keep moving to the station," he said. "I'll talk to Joseph in the car. I can drive."

In the car, Joseph stared ahead. Drew talked, trying to convince him to delay their departure, but no matter what he said Joseph would not listen.

At the station, Drew went off to get a trolley, then hurried back to organize the bags. They only just had enough time. On the platform, the ticket inspector came over to them. Drew showed him their tickets, and the inspector nodded and pointed to the yellow machine that would validate them. He mimed putting the tickets in to be punched.

Joseph sat motionless. The train was arriving in two minutes. The ticket inspector took them to the part of the platform where the first-class carriage would stop, repeating "I will help you." Isabeau followed, a spectator to the unfolding departure.

Drew looked at Isabeau. "I can't thank you enough for all you've done," he said.

Out of the corner of her eye she saw Joseph flinch.

"I'm sorry."

Drew put his arm around her shoulders and turned her away from Joseph. He talked softly.

"This is going to work out, when he calms down."

"Joseph's right to be angry," she said. "I misled him. His father's ashes. They're lost. Perhaps gone with the rubbish."

"He'll calm down. When I arrived back yesterday, he was looking better than I've seen him in months." Drew hugged Isabeau to him and whispered in her ear. "Take care. I don't know how, but I'm sure it's going to be all right. Find Uncle George, and I'll phone you when we get home."

The train pulled in to the platform.

"I'm sorry, Joseph. I'm really sorry." In her bag, Isabeau's hand squeezed her inhaler until it hurt.

"So am I," he said.

Drew helped Joseph up the steps and then took the bags. When he came back for the chair, he paused beside the carriage door.

"Bye, Isabeau. Take care. It's going to be okay," he called to her.

The doors shut. The guard blew his whistle. Joseph was seated at the window, looking out at her. His eyes were empty. She raised her hand. He didn't move. When the train had disappeared from sight she blew a kiss.

PART IV

In the kitchen, Isabeau stared at Joseph's half-eaten piece of baguette. She still wasn't hungry. All she could think of was Joseph pushing the bread away. Joseph staring at her from the train. Joseph who hated her now, and hadn't even said goodbye.

She fetched the photo of George and Joseph.

"I'm sorry, George. Forgive me. Please be safe. Please can Pierrot not have thrown you away."

She had to ring Pierrot. She thought about looking up his address on the Minitel and driving to his house. But maybe he'd already left on holiday, earlier than planned, annoyed about her and Joseph at the wedding. Was that why he had cleared everything out of the house? It was only 7 a.m., but she picked up the phone and dialled. It rang a long time. She was about to hang up when he answered.

"Allô, Pierrot."

"Isabeau! I wasn't expecting it to be you, especially this early."

"I'm sorry, sorry to bother you."

"I've been up for a while. I was just walking out the door when the phone rang. You're actually lucky you caught me."

"I see you've taken your gear and boxes from the house."

"Yes. I've had a change of plans. I'm heading to Brest. My brother needs a hand; he's had a burst pipe at his apartment. I called in to the house last night – thought it was easier to pick up everything. Is that a problem?"

"No, no, of course not. It's just that by mistake I put something in one of your rubbish boxes."

"They're still sitting in the back of the van. I didn't notice anything though."

"The thing I misplaced is a small wooden box, wrapped in one of my scarves. I need to get it back. It's of sentimental value. It might be under some other things. Would you mind having a look?"

"Now?"

"Please."

"Er, okay. Hold on."

Isabeau rubbed her temples while she waited for Pierrot to come back to the phone.

"You were right. It was under the rags. A little box in a green scarf."

"I could drive over and pick it up," she said.

"Sorry, I can't wait around. I need to get to Brest; I'm already running late. I'm coming back through on Sunday. I could drop it off to you in the afternoon."

"Thanks. I would really appreciate that."

"Are you okay, Isabeau?"

"I've got a really bad headache, that's all."

"Is your New Zealand friend there?"

"He and Drew, his cousin, they ... left ... this morning. I'll be fine. My headache should pass."

"Well, look after yourself."

"Take care of the box, please."

"Will do. See you Sunday."

Isabeau wandered around the house. There was a used shaving cream can in the bathroom rubbish bin and tourist brochures beside Drew's bed. The empty space at the table where Joseph had sat with his wheelchair. There wasn't much else to show that Joseph and Drew had been in the house.

She ran her hand along the journals in the bookcase. One of the ones that she'd been writing in when Joseph had been there was slightly poking out, and caught her eye. She took it out and flicked through the pages. In the middle was a little note.

Isabeau,
Words for you
words for me
say many things.
Songs for you
songs for me
sing many things.
Joseph XXX

In the alcove, Isabeau undressed and got into Joseph's bed. The tension behind her eyes was painful. The tears had been waiting all morning. Now, she couldn't stop them. "Joseph, Joseph, Joseph," she sobbed. Under the pillow her hand felt something hard and smooth, attached to a cord. Joseph's pendant. It was cold when she held it against her cheek. It almost smelled of him, like the sheets. She pulled the duvet and sheet tightly around her and cried while she whispered into his pillow everything she wished she had said.

A dull ache inhabited Isabeau's head, and the tension stretched an uncomfortable band behind her eyes, which made it difficult to focus. She rubbed and rubbed her forehead, but it wouldn't budge. She couldn't clear her vision or her thoughts. She'd spent three days curled up in Joseph's bed. She rubbed the bone pendant, her fingers following the spiral to the centre and back outwards. Always the same movement, which could lead nowhere new. It was like the mess she'd got herself into. She could go nowhere now.

Drew had phoned, but it hadn't made any difference. In his calm voice he'd told her that he and Joseph had arrived home safely, and he'd reassured her several times that everything would be all right. But how could it? Joseph didn't want to speak to her, and Drew said that he refused to talk about the ashes. "He'll come around," he had concluded. "It's been an intense year for him. He needs some time."

Pierrot would be there soon. Isabeau decided to have a shower to make herself feel better, to try and clear her head. But in the shower the shampoo and conditioner bottles went flying and slipped out of her hands when she picked them up. She stamped her feet. She raised her face to the water, and the tears kept coming.

She got dressed and tidied the kitchen. She pulled shut the alcove curtain, cleared the table and piled the dirty dishes in the plastic basin under the sink. She wiped the table. One little task at a time in the mental fog, talking her way through it, as if there was someone else there to guide her.

Getting George back was all that mattered. Hopefully Pierrot wouldn't mention the wedding. She made coffee. The smell of coffee: such a normal thing. If she appeared matter-of-fact it couldn't possibly be someone's ashes in the box.

Pierrot arrived around three o'clock.

"I'm a bit of a delivery man again," he said on the doorstep, as he handed her the box wrapped in the scarf. "It seems like it's very important?"

"Thank you. I really appreciate it," said Isabeau.

"Are you feeling better?"

"I've still got a headache. I'm sorry; it was getting the better of me when I called you the other day. I'll be fine, though." She forced herself to smile as she spoke. "Would you like to come in for a coffee?"

"No, thanks. I'd better get going. My brother's waiting for me. We're going to get our camping gear organized and then head off early tomorrow."

"How long will you be away?"

"We'll be in the Cévennes for a week, then we're heading to Corsica. With our tent we can stop where we want."

"Have a great holiday."

"Thanks." Pierrot looked at his hands. "Marianne and François should be having a great time on their honeymoon. Great wedding, wasn't it? We've had some good weddings in our family, but nothing like that. The music and singing at the breakfast ..." He met her eyes. "Joseph ... well, it seems like you two are ..."

"There's not really anything between us," she said. "And he's gone now."

"Are you sure you're okay, Isabeau?" Pierrot glanced at the box.

"I'm fine, really. I'm sure I'll feel better after a nap."

"I'll be in touch when the holidays are over," he said. "I'm not sure yet how I'll be placed with work, but I should have some time for the bathroom."

"Please don't worry about it. I think I need a break from the renovations for a while. I'd better let you go." She didn't wait for him to answer. "Have a great holiday, and thanks again for the box," she said, and closed the door.

Grubby feet marks covered the bottom of the sheets, and the pillowcase was stained. Isabeau pulled at the duvet, forcing it out through the opening of the cover, and added the cover onto the pile of Drew's bed linen on the floor. She punched the pillow and yanked the top sheet from the bed. Grabbing the fitted sheet, she tugged as hard as she could. The elastic around the corner piece stretched and resisted, and then the seam cracked and ripped. She wanted to rip it all to shreds. She threw it down on the rest of the bedding and stomped on the pile. Finally, she took it all to the washing machine. She jammed the sheets in, clipped the barrel shut, put powder into the dispenser, closed the lid and turned the knob to cotton, ninety degrees. Click, click, click. "You – de – serve – this – you – de – serve – this," she said, and pulled the knob to start the machine.

Today was the first day of the Assumption Day holiday weekend. There had been a lot of rain, but the weather had improved, and it was sweltering hot. It felt strange to step out through the front door after being inside for several days. The sunlight hurt Isabeau's eyes and tightened the band of tension in her head, but she had to finish what she'd started. She stretched the sheets on the line. The washing smelled fresh and good, in the way that bakery smells did, but today this brought her no pleasure. Joseph's scent – the faintest trace – was gone.

The bed linen dried quickly. She laid it on the kitchen table. Even though she worked slowly it was all soon folded flat and smooth, and sitting perfectly in line on the piles in the cupboard. Nothing out of place. Everything as it had been before. The piles were short. You don't need a lot of linen when you live alone. She slammed the cupboard door shut.

In the alcove, she sat on the bare mattress on Joseph's bed. The pendant swung between her hands. She placed it over her head. The bone was cool against her skin. She pressed it against her heart to warm the spiral.

"**C**hocolate éclairs for afternoon tea," said Marianne. "There's nothing quite like a good éclair: my father's favourite, even out of all the fancy pâtisseries he makes." She looked around the kitchen, taking in the mess. "I'll give you a hand with the dishes first."

"You don't need to do the dishes." Isabeau pressed her hand to her chest, checking again that the pendant was inside her shirt.

"They'll be almost done by the time the coffee's ready. You can dry." Marianne threw the tea towel at Isabeau and began to fill the sink. "Nothing like working up an appetite for an éclair." Marianne had that look in her eye that meant you couldn't say no. "Well, how are you? When will you be going back to work?"

"I haven't even asked you about your honeymoon," Isabeau protested.

"I asked first."

"How did you know I was on sick leave?"

"Easy. My first day back and you didn't come in. Then Madame Morel came in. She said that you're on leave and that they've been popping in regularly to see you. And then François saw Pierrot, and even he seemed to know that you weren't well." Marianne stopped washing. "How are you?"

"I have a headache – tension behind my eyes – and it won't budge. I wake up tired. I don't know where I'm going to find the energy to go back to work."

"I used to get these tension headaches from my neck up into my head," said Marianne. "I changed pillows and that helped. And sometimes François gives me a massage. It's divine. There's something about his hands – maybe because he's used to kneading dough. When he's sore from working in the bakery, I do the same for him; I always feel though that I'm getting the better end of the bargain. Here, I'll try it on you." She gestured towards the chair.

"I don't know. I've never had a massage."

"We need to do something about that then." Marianne pulled out the chair and sat Isabeau down. "Close your eyes. Just think how good that coffee and éclair are going to taste."

The coffee did smell good, a hundred times better than when Isabeau made it on her own. She closed her eyes and tried to think of nothing except the smell of the coffee. Marianne eased her back until she rested against her, put a hand on each side of Isabeau's head and held her for a minute. Marianne's hands sat with exactly the right pressure. She started to stroke outwards from between Isabeau's eyes across her forehead and then over her cheeks, and little by little down to her chin and neck. Isabeau started to let go. She felt like a cat who wanted to purr. Marianne worked around the thin leather cord holding Joseph's pendant. *Please don't notice it, please don't say anything,* she silently implored Marianne. *Please can Pierrot not have talked too much about the box.* On Isabeau's shoulders Marianne pressed harder. It hurt, but Isabeau didn't want her to stop. She started to feel pleasantly heavy. Maybe, just maybe, she could sink into the kind of sleep that erased fatigue.

"You don't have to open your eyes straight away. Wait till you're ready," said Marianne as she finished, once again holding Isabeau's head in her hands.

"That felt amazing. Thank you."

"Your shoulders are very tight; no wonder you've got an awful headache. Now you need something to eat and drink." Marianne's eyes flitted around the room to the alcove. "Did Joseph get away okay?"

"Yes."

"Seems like you two had a great time."

"We did. What about your honeymoon? How was it?"

"Fabulous. We stayed in Montpellier, in an apartment close to the beach, and then François surprised me with a week in Collioure, and took me to Spain a couple of times. It's been the most amazing time, with the wedding and this past month away, just the two of us. Seems like a dream." Marianne twirled her rings.

"The wedding was incredible, and your family were so friendly. Joseph couldn't believe how welcoming everyone was."

"When he sang, it was beautiful. Everybody was touched. It was like Thierry was there, in a way," Marianne said.

"Your brother? Did he sing?"

"He was musical, similar to Joseph. And he was in a wheelchair." She sighed.

"You didn't say anything about that."

"When I met Joseph at the bakery, I couldn't stop thinking about Thierry, and I wanted to tell you. Then it was full on and there was never the opportunity, and at the wedding there was so much happening."

"Why was he in a wheelchair?" Isabeau asked.

"The accident," replied Marianne.

"So he wasn't killed in the accident?" Isabeau was confused.

"No, he had the accident when he was nineteen, driving with his girlfriend, Stéphanie. The road was icy. She was killed. I think he felt that his being in a wheelchair was a way to pay for the accident – for what happened to her – but he still never forgave himself." Marianne paused. "He committed suicide three years later. We didn't see it coming. Afterwards, we all felt we'd let him down – that we hadn't helped him enough. We all thought about him at the wedding, not being there. And then Joseph turned up, and it was as if Thierry was there in a way. I know it's stupid."

"Not at all." Isabeau knew how mixed up things could become.

"Anyway, tell me about Joseph and what you two got up to in July. Seemed to be more than you had *planned*." Marianne rolled her eyes. "I might add that you two were not the only surprise at the wedding. Pierrot and Véronique hit it off too. Love was certainly in the air!"

"I'm glad about Pierrot and Véronique." Isabeau finally smiled.

"Turns out she really likes him. I must admit I was thinking that you and Pierrot would be great together. You seemed to be getting on so well. But I don't think you're going to be too disappointed about that now, are you?"

"No." Isabeau shook her head. "I felt bad about not going to the wedding with him and then the way things worked out."

"Especially after that mix-up with the studio unit!"

"Yes, things were going well, but then there was a problem." Isabeau took a deep breath. "It doesn't really matter at all now. It's finished." She wanted Marianne to keep asking questions. It might take some of this weight away. And yet she didn't want her to keep asking questions. She might talk about George. She might cry too much.

"What kind of a problem? Is that why you got upset at the wedding dance?"

"No, it happened the day he left with Drew. There was a misunderstanding."

"Pierrot mentioned something about a box."

"Yes, a box. Joseph gave it to me. It was precious. It meant a lot to his father and to Joseph too, of course. I thought it would look good in my new kitchen up at the house. I don't know how, but it somehow got put into the rubbish." Isabeau bit her lip. She tried to not think about the lie. It was too hard to explain about George, even to Marianne.

"Did Pierrot throw it out?"

"No, no, no, no. I was sorting out and somehow put it in one of Pierrot's boxes."

"If it was just a mistake, Joseph should understand that."

"Maybe. But I don't think it was meant to be." Isabeau couldn't control her voice any more. Her lips tried to articulate what she wanted to say, but the tears were running down her cheeks. Each word came out on the wave of a sob. "He doesn't want to know me any more."

"I can't imagine it's that bad. It's only a box. Love is a powerful thing; it can always find a way. Didn't he say that he was coming back next summer to perform in Nantes?" Marianne put her arms around Isabeau.

"Yes, but it's probably for the best this way," Isabeau cried into Marianne's shoulder.

When Marianne left, she made Isabeau promise that she would call at the bakery the next afternoon, threatening to come and get her if she didn't.

Isabeau put Joseph's cassette on and picked up the tiny note he'd left. She caressed the paper between her fingers and stared at the words. She thought of Marianne's brother. Thierry. Marianne was sad too, yet she was sure of herself and of most things in life. She was able to be happy. What if it was true, what Marianne had said? What if love could find a way to sort this out? A tiny doubt began to creep into Isabeau's unhappiness.

68

The Morels kept calling in, with a lettuce or cucumber from their garden, a jar of green beans that Madame Morel had bottled, homemade tomato sauce that "wasn't quite enough to fill another jar" and fresh butter biscuits, exactly like the ones Madame Morel had made when Isabeau was a child. While Docteur Morel and Isabeau chatted, about topics Isabeau could never afterwards remember, Madame Morel quietly moved about. When they were gone, the bench was always wiped clean, freshly washed dishes were drying in the rack and the kitchen floor was swept. The house felt better.

And Marianne arrived at unexpected times, bringing leftover sandwiches from the bakery. Each time, she gave Isabeau a short massage, and left calling over her shoulder, "I'll see you tomorrow at the bakery." She talked about Christmas and wanted to take Isabeau to Saint-Laurent-de-la-Plaine. Isabeau didn't know if it was a good idea, but it was the only possibility in front of her.

She could have been going to New Zealand for Christmas. Not now.

The band of tension behind her eyes came and went, but it was never far away. Docteur Morel assured her even so that it was best to return to work – it would do her the world of good to be active. At least work was a reason to get up before midday, and a good reason to get angry at something else, rather than her parents or herself or Joseph.

Although the days were shortening, Isabeau started walking again to the cemetery and back to the menhirs. She avoided the house. She didn't want to think about the renovations, and the garden was getting overgrown. It was easier not to go there any more. She walked slowly, touching the pendant as she went, as if it was a bone genie and rubbing it would somehow give her an answer, make things clearer.

She returned to the Giant. It was ages since she had been there. It was All Saints weekend again, more than three months since Joseph had left, and a whole year since George had arrived.

She wondered whether that was why Drew had phoned that morning. She stood in front of the Giant and went back over the conversation in her mind. She wasn't sure what she'd said, how she'd answered his questions. Drew had been his usual cheerful self. His voice had sounded concerned, though – or was she imagining it? Was he worried that Joseph was spending so much time engrossed in writing songs for a new album, or was he pleased? Apparently Joseph wasn't giving anything away, although his inclusion in the festival line-up had been confirmed.

Finally, Drew had brought up the subject of the ashes.

"Joseph refuses to talk about it," he told her. "He's cutting off his nose to spite his face. I'm sure he'll come round, but I think you'd better hold on to them for the time being. This will all sort itself out one way or another, at the latest when he comes back for the festival."

What was she supposed to do? Isabeau stomped around the Giant.

"Cutting off *his* nose to spite *his* face," she said to the stone. "Well, what if I want to play that game too: to cut off *my* nose?" Now she shouted at Joseph himself. "I didn't ask you to send the ashes to a *stranger on the other side of the world*! You had a secret, too. You didn't tell the whole story about your leg! Your absence of leg! What do you say to that?" She sat down at the base of the stone and cried.

69

No more news from Drew. Nothing from Joseph. Nothing from Nantes. "Why should I be surprised?" Isabeau asked George. Should she send a card to Drew? Phone him? What would she say, though? With the time difference, she would have to ring in the early morning or the evening. In the morning, there was never time. In the evening, she was too tired. When she questioned George, all she heard was the sound of her own voice. It was a dead end. Dead like George.

She talked to him in the evening and when she went to the cemetery at lunchtime during the week. The All Saints bouquets wilted and dried up and then disappeared, and the chrysanthemums and cyclamens slowly died. The cemetery became more deserted, quiet again, as everyone's focus shifted to Christmas.

The only thing to look forward to was spending Christmas at Saint-Laurent-de-la-Plaine with Marianne and her family. Isabeau tried to concentrate on that, to get through the weeks one day at a time. Buying presents for Marianne, her parents, François, Christian and Sophie was a welcome distraction. It was a new experience to have so many presents to buy, to have shopping to do. Just like Corinne and her other colleagues. For Marianne, she found a book on Celtic embroidery, and for François two packs of good quality Cholet handkerchiefs. Isabeau remembered Marianne had complained that he always ended up wiping grease on his handkerchiefs when he did maintenance on the bakery oven. She bought wine for Marianne's father, and soap for her mother, taking time to find the right one. She didn't really know Christian and Sophie very well, so she questioned Marianne discreetly about what they were interested in. They loved going to the cinema, she said. Just when Isabeau thought she'd never find anything, she came across mugs decorated with scenes from old films and bought them one each.

Marianne's life was hectic. When Isabeau saw her at the bakery she was always taking orders for Christmas bûches and chocolates. She and François could only get away from the bakery for Christmas Eve and Christmas Day. It was enough for Isabeau.

She wanted to talk to Marianne about Thierry, but there was no time, no space for that. Isabeau couldn't stop thinking about Marianne's brother. It was like a coin. Joseph was on one side, and sometimes the coin fell the other side up and Thierry was there. He and Joseph were connected now. Thierry gave her another link to Joseph: a link that would remain even if she never heard from Joseph again.

But she had to hear from him again, she kept telling herself, because she still had George. Something had to happen.

At work, the volume of mail increased. Isabeau couldn't stop herself from checking her letterbox every time she went past it. Maybe Drew would manage to talk Joseph around, she thought. But her letterbox stayed empty except for the bills.

The little envelope that finally turned up was hidden in amongst them, and she didn't see it at first.

Her excitement was short-lived. No airmail sticker. Round handwriting she'd never seen before. She didn't know whether she wanted to laugh or cry at the irony of it. She'd no longer hoped – almost forgotten – and yet here it was in black and white in front of her. Finally, some information about her father.

Mademoiselle,

I am writing to you concerning Monsieur Paul Martin, who is, I understand, your father. I apologize for the delay in answering your enquiry, but my grandson has only just spoken to me about this matter.

Paul and his wife Ghislaine rented a small apartment on the third floor of our house for two years in the late sixties. They kept very much to themselves but were good tenants. During this time, Paul worked in a bar in the centre of the city, and Ghislaine was a cleaner at the local school. Paul often talked about Brittany and his work on the fishing boats. When they left Nantes, they went to Quiberon.

I forwarded their mail on to a café in Quiberon, La Presqu'île, but I had no further word from them. I have taken the liberty of sending a note to the café with your details, asking for anyone with news of him to contact you.

I regret that I do not have any information concerning your father's present whereabouts and only hope that this may be of some help to you in your search for him.

Yours faithfully,

Huguette Goudeau

Isabeau needed to sit down. Quiberon. So close. Just like Pornic.

70

"Welcome back to Saint-Laurent, Isabeau," Madame Fournier greeted her. "We're all really pleased you could come for Christmas." She wrapped her arms around Isabeau. Behind her, the dining table was covered with trays of chocolates of different sizes and shapes, beautiful shiny boxes, rolls of ribbon and cellophane. Isabeau had never seen so much chocolate.

"Sorry, things are a bit of a mess," said Marianne's mother. "I've just finished the last of the orders to be picked up tonight. The rest will be for New Year. The shop will be closed in an hour, then things will quieten down."

"It's very kind of you to invite me. I'm sorry if I'm inconveniencing you," Isabeau said.

"Not at all, we're very happy to have you. It's always like this at Christmas. Why don't you take your things upstairs?"

Marianne and Isabeau said a quick hello to Monsieur Fournier in the bakery, where Christian, Sophie and François were helping him and the apprentices tidy up, then Isabeau followed Marianne up the open wooden staircase on the back wall of the dining room to the third floor. Marianne showed her around. There was a bathroom on the left, then, opposite the stairway, Marianne's old bedroom, and the next one was Christian's room. She led Isabeau to the last bedroom on the right and left her to get settled in, telling her to come back down when she was ready.

Isabeau sat her bag on the double bed. It was covered with a thick patchwork quilt of blue- and green-patterned materials and a long round bolster pillow that spanned the width of the bed. She ran her hand over the quilt. A lot of stitches and love had gone into it. The colours had faded, as if it had been on the bed forever. She walked around the room. The walls were cream, and the furniture was all dark wood. A square alarm clock sat on the bedside cabinet. This was a man's room. In the wardrobe, several boxes were stacked in the corner, and half a dozen of the hangers held men's clothing: mostly jackets. Isabeau picked up a pen from the pot on the desk. She could have been in Joseph's house for Christmas. Instead, she'd ended up in Thierry's room. She smiled to herself, and a tear ran down her cheek. She wiped her face and sat down on the bed.

When she went back downstairs she helped Marianne clean up the boxes of chocolates and packaging, Marianne apologizing for roping her in to help. But Isabeau was quietly pleased to have something to do and to be part of the activity. Marianne put the last rolls of ribbon away and pulled out an old box of decorations.

"My parents don't have time to do any of this," she said, "so Christian or I normally put them up at the last minute. Hope you don't mind?"

"On the contrary, it's nice to be able to do it with you. Your mother is so welcoming. She really makes me feel at home."

"My parents are happy to have you with us. We all are."

They attached garlands to the chandelier light and stretched tinsel across the top of the sideboard before they started on the little tree in the corner. All the time Isabeau couldn't help looking at the family photos, trying to find Thierry in each one. There was a picture of him when he was a child, running out of the waves, carefree, and a portrait of him in what she imagined would have been his early twenties. He must have been in the wheelchair then. Like Marianne, Thierry was dark-haired, but his hair fell in the same way as Joseph's did, and his face was similarly long. Now, when she looked closely, she saw a little something in his face that reminded her of Joseph too.

"That was one of the last photos taken of Thierry," said Marianne. "I miss him. He always gave us so much pleasure with his singing, like Joseph. You would've liked him." She handed Isabeau a little angel to put on the tree.

"Did he play any musical instruments?"

"The guitar. He was always strumming on it." Marianne looked happy to be talking about her brother. "Christian's musical too. The music gene must've just been on the male side, though, because I didn't get any of it. Thierry started studying architecture, then he gave it up to spend more time on his music. Maybe he would've ended up as a professional singer like Joseph. Who knows?"

Isabeau's free hand pressed on the bone pendant under her roll-neck sweater. Marianne glanced at her hand.

"Sorry. Are you thinking of Joseph? I must admit I can't get him out of my thoughts whenever I think of Thierry. Have you had any news from him for Christmas?"

"Still no news since Drew rang at All Saints. I doubt that he'll get in contact with me now." She put down the garland she was holding.

"Why don't you contact him? You've got nothing to lose."

"It's not that easy."

"Someone has to make the first step. You can't give up. That's part of what love is about: taking a risk."

"It's not like you and François. It's a bit more complicated."

"Things aren't always as complicated as you imagine," Marianne persisted. She sighed. "Sorry, I'm not meaning to lecture you. Let's enjoy Christmas and remember those absent. Here, pass me that Father Christmas, will you?"

When they had put up all the decorations, Marianne laid a large red linen tablecloth on the dining room table and from the sideboard pulled out plates that had belonged to her grandparents, cutlery that had been one of her parents' wedding presents and delicate old wine glasses. Everything had a story. Isabeau couldn't imagine having so many family treasures and each thing being a part of the family history, all connected. She thought of her lonely bowl and George at home in her bedside cabinet.

By eight thirty the bakery and shop were clean and tidy and the house was finally calm. Marianne's tired parents went upstairs to have a shower and get changed, while Marianne and Isabeau finished the dishes. Half an hour later they all sat down to eat. They bowed their heads and held hands in a circle around the table while Monsieur Fournier said grace. Isabeau also silently gave thanks to Marianne and her family for inviting her to share Christmas with them.

Oysters, smoked salmon with a chive cream sauce and turkey with apple, raisins and pineapple, instead of the classic chestnuts. The fire in the large stone fireplace. Roquefort, reblochon and gruyère with baguette, and then praliné and chocolate bûches. Even the sore place deep inside Isabeau was fed and warmed. It made her want even more to have family. To have Joseph.

"I'll prepare a herbal tea," said Marianne's mother, "and we can drink it while we exchange our gifts, before we go to church." She went to the kitchen, and Monsieur Fournier started to arrange the chairs around the fire place. Marianne, Christian and Sophie headed upstairs to fetch presents. Isabeau followed. Marianne had to make two trips to bring all her parcels down. Back downstairs, Isabeau added her presents to the collection under the tree. She crossed her index and middle finger behind her back, hoping that everyone would like her gifts, especially as she had seen that there were presents with her own name amongst them.

Once Marianne had handed out all the presents, they pulled their chairs in closer around the fire and opened them, showing them off to each other. Isabeau couldn't stop smiling. She had a bottle of body lotion from Christian and Sophie, a beautiful gold and purple notebook from Marianne's parents, and embroidery linen and thread from Marianne and François.

"I know that you already have plenty, but this is for a new project," said Marianne. "I'm sure you've got some ideas."

"Embroidery materials! Who would've guessed?" said Christian.

"You can never have too much." Marianne lightly punched her brother on the shoulder.

"It's perfect. Everything's perfect. You've all spoilt me so much," said Isabeau, and wiped her eyes.

"I think I'd cry too if Marianne gave me linen and thread!" joked Christian.

"Well, you've also spoilt us," said Madame Fournier.

"I agree," said Sophie, and everyone nodded.

They finished their hot drinks, put on their coats and walked out the back of the bakery to the church nearby. Marianne's mother took Isabeau's arm. Everyone knew the Fourniers, and Isabeau recognized some faces: people from the village who had been at the wedding. They all said bonjour to her and asked her how she was.

It was a long time since she had been to church. She was surprised at how good it felt to be celebrating Christmas with so many people, even though the majority of them were strangers. It brought back distant memories of the few times Papa had taken her to Christmas mass. And then at the first notes of Silent Night she felt the past pull at her even more strongly. Suddenly she was back sitting on a pew beside Papa, many Christmases before, pressed up against his warm side.

When they returned from mass, they gathered briefly around the fireplace. Monsieur Fournier, Marianne, François, Christian and Sophie all said goodnight and headed up the stairs. Isabeau lingered, looking at the photos again. Madame Fournier joined her. Her eyes were fixed on the photo of Thierry as a child, running out of the sea. She stared into it as if the next wave might bring him back again.

"How is your Joseph?" She turned to Isabeau. Her eyes were kind.

"He's fine, I think." Isabeau said.

"In his wheelchair, he reminded us of Thierry," said Madame Fournier, turning back to the photos.

"Marianne told me about Thierry. I'm sorry."

"Thank you. We don't know what might have been. All we know is that we loved him, and we always will. From that love we draw strength." She embraced Isabeau. "Goodnight, Isabeau. Sleep well, and Merry Christmas."

In bed, Isabeau hugged the bolster. Like Goldilocks in the little bear's bed, she felt that the mattress was just right, and she was warm and cosy under the pleasantly heavy woollen blankets and patchwork quilt.

Could she have been with Joseph for Christmas? She would never know. Where would she be without Marianne and her family? That she did know. If it wasn't for them, and the Morels, she'd be two centimetres from the edge. It would be easy to lose her breath, her balance. She whispered what Madame Fournier had said, as the words repeated themselves in her head. "We don't know what might have been. We don't know what might have been. All we know is that we loved him, and we always will. We always will. I don't know what might have been. I don't know. All I know is that I love him, and I always will. Always will."

They were having a late breakfast when there was a knock at the kitchen door.

Tonton Aimé, dressed in a dark suit and black hat, entered. "Joyeux Noël to one and all!" He squeezed Isabeau's hand as he kissed her firmly on each cheek. She felt like a special niece too.

"You always seem to know when there's fresh coffee, Tonton," joked Christian.

"Well, boy, I can tell you, it's like many things in life – a real art," he said with a flourish as he sat down. "I'll just sit here between Marianne and Isabeau. I like to surround myself with lovely young ladies. A man's got to do what a man's got to do to keep young."

Tonton Aimé was the centre of attention, but after a time, as the conversation turned elsewhere, he quietly addressed Isabeau.

"And how are you, ma petite Isabeau?"

"Okay, thanks. I'm really enjoying spending Christmas with Marianne's family. And how are you? I must say, you're looking very well."

"Thank you. I feel like a new man."

"You haven't been smoking?"

"No. Report for the year: seriously tempted twice, but still zero cigarettes. I feel better. It's never too late." He chuckled. "And you? I presume you are answering correspondence promptly?"

"Things were going better earlier in the year; lately I haven't received many letters."

"What about your singer friend, Joseph, my penfriend? I remember how he sang. It put a tear in my eye."

"I think he's busy, writing songs."

"Too busy to write to you?" Tonton Aimé's eyebrows arched.

"I don't know. I ... well, he's not very happy with me. I disappointed him ... it was something quite important."

"Well, that can happen to everyone. We all make mistakes."

"Yes, but this was really bad."

"If he doesn't forgive you," said Tonton Aimé, "he's an idiot."

"I wish it were that simple."

"Well, it'll soon be New Year: time for resolutions and especially new possibilities. And, just remember, ma petite Isabeau, Rome wasn't built in a day. Carnac either, no doubt."

71

"I know you don't feel like it," said Marianne over the phone. "That's what you said about Christmas too, but look how much you enjoyed it. You'll have fun once you're there."

"I appreciate the invitation," said Isabeau, "but I've got another headache. I really need to get to bed early."

"Well, look after yourself. I'll pop in and see you next year!" Marianne laughed. "We can have a catch-up over a galette des rois. Bonne année."

"Don't worry, I'll be in bed soon. Have fun. Bonne année to you, too."

Isabeau hung up the phone and pressed her hands to each side of her head, rubbing her temples. Since Christmas, it was as if what Madame Fournier had said about Thierry had been stuck in her head. And she was waiting again. The house. Joseph. George. Quiberon. If she didn't get her resolutions sorted out before the new year began, she would have missed the opportunity. She would be on the back foot from Day One.

"Okay, George. I need your help. Let's have a look at last year's resolutions."

Isabeau put on an Aznavour cassette and turned the volume down till the music was soft in the background. She lit a candle and placed it beside George's box in the middle of the table and then opened her journal and read down the list.

"*Scatter George.* Well, maybe we'll start with something else, George. Something easier: Clothes – better. Hair – better." She untied her ponytail and shook her hair free.

"On the whole I'm dressing better, especially at the engagement party and wedding, but I just need to develop my own style more."

Isabeau picked up the notebook the Fourniers had given her. Its gold cover was decorated with rich purple flowers, and there was a satin ribbon to tie it shut. It was gorgeous. It must have been Marianne's idea, she thought. She undid the bow, picked up her special Waterman pen and started a new list.

Appearance. Try to make an effort on clothes every day, especially for work. Wear hair loose more often. Work on developing my own style.

"That's me," she said aloud. "Now, the house. Kitchen-living room, check. Done. Bathroom still unfinished. House still unfinished: still so much to do, and the garden is overgrown again. Too many *stills*. Do I still want to carry on with the house project?"

After the wedding, and the box incident, Isabeau felt awkward about contacting Pierrot. He'd said he should have some time for the bathroom after the holidays, but did he really want to carry on working on her house? "But I can't leave the house half-finished now," she said to herself. That phrase kept surfacing in her thoughts. "Maybe I could ask Marianne to talk to him and see what he says." Isabeau drew a small picture of the house and wrote beside it *Ask Marianne to talk to Pierrot. Tidy garden: start in April when weather improves.*

"Friends. At least I made progress there, didn't I, George? Invited Marianne: check. Visit Morels regularly: check. Okay, maybe not so much since July. More often, they visit me." Isabeau added to her list: *Invite Marianne again (to say thank you for Christmas). Go and see the Morels at least twice in January. Complete embroidery project with materials from Marianne and François. Write at least one happy poem in this journal.*

"And I actually like Corinne at work," she pondered out loud. "I'll try and talk to her. Shall we add that to the list? Now, correspondence. Answer promptly. Okay, I should write and thank Huguette Goudeau, for a start. And I'll send Happy New Year cards to the Fourniers and Tonton Aimé. At least they might write back."

Isabeau's hand went instinctively to the pendant. If she did write to Joseph, would he answer? Was he still cutting off his nose to spite his face, as Drew had said? She'd already told Joseph that she was sorry. What else could she say? She still felt raw each time she thought about the day he'd left and the way he'd spoken to her.

"Okay, I know it's all my fault, George, but was he always that stubborn? He didn't need to get so angry; he could have let me explain." She stared at George's box. "You're not really saying anything, are you? I think you might agree with me."

She picked up the box. "And what are we going to do about you?" She ran her fingers across the lid. "I can only promise you one thing. You're with me till July – till the festival – then somehow I'll have to give you back to Joseph."

The last heading was "Papa". Should she do anything about Quiberon? And this Ghislaine? Now Papa was linked to this woman. It wasn't just him, only him, any more. Isabeau hated her.

"Why don't I get started with the easier resolutions first? Like Tonton Aimé said, Rome wasn't built in a day. If there's no word from this café by March, I'll go there in April, when it's a little warmer. Deal, George? I think that's enough change for 1988."

Isabeau shut the journal and stretched back in her chair. Aznavour sang "Nous nous reverrons un jour ou l'autre". It was 11.55 p.m.

"And Bonne année to you, too, George."

72

The first time Isabeau saw Marianne in early January she invited her to come round for an evening meal and to do some embroidery. Marianne said she'd love to, but she'd have to wait until things quietened down. After the Christmas and New Year rush, the bakery was busy again, this time with galettes des rois.

The galettes filled two of the long shelves in the glass cabinet in the shop, and although Three Kings' Day – the celebration of Epiphany – was usually held the first Sunday of January, they would be sold until the end of the month. Marianne had spent a lot of time choosing the right fèves, charms, to be hidden inside the galettes. This year they were little porcelain Châteaux de la Loire fèves, and Marianne had decorated the bakery in a similar theme, with pictures of each of the castles featured on the fèves. Along the top of the glass cabinet, several of the cardboard crowns that the bakery was giving out with the galettes completed the decoration.

The first galette des rois Isabeau had was at work one day during the morning tea break. Instead of going for her coffee towards the end of the break, when most of her colleagues had finished, as she usually did, she followed Corinne out to the staff room and took the seat beside her.

Isabeau pretended she was sitting at the engagement party or the wedding. She straightened her back, tried to relax her shoulders, and smiled at Corinne.

"Nice earrings," said Corinne. "They suit you. Looks like you're going for a bit of a different look this year?"

"Thanks. I'm tired of wearing trousers. I'm trying to have a change. The earrings were a Christmas present – last year, though."

"How was your Christmas?" asked Corinne. "This year, I mean."

"Good, thanks. And you?"

"Well, I ate too much. My parents feed us as if they have eight children, and there's just my sister and I! It was good to catch up with my sister. She lives in Paris. Speaking of eating – here, a piece for you." She handed a piece of galette to Isabeau.

Isabeau took the piece. She recognized that it was from Marianne and François' bakery.

"Wonder who will be king or queen," said Corinne. "I hope I'm queen. It's a Châteaux de la Loire fève. I'm trying to get the full set."

"Then you could choose Monsieur Poulain as your king!" said Isabeau.

Corinne started giggling, and Isabeau joined in. When they had stopped laughing, Isabeau bit into her piece of galette. It brought back childhood memories of all the times she'd eaten galette at the Morels' house, hiding under the table to say who each piece should be for while Madame Morel cut the galette. Isabeau smiled to herself, then her teeth hit something hard.

"I think I got it," she whispered to Corinne.

"Looks like you're queen for the day," said Corinne, as Isabeau pulled the charm out of her mouth. "Who will you choose to be your king?"

"I guess it will have to be Monsieur Poulain!" she said to Corinne. "You can have the fève. It's the one of the Chinon Castle."

"Thanks, Isabeau, that's nice of you."

The following weekend, when the Morels invited Isabeau to share a galette, Isabeau insisted they come to her house, saying that she'd make one, as a thank you for all their help when she'd been on sick leave. Madame Morel was a great cook and baker, and Isabeau had never made a galette. But there was a first time for everything, she told George, as she started mixing the ingredients.

Isabeau put her best tablecloth on the table. She washed the tea set and set it all out, as well as her best coffee cups. The Morels arrived at three o'clock and ended up staying until dinner. After she had told them all about her Christmas at Saint-Laurent, and they had in turn recounted their own celebration at Docteur Morel's brother's, and also told her how Chantal and her family were, Isabeau pulled out Huguette Goudeau's letter to show them. Then they spent the rest of the afternoon talking about her parents, and Isabeau remembered the happy times with her father. If felt good to talk about him with the Morels. There was nobody else who had known him that she could talk to.

After the Morels had left, she sat back down and ate the last small piece of galette with George. "Well, I think that went rather well," she told him. "Wasn't there a king by your name? King George?"

As she ate, she scribbled on rough paper: ideas for a poem about galettes and first times and Tonton Aimé. Once she was happy with the happy poem, she would write it in the Christmas journal.

A few days later, activity in the bakery had calmed down enough for Marianne to have time to bring round a galette for the two of them to share. During the course of their conversation, Isabeau asked her to discreetly bring up the Alouettes house if she had the opportunity when she was talking to Pierrot – to see how he reacted, and whether he was interested in carrying on. "Please don't bring up the incident about Joseph's special box that ended up in the rubbish," Isabeau said, hoping she sounded concerned in a casual kind of way. "I'm too embarrassed about the whole thing."

She also asked Marianne if she could borrow her *La Redoute* catalogue. After looking through it several times, she decided to buy herself two winter skirts and a new coat. When the items arrived, Marianne insisted on coming back for a modelling session, and it turned out to be the perfect opportunity for her to stay for dinner and some embroidery.

Isabeau's new woollen coat was warm and comfortable. She was wearing it every day, and she walked differently when she wore it. In spite of the winter cold, she kept walking up to the Ménec and Kermario Alignments and to the Giant. She sometimes called in to see the Morels, but every time she saw her own house all she could think of was the last time she'd been there with Joseph, and she didn't want to go inside.

In mid-January, she wrote to Huguette Goudeau to thank her, and she bought three cards. One went to the Fourniers, wishing them a happy New Year and thanking them for sharing their Christmas with her. She asked Marianne for Tonton Aimé's address and sent the second card to him. Madame Fournier replied, wishing Isabeau a happy healthy New Year and all that Isabeau desired in her heart of hearts. Upon reading the card's message, Isabeau cried. Tonton Aimé's card arrived soon after, addressing her as "My Dear Isabeau, my Little Penfriend". His beautiful writing, in fountain pen, wished Isabeau "a magical 1988, amongst the menhirs, and, because Rome wasn't built in one day – and it is a leap year – 366 days of fulfilling resolutions." It ended with a general wish for good health and happiness, and was signed "Still Non-Smoking Tonton Aimé." It also contained a P.S.: "You may find this useful."

Inside the card, there was an old brass letter opener. Isabeau turned it over in her hands, examining the unicorn head and fleur de lys that decorated it. It was like a late Christmas present, and it was perfect. Precious. She replied the next day, to thank Tonton Aimé, telling him that she was starting the year well with her New Year's resolutions and that she was very happy that he had thought of her.

She stood the two cards up on the sideboard, with the letter opener, and picked them up several times a day to reread the good wishes.

The third card she'd bought stayed propped up beside George. She couldn't write it, no matter how many times she held her pen in a certain way, to remind herself of how it had actually felt when she had written to Joseph.

*T*hings come in threes, was Isabeau's first thought, when she found the small envelope in her letterbox. Across the standard stamp the postmark was unsmudged. Quiberon. There was no sender's name or address. The spindly writing sloped to the left, and Isabeau's name, in large capital letters, looked like it had been written by a shaking hand. It wasn't Papa's handwriting. She tried and tried to tell herself it could be good news, but there was nothing she could do to stop the bad feeling she felt developing inside.

She stood for a long time in the courtyard with the letter in her hand. She should go inside, turn the heating up and make a hot drink, she thought. Instead, she put the envelope in her pocket and set off to the Giant. In the clearing, she leaned back against the stone and slit the envelope with the house key.

Mademoiselle,

I have received a letter from Madame Goudeau in Nantes. The letter was sent to the café in Quiberon where I used to work. I have recently been in bad health, and the letter sat in a drawer at the café for some time, until I finally called in there last week.

From what I understand, you are looking for Paul Martin, your father. Paul was my companion. It is with regret that I have to inform you of his disappearance at sea in October 1975, when the fishing boat he was working on, Le Rêve, capsized during a storm.

Paul often spoke of you. It was a constant regret to him that he had no contact with you after he left Carnac.

I would like to meet you. I think it is very important for both of us. If you are able to come to Quiberon, I would appreciate if you would come and visit me. I have a letter to give you.

Yours faithfully,

Ghislaine Bourdain

Isabeau's numb hands pressed against the cold, rough, hard stone. It was like she was touching her insides. Everyone else was at home in the warmth. Everyone else. Papa was dead. Dead. Dead. Dead. Forever somewhere and nowhere in the sea. After all those years, it felt like a gigantic blow had crushed her tiny grain of hope.

It was terrifying to be drawn to the thing that frightened you the most. Isabeau crossed the causeway and drove straight towards Quiberon. No going back. It was the end of February, and the roads were quiet. The street she was looking for was on the left, before the shops and port. Easy to find. She had driven past it with Joseph before they had parked and he had bought his marinière. How could she have not even glanced at it as they drove along? The street where this woman lived. Ghislaine Bourdain. The woman who was the only link she had to Papa. Funny how an ordinary street suddenly became the centre of the universe. Number 15. It was the right number, but nothing felt right.

Isabeau took a puff on her inhaler and knocked lightly, almost not at all. What if this Ghislaine wasn't there? What if she just happened to be out at the shops? Isabeau didn't know if she would have the courage to wait, or come back. Joseph wasn't there to pick up the pieces this time, and she hadn't told Marianne or the Morels about this. She wanted to go home. But her hand knocked again, louder this time. She swallowed hard. She was not going to cry in front of this woman.

There was a faint sound, and the door opened. A woman, possibly in her mid-sixties, her long hair tied up, stood, leaning on crutches.

"You've come!" she exclaimed.

Isabeau couldn't move. Couldn't speak.

"You look so like your father. I'm sorry, I haven't even introduced myself. I'm Ghislaine Bourdain." She held out her hand. "Please come in. It's bitterly cold outside."

Isabeau couldn't take her eyes off the woman's face as they settled in armchairs beside the radiator. She must have been striking when she'd met her father, but now her beauty was tired. The bags under her eyes were dark violet. Her skin was sunken, sad. She was the only lifeline to what was left of Papa, but she was like a broken fragment smashed by the storm.

"I know this isn't easy for you, but I'm glad you've come." The woman hesitated. "I couldn't believe it when they gave me Madame Goudeau's letter at the café. It was a relief, in a way. So many times I've wondered whether I should try to find you. I needed to see you for

Paul's sake. It's been a burden to keep the letter he wrote to you. And you're all that's left of him."

"*I've* waited more than twenty years. And then your letter arrived, only to say that he's ... dead." Isabeau didn't know where her words were coming from. "He never came back. He could have found me." The anger was already rising in her throat.

"He tried," said Ghislaine. "He went back to the house shortly after he left, and it was empty. You and your mother had gone. He was heartbroken. He tried over the years to find you, but your mother's solicitor had been instructed not to speak about her, and she wasn't listed anywhere."

Ghislaine got up and rummaged in a desk drawer. She pulled out a letter with a lilac ribbon tied around it, and handed it to Isabeau. The stained envelope was postmarked September 1975. It must have been just before he was killed. And it was stamped with "Return to Sender". It was unopened. Isabeau recognized her father's handwriting. And the ribbon. It was one of the ribbons he used to tie around her ponytail.

"Your father would be happy that you finally have this," Ghislaine said. "I've been waiting too, all these years, to give it to you. I found it hidden away in his things after he was gone. I think there were more, but I don't know what happened to them. This is all that's left."

Pressure was building up behind Isabeau's eyes, and her throat was tight. Everything was blurring in front of her. Blinking hard, she felt for Joseph's pendant under her clothes.

"I met your father when I was working at a café in La Trinité-sur-Mer," said Ghislaine. "My husband was an alcoholic. I sympathized with Paul as he talked about his wife and the problems he had – your mother's mental illness – but when he spoke of you his eyes would light up. We began seeing each other, and then we, well, we hadn't planned it like that in the beginning, and we didn't go far: just to Pornic and then Quiberon."

"He could have taken me with him." Isabeau stared at the letter in her hands.

"He regretted it, all those years. It was difficult for him to live with." She paused. "Eventually we went to Nantes and rented a small apartment in Madame Goudeau's house. We stayed there for two years, but Paul was drawn back to the sea, to Carnac. We settled in Quiberon, and he worked on the boats. And then there was the storm. They never found the bodies, and since then there's only been the wide open sea. No body, no headstone, nothing. Only the wide open sea. I haven't been able to leave Quiberon since then. I don't have any family left now."

The tears rolled down Ghislaine's cheeks, and she started to sob. Isabeau blinked and blinked, but she couldn't hold back the tears either. She wiped her eyes as best she could and stood.

"I think I'd better go. Thank you for the letter."

"Perhaps one day you'll come back and see me?" It was all Ghislaine managed to say before Isabeau turned and walked out.

The weight had gone. But in its place there was nothing. Isabeau felt as if her chest would collapse in on itself, into a deep void. She sobbed as she drove to the port and stood at the sea wall, looking at the ferry terminal. She crouched behind the wall and opened the letter.

15 September 1975

Dear Isabeau,

Today is your birthday. I write to you every year on your birthday, but the post office has sent all of the letters back to me.

I used to promise I would take you on the ferry to Belle-Ile. Today I would have taken you, just the two of us out on the ocean. I promised you a lot of things, but I have not kept any of my promises. I'm sorry. I wonder what kind of a young woman you are growing into. I hope you make something of your life. I hope you will be happy. I hope that the love I have for you is still somewhere deep inside you and will never leave you. You were the best part of me. I am sorry I left you with your mother. I am sorry I wasn't a better father. I have never been able to forgive myself. There is not a day goes by that I don't think about you – that I don't love you.

With all my love.

Papa

One letter was all that was left. Isabeau picked it up and took a long sip of coffee. It was her third cup of the evening, but it didn't make any difference to her sore prickly throat. She read the letter. Again. She couldn't help herself, even if she knew it by heart now. So, he did care what kind of a young woman she was growing into. So, he did try to find her. So, he did regret leaving her.

"So what, George? What does it matter, anyway?" Her voice rose with each word. She'd written to him, and he'd written to her. How could they not have made contact all those years? "Return to sender." Isabeau was shouting now. "Pornic. He wasn't far at all, but he might as well have been in New Zealand!"

No matter how many times she read the letter, it changed nothing. The tapestry of tragedy couldn't be reworked. She couldn't undo a single stitch, snip a thread, change the colour, start all over again. She was used to not having him. How come it hurt so much?

It was too late to go to the bakery or go for a walk. She stomped around the kitchen.

"All I know is that I love him. What good is that if he's dead? Dead – just like you, George."

She screwed up the letter and threw it on the floor. Then she grabbed the card she still hadn't written to Joseph off the sideboard. What was the point of anything? Even if she did manage to write it, it probably wouldn't change anything any way. She ripped the card to pieces.

The walk home from work seemed twice as long as usual. Isabeau slowed her steps and coughed. She looked along avenue du Roer and wished she was already home, in her pyjamas, beside the radiator or in bed. She tried to tell herself that at least work was a reason to get out of bed in the morning. It seemed like the only reason, these days, but she wasn't sure how much longer she could keep making the effort. The days were lengthening and the cold easing, but she still couldn't shake off her sore throat.

At home, sitting at the kitchen table, she peeled a banana. That would do for dinner. She should have gone to the traiteur and bought something, or even a sandwich from the bakery. By now Marianne would have finished clearing out the unsold pâtisseries and bread, and bolted the door. Marianne, who was waiting for an answer as to which evening would suit her to get together and do some embroidery. Marianne, who kept asking "How are you?" If only she'd ask "Have you had any news about your father?" There was more chance that the Morels would ask, Isabeau knew, but she hadn't seen them for three weeks.

She ran her hand across the crumpled letter, trying to gently iron out the creases.

"Stupid, stupid, stupid Isabeau. How many times are you going to read this damn letter, Isabeau Martin?"

She was going round in circles. Going crazy. She had to do something. She grabbed her Waterman pen and the paper she had used to write to Joseph.

Dear Papa,

The letter you wrote to me has waited a long time. Like me. It hurts more than I can make the words say that you left, without me, and all the years that I waited you didn't come back, not even once. How could I ever know that you wrote to me and that you came back? And then that you were dead, and I was only chasing memories, chasing a ghost?

How could you just pack up your things and walk out? When I found out about Ghislaine Bourdain, it didn't feel as if you had left Mother for another woman – you had already left Mother long before – it felt as if you had left me for this woman.

How could you leave me with Mother? You knew better than anyone that she was sick. I know you never had a father of your own, but why did you have to leave me to the same fate? I have struggled for years to understand. What did I do to deserve this? It has always felt as if I must have done something terribly wrong, and it was all my fault. And if I was not worthy of your love, how could I be worthy of anyone else's?

After you left, Mother took me away from Carnac. She took me away from the stones, and it was as if she was taking you away all over again. Since you left, my life has been absence. You weren't there when I had my asthma attacks. You weren't there when I was sick. You weren't there when the children at school teased me ...

Isabeau continued. She wrote quickly. Her writing was rough, but it didn't matter. She filled the page and took another and another. Her hand and arm started to hurt, but she couldn't stop writing. She had unleashed a massive poem detailing her miserable childhood and growing up years. Each line or paragraph started with *You weren't there.* Things rose up from deep in her memory, each one pulling up another hurt or disappointment. She wrote until there was nothing more to extract from the well of pain and broken promises.

... You weren't there when I cared for Mother all those years. You weren't there when Mother died and I stood alone, surrounded by a handful of neighbours and acquaintances.

If you had stayed, if you had been there more and tried to help Mother, she might have been better. Maybe I would have had a loving mother. Maybe we could have been a family.

My life has been full of ifs and maybes. A series of questions. There are not a lot of things I am sure of; I don't know what might have been. All I know is that I loved you, and I always will. From that love I draw strength.

Your daughter

Isabeau

Isabeau put her head in her hands. She was spent, but there was something else she needed to do. She took another sheet of paper.

Dear Mother,

You were always there, in your bedroom. And I was always alone. Your presence was empty. I don't have any memories of you cooking or doing housework. Smiling. Laughing. Standing at the school gate with the other mothers. I don't have any memories of you looking after me. Hugging me. Giving me a kiss. I know you lost your own mother and your father, and that must have been very hard. But why couldn't you have been there for me? I had so much love I wanted to give you.

I had to look after myself. I had to look after you. So many times I wanted to walk out the door, like Papa, and leave you. And then when you were gone, I thought I was finally free, only to discover that I was chained to the memory of a mother who never showed me any care or love. You never showed any love for me, no matter what I did, no matter how much I looked after you. I hated you for that. Nobody should be made to hate their mother. Did you ever love me? It was impossible to know. All I ever wanted you to do was show me you loved me.

I don't know what might have been. All I know is that I have so much love I wanted to give you. From that love I draw strength.

Your daughter

Isabeau

She found an old enamel pot, a candle and a packet of matches. She took it all outside in the dark. She started with the letter to Mother. The flame slowly curled and engulfed the paper. Then she fed the letter to Papa into it. The flame grew bigger, and the pages shrivelled as they were sucked in, until there was no paper left. Back inside, she searched and found a small tin that had contained caramels flavoured with Guérande salt. She carefully transferred the black flakes of burnt paper from the pot into the tin, closed the lid tight and looked up at the sky. The full moon shone. There was one last thing she had to do.

O n the upper deck at the back of the ship the only other passengers were a group of elderly tourists and a young man in tramping boots with a backpack. The other passengers were below, inside: islanders returning home from shopping and errands on the mainland, and a few visitors. Isabeau put her raincoat on over her jacket, pulled her beret down further and wound her woollen scarf up around her neck as far as it would go. She dug her hands deep into her pockets and clenched her inhaler in one hand and the little tin in the other. The group of tourists pointed towards Belle-Ile-en-Mer and talked excitedly as they settled into their seats. She wished that they would go downstairs and that the young man with the backpack would stay.

Isabeau had bought her ticket, but when the time had come to board she had stayed in the terminal, trying to drum up the courage to actually get on the ferry. Time was running out. She had been about to turn around and leave, go home, when the young man with the backpack had arrived at the last minute. She watched him buy a ticket too. He had a black woollen hat pulled down over his ears; wisps of hair escaped at the sides. Her eyes were drawn to his backpack. It was covered in travel patches. On the top flap, in pride of place, was a Canadian maple leaf. Below it there was a Union Jack and an Australian patch with the outline of the country and a kangaroo. As he turned, a patch on the side caught her eye. It was black and white, and it looked like a fern. She stepped closer, coming up beside him, and just as she caught a glimpse of the words "New Zealand" and "Silver Fern" he turned and raced out of the terminal towards the ferry. She followed him, trying to get another glimpse of the New Zealand patch, while she fished her ticket back out from the bottom of her bag. Maybe this was a sign. Maybe.

Please go up on deck. Please don't go inside, Isabeau had silently implored him. If he went inside, she thought, she might not have the courage to do this.

As she'd hoped, he continued up the steps to the deck and found a seat near the tourists. Isabeau settled on a seat in the middle, as far from the rail as possible. She pressed the bone spiral against her skin under the thick layers of clothing. She thought of Drew and his similar bone pendant, in the shape of a fish hook. Perhaps the pendant would protect her.

The ferry made its way out of the harbour, across the choppy dark sea. Isabeau gripped her seat and tried to get used to the movement. Quiberon became smaller, and the wide end of the peninsula sank behind the waves as the sky and sea grew bigger. Papa was here. Somewhere or everywhere. She tried to look at the sea and think of him, but she had to shift her gaze closer, otherwise the vastness would swallow her, and a wave of nausea would rise inside her. She glanced at the young man out of the corner of her eye. He was at ease on his seat with his backpack beside him. She closed her eyes and hugged her legs, trying to cut out the rise and fall of the ferry.

Her throat was prickly, and her chest was tightening. She wished she were anywhere but on the boat. She might be sick. Or something really bad might happen. She might have an asthma attack, or be sucked overboard when she threw the tin into the sea. Or the ferry might arrive in Belle-Ile before she had the courage to do it.

The journey only lasted forty-five minutes. If she didn't do it, it would be like when she hadn't told Monsieur Poulain about Joseph's parcel, and when she'd gone to the Giant with George's ashes. She'd been stuck in that place ever since. No – she'd been stuck since Papa left. She'd be stuck all over again.

From that love we draw strength. From that love we draw strength. Isabeau remembered Madame Fournier's words. She stood, but as soon as she'd taken a couple of steps she needed to sit down again. She was shaking, freezing, afraid. The young man with the backpack was staring straight ahead, and the tourists were studying a map. She had to throw the tin overboard. Now. While they weren't looking. Before she was too seasick. She staggered to the rail and gripped it with all her might. The waves rose and fell. She felt as if they wanted to draw her in, but she couldn't pull herself away. The salty spray smelled of Papa. For a split second he was there, dressed in his blue woollen jersey and hat, kissing her cheek, his hand caressing her hair. Isabeau took one hand off the rail and retrieved the tin from her pocket. She eased the lid open a little, brought the tin to her frozen lips and then hurled it as hard as she could. "Goodbye, Papa," she shouted to the wind. The tin hit the water, bobbed for a few seconds and disappeared under the waves, in the wake of the ship. Isabeau gripped the rail and turned her face upwards, and for a moment she felt as if she was suspended in the movement of the waves and the wind. The menhirs were far away, and she was anchored to nothing, suspended in time and place. Nothing was as it had been. Nothing would be the same again. Papa was gone forever – she knew this now – but he was there forever too. A large wave hit the ship, and as the ferry pitched, the bile suddenly rose in her throat. Weak, dizzy and sweaty, she pressed against the rail and vomited the entire contents of her stomach overboard.

At the small port of Le Palais, the breakwaters extended like two arms, as if they were welcoming the ferry through their narrow opening into the harbour. As Isabeau stepped back onto firm ground she felt a thousand kilometres away from Carnac, and it felt like a thousand hours since she'd left home at one o'clock. Her legs were shaky, and she felt as if her head was floating and not connected to her body. She was numb with cold. Her mouth was dry and had a bitter taste.

She had forty-five minutes until the ferry left again for the return trip to the mainland. She wandered into the first café she came to. She kept her jacket on and rubbed her hands together as she waited for a glass of water and a hot chocolate. As soon as the waiter brought her drinks to the table, she gulped down the water, and it made her feel colder. She sipped at the hot chocolate, but it wasn't enough to warm her up. She asked for another glass of water and a cognac. She didn't care that the waiter asked her to repeat her order. She didn't care what he thought. She needed to warm up. He came back with the cognac, and she drank it straight away. The strong liquid was a stark contrast to the sweet milky chocolate and made her face screw up, but she swallowed it.

The warmth from the cognac stayed with her while she reboarded the ferry for the return trip. She settled inside. Sick bag at the ready, she gripped the seat, planted her feet on the floor, closed her eyes and tried to block out the rise and fall of the boat.

Disembarking at Quiberon, the sky was darkening and the wind was sharp. By the time Isabeau reached her car, dizzy and disorientated, the warmth of the cognac had long worn off. Her throat was raw. She wanted to be in her bed, but she still had to drive home. She gasped as she collapsed behind the wheel of her car, wheezing, and lay down across the front seats, gripping her inhaler.

When she finally made it home, it was late. Isabeau couldn't remember which way she'd driven. She went straight upstairs and rolled herself in her duvet. She wished she could lie back and savour the fact that she had taken the ferry and said goodbye to Papa. If only she wasn't so cold. If only she could stop shivering. It was a long cold night, but by the morning she was burning like fire.

Docteur Morel sat down on the side of Isabeau's bed.
"I've been coughing all night," she told him. "My chest is so tight, and my inhaler doesn't make any difference." She burst into tears.

"Let's have a listen," said Docteur Morel. He helped her to sit up, and put his stethoscope against her chest. After he had listened to her front, he listened to her back. "Your left lung is rattling. It sounds like pneumonia. I think you're going to need a blood test and chest x-ray, antibiotics. You need to be careful, what with your asthma. We'll take you around to your doctor."

Isabeau sank back against the pillows and started to cough.

"How long have you been like this?" asked Docteur Morel, and waited for her to finish coughing before she answered.

"A few days. I'm not sure. What day is it? It was a sore throat and fever, then I started coughing two nights ago, I think. I haven't slept at all."

"It's Wednesday," said Madame Morel. "Thank heavens you rang us." She looked around Isabeau's bedroom, at the dirty dishes on the bedside cabinet and the piles of tissues strewn on the floor. "You can't stay here on your own."

The Morels offered to have Isabeau, and she didn't have the strength to refuse. Madame Morel helped her get dressed and pack some clothes and toiletries. "I'm sorry to put you to all this trouble," said Isabeau as Madame Morel folded her pyjamas and flattened them into her bag. She picked up Cosette from the end of the bed.

"You've had her a long time, haven't you?"

Without saying any more, Madame Morel carefully placed the rag doll in the bag, too. She picked up the bag, took Isabeau by the arm and helped her towards the door. As they left the room, Isabeau looked over her shoulder at her bedside cabinet, and then she went with Madame Morel down the stairs.

Madame Morel installed Isabeau in Chantal's old bedroom, on the ground floor. She brought her a radio, magazines and books, pen and paper, and a little bell that she insisted Isabeau ring if she needed anything. Isabeau picked up a magazine and flicked through it, then put it back down. She needed a shower, but after the x-ray she didn't even have the strength for that. It took all her energy just to breathe. The slightest movement disturbed the cough. She sat motionless, eyes closed, in the armchair beside the window. Her body was empty, exhausted, sore, sad. Papa was dead.

Time slowed. The nights were longest. Isabeau longed to lie down and let her aching muscles sink into the mattress, to sleep. Each time she tried, the cough awakened. She sat up in bed, or returned to the armchair. When she could take it no longer, she wandered, as quietly as she could, to the kitchen. Like a ghost. She sipped hot water and honey. It helped for a short time, but the cough was never far away.

Insomnia left her lifeless during the day, unable to think clearly, but at night the questions were urgent and incessant in her head. She wanted to tell the Morels about Papa and going on the ferry. She wished she had the strength to start talking about it. Instead, she talked quietly to George, who seemed so far away – although it wasn't that far to the little house in town. She wished she had brought his box with her. She hugged Cosette and stroked Joseph's pendant. Her night was his day, on the other side of the world. Did he think about her? Would he ever write?

Isabeau grabbed on to the little daily rituals: Docteur Morel checking on her and listening to her chest, Madame Morel coming and going, sitting on the bed to talk when she brought Isabeau her meals or a tisane and home baking for afternoon tea at four o'clock. Isabeau ate small amounts. She took the antibiotics. She moved slowly, carefully. There was no energy for anything else.

79

Marianne put her basket on the chair. It was full of magazines and a pâtisserie box.

"My family send their best wishes," she said. "They're sorry to hear you're sick and hope you get better soon. So do I. Maman said to give you lots of love."

Marianne gave Isabeau a long hug that reminded her of Madame Fournier's welcome at Saint-Laurent.

"And before I forget, Corinne said to say hello and pass on her good wishes. She popped in to the bakery at lunchtime." Marianne pulled out a tiny parcel containing a strip of linen, a needle and two small hanks of embroidery thread. "Just in case you feel like some needlework. I've also got something for afternoon tea."

"Don't tell me there's a *La Redoute* catalogue in your basket too."

"I knew I'd forgotten something. Now I know why you're sick; you're obviously in withdrawal. Not enough clothes shopping!"

"Don't make me laugh," said Isabeau, starting to cough.

"You'll just have to do with some magazines." Marianne pulled out a *Broderie Aujourd'hui,* a *Marie Claire* and half a dozen decorating magazines. "I thought you might like some inspiration for your house. I sounded out Pierrot, and he still seems keen."

"Really?"

"Things have a way of working out. He's probably grateful to you because he's getting quite serious with Véronique."

"Already?"

"Mmm." Marianne picked up one of the decorating magazines. "I had a look at your house on my way in. Looks full of potential – lucky you. At least at the moment you've got plenty of time to think about what you want to do with it, how you want it to be." She opened the magazine at an article on bathrooms. "I mean, look at this. Isn't it gorgeous?" She pointed to photos of a bathroom in pale blue and white.

"Yes, nice and fresh. I really like it. It looks light and spacious."

"Wish I had a bathroom to do up. The bakery's starting to grow on me, but I'd love to have our own house. François's said I can redecorate the living quarters, but I don't want to change it too soon. His parents have only just moved out. And if I do take him up on the idea, he might wonder what's hit him."

Madame Morel brought in a tisane, and Marianne opened the pâtisserie box. As they had afternoon tea Marianne flicked through the magazines, talking about decorating, from time to time asking Isabeau what she thought of different makeovers and décors. Isabeau took small bites of a chocolate éclair and forced herself to answer and to think about something other than her tight chest and sore body. She hadn't yet finished her éclair when Marianne put the magazines on the bottom shelf of the bedside cabinet.

"I'd better let you get some rest," Marianne said. "I'll leave you the magazines. No hurry." She stood up to go. "There's one more thing. Madame Morel asked me to clear your letterbox."

Marianne slipped an envelope out of her jacket pocket. In a glance, Isabeau recognized the stamps, the writing. She took the envelope and turned it over in her hands.

"I'll leave you to read it," said Marianne, and hugged Isabeau again before she slipped out of the room.

Isabeau picked at the back flap on the envelope and then worked her finger in the crease, slowly cutting a jagged opening. She tried to take several deep breaths as best she could.

Dear Isabeau,

The festival is finalized. I will be performing. If you would like to come to the concert I can organize a ticket for you.

Joseph

Twenty-seven bare words. Not a single drawing. A small sheet of paper. Large writing. If Joseph wanted her to read between the lines, there weren't many. Isabeau thought back to what Marianne had said. Someone had to make the first move. It was a small step. But was it just about the ashes, or did he really want to see her? She didn't know what to think, what to hope.

"George," she said, "I guess it's better than nothing. At least, it would be an opportunity to give you back to Joseph."

Isabeau slipped the letter under her pillow, leaned back and closed her eyes.

80

Isabeau looked at her reflection in the mirror beside the door. She smiled. She frowned. She moved her head from side to side, poked out her tongue and grimaced. The pale thin face in the mirror still didn't look like her face. As she stepped out the door, Madame Morel called out "Enjoy the sun. See you later." Isabeau pulled the jacket around her. In spite of the spring weather, she was wearing Docteur Morel's jacket, a scarf and a woollen hat. The jacket was too big, but even her own clothes were loose now. She mouthed "bonjour" to her house before taking the path to the Ménec Alignments. She tried to forget her chest, her asthma, but it was hard not to press against the jacket pocket to check her inhaler was there.

At the alignments, she looked up and down the rows of stones, taking her time to choose. She picked the furthest away row on the right and walked down it, touching each stone lightly as she passed, saying over and over again to herself and the stones in a quiet voice, "I did it. I went on the ferry to Belle-Ile to say goodbye to Papa. I did it."

When she came back, instead of walking towards the Morels' house, she continued on allée des Alouettes and headed into the Cité du Runel, a housing estate that had been built in the 1970s. She'd avoided this place as a child. Too many other children. The sun was pleasantly warm on her back, and she kept walking, studying the houses and their front gardens. There were plastic toys in the grass, trikes, and bikes leaning against garages. It was still a place for families with young children.

A front door opened and a young woman stepped out with a toddler on her hip, balancing a large bag on her opposite shoulder. Isabeau slowed her steps and watched the mother open the station wagon parked in the drive and then strap her daughter into the car seat before they drove off.

Isabeau loosened the scarf a little. It felt good to be out in the fresh air and to move – to be walking again – even if she wasn't going far, and her body was stiff and her steps slow. She still hadn't been back home. She thought of George, alone. She missed him. She thought of Joseph. She took her hand out of her pocket and held it out in the sun, trying to remember the warmth of his touch. It was like another ache, deeper than the one in her muscles, which were tired from coughing and sitting. She wished he wasn't so angry. She wished he was beside her rolling along in his chair. She wished she had the energy to find the right words to reply to his card. It was still under her pillow. If Madame Morel had seen it she wasn't saying anything. She had pen and paper, and Madame Morel would no doubt be happy to go to the post office for her. The answer was only one word. In her mind Isabeau had answered the card a thousand times, but she still hadn't managed to actually put pen to paper. Even that still seemed too much, too hard. The days were passing.

"Such a beautiful day. I should have come with you," said Madame Morel as soon as Isabeau came through the gate. Madame Morel was working in the front garden, while Docteur Morel was pushing a wheelbarrow of weeds towards the garage. They both stopped what they were doing and sat down at their outside table with Isabeau.

"The sun was lovely," said Isabeau. "I walked into the housing estate, almost down to the pond, then I had to sit down on the grass for a breather before I came back."

"Have you ever seen the old bread oven?" Docteur Morel asked her. "It's an interesting old piece, in a field past the pond. You should show it to your friend Marianne. I could take you down there one day."

"Thank you, I'd like that. You've both done so much for me. I don't know how I can ever thank you for your kindness." She looked from Docteur Morel to Madame Morel. "And I need to tell you something. I had some news about my father, all because of the Nantes address you found. I was going to tell you, but then I got sick."

"You haven't been in any state to think about that," said Madame Morel.

Isabeau nodded. "His landlady at that address in Nantes finally contacted me, and she remembered Papa and Ghislaine. She wrote to the café in Quiberon where she had forwarded their mail when they left Nantes."

"That's good news," said Docteur Morel.

"Then I received a letter from this Ghislaine. Ghislaine Bourdain is her name. She wanted me to go and see her."

"What! *She* contacted you?" said Docteur Morel. His mouth dropped open.

Madame Morel stared, wide-eyed, at Isabeau. "Have you been to see her?" she asked when she had got over her surprise.

"Yes."

"And?" asked Docteur Morel gently.

Isabeau composed herself before she continued.

"My father is dead. His fishing boat went down in a storm. In 1975."

"Oh, no," the Morels both said at the same time. They looked from one to the other and then back at Isabeau.

"I'm so sorry, Isabeau," said Madame Morel. "After all this time to find out that he's dead." She stood up from her seat and gave Isabeau a hug. "I'm surprised we didn't see it in the paper," she said as she finally sat back down. "We must've been in America. That was the year we went for the first time."

"You said you went to see this Ghislaine. What else did she say?" asked Docteur Morel.

"She was very happy to see me. She said that Papa did try to find Mother and me. And after his death she found a letter he'd written to me, and she kept it, hoping that one day she'd have the opportunity to give it to me. So we both had unfinished business."

"That's incredible," said Madame Morel. "A letter?"

"He wrote it shortly before he died. He said that he was sorry for all his broken promises, sorry that he left me. I still can't believe that we never made contact over the years. It all seems crazy." Isabeau stopped talking and blew her nose, dried her eyes. "Once I had the letter, it was like I had to answer it. I wrote to Papa, and then I wrote to Mother too."

"I understand," said Madame Morel.

"I felt better, but I still had to do something with the letters." Isabeau needed to say it all. "I burned them. And then ... Papa always promised to take me to Belle-Ile-en-Mer. I don't like the sea, but I went on the ferry. And I threw the letter ash overboard."

"Oh, Isabeau, that must have been awful on your own," said Docteur Morel.

"It was freezing. That's when I caught cold. It was stupid to go. I already had a sore throat. But I had to do it."

"He loved the sea. It's fitting that he's resting there. You'll both be at peace now," said Docteur Morel. "And you're getting better, Isabeau. You're going to be okay."

"Yes," she said. "I am."

81

"You can open your eyes now," said Marianne, as she led Isabeau into the bathroom at the Alouettes house and let go of Isabeau's hands.

Isabeau blinked. Her mind was struggling to understand what she was seeing. White tiles around the bath and basin shining against freshly painted light blue walls. A new toilet in the corner, and a new basin and bath. And the little wooden cabinet looked brand new with its coat of white paint. The grotty bathroom had vanished as if by a magic spell.

"I don't know what to say. This looks like one of the bathrooms out of the magazines. It's beautiful. How is it possible? How did you manage it?"

"I'm not sure myself, but I did have a *little* help from Pierrot, and even François. They did the tiles, and I did most of the painting. Once we got started it was fun. The Morels brought over coffee. You have no idea how hard it was to keep it top secret from you. We had to park around the corner further down and get the Morels to make sure you didn't come over this way when we were working!" Marianne laughed.

"Now I understand the magazines," Isabeau smiled, "and why Madame Morel kept saying not to worry about the house, that it could wait."

"I hope you like it. I thought it was better to keep it simple. It's ended up looking quite coastal and beachy, with the blue. I must admit it was a bit of a risk doing it without your approval, but it seemed right in the circumstances. I hope you don't mind?"

"Mind! How could I mind? And it's perfect. I couldn't have done it better myself." Isabeau kissed Marianne firmly on the cheeks. "You really fooled me, talking about wanting your own house."

"Well, that is true, and doing this with François was a good opportunity to make a few hints and show him it would be good to have our own place one day." Marianne ran her hand along the basin. "It was good to do something together, outside of the bakery for once."

"I can't thank you enough – and François and Pierrot too."

"You'll have to sort out the accounts with Pierrot. He also organized the plumber. He got the toilet, basin and bath for a good price from a builder friend who's doing up a luxurious house. The owners have just bought it and wanted to revamp everything – can you believe it? – even though the bathroom was only a year old. They're practically brand new."

"It's beautiful." Isabeau's voice wavered. "No one's ever done anything like this for me."

"Well, when you have your house-warming, you can thank us properly. That'll be something for us all to look forward to."

Marianne had a way of talking that left no room for Isabeau's questions and doubts, and Isabeau liked that. There would be a house-warming; that's just the way it would be.

"You three will be my guests of honour." Isabeau made an effort to make her voice sound confident.

"When do you think you'll move in?"

"Sorry?"

"Now that the bathroom and kitchen are done," Marianne said. "The rest may not be tip-top, but it's liveable."

"Haven't really thought about it yet," Isabeau replied. She shrugged. Her mind was racing to keep up. The new bathroom. And now a house-warming.

"I can really see you here in the house," said Marianne, "near the menhirs. You're so lucky to have it. Now, that's enough of being good to you! You need to get your hands dirty. There's something you need to put in the garden." Marianne went out the back of the house and came back with a small rose bush covered in tiny pink roses. "This is to celebrate you feeling better, but in return, I'd love more tapestries to hang in the bakery. I want to do something different around the theme of megaliths, and I know you've stitched plenty of them. I have this idea of a sort of exhibition in the bakery this summer, something original and different."

"Where do you get the energy?"

"I love the bakery, but I'd go crazy just selling baguettes. And François's working on a new chocolate and a pâtisserie, both shaped like a menhir. Deal?"

"Deal," Isabeau replied, and they shook hands.

Marianne said she could help Isabeau plant the rose bush and do a bit of gardening before she had to get back to the bakery. They started digging over the garden along the front fence, removing the weeds and the convolvulus that was growing back with renewed vigour.

"I'm not going to let it win the battle," Isabeau shouted. She pulled out a long root, held it and her trowel aloft and started to laugh. Suddenly she wanted to tackle the whole garden. The sun and fresh air; the new bathroom; all Marianne, François and Pierrot's efforts for her; and Marianne's company – it all made her forget the tiredness she'd been feeling after her first week back at work.

Despite that fatigue, the return to work had been better than she had expected. Monsieur Poulain had spoken kindly to her, and Corinne had helped to clear her desk.

Marianne interrupted Isabeau's thoughts. She was standing beside her with an armful of weeds.

"I wish I could stay longer," she said, "but I have to get back to the bakery soon. Madame Morel mentioned you had news about your father. She said I should ask you. Good news? Bad news?"

"Yes and no," said Isabeau, shaking her head, and she began to tell Marianne about going to see Ghislaine Bourdain and what had happened to her father. "After that, I went on the ferry to Belle-Ile to say goodbye to him. That's all about the time I got sick, and I didn't have the energy to talk about it. Now I know I won't ever see him again. At least I know ... I know he tried to find me."

"I'm really sorry." Marianne hugged Isabeau. "Whatever happened, it wasn't going to be easy. Uncertainty is the worst thing, though. It's better that you know. Now, at least, you can look to the future. And while I'm asking questions, dare I ask about Joseph?"

"In the letter, he said he's coming to Nantes for the festival. He asked if I'd like a ticket."

"Of course you wrote back and said yes."

"Not yet. I've bought a postcard. I'm just about to send it to him."

"Oh, come on, Isabeau!"

"I'm going to write, really. I have to. I have unfinished business with him."

"Of course you do. You two definitely have unfinished business, I would say." Marianne winked.

"It's not like that."

"That's what you always say."

"Look, I know you're still tired, but you have to promise me you'll write today – when you get home. Otherwise you'll let your chance slip through your fingers. Promise?"

Isabeau nodded.

"That's not very definite. You promise?" Marianne insisted.

"Yes," said Isabeau firmly.

"That's better. Well, that's our second deal of the day!"

Sinking into her armchair, Isabeau sighed long and loud. When she'd finished in the garden she'd called in to see the Morels. It had been five o'clock by the time she'd left to drive home. "More than once I thought we'd let the cat out of the bag," Madame Morel had laughed. "You have to stay for lunch to celebrate!"

Isabeau closed her eyes. She'd done too much. When would she stop feeling drained and tired, this dryness in her bones? Her body ached, but for the first time in a long time she also felt a little of the good tiredness that came from working in the garden and walking: the good tiredness that would help her wake feeling rested and refreshed. She was almost sleeping with her pillow flat again now, and she was walking a little every day, discovering a freedom in her shoulders, arms, legs, chest. The freedom was creeping into her head too.

Isabeau laughed out loud. She still couldn't believe how Marianne had managed to renovate the bathroom. It was crazy.

"George," Isabeau called, "you won't believe it. Marianne has done some kind of a miracle with the bathroom at the Alouettes house. Some kind of magic. I'll have to show you. Don't worry, I won't leave you in the rubbish again."

I know.

The unfamiliar, familiar voice was back.

"Thank you," she whispered.

Isabeau went upstairs. She wanted to lie down, but she took out a pen and the postcard from her bedside cabinet. It showed three scenes of Belle-Ile-en-Mer: an aerial view of the port of Le Palais; the smaller port of Sauzon, with its little lighthouse; and Locmaria, a sandy beach with green clear water. She looked closer at the map of Belle-Ile that was superimposed in the middle of the three photos. Maybe she should have stuck with a postcard of the alignments, she thought. But it was too late now. She had promised Marianne. Today.

Dear Joseph,

I'm sorry it's taken me this long to answer. I had intended to reply sooner, but I have been ill with pneumonia. I'm finally feeling better now. Spring has arrived, and today at the house, I planted a rose bush with Marianne.

Thank you for the offer of a ticket. Yes, I would like to come to the festival. It would be good to hear you sing and to see you, to give you back your father's ashes.

Sincerely,

Isabeau

"P.S. Tonton Aimé said you are an idiot!" She slipped the postcard into an envelope. "Don't worry, George, I haven't put that."

Monsieur Tatibouet shuffled the papers on his desk until they formed a neat pile. Isabeau straightened her back. It seemed a lifetime ago since she'd been sitting in this beige chair opposite his desk, saying for the first time that she was going to renovate her house. Now it was true. She waited for him to speak.

"Mademoiselle, how are you? I must say you're looking remarkably well. Carnac obviously agrees with you." He rubbed his hands together.

"Thank you."

"You must be wondering why I asked you to come today. We're certainly very happy with the way you're looking after the house. However, I'm afraid an unforeseen situation has arisen." He cleared his throat. "My son's contract has been renegotiated, and he'll be coming back earlier than anticipated, in September. It may be for only a month or two, or it could be indefinitely. I was hoping things were progressing with your own house. How is it coming along?"

"Well, um, things have taken a lot longer than anticipated, and I was unwell during the winter, but now the house is looking much better."

"So it won't be a problem if you have to vacate the house at the end of August, for example?" He shifted forward and smiled.

"That shouldn't be a problem."

"Good, then. Arnaud appreciates the care you've taken of his house. We're sorry that we couldn't give you more notice. Let me know when you can shift out, and we can organize the final inspection." He stood up, shook Isabeau's hand and led her out of his office.

Isabeau was almost dizzy from what she'd just said. It had only been a week since Marianne had asked her when she was going to shift into her house. She hurried home to look at the calendar, but before she'd even reached the alley she knew the perfect time for her house-warming: mid-September, around her birthday. A house-warming birthday party. Her first proper birthday party. Her first house-warming.

At home, she studied the calendar. If she shifted in mid-August, she would have a month to get settled in and do some more work on the house. The Assumption holiday, 15 August, would give her a long weekend.

She was still tired, but suddenly she felt that she couldn't wait any longer. She wanted the house to be new, fresh, finished, with her embroidery chair beside the window, her things installed.

There wouldn't be much left of her savings once she'd paid Pierrot for the work. Marianne had said he was going to drop the invoice in at the bakery on his way through during the week. Isabeau started a list, trying to think of everything that she could do herself before the party. The downstairs was now clean and tidy, but the kitchen and living area still needed to be repainted or limewashed. The parquet wasn't in the best condition, but it would do in the meantime; she could give it another coat of wax. Upstairs, however, hadn't been touched. And she would have to sleep up there.

Isabeau opened the upstairs shutters and windows, and the sunlight entered in slanting shapes across the dirty parquet. She walked back and forth between the three bedrooms. In her mother's bedroom, the musty air and faint cigarette smell made her cough, and the orange and green flowery wallpaper almost gave her a headache when she looked too closely at it. Still, she kept coming back to Mother's room. She pushed the windows further open and unhooked the heavy curtains, stained and dusty. She took them outside to the growing rubbish heap behind the shed. The room already looked better. Beside the door, the wallpaper had come unstuck along the edge. She wedged her scraper underneath, and the paper lifted enough for her to pull on a corner of it. It ripped up the wall in a short strip. Isabeau stood there and tried to imagine the room light and clean, with cream walls. And she tried hard to imagine that maybe her mother would have been happy about such a change, if she'd been well and able to appreciate such things. She had intended to start with her own bedroom, but what did it matter, as long as she got one room done over the weekend?

She had just driven to Vannes and picked up the machine to strip wallpaper. She'd left straight after work Saturday lunchtime, eating a sandwich in the car as she drove. She went back downstairs and got the machine ready. She filled the reservoir and, while the water heated, covered the floor with a large sheet of plastic. Once the machine was hot, she placed the steam plate on the wall beside the door, systematically working her way over the first strip of paper like the man at the equipment hire company had explained. Small patches of the paper lifted. She groaned. There was another layer there, an all-over floral pattern, and then under that yet another one, with a striped design, before she hit the jackpot of bare plaster. She gathered her strength and continued. On the stubborn pieces, she tried making a series of diagonal cuts and applying the steam for longer, but there were places where the paper refused to budge, as if it was bonded to the wall. Her arms were already starting to ache. And standing holding the plate against the wall gave her too much time to think. Once she'd gone through the house-warming party and the shifting process in her mind, she always came back around to Joseph. He hadn't answered her letter yet. No ticket.

In the evening, Isabeau slumped down on the floor. She couldn't hold her arms up any more, and her neck and shoulders were tight. Her hair was stuck to her forehead and her t-shirt damp against her back. She smelled of wet wallpaper. She stared at the wall that she'd spent all afternoon working on. Only two strips of wallpaper were gone, and not completely. There were still obstinate patches. Merde. She hated the wallpaper, and she hated the man at the machine hire place for making it sound easy. At this rate, there was no way she was going to get it finished in a weekend, or two. Even the holiday coming up wouldn't give her enough time to do this one room before September.

She locked up the house and went home, arriving with barely enough energy to stand under the shower and wash her hair. When she dried herself she could still smell damp wallpaper. In the kitchen, she pulled out bread, pâté and cheese, and devoured leftover potato salad directly from the container. Between mouthfuls, she talked to George.

"Ha, ha – so I thought I was going to get a bedroom done this weekend!" She tried to laugh, otherwise she'd cry.

When the alarm went off early the next morning, Isabeau turned over and tunnelled into her pillow. Her body didn't want to co-operate with this project any more, but she couldn't stop now: the wall she'd been working on was a motley unfinished mess. Compared with the bathroom it was pathetic. And she had to make the most of the stripper; the machine needed to be returned the next day. It was as if there was an insistent voice, George's voice, in her head repeating *Just get up!* She pulled back the covers.

Today, with everything already in place, it was quicker to get started. She got into a routine, lacerating the paper first, steaming it for longer, and she was pleasantly surprised to find she was developing a knack for lifting the paper with the scraper and getting the steam under it. She forced herself to work through one layer at a time. Bigger pieces lifted off cleanly. She made a habit of finishing a whole strip before going back to work on the obstinate pieces. The ones that wouldn't budge would have to wait until she'd worked her way around all the walls.

By two o'clock Isabeau had finished the first wall. Outside, she bit into her sandwich like a hungry dog. When she'd finished eating she gave herself twenty minutes lying on the grass. She tried to relax her breathing and refill her lungs with fresh air. She had to pace herself if she wanted to work until the evening. She couldn't afford to have any more time off work. She'd rebook the machine for the following weekend, she decided. She closed her eyes, and when she breathed out she hummed parts of Joseph's songs. She wished she could show him what she was doing.

"I'm so slow at this, George. I'm a snail stripping wallpaper, but Rome wasn't built in a day – nor Carnac. Tonton Aimé said so. At least I'm doing it, and I'm doing it on my own. You would be proud of me. You too, Papa."

84

Isabeau hugged the cardboard box of embroideries to her chest. The sooner she gave it to Marianne, the better. Then it would be out of her hands. "As much variety as possible," Marianne had said. In the end Isabeau had also put in some of her sketches. She was no longer sure it was a good idea, but she'd promised.

Walking around the outside of the church, she glanced at the paintings in the little art gallery on the corner. Breton ports and fishing boats. Maybe she would buy one to hang in the house. She stopped. She wasn't even sure why. Her eyes were unconsciously drawn to the posters stuck on the gallery door. She looked at the top one: "Festival de Nantes, 2–30 July".

On the poster, the sun rose above a blue and green planet earth, with photos of the artists featuring at the festival amongst the sun rays. Right there in the middle of the horizon, "From the Antipodes, singer-songwriter Joseph Turner" smiled at Isabeau. She almost dropped the box. Joseph had a closely cropped beard, and his hair was longer. His long thin face had filled out a little. He looked good. She sat the box down and ran her fingers across the door glass and Joseph's photo. "Joseph Turner. Why don't you write? Where is the ticket?"

He was performing Saturday 9 July. The festival was only three weeks away. Isabeau realized with a pang how quickly time had passed as she'd been working on the house and garden and preparing for the shift. She was making good progress, but each day's "maybe it will be here tomorrow" had changed to "probably it won't come at all". Letters did go missing, she knew, but not that often.

She didn't blame Joseph if he'd changed his mind. She could remember the look on his face when the train pulled away better than how he smiled, like he was smiling on the poster. She still had to give George back to him, though. And there was his pendant. Now, with summer clothes, it wasn't always hidden any more.

At the bakery, the same poster was stuck on the glass door.

"Great," said Marianne, coming out from behind the counter and opening the door for Isabeau.

"Thanks. It feels good to finally be giving it all to you."

"It's going to look amazing when it's set up! It'll be something different for a bakery. I can't wait. So, what do you think?"

"There should be more than enough material." Isabeau held out the box. "I wasn't too sure, so I put it all in, even some sketches. You can choose."

"No, not that – this!" Marianne pointed at the poster. "He looks good, doesn't he?"

Isabeau blushed. "I've just seen the same poster on the door of one of the little art galleries." She touched the poster.

"The woman came in an hour ago with it. I was so excited. Must admit I was hoping I'd see your face when you discovered it," said Marianne, smiling. "And there was something on the radio about the festival this morning. I only caught the end of it, but it sounds like Joseph's one of the major acts. They're making a big thing about him being from so far away. The song they played sounded like what I heard at your place. I'd love to hear him sing at the festival."

"So would I." Isabeau's shoulders dropped.

"Don't give up. I'm sure the ticket will arrive. There's still time."

"He's probably changed his mind."

"I can't believe that." Marianne shook her head.

A group of tourists entered the shop.

"I'm sure it's going to be okay," Marianne said, and put the box behind the counter. "Anyway, I'm hoping to have the exhibition up by then. François will be ready to put the new chocolate and pâtisserie – it's a meringue – on sale then too. I'd better go. Talk to you tomorrow."

Isabeau stared at the poster. It gave a number to call for reservations. She wondered whether she should reserve a ticket in case. She left the bakery and walked away, heading towards the alignments. When she reached the house, she didn't stop. Putting the undercoat on the window frame in Mother's room would have to wait. If her feet stopped, her thoughts caught up with her and hurt too much. She had to remind herself of all the good things as she walked, otherwise that one poster would be enough to make it all seem pointless.

85

NOUVEAU
Exhibition and tasting
Le Ménec: Praliné and mousse rocher
Le Kermario: Chocolate, praliné meringue
Come in and admire the menhirs
Eat one too!

The sandwich board on the pavement in front of the bakery stood out from a distance with its red, blue and white chalk writing and the three small black and white Breton flags attached to the top. Isabeau saw it as soon as she turned the corner of the church. The double glass doors of the bakery were wide open, and the bakery and pavement were full of people sipping cider and holding serviettes on which sat chocolates and meringues. She wished she'd picked up the Morels earlier or waited until much later in the day.

"Come on," said Docteur Morel. "The artist should be in on the action."

"I didn't expect this many people." Isabeau stopped. She wanted to go home and come back when there was no one there.

"Don't be shy," said Madame Morel, linking her arm through Isabeau's.

They joined the crowd and slipped into the bakery when a group of people came outside.

Isabeau's embroideries and sketches were everywhere: on every piece of available wall space and on an old wooden stand that had been set up in the corner. Along the wall shelves, the usual bags and boxes of sweets and treats had been replaced with small embroideries, Isabeau's sketches and biscuit tins featuring scenes of Carnac and the Breton flag, with its stripes and ermine spots. In the pâtisserie cabinet, rows of meringues in the shape of menhirs, all slightly different, were set out in unruly lines, next to a little sign marked "Les Alignements de Kermario". On the shelf above, there was a similar presentation of menhir-shaped rocher chocolates: "Les Alignements du Ménec". There was a queue of customers at the counter, and Julie and François' mother were busy serving them and boxing up the meringues and chocolates.

Holding a tray of meringues, Marianne worked her way carefully through the crowded bakery. Her black-and-white-striped apron matched the Breton flag perfectly. Isabeau noticed three little black ermine spots stitched on the white stripe on the top left-hand corner.

"Isabeau!" Marianne greeted her. "Finally, our star has arrived. Docteur Morel, Madame, it's good to see you too. Here, you all have to try the new meringue: François' creation." She held out the tray. "I'll be back around with the chocolates next, and help yourself to some cider too, over in the corner."

They all took a serviette and a meringue. Isabeau bit into hers. It was slightly chewy, and contained pieces of dark chocolate and hazelnut and little blobs of soft praliné.

"Mmm, these are amazing," said Isabeau.

"So are your embroideries and sketches!" said Marianne.

"Shh, not so loud."

Marianne smiled and raised her voice a little more. "Oh, Isabeau, enjoy it! Your work is beautiful."

"It's not every day you get to have your work exhibited. You're very talented," said Madame Morel, and Docteur Morel nodded in agreement.

"Thank you," said Isabeau.

"And, Marianne, I must say the way you have set it all out in the bakery is quite incredible. Well done," said Madame Morel. "I don't know how you've managed to get it all set up so quickly. When I came for my bread yesterday, the bakery was, well, the usual bakery."

"Must admit I didn't get much sleep last night," said Marianne. "But I did all the preparation during the week, so it was only the setting up. I requisitioned Pierrot to help me."

"He didn't mind?" asked Isabeau.

"You can ask him yourself."

At that moment Pierrot came through from the back of the bakery with François, who was carrying a tray of meringues to refill the empty spaces in the pâtisserie cabinet. Pierrot squeezed through from behind the counter and joined them. He said "bonjour" to the Morels, and then they went to get bolées of cider from the small table Marianne had indicated, and Marianne herself headed outside with her tray of samples.

"I didn't expect to see you here," said Isabeau. "Actually, I didn't really expect to see anyone here."

"Marianne is very persuasive," said Pierrot.

"I know what you mean." Isabeau smiled.

"But seriously, I wanted to help, and I'm glad I could make it today."

"I'm sorry I haven't been in touch earlier. I've been busy working on the house, in fact."

"So I hear."

"And I haven't seen you since the bathroom was renovated. Thank you. It's beautiful. It couldn't be more perfect. You went way beyond what I've paid you for."

"No worries. Marianne passed on the thanks."

"Is ... Véronique here at all?"

"No, she has to work."

"That's a shame."

"Yeah. Marianne mentioned that Joseph's coming back too. I hope you get to see him."

"Thanks. I'm not sure that I will, but I appreciate that. Have you tried the meringues?" Isabeau took another bite of hers.

"I've already overdosed on them," said Pierrot. "Every time I've called in these past few weeks, François's made me try the latest version."

"That must have been hard!" Isabeau laughed. "They're so good."

"I'd better get going," he said. "Good luck with your house. I might call in and have a look at your progress sometime."

"I'd like that," she said. "I'm shifting in soon. And I'm having a house-warming in September. I would really like you to come, and Véronique too. You'll be one of the guests of honour."

"I look forward to it. See you later."

The Morels came back with a bolée of cider for Isabeau. "Now let's have a good look at your work," said Madame Morel.

86

Isabeau sat on the front step and brushed her hair. She'd been up since five. Hope hadn't made the ticket arrive. *Should* was the word that obliterated all else in her mind. She should have been in contact with Joseph again. No – she should have reserved her own ticket. Why hadn't she rung him? But that was like asking why she hadn't scattered George. It seemed simple, now it was too late. Perhaps he hadn't received her card. But perhaps he had. She didn't know if she was angrier with Joseph or with herself. And she hadn't heard from Drew, either. She was starting to get angry with him too. She got up and walked around the courtyard, counting each time she circled. When she got to twenty, she threw her arms up and grunted and stamped her feet. She went inside and grabbed a piece of paper and pen, and then headed out the gate and straight up to the gallery window where she'd first seen the poster. Back at the house, she reread Joseph's letters with George beside her. Then she dialled the number she'd scribbled down.

The woman on the other end was pleasant and full of enthusiasm for the festival, but very sorry. The concert was sold out, had been for several days. She repeated that three times. Now Isabeau was angry with this woman, who had no right to tell her that in such a pleasant voice, especially after all the effort it had taken her to make the call. Where would Joseph be staying? Maybe she should have asked, but how would the stupid woman know anyway?

"Yes, I know, George, time is running out!" Isabeau stomped up the stairs two at a time. She changed into the halter top and skirt she'd worn when she'd been to the beach with Joseph, put on her special earrings from Marianne, shook her hair and took off the bone pendant and put it in her bag. The only cloth she could find to wrap George's box in was a piece of linen with a half-started standing stone embroidered on it. She tied up the precious parcel with a ribbon and put it in her bag with Joseph's last two letters.

She left home in the car and drove along the Ménec Alignments, where she saw the usual high-season holiday crowd wandering around the menhirs. She slowed the car. "There they are George, the stones, all lined up. I'll take you to the Giant one last time, and then I have to somehow get you back to Joseph." At the car park leading to the Giant, she got out of the car and hugged her bag against herself. She forced herself to walk slowly down the path, to keep at bay the urge to get to Nantes as soon as possible, to stay calm. She wandered amongst the tourists around the Giant and the quadrilatère. In her head, this was her farewell conversation with George. *Goodbye, George. It's time to go. Thank you.*

Back in the car, she gripped the steering wheel. "Joseph Turner, you are getting your father's ashes back, whether you like it or not," she shouted. She picked up route du Purgatoire again and accelerated towards the main road. She didn't stop until she reached Nantes. When she had pulled into the Ile Gloriette car park in the centre of the city and turned off the motor, she closed her eyes. It was two o'clock. She was hungry and thirsty. She had no plan, and no ticket, and no idea where Joseph could be. She went straight to the Tourism Office, on the Place de la Bourse, and climbed the steps of the old stock exchange.

"I'm afraid it was the first show to sell out," said the woman behind the counter in answer to her enquiry. "They've been playing his music on the local radio, and it's created a lot of interest. Sorry."

This woman had a voice like the one she'd spoken to on the reservation line, and she was saying the same thing. Isabeau shouldn't have been surprised that so many people had bought tickets. She should have bought one too. She still wanted to shout at the young woman, though – "Joseph promised me a ticket!" – or to ask her if by any chance she knew how she could contact him. But she said nothing. She hurried outside before the tears rolled down her cheeks.

She wandered back towards Place du Bouffay, turned to the right and stopped at the Crêperie Jaune, where she and Joseph had had dinner. The waiter was cleaning up around the last midday customers. "Can I help you?" he asked.

"No thanks," said Isabeau. Her hand brushed the table where they had sat, and then she carried on through the narrow cobbled streets towards the castle. The smell of grilling meat and French fries came from a kebab stand nestled in amongst the little restaurants. From a juicy slab of meat on a vertical spit, a dark-skinned man sliced pieces onto a large hamburger bun covered with shredded lettuce and slices of tomato. He added sauce, a scoop of French fries and the top of the bun, and handed it to a teenager at the counter.

Five minutes later, Isabeau was installed at the white plastic table next to the stand, biting into a kebab. The stallholder wished her bon appétit and asked if she was enjoying the food, and she nodded between mouthfuls. Then another customer arrived, and he turned away into his kitchen.

Isabeau stared down the street and watched the people passing. Some sort of crazy optimism made her hope she'd see Joseph. Or would he be preparing for the concert? She finished off the bottle of sparkling water she'd bought and pulled out her map of Nantes.

She followed the route she had mapped out to the concert venue in rue Basse-Porte. It was opposite the Talensac Market, which was already closed for the day. The ground outside the covered market was still wet from being hosed down. There was a large shutter over the main entrance of La Bouche d'Air concert venue, which had the Salle Paul Fort inside, where Joseph's concert was taking place. Isabeau knocked on the door to the left, but there was no answer – no one to see or ask – and the concert didn't start until eight o'clock.

She went back down rue Basse-Porte and rue Paul Bellany and headed along the banks of the Erdre River until she came to l'Ile de Versailles. It was quiet on the little island with its Japanese garden. She hid away in one of the spaces enclosed with bamboo and large stones. She closed her eyes and tried to conjure up Joseph. She only had to hold out her hands and give the parcel to him. How was it possible to be so afraid of seeing someone you loved? Easily. It would have been the same if she had been able to see Papa before he died, no matter how much she had wanted to see him.

At half past seven Isabeau was back on the other side of the street to the concert hall. She stood under the covered outside area that ran the full length of the Talensac Market, hoping she looked like someone waiting to meet a friend. She was, but not in a way that any of the passers-by – mostly couples and groups of friends – could imagine. By five to eight the flow of concert-goers into the hall had dwindled. There was only the odd latecomer, who went straight inside, and a young woman waiting beside the entrance.

Isabeau had seen her arrive a quarter of an hour earlier. She watched her pace up and down. She had tickets in her hand and she fiddled with them. Isabeau tried to catch her eye, but she kept looking down rue

Basse-Porte and glancing at her watch.

It was eight o'clock. Isabeau reread Joseph's card, took out George and held him for a few seconds. She had to do something. She squared her shoulders and crossed the road.

"Excuse me," she addressed the young woman.

The young woman turned towards Isabeau. "Sorry?"

"Are you waiting for someone?"

"Yes." She blushed.

"Me too. Well, sort of ... And the concert's about to start." Isabeau moved on her feet.

The young woman looked at her watch again. "I should have known he wouldn't turn up."

"I'm sorry," said Isabeau. "I understand."

"Thanks. Don't know if I even want to see the show now."

"You should; he's really good. It would be a shame to miss it. I was promised a ticket, but my friend, well, he didn't come through either."

"Sorry." The young woman gave Isabeau a commiserating smile.

"Would you be willing to sell your spare ticket to me?"

"Sure, but they're not the best seats. I think I got the last two tickets."

"I don't care. How much did you pay?" Isabeau pulled out her purse.

"It was a hundred francs for a ticket."

That was exactly what Isabeau had left in her purse. She grabbed her two fifty-franc notes and gave them to the young woman. "Come on, we'd better be quick. I hope we're not too late."

Isabeau's heart was beating fast. She sank into the seat. It was right at the back, on the end of the row, beside the wall. Next to her was the young woman, who, on the way in, had said her name was Nicole. The ticket lady had told them the concert was about to start, and they had only just made it. Isabeau smoothed her hair behind her ears and tried to look as if she wasn't a complete mess inside. She kept her bag on her knee. *We've made it, George. We've made it.*

The lights were dimmed and musicians – a drummer, a pianist, two guitarists and a violinist – were taking their positions. The central microphone waited. Harmonica notes came from offstage. Isabeau shivered. There was a gradual hush in the audience, and heads turned to the side of the stage. The notes reached a crescendo, and then the musicians started to play. Isabeau squeezed George through the material of her bag.

Joseph entered, playing his harmonica. Walking.

He was so tall. Joseph. Joseph. Isabeau gasped. He had a slight limp, but it was still a shock to see him walking, almost normally. It was hard to know if anyone else could see the limp. He was dressed in jeans and a white t-shirt with a black motif that reminded her of the bone pendant. His hair was longer, and he had a short beard, like on the poster. He stopped behind the microphone, lowered his harmonica and started to sing.

"The mountains pinched and tucked by father time
The mountains set in a perpetual mime
They guard the land, they watch over the coast
They guard everything I love the most ..."

Joseph cupped the microphone and between verses took up his harmonica to play the refrain.

At the end of the song the applause was loud. Isabeau released her bag and clapped with all her might. When the audience quietened he started speaking in French.

"Merci, bonsoir. Je suis content d'être avec vous ce soir, je rêvais de revenir en France depuis mon séjour à Carnac l'année dernière, qui m'a beaucoup inspiré. Thank you, good evening. I'm happy to be with you here tonight. I've been dreaming about coming back to France since my stay in Carnac last year, which inspired me a lot. But more of that later. To start, I'm going to do some of my earlier material, some songs off my first three albums. A lot of them were inspired by where I come from, New Zealand: la Nouvelle-Zélande!"

Isabeau couldn't help but smile. He sounded so much more fluent in French; he must have been working on his pronunciation. He started to sing. She wanted to close her eyes and lose herself in the music and let the tears stay hidden, but she couldn't take her eyes off Joseph: every movement, every expression. Between songs, the applause was long, and Joseph simply said "Merci, thank you." After several songs, he took the microphone off the stand and walked to the front of the stage.

"Maintenant je voudrais interpréter une chanson classique française. Cest un honneur pour moi. J'ai eu le privilège de la chanter pour la première fois en France l'année dernière à un mariage. Now I would like to perform a classic French song. It's an honour for me. I had the pleasure of singing it for the first time in France last year, at a wedding."

An accordionist walked on playing "L'Hymne à l'amour". The crowd whispered and clapped, then quickly fell silent as Joseph started to sing. Isabeau was back at Marianne and François' wedding. She could remember exactly how it had felt when Joseph had sung then. It hurt. It wasn't fair that he sang that song here.

Joseph looked into the distance. Could he somehow see her in the dark? The tears ran down her cheeks.

After the song, Joseph picked up a guitar and started to pluck at the strings. He spoke slowly.

"I'd like to play some new material now, which I've written since my visit to Carnac last summer. I was inspired by the standing stones, and also by the people I met there. My father always wished to visit the stones, but sadly this was not possible."

He began to sing.

"Sing to me, cry to me, over the big blue sea
Send a bird with a bare branch of pain
and I will paint the leaves on with love and care
and send it back again and again
I want to touch the stars in your sky
I want to see myself in your eyes
I want to come to you

I want to fly ..."

Still clutching George, Isabeau slid down into her seat. Sitting outside last summer with Joseph. It all came back to her. The pain felt like it was in her heart. If only he really were singing to her, but he couldn't be. She would have received a ticket. She wouldn't be hiding here in this back seat. He would have contacted her when he arrived. She wouldn't hurt the way she did.

She listened to the lyrics of his new songs and tried to make sense of it all. The concert was going too fast.

At the end, as Joseph left the stage, she clapped wildly like the rest of the audience, and stood.

Joseph returned to the stage with the musicians.

"Merci beaucoup. You've been an amazing audience, and I've really enjoyed tonight. I hesitated over whether I would sing this song, but I need to. I hope you enjoy it."

"Across the miles I reached out for help

Across the miles, in search of myself

Caught in a cage of despair and rage

The cage of regret means I cannot forget

Your pain in me is set

I thought we were through

but I can't forget you

Forgive me

Set me free ..."

Joseph finished the song, and then he lined up with the other musicians, and they linked hands and bowed. He applauded his fellow performers, and they turned and acknowledged him. His eyes swept slowly around the concert hall, and as he left the stage he called out "merci" and blew a kiss into the audience. And then he was gone. Gone again. Like the day he'd left with Drew, the train disappearing down the track.

The lights came on, and everyone started talking. Isabeau blinked and wiped her eyes, conscious of Nicole's gaze.

"Boy, you were right," said Nicole. "I'm glad I didn't go home. Thanks."

"Me too. Thanks for the ticket. I appreciate it more than you can imagine."

Isabeau said goodbye to Nicole and went straight to the toilets. In the cubicle, she couldn't hold back the tears any longer. Who had Joseph been singing the last song to? If it wasn't her, who was it?

Other women came in to use the toilets, and Isabeau tried to silence her sobs and get her breathing back under control. She listened to them talking about what a great concert it had been and how Joseph was an amazing singer: the best at the festival, according to one of the women whose voices filled the washroom. When they had gone, she waited until she was sure there was nobody and came out. She splashed water on her face and patted it gently, trying to calm her red eyes. If she wasn't careful she might end up locked in the building with George. She brushed her hair, put on some lip gloss and tried to hold herself like Marianne. When she returned to the entrance it was empty, and the ticket lady was standing beside the door.

"Well, I think you were last to arrive, weren't you? And you're last to leave," the ticket lady greeted her. "Did you enjoy the concert?"

"Very much so, thank you." Isabeau smiled the best smile she could at the woman. "I was wondering if, by any chance, it would be possible to see Joseph Turner? I have something to return to him. It's very important, personal. Something that belongs to him." Isabeau held out the parcel.

The ticket lady looked down at it. " Er, I doubt that will be possible, dear. I don't even know if he's still in the building."

"Please! This is very important. I'm not a fan. I'm a ... friend of Joseph Turner's. Here, he meant to send me a ticket." Isabeau pulled Joseph's card out of her bag and showed the woman.

"There, there, dear. I have a niece your age. She has her favourite singers too. This one's certainly drawn a lot of female interest."

"Look, please can you just go and see if he's there? Tell him that Isabeau is here and has something for him. It's to do with his *father*."

The woman hesitated. "Alright, but I'm not guaranteeing anything." She turned on her heel and went off.

Isabeau was getting short of breath, dizzy, and her heart was beating fast. What would she say? She squeezed George and tried to concentrate on the pattern on the embroidery.

The ticket lady returned a very short time later. "I'm sorry, dear, it's not possible." She sighed. "There's a commotion out the back. The singer's had a problem with his leg, and there are also a couple of journalists wanting to speak to him as well."

"What do you mean, a problem with his leg?"

"I'm afraid I don't know."

"Would you be able to give it to him? It's extremely important."

Isabeau was about to hand over George when two men walked into the foyer.

"Olivier, there's a guy from some magazine insisting about his interview," said one of them.

"He'll have to wait. I need to talk to the television guy. Where's he got to?" asked the other man, looking around the foyer. He was tall and slim, with glasses.

Olivier. Isabeau walked towards him.

"Excuse me."

Olivier turned around.

"Please could you give this to Joseph Turner? It's very important." She pushed the parcel towards him.

He looked surprised and annoyed, and stepped back from her. "Look, I don't have time for this. The concert's over." He walked away.

Isabeau ran after him and thrust the parcel into his hands. "Please, give it to him. It's very important – extremely. Believe me, he's waiting for this."

Olivier didn't answer, and he strode off with the parcel in his hands.

88

Isabeau paced up and down in front of La Bouche d'Air. Her feet were sore from wearing her high-heeled sandals all day, but she couldn't stand still.

"Stupid. Stupid. Stupid." Why had she given the parcel over, just like that? She should have explained to Olivier who she was. It had all been over so quickly, and then the ticket lady had ushered her out of the building. She was just about to go back into the foyer when the lights went out, and the automatic shutter across the main entrance began to descend.

"Wait!" Isabeau banged on the door to the left of the entrance. She crouched down and called again before the shutter cluttered to the bottom. The shadows along the Talensac Market suddenly looked darker than before, and she felt vulnerable. There must be a back entrance. She should have thought of that earlier. She quickly headed up rue Basse-Porte, trying to run, swearing at herself under her breath. When she came to the corner and turned left, she found rue de Bel-Air, which cut back on a forty-five-degree angle. She hurried down it, but there was no back entrance anywhere. When she arrived at Place Saint-Similien she turned left again on an angle into rue Jeanne d'Arc. Surely it had to be down there.

She finally reached a stone wall at the back of La Bouche d'Air. There was a billboard with a poster for the festival beside two green iron gates with "no parking" signs on them. Both shut.

A van was heading down the street. Isabeau waved and started to run. The van reached the end of the street, turned right and disappeared. She rubbed her feet and pulled her jacket around herself. It was almost midnight. Why hadn't she worn sensible shoes, sensible clothes? Now she hated the sandals, the halter top. What good was it all? She hadn't even spoken to Joseph. She headed up rue Jeanne d'Arc towards the tall Tour de Bretagne, which loomed dark and foreboding, and then continued in the direction of the Ile Gloriette car park. She put her head down and limped along in her heels. It felt like walking all the way back to Carnac.

The smaller streets were quiet, and Isabeau wasn't used to being out this late in a big city. She tried not to think about it and talked quietly to George: George, who was gone. "Well, if he wanted to be sure to get his father's ashes back, he should have sent the ticket," she told him. "He should have contacted me."

She was pleased to arrive at Place du Commerce, where a late tram was pulling in. People were still sitting at the café tables, groups of friends were coming out of a film at the Gaumont, and young couples walked along with their arms wrapped around each other. Another two hundred metres and she was at the car park. As soon as she reached her car, she grabbed the rug from the back seat and wrapped herself in it.

The last time she'd driven from Nantes to Carnac in the night had been with Joseph. The Goldman cassette they had listened to was still sitting in the tape deck. Isabeau pushed it in. She turned the volume up high and drove. She just wanted to get home and try to forget about George. And Joseph. But by the time she got out of Nantes and had been on the N165 for twenty minutes, she was having trouble keeping her eyes open. She felt like she'd been in Nantes for a week. A week of late nights. She turned off towards Guérande. She needed to find somewhere to stop for a nap.

Isabeau tried to stretch her arms and back. She was cold and sore everywhere, and she had a headache. She was curled up, half lying, across the front seats of her car, in the car park in front of the main entrance of the walled city at Guérande. It was six o'clock. She got out of the car and stretched, walked around. She rubbed her temples.

Almost two years of taking good care of George, and she had handed him over just like that. She'd done what she'd set out to do, but now it seemed like a very bad idea. Olivier could have thrown the strange parcel, wrapped in a half-finished embroidery that didn't look like anything recognizable, into the nearest rubbish bin, muttering "crazy fan". Or he could have kept it to himself, not wanting to bother Joseph when he was having problems with his leg.

Was Joseph okay? Had he fallen? Was it bad enough to go to hospital? And she hadn't given the pendant back; it was still in her bag. She didn't know whether it was better that she had forgotten to hand it over or not.

Isabeau rubbed the sleep from her eyes. She needed coffee. One of the cafés near the car park was opening. She walked over to it and entered. She stood at the bar and stretched, then ordered a café noir and croissant. She was served quickly, and the coffee tasted good. It took the edge of panic off her thoughts.

Even though she drove slowly, she arrived home early. There was no bed linen to wash and nothing to tidy or put away, yet it felt like it had when she'd come back from taking Joseph and Drew to the station. Funny how empty the house seemed without that little box of ashes in it.

She took a long shower, pulled on an old loose t-shirt and fell into her unmade bed. It was nine o'clock in the morning.

She woke much later in the day. The phone was ringing. She'd been dreaming. She had an appointment to keep and no matter how much she hurried – how much she ran – she was always late, always late. The phone continued ringing. It was like she was still somehow in the dream. She jumped from the bed and ran, taking the steps two at a time. Her foot slipped, and her ankle bent to the side. She fell forward, taking the last four steps in one great leap, only just righting herself as she landed at the bottom. Heart pounding, she rushed forward to the kitchen. As she grabbed the receiver, the phone stopped ringing. The dial tone was dead.

89

"I gave George back. I did it. Okay, I don't know if Joseph has him or not. I saw Joseph sing. Please, please, please can Joseph have George." Isabeau reached out and stroked the Giant. She'd taken her time over breakfast in case the phone rang again, but there had been no more calls since the one she'd missed the evening before. She had no idea where she could try to ring Joseph or how she could check whether he had George. What would she say? "Did you get the ashes?" "Are you okay?" "Why didn't you send the ticket?" "Did you try to phone me?"

There were steps behind her. She stopped talking to herself. A hand touched her shoulder and squeezed. Isabeau screamed.

"Easy does it, Isabeau. I didn't mean to give you the fright of your life." Drew looked serious, but in a split second the smile had come back to his face. "It's good to see you. And that looks good on you – better than it did on Joseph." He pointed to the pendant.

Isabeau was mute. Drew wrapped his big arms around her.

"We've been looking everywhere for you."

"Drew!" she finally managed to say. "I didn't know you were here too."

"When it came down to it, I felt like I also had unfinished business with Uncle George, and with Joseph, so here I am."

"I didn't see you at the concert."

"You were there after all? I was backstage. I ended up helping set up some of the equipment."

"Where's Joseph?" she asked.

"In the car, asleep. He's exhausted, but I can tell you, even if he won't admit it to himself – or at least not to me – he's been waiting a year for this."

"Did he get the ashes? I gave them to Olivier."

"Yes, once things settled down. After the concert, Joseph had problems with his leg: phantom pain. I've never seen him like that." Drew winced as he spoke.

"He said he would send me a ticket, but he didn't. I don't think he really wants to see me."

"Believe me, he does. It's just been crazy since we arrived in Nantes.

We've been flat out. He's been mobbed by the press since we got here. He tried to ring you several times the day of the concert and again yesterday, but there was no answer. And then yesterday, they asked him to perform in an impromptu concert at the castle with some of the other performers from the festival. This morning, I told him he was a bloody idiot, and if he didn't get in the car to come here I was going to forcibly put him in!" Drew looked towards the path. "It's a white Peugeot 205. I'll have a wander around here for a while. I kind of feel an affinity with this stone, and I need some fresh air." He gently pushed her in the direction of the path. "I'll be along soon."

Isabeau didn't know whether to laugh or cry, to run or walk, but she found her steps quickening as she advanced along the path.

In the car park, the Peugeot was the first car. She stopped and caught her breath. Joseph was asleep against the side window, dark lines under his eyes. He was wearing the marinière over jeans with two legs and two shoes. On his knee sat George's box, still wrapped in the cloth, his hand draped over it. She stepped back from the car and watched him for a long time. It felt good to see him, and she was glad of the moment. She needed time to calm herself.

His eyes flickered and he stirred. He got out of the car. Isabeau studied his face, but it was hard to see what he was thinking.

"Isabeau! I felt like someone was watching me. Thank heavens it's you."

"You got the box."

"Yes." He glanced over his shoulder at it on the seat of the car.

Isabeau's words came out in a rush. "Your father ... I didn't mean to deceive you, but the longer it went on, the harder it became to say. And I really did feel as if he wasn't ready to be scattered, as if he was helping me find my own father. I did intend to scatter the ashes. It was just too soon. I –"

"It's okay, Isabeau." Joseph stepped towards her. "I've had a lot of time to think, and I've thought about what you said about feeling Dad's presence with you. I remember how I felt close to him in Carnac, and it felt right. I think you needed him. He turned up at the right time for you. And you took good care of him, I can see that now." He sighed and ran his hand through his hair.

"But you didn't send the ticket?"

"Olivier told me he'd sent it! He didn't think it was important. I should have made it clearer to him. I found out that he hadn't at the last minute before the concert. By then it was too late. But I should have been in touch with you earlier, anyway. Drew kept telling me I was too stubborn. He was right." Joseph shook his head. "Then yesterday Olivier gave me the box. I couldn't believe it." Joseph reached out to her and put his hands on her shoulders.

"I had no choice but to hand it over to him. It was sheer luck I got into the concert, and then the songs ... some of the words; it was as if you were explaining." Now that Isabeau had started, she couldn't stop. "You didn't get in touch. You left me with your father's ashes ... You left me ... You left." She was crying and shouting. "And my father's dead too. He's dead."

"I know. We called in at the bakery on our way here. I'm sorry, so, so sorry."

Joseph put his arms around her. She pushed her fists against his chest. He didn't move, and then she gave way and found herself sobbing into his marinière. He let her finish crying before he began to speak again.

"So many times, I almost picked up the phone to ring you," he said. "I should have done it long ago. To apologize. My outburst – I hate to think about it. I'm sorry. I tried to ring you, and when there was no answer, I was afraid you'd gone away for the summer and I wouldn't see you. Then the whole festival thing took over, and it was mayhem. Isabeau, it isn't just about the ashes any more; it's also about you."

Joseph kissed the top of her head and started to sing, his voice quiet and gentle, whispering the song in her ear.

"Sing to me, cry to me, over the big blue sea
Send a bird with a bare branch of pain
and I will paint the leaves on with love and care
and send it back again and again
I want to touch the stars in your sky
I want to see myself in your eyes
I want to come to you
I want to fly."

Isabeau relaxed into his chest. His arms relaxed too and encircled her more fully. It felt good to be held. Safe. And all the tension of the preceding days and months fell away. She almost felt lightheaded with happiness. When she looked up at him, he touched the pendant around her neck.

"I forgot to give it back with the ashes."

"It looks perfect where it is."

Joseph's face was drawing slowly closer, and Isabeau could feel herself pulled towards him. She met his gaze. She wasn't afraid any more. He knew who she was; there was nothing to hide. Their lips met.

Beyond the bare ground around the Giant, Isabeau, Joseph and Drew found a space amongst the trees. Joseph untied the ribbon and unfolded the cloth and handed them to Isabeau. He opened the box. She had never looked inside. George had been so many things to her, and yet here he was, just grey ash, much coarser than she had imagined.

Joseph closed his eyes and bowed his head. Isabeau and Drew did the same, and they all stood in silence for several minutes. When Joseph opened his eyes, he tipped up the box and scattered most of the ash around the trees. He left a little ash in the box and slid the lid back on it. "I know exactly where I want to scatter what's left," he said, holding up the box.

They walked slowly back down the path, without speaking. Joseph took Isabeau by the hand. In the car, on the way to the Alouettes house, there was a comfortable silence. Drew drove, and for once he was quiet. It seemed so unreal. Isabeau felt as if she was in a dream: the best dream she could imagine. She wanted to reach over to the front seat and lay her hand on Joseph's shoulder, but she sensed it was important to leave him to his own thoughts. They parked in front of her house and got out of the car.

"The garden looks good, Isabeau, really good," said Joseph. "We called in here before, after we'd tried your house in town and the bakery. Your neighbours were pretty surprised to see us. They told us to try the Giant."

"I've been working hard on the house. I'm shifting in next month. I'll show you later," she offered.

"Once we've finished this," said Joseph. He led them along the road to the small field of menhirs opposite allée des Alouettes. They crossed the road and went to the furthest corner of the field and continued a little way into the trees. "I had intended to spread the rest at the Ménec Alignments, but I think here will be perfect. I think Dad would like this spot, away from all the crowds and not far from your house."

Joseph raised the box and tipped the last of the ashes into the grass, where it was long. "Goodbye, Dad. I love you. Rest in peace," he said.

"Rest in peace, Uncle George," said Drew.

"Rest in peace, George," said Isabeau. She could still see some of the ash amongst the grass. It wasn't a goodbye. It was a homecoming. Joseph put his arms around her shoulders. She didn't want him to let go.

"You have a beautiful home, Isabeau." Madame Fournier followed Isabeau back into the living area.

"I told you it was gorgeous," said Marianne to her parents. "Especially the bathroom!"

"What a transformation," said Madame Morel. "It's incredible."

Transformation. The word kept coming up. Isabeau wasn't sure if they were just talking about the house or about her as well.

"Magical: just like the menhirs," added Tonton Aimé.

"Thank you," Isabeau said to them all. "It certainly looks better now, with all the furniture. Shall we join the others?" François, Pierrot and Véronique, Marie-Claire and Benjamin, and Corinne had already had a tour of the house, and were installed outside, at the tables set up at the back. Isabeau glanced at the clock.

"They shouldn't be too much longer," Madame Morel whispered in her ear. "Don't worry."

It was a perfect September day, warm and balmy. The front door was open. As if on cue, Isabeau's car pulled up outside, and Docteur Morel manoeuvred it between the parked cars. Joseph got out of the back, opened the passenger door and helped Ghislaine Bourdain out of the car.

"I'll start organizing the apéritif," said Madame Morel, "while you greet your guest." She gave Isabeau a quick hug and followed everyone outside.

Isabeau came out to the front step and watched Ghislaine walk across the lawn. She didn't have her crutches. She took Joseph's arm and advanced with slow careful steps. Her hair was up in a loose bun, with a flowery silk scarf tied around it. In her hand she clasped a small packet. After a few steps she stopped. She looked around the garden and then studied the house. Joseph waited by her side, and Docteur Morel joined them.

"The garden's very pretty," she said to Isabeau.

"Thank you. I've enjoyed working in it."

"For you." Ghislaine advanced and handed the parcel to Isabeau. Both her voice and her hand shook.

"There's no need, really."

"Yes, there is. I think you should have it."

Isabeau looked down at the small parcel and hesitated.

"Please," said Ghislaine, "do open it."

Isabeau lifted the tape. Wrapped in tissue paper inside the parcel was a small wooden photo frame. It contained a photo of her father on the beach. Smiling and waving. He was older than she remembered.

"Papa."

"I took the photo when we went to Noirmoutier," said Ghislaine. "It's one of the last photos of him. He bought the frame for me there. I wanted you to have it."

Isabeau swallowed. "Merci. I don't have any photos of him." She stared at the photo in her hands.

Joseph broke the silence. "Entrez, entrez," he said to Ghislaine, and helped her up the step.

"Of course," said Isabeau. "Oui, welcome ... Madame Bourdain, please come in. Thank you for the photo." She kissed the older woman's cheek. Her sagging skin was soft and smelled ever so faintly of salt, or something that reminded Isabeau of her father.

"Merci bien. Thank *you* for the invitation."

"Let's get you a chair, Madame," said Docteur Morel. "Everyone's outside. Come and meet my wife and Isabeau's friends." Docteur Morel accompanied Ghislaine outside.

Isabeau took the photo to the sideboard and set it down. Joseph put his arms around her and held her.

"Come on, Isabeau, now it's time to enjoy your party. And you've got other presents to open."

Everyone was seated around the trestle tables Isabeau and Joseph had set up earlier in the day and covered with tablecloths borrowed from Madame Morel. Ghislaine was seated between Tonton Aimé and Madame Fournier. Joseph helped Isabeau bring out the taboulé and Niçoise salad that was the entrée. Marianne wanted to help, but Isabeau wouldn't hear of it. "You are one of my guests of honour today," she said.

They took their time eating and sat and talked before they started the paella that Isabeau had ordered from the traiteur.

When they had finished, Tonton Aimé came over to Isabeau. Joseph stood up and offered him the chair.

"Good, always a gentleman," Tonton Aimé said to him. "Isabeau, you must have improved on your correspondence." He nodded towards Joseph.

"No need to write at the moment. Things have worked out differently to what I thought."

"Often happiness is not where we expect it, when we expect it. It catches us by surprise. You just have to make sure you grab it and don't let go."

"I'm trying."

"There could be new resolutions involving travel, perhaps, then?"

"I'm not sure what next year will bring," Isabeau told him, "but Joseph's taking me to Besançon at All Saints, and we're thinking of going to England for a trip too."

Tonton Aimé raised his eyebrows and turned to Joseph. "Voyage? Isabeau?"

"Oui, oui," laughed Joseph.

Isabeau smiled to herself. She couldn't but help think of Drew, who had made her promise that she would go to New Zealand. "You can't get out of it. Don't worry about that Joseph bloke. Come and see me instead." It was the last thing he had said to her, through the car window as he left to drive back to Nantes, to return the rental car and catch the train.

Madame Fournier came over. "And your singing, Joseph? How is it going?"

"Olivier's lined up some gigs, and he's helping to organize a visa for me to stay longer."

"Excellent! That's good news. I hope we have the opportunity to see you perform. And, you must come back to Saint-Laurent with Isabeau. We would like that."

Marianne and François went to the kitchen and came back with the fraisier that François had made, covered with burning candles. Marianne put the cake on the table in front of Isabeau, and everyone burst into "Happy Birthday", in French and then in English.

"Make a wish," said Marianne.

Isabeau closed her eyes tight. No one spoke. She opened them again and blew hard.

"I thought it was going to be fraisier flambé," said François.

"You can't hurry wishes," said Tonton Aimé.

Isabeau removed the candles and cut up the cake. When everyone had a piece, she raised her glass.

"I'd like to propose a toast. First of all, to Marianne, Pierrot and François, for the amazing bathroom. And to Joseph, who has carried on a lot of the work since he's been here. To the Morels, who, well, I don't know what I would have done without you. And to you all, for helping me to complete the house, to be here, where I am today. To good friends." Isabeau swept her glass around the group, making eye contact with each person.

"To good friends" rang out in the garden as everyone raised their glasses and drank.

"And to those absent," added Isabeau.

"To those absent."

Isabeau gave a half smile to Ghislaine, and exchanged a glance with Joseph.

As everyone watched, Joseph picked up his guitar. "This song is for Isabeau," he said. "I've written it as my secret house-warming present." He reached for Isabeau's hand and raised it to his lips before he started to play.

"I wasn't looking for you
but I found you on the way
You brought me here
made me want to stay
It's been a long time coming
back to the place I call home
It's been a long time coming
back to the stones
It's been a long, a long, a long time coming
I'm no longer alone
I am home."

Author's Note

In 1986, when Isabeau returned to Carnac in this story, the alignments were freely accessible. However, in 1991, in order to protect the standing stones from damage – in particular, loosening of the earth at the base of the stones caused by the ever-increasing number of visitors – the main alignments were fenced off.

Now, from October to March, it is still possible to freely visit the alignments. From April to September, it is only possible to enter the site by taking part in a guided visit, organized by the Centre des Monuments Nationaux. The most up-to-date information on access to the alignments can be obtained from the Maison des Mégalithes, situated at the Ménec Alignments.

Also, in 1986, when the ashes arrived at the post office in Carnac, no law specifically governed the storage or scattering of ashes in France. This has since changed with legislation being introduced in 2008.

Acknowledgements

Writing Isabeau and Joseph's story has been a long labour of love. Along the way many people have helped me, and my heartfelt gratitude goes to them all.

Thank you, Damien, for love and support and patience, and for even writing several drafts of a novel yourself, just to get me started on and fully committed to mine! It worked. And Félix and Gwenaëlle, for your love and laughs and not too many interruptions when the "Do Not Disturb, Creation in Progress" sign, made by Gwenaëlle, is on the door of my office. Thanks, Gwenaëlle, also for creating a great cover. And to Mum and Dad, and my in-laws, Marc and Marie Lou, for always supporting me in so many ways in all endeavours. I really did draw four lucky life straws in the parents' lottery. Thanks also Mum for being one of my precious readers. And merci Marie Lou for sharing your passion for embroidery with me.

My sincere thanks to the Penpushers Writing Group: Pat Braithwaite, Briar McMahon, Hugh Adams, Kathryn Kearns, Penny Olds and the late Ann Hughey all offered support and encouragement for my writing during our weekly writing group meetings for almost a decade. We don't meet so often now, but the encouragement keeps coming. Extra thanks also to Pat and Briar, who both helped with editing in the final stages, and Briar sowed the seed for the title.

We all met at a Gifting Your Stories to Your Grandchildren course at the Centre for Continuing Education at the University of Canterbury, taught by Grant Hindin-Miller. Grant read one of the first drafts of this book that I released into other hands, and gave me much appreciated constructive feedback.

At the Hagley Writers' Institute, director Morrin Rout, tutors Kerrin P. Sharpe and Frankie McMillan, and my fellow writers in class all encouraged me on the writing journey. My mentor, writer Coral

Atkinson, also gave me enthusiastic guidance and the opportunity to have my manuscript read by students at the Whitireia Publishing Course. A big thank you to Robyn Anderson and Fiona Tyson, fellow students, who kept the critique going as the manuscript was further reworked and reworked, and who were happy to keep reading and were never afraid to push me and my writing harder.

I am indebted to other readers along the way, avid readers and fellow school mums: Heather Holder-Lunn, Jayne Stewart and Heather Mitchell, who were happy to give their time to read earlier drafts.

Gratitude goes to my good friend Nickei Falconer, who has offered encouragement and critique as well as love and care as we have shared our creative endeavours, especially since that special peach bath under a full moon in Nickei's beautiful Tancred St garden. Also, Nickei introduced me to my editor, Daisy Coles, and I don't know what I would have done without Daisy.

Thank you, Daisy, for your incredible work, which helped make *Alignment* what I wanted it to be. You really took Isabeau and Joseph to heart, cared about them, and with your skill took the story to another level that I hadn't ever imagined possible.

Merci to my soulmate sister-in-law, Roselyne Le Saux, who proofread the French in *Alignment* with precision and love.

Other people have helped with practical matters. My thanks go to Joanne Boereboom and Daryl Humberstone who willingly talked about their experiences of life as amputees, Vicki Moore at the Cremation Society of Canterbury who was helpful with information about ashes, Lachie Hill for answering carpentry questions, Sandra and Hamish for their memories of the Gladstone, and Lauren Brunt for enlightening discussions on mental illness. Any errors in the information everyone has been happy to share with me are entirely my own.

I'd also like to thank Jennifer Manson, who generously shared her knowledge and experience as a writer, and TBG, who arrived on the scene late in the piece and encouraged me over the finishing line.

By the time this is available to the reading public, I will also owe a huge debt of gratitude to many people who will have helped me throw the biggest party of my life to celebrate *Alignment*: the realisation of the book and the dream.

Finally, if you are reading this book: thank you. It's for you.

About the author

Tracy Chollet is a New Zealand writer who lived for many years in France. She studied French in New Zealand and France, and has Bachelor's and Master's degrees in French and French literature respectively. She has been writing for many years, including as a freelance journalist. *Alignment* is her first novel. With her French husband and two children, she regularly returns to France. Tracy's many experiences in France, including living in her husband's family's village bakery and holidays spent in Brittany, have provided inspiration for *Alignment*.

Find out more about *Alignment* at www.tracychollet.com

Connect with Tracy at www.facebook.com/TracyCholletAuthor

47309619R00202

Made in the USA
San Bernardino, CA
27 March 2017